LAST
DAY

Center Point
Large Print

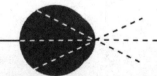

**This Large Print Book carries the
Seal of Approval of N.A.V.H.**

LAST DAY

LUANNE RICE

CENTER POINT LARGE PRINT
THORNDIKE, MAINE

For Audrey Loggia
and Joe Guccione

PART I

1

July 11

Beth Lathrop lay on her side, one arm flung across her eyes as if to block the bright morning sunlight that streamed through the east-facing window. She was covered by a pale-blue percale sheet that draped over her pregnant belly and clung to her left hip. It was mid-July; the baby, a boy, was due October 4. The distinct peace of white noise made the room a separate world from the rest of the house: the hum of the air conditioner, the low buzz of a single fly circling the odd, shocking, dark-red jewel behind her ear, the muffled sound of a dog just outside the door.

Outside, a salt breeze blew off the protected cove down the hill. July in Black Hall could be humid, waves of damp heat rising from the marsh and tidal flats, but although it was already eighty-five degrees, the air was clear, and this was one of those sparkling summer days Beth loved so much, looked forward to all winter.

If the windows had been open, the white curtains would have lifted and rippled, and the cross breeze blowing across the marshes, off Long Island Sound, would have cooled the whole house. But the house was closed up, the bed-room door shut tight, the window air conditioner running on the highest setting—so high that despite the hot day, a thin film of frost had formed on the vents and the sill. Beth's golden-red hair, loose and wavy, cascaded over her bare shoulders.

Her iPhone on the bedside table lit up with an incoming call from her sister, Kate. The phone was set to "Do Not Disturb," so it neither rang nor vibrated. When Kate disconnected, a message banner showed on Beth's screen. It was the most recent of twenty-one missed calls. Nearly as soon as the message appeared on the iPhone, the landline began to ring. It was downstairs, in the kitchen, and the tone was muffled by the rooms and stairs and closed door in between it and Beth.

Popcorn had been scratching at the bedroom door, but he had given up and now lay on the top step, whimpering in the hall. The family's yellow Lab loved his morning beach runs. It was 7:35 a.m., and he was used to being fed and walked around 6:00. With Pete gone on his sailing trip, Beth under her sister's orders to grab a little extra sleep because it had been a com-plicated pregnancy, and their sixteen-year-old daughter, Samantha, away at camp, Popcorn had to wait. He kept glancing at the bedroom door—lifting his head, whining, resting his chin on his paws.

Through the closed bedroom door and over the air conditioner's loud hum, the doorbell could barely be heard. It rang three times. Popcorn let out a whooping yelp, bounded down the stairs, and ran back and forth in the entry hall. Then came the sound of rapid closed-fist pounding on the front door. Then the sharp clank-clank-clank of the brass door knocker. Popcorn barked wildly.

The noise at the front door stopped. Footsteps sounded on the brick walk along the side of the house, voices carrying as the white picket gate squeaked open. Popcorn tore into the kitchen, wailing at the two women and a man who had entered the backyard and were standing just outside the back door. They peered in, hands cupped around their eyes to block the sunlight.

Popcorn pranced with excitement, his tail thumping. One of the women knew him well—Kate Woodward, Beth's sister. He reared up, front claws clicking on the glass. Kate went to the gas grill, opened the lid. The Lathrops usually hid a spare key inside, and although she had looked earlier, before she had called the police, before they had pulled up in their cruiser, she had to double-check to make sure it really wasn't there.

The other two visitors were uniformed Black Hall police officers, Peggy McCabe and Jim Hawley. McCabe knocked hard, the rap of her knuckles sharp and staccato.

"Black Hall Police," she called. "Beth, are you home? Anyone in there?"

"Is the dog friendly?" Hawley asked warily.

"Yes, very—Popcorn's very friendly; don't worry," Kate said. "Just break the door, will you? Please?"

Hawley crouched down, looked the dog in the eye through the slider. "Hey, Popcorn; hey, Popcorn," he said. "You're not going to bite, are you?" Popcorn slimed the glass with his nose, his tail wagging.

"There's nowhere else they could have hidden a key?" McCabe asked.

"I don't think so. I don't know. The spare is always in the grill. Beth would never go this long without calling me. Will you please get us in there? I should have broken in myself. Something's wrong."

"Did you have a fight?" McCabe asked.

"No!" Kate said.

McCabe knew they should get a search warrant, but Kate's panic was compelling. Beth Lathrop was six months pregnant and hadn't been heard from in three days. Her silver Mercedes was parked in the driveway, and at least two days' worth of dog waste was visible through the window. These facts, plus Kate's demeanor, told McCabe that she and Hawley could claim exigent circumstances if they faced a problem in court later.

"Is there an alarm?" she asked. "Is it silent?"

"Yes, there is one. No, it's not silent. It's a siren," Kate said. "But I know the code. I can disarm it."

"Get back," McCabe said. She pulled on latex gloves, took her baton from her black leather belt, and smashed the door. The glazed glass shattered into a thousand tiny squares, but they held in place. She gave it one extra-forceful tap with the butt of her baton, and the pieces rained down onto the blue tile floor. She reached in to unlock the door from the inside.

The alarm didn't go off. It hadn't been set.

The officers stepped into the kitchen, but Kate pushed past them.

"Beth!" she shouted.

"Wait," McCabe said, grabbing Kate's arm. "Please step outside until I tell you to come in."

"There's no way," Kate said and disappeared through the kitchen.

McCabe kept her hand on her hip holster, following Kate. Hawley petted the dog, let him outside into the fenced yard, and then followed the other two up the stairs.

"Beth!" Kate called. She was on the stairs, mounting them two at a time, McCabe just behind her. McCabe heard the air conditioner humming behind a closed door at the top of the staircase. Kate started to grab the knob, but McCabe clamped her wrist to stop her. Kate's hand was shaking.

"Wait out here, Kate," McCabe said.

Kate took a step back, letting Hawley pass, seeming to comply.

McCabe turned the brass knob—even through her glove, the metal felt like ice.

Inside, the bedroom was freezing cold, the air conditioner running hard. The room smelled sickly sweet and rotten. Beth lay on her right side facing the window, her back to the door. Flies, sluggish in the chilled air, buzzed around her head. Kate ran past both officers to her sister.

"Beth," Kate said, crouching down to look into her face. She let out a sharp, instant shriek of wild, immediate grief. "No, Beth, don't let it be this—don't let it."

"Don't touch her," McCabe said.

"Oh, Beth," Kate said.

Hawley and McCabe approached the bed.

Beth's eyes were half-open, her lips parted and protruding tongue blue and swollen. There was a purple line around her neck, a lace pattern imprinted into her skin. The left side of her face was bruised, her head split open behind her ear, her hair caked with dried blood. The blue sheets were disheveled and stained with fluids, the top one pulled up just enough to cover Beth's pregnant belly. Black bikini panties, the filigreed elastic stretched and torn, lay bunched on the floor. A lacy black bra, sides and straps ripped, hung off the side of the bed.

Kate stood still, fists pressed to her chest, weeping. McCabe put her arm around her shoulders, led her to the bedroom door. Kate didn't put up a fight. Her body felt rigid, her chest heaving with sobs.

"Who should I call?" McCabe said. "To come and get you?"

"I'm not going anywhere," Kate said.

"You can't be in the room, though," McCabe said.

She looked into Kate's tear-flooded green eyes to make sure she understood, really got it. Kate shook her head, paced back and forth a few times, went into the hall, and sat heavily on the top step.

McCabe started to tell her she couldn't, that the stairs were part of the crime scene, but instead she just tapped Kate's arm.

"Don't touch anything, Kate," she said. "Not the wall, not the banister, not anything."

Kate didn't reply, just sat there crying.

McCabe returned to the bedroom, closing the door behind her.

"Jesus," Hawley said.

McCabe glanced at him and nodded. She knew it was his first murder scene—hers too. Black Hall was one of the quietest, most affluent towns on the Connecticut Shoreline, and nothing like this ever happened here.

"You want to call it in, or should I?" he asked.

McCabe unclipped the radio from her belt and called Marnie, the dispatcher.

"We have a homicide at 45 Church Street," McCabe said.

"The Lathrops' house?" Marnie asked, taking in a sharp breath. This was a small town. "Good Lord. Is it Beth? Or Pete? Not the girl; gosh, what's her name—she's two years behind Carrie. I can't remember . . ."

"Call Major Crime for us, Marnie," McCabe said, referring to the Connecticut State Police's squad of detectives assigned to murders and kidnappings and bank robberies and deliberately not answering the question.

"Roger. I'll do that now," Marnie said.

McCabe disconnected.

She glanced down at the iPhone beside the bed, touched the home button with her gloved thumb, and saw the screen light up. It didn't ask for a password, which told McCabe that Beth had trusted the people around her. "Look at all these calls and texts. Two days', three days' worth?" There was a slew of messages and missed calls from Kate, but the three most recent came up as "Pete."

"And the dog hadn't been out in a while, from the looks of all that shit by the door."

"Yeah," McCabe said.

"Rape too?" he asked, gesturing at the torn panties and bra.

16

"Maybe," McCabe said. She crouched by the bed. A marble sculpture of an owl lay half-under the fabric skirt. The bird's head was smeared with red-brown dried blood.

"Murder weapon?" Hawley asked, pointing at the gash behind Beth's ear.

She stood up, staring. Blood had coagulated around the wound, bizarrely bright red in the sunlight. Her gaze moved to the bruised indentation around Beth's neck. "That or strangulation," she said.

"Nice house for something like this," Hawley said. "Expensive everything. Mercedes in the driveway."

"I know," McCabe said, looking around the room. The Lathrops obviously liked order. Except for the lingerie, there were no clothes strewn around. Books on the nightstand were perfectly stacked. The furniture looked to be antique—fine wood, burnished with age. Landscapes of local scenes, framed in museum-type gilded frames, hung around the room. McCabe looked at one, saw the signature *Childe Hassam* in the lower-right corner. She had grown up in town and recognized the name of one of the most famous Black Hall artists—a fortune right here on the wall. There was also an empty frame, with ragged shreds of canvas fiber clinging to the wood.

"Look," she said. "What was there? Think someone cut the painting out?"

"Could be," Hawley said. "The husband owns the Lathrop Gallery, right?"

"Isn't that a little sexist?" McCabe asked. "Assuming he owns all this?"

"He doesn't?"

"It used to be called the Harkness-Woodward Gallery," McCabe said. "It's always been in the victim's family." A high-end art gallery in the center of Black Hall, it specialized in the same kind of paintings that hung on the walls. McCabe's mother had taken the kids there on Saturdays, after their father had died—anything to distract them.

As soon as she'd heard Kate's last name, it had all come back to her. The gallery had belonged to Kate and Beth's grandmother. There had been a scandal associated with it, back when McCabe was just a kid. A robbery and a death, she remembered. Paintings stolen, a mother and her daughters tied up. People in town had talked about it nonstop. Even on the beach, on the most perfect days of summer, the whispers had been about cheating, greed, and murder. Sometimes she wondered whether that crime, burned into her consciousness at such a young age, had been the impetus for her to become a cop. And now, staring at Beth: Had she and Kate been those girls in the basement?

McCabe wondered what the missing painting might have to do with Beth's murder. Seeing the torn lingerie made her feel sick; what had the killer put Beth through? "God, it's freezing in here." She shivered in the blast of icy air.

"Time to turn that thing off," Hawley said, heading toward the air conditioner. The compressor cycled, pumping hard; it sounded ready to give out.

"No, leave it till the Staties get here."

McCabe had two years more than Hawley on a force so small the selectmen were considering merging it with the department in the next town. She lived in Norwich now, a tougher place to work, and she felt lucky to have gotten a job in sleepy Black Hall. It was a postcard-beautiful village on Long Island Sound, a beach resort in summer, a place that had attracted artists since the late 1800s, and a bedroom town for executives of Electric Boat and professors at Yale, Connecticut College, and the Coast Guard Academy. Until today, her worst calls had been domestics and bad car accidents.

She leaned closer to Beth, looked at her injuries. The edge of the panties had left a pattern of lace in the deep-purple bruised circle around her neck. She cringed at the sight but couldn't look away. It was at least as brutal as the cracked skull, even more disturbing with its hints of sexual violence.

"The husband is always the killer," Hawley said. "But not this time. What did the sister say?

He's on a boat out in the Atlantic somewhere. Besides, I can't imagine a husband doing this."

McCabe didn't answer. She'd learned early, from a case very close to home, that even nice-seeming people could do terrible things.

"We've got to notify him," Hawley said. "That's going to suck for him, off on a nice sailing trip, getting news like this. If we can even get through. There's probably no cell reception. I go fishing in the canyons behind Block Island; there's a major dead zone out there."

"There'll be a radio."

"Yeah, forget that. A bunch of guys on vacation aren't going to be listening to the marine band."

"It's Major Crime's problem," McCabe said. Kate had said Pete took the sailing trip every summer, with the same bunch of guys, and that this voyage would be the last before his new baby was born.

That thought made McCabe stare down at Beth's belly.

The baby was dead too.

2

Detective Conor Reid parked in front of 45 Church Street, the Major Crime Squad van not far behind. He'd been investigating a credit union robbery in Pawcatuck until late last night, and he still had on the same blue blazer and gray slacks. He'd changed his white shirt, though, and put on a striped tie. His brown hair, a little too long for the Connecticut State Police, was salty from an hour spent fishing. Instead of going straight home after leaving the scene at dawn, he'd hit the Charlestown Breachway to go surf casting. It was the second week of July, and stripers were just starting to run. He had a heavy caseload, and there never seemed to be enough time for fishing or haircuts or much of anything but work.

The dispatch call had pulled him away from the fish. Hearing the Black Hall address was a bullet to his heart. He had sat in front of the house often enough, wondering about the woman inside. The fact a crime had occurred to this family hit him with a bolt from the past. The news was all he needed to throw his rod and tackle box into the trunk of his car. Speeding south toward Black Hall on I-95, he knew this case had to be his.

After getting out of his car, he took in the scene—a large white sea captain's house, typical of this affluent part of Black Hall. A boxwood hedge surrounded the property. Mature oak and beech trees shaded the lawn, and blue hydrangeas bloomed along an old lichen-covered stone wall. He noticed pink gardening gloves, clippers, and a flat basket full of wilted cut flowers at the foot of the wall. A white canvas sun hat lay on the ground. A green hose was draped over the wall, water trickling from the spray nozzle, sending a thin stream down the hill toward a wild meadow. Someone had been interrupted while gardening.

He walked over to the hat, crouched on his heels, and saw that the fabric glistened with morning dew, as if it had been left on the grass overnight or longer. The crime techs had arrived, and he gestured at the hat and gardening equipment, letting them know to photograph and process them as part of the crime scene.

Black Hall police officers had been the first to arrive. He spotted two uniforms next to a cruiser and headed toward them. A dark-haired woman, clearly distressed, stood between them. The sight of Kate stiffened his spine. He stared at her, thinking how she had changed yet somehow looked the same.

The female officer caught his eye and broke away from the others.

"Hello," he said, holding out his hand. "I'm Conor Reid."

"I'm Peggy McCabe, and that's my partner, Jim Hawley. Beth Lathrop is the victim here," McCabe said. She nodded toward the woman standing with Hawley. "That's Kate Woodward, her sister."

Reid stared at Kate, wondering if she would recognize him. He tried to control his breathing.

"Who called you here?" he asked McCabe.

"Kate. Before I tell you anything else, we did break the door to get in. We went upstairs and discovered the body. We debated getting a search warrant."

"Okay," Reid said. He shoved his emotions aside, thinking down the road to some defense lawyer using it against them.

"Kate had been trying to reach Beth for three days. She was pretty frantic. The sisters were close. They spoke every day—sometimes many times a day. Beth was pregnant, and apparently the pregnancy wasn't easy. Kate felt nervous after the second missed call, but at first she assumed Beth was working at the family business."

"The art gallery," Reid said.

"Yes," McCabe said. "Or out on the beach with the dog, in the garden, whatever. She wasn't a big cell phone user. She often left it at home."

"But there were missed calls?"

"Oh, lots. The sister was out of town, calling

and calling. Other numbers in the call log too, including from the husband. Kate couldn't get here to check until this morning. She cut her trip short, flew home first thing to get here."

"What kind of trip?" He felt dishonest asking questions to which he already knew the answers.

McCabe looked blank, then reddened. "Sorry, I didn't ask."

"Don't worry," Reid said. He looked past her toward Kate Woodward. He couldn't keep his eyes away.

"Anyway, the husband is sailing—a yearly thing with the guys, several days offshore. And sorry, I didn't ask where."

"We'll find out," Reid said. He nodded with what he hoped was reassurance at McCabe. He had started out as a police officer in New London, then had spent two years as a trooper for the state police before becoming a detective with the Major Crime Squad. It wasn't the local cops' job to investigate a crime. It was his, and in the byzantine world of his relationship with the Woodward sisters, he knew more than he would ever tell this officer.

"She was hit here," McCabe said, tapping her own head just behind her left ear. "And she was strangled."

Reid nodded, trying to keep his composure.

"What else did you notice?" he asked.

"Marble owl statue, covered with blood, under the bed—obviously the weapon he hit her with." She paused. "And a weird thing—an empty frame on the bedroom wall. Some threads stuck to the wood as if maybe a painting was cut out."

"A painting?" he asked, electricity zapping his bones. *But it couldn't be the same one,* he thought.

"Looks that way to me."

"Okay," Reid said. "Thanks."

He walked toward Kate Woodward. He wanted to go into the house, to sit with Beth Lathrop. He always thought of his first encounter with a homicide victim as two people meeting. An encounter every bit as important in death as it would have been in life, as revelatory as a conversation—in some ways more so. But this would be different from any crime victim he'd ever met: he knew Beth and had rescued her after what, until today, had been the most traumatic event in her life.

He said hello to Officer Hawley, who was savvy enough to peel off and leave him alone with Beth's sister. He took a deep breath, looked into Kate's eyes. She stared at him, unrecognizing. He wanted to hold her hand, as he had that day in the art gallery twenty-three years ago. She had been sixteen, Beth a year younger. His heart beat so hard he figured she'd see the vein throbbing in his neck.

"Miss Woodward, I'm Detective Conor Reid. I'm very sorry about your sister."

"I knew, I knew," Kate said, digging the heels of her hands into her eyes. "I should have come home the minute she didn't answer—I felt it."

"What did you feel?"

"That something was wrong."

"She always answered her phone? Every time you called?" Reid asked, remembering what McCabe had told him.

"Not always, not before this—but both Pete—her husband—and I were away this week, and Beth was having a rocky time, and I made her promise she'd carry her phone and answer when I called. Even so, when she didn't pick up, I tried telling myself it was just her old habits."

"What kind of rocky time had she been having?"

"Well, she had wicked morning sickness the first three months, and then her blood sugar spiked. She had gestational diabetes with Sam—their daughter—and it went away after Sam was born. Her doctor said there was no guarantee she wouldn't have it again with this pregnancy."

"They have other children?" he asked.

"No, just Sam. And, almost, Matthew."

"Matthew?" he asked.

"That's what they were going to name him," Kate said, her voice cracking. "The baby. Did he, is he . . . did he die too? He did, right? He's dead?"

26

"The medical examiner will tell us," Reid said, although according to the officers' report, he knew the answer was yes. He knew many details about her sister's life, but not specifically why there were so many years between the children.

"And Pete's off sailing," Kate said, the anguish in her eyes giving way to anger. "Who would leave his wife for a week, knowing she wasn't completely okay? Especially because I was gone too?"

"Where did you go?" Reid asked.

"I had a charter from Groton to LA."

Reid waited for her to explain. He had to be careful here and pretend he didn't know about her career.

"I'm a pilot for Intrepid Aviation," she said. "Private jets."

"And you flew back this morning?"

"Yes. It was supposed to be a deadhead, but then the clients decided they wanted to come back. He's a studio executive, and they have a summer place in Watch Hill. So I'd thought I would be home a day and a half ago, but I had to wait for them. I should have left them in LA— my first officer could have taken over for me. I could have booked a commercial flight home."

"Where is Pete sailing?"

Her brow furrowed. Her eyes shut tight for a moment, as if in a private moment, lost in recriminations over her own delay in returning.

27

Then, "I'm not sure. They meet the boat in Nantucket and sail from there. Every year in July, Pete and a bunch of his friends charter a Beneteau and take off for a week."

"A Beneteau?"

"It's a sailboat. Fifty feet or so long. It's fancy. Well, expensive."

"Okay," Reid said. His brother, Tom, would know all about it. Tom was a commander in the Coast Guard, and he knew all things nautical. He was Reid's secret weapon when it came to certain local investigations, especially the last one involving the Woodward sisters. *I couldn't do it without him* was an overused phrase, but when it came to Tom, that's how Reid felt.

Kate was silent, her lips tight. Reid had the feeling she wanted to say something more about Pete. Why hadn't she suggested they call him?

"What does your brother-in-law do?" Reid asked.

"He's *president* of the Lathrop Gallery," she said, clear derision in her voice.

"Why do you say that?"

"As if he does anything at all."

"I know the gallery well," he said carefully. "And that it originally belonged to your grandmother."

Her expression didn't change. She didn't seem surprised that he knew that. Then again, the gallery was well known in the art world, a

28

mainstay in art-centric Black Hall. But did she remember him?

"It's been in my family for generations. It eventually came to me and Beth."

After their mother's death and their father's conviction. He stared at Kate, debating how much to tell her about his role the day she was rescued. Could she be assuming Beth's murder might be connected to what her father had done? He began to formulate an idea about who might have been inspired by that crime.

"You changed the gallery's name," Reid said. "Is your brother-in-law an owner?"

Kate shook her head. "No. Beth and I are. I let my sister make most decisions regarding the gallery, and she gave him the title. President."

"Is it just a title?"

"Pretty much," Kate said. "He just sits back and thinks about . . . himself. Whatever he wants to do next."

That's what people had said about her father years ago.

"Why did she give it to him?"

"He's an arrogant jerk with an inferiority complex. He acts as if he's better than everyone— even Beth. But his feelings get hurt if you look at him sideways. Beth decided it was easier to let him have what he wanted. She isn't someone who likes to fight."

"But he is?" Reid asked.

"He likes getting his own way," she said quietly. Again, Reid thought of the girls' father. There were such parallels with Beth and Pete, two generations of secret lives. Kate and Beth's mother had had the money and the gallery; she had given her husband a title and the power to run it the way he'd wanted, just like Beth and Pete.

How much did Kate really know about her sister's marriage? The sisters had been traumatized by their time in the basement. He didn't need a psychology degree to understand they would be deeply affected for the rest of their lives. For some time now, he had believed Beth's earlier experience made her vulnerable to a predator—the man she had married.

Some nights, unable to sleep, Reid felt Kate's small cold hand in his. He heard Beth's high, thin animal wail. Twenty-three years ago, the Woodward sisters and their mother had been forced into the gallery's basement, bound to each other with ropes and duct tape, while upstairs thieves had stolen priceless nineteenth-century landscapes. Reid had been the resident trooper and first on the scene.

Helen, the girls' mother, had choked on the gag and died. Kate and Beth had been thrashing, screaming into the cotton wadded into their mouths behind the duct tape. Reid had cut them loose. He exhaled slowly now, remembering how

Beth had thrown herself at her mother's body, holding her and sobbing. Kate had gone silent. She had stood stiff and numb, in total shock, backing away from her mother and sister, eyes like a zombie's. That's when Reid had taken her hand, tried to get her to look at him, to focus on him instead of the horror right in front of her.

He stared at her now, her right hand clenched. He had to hold himself back from reaching for it. He felt dishonest, not being straight with her about his involvement—and not just with the previous case. The day he had pulled the Woodward girls from the basement, he had vowed to protect and keep track of them. He believed the old rule, that if you rescued someone, you were responsible for them forever. He had kept an eye on them as much as possible, and it was killing him right now to know that Beth was dead inside the house, to realize how badly he had failed.

After a few moments, Kate seemed to compose herself. She sighed, gave her shoulders a small shake, as if bringing herself out of a trance. Reid was wound tight, forcing himself to breathe, to be right here with Kate and hear what she had to tell him.

"Pete called me, looking for her too," Kate said.

She hadn't mentioned that before. Reid had a million questions, but he kept quiet and listened.

"Twice," Kate said. "Once while I was in the air, and I didn't get the message till after I landed in Van Nuys. That time he just asked if I knew whether Beth had plans. It seemed strange, but I didn't think much of it. I didn't even call him back before he rang again. He said he'd been trying her, not getting through. He knew she was tired, thought she might have been catching up on extra sleep. I told him that was definitely possible, but then I started getting nervous. And I couldn't get her either."

"Did you call anyone to go check on her?"

"Our friend Scotty Waterston," Kate said. "She had been over very early, gardening with Beth. Then she came back, with muffins or some-thing—they were going to have coffee—and saw that Beth had left a note on the front door for the UPS driver. It said she'd gone out for the morning, that he should leave packages without a signature."

"Where's the note now?" he asked.

"It's still there. Scotty left it." Kate pointed at the yellow paper taped to the doorframe.

"Is it Beth's handwriting?" he asked.

"Yes."

"Were there boxes?" he asked.

"What?" she asked.

"Left by the UPS driver," he said.

"No," she said and frowned. "But the note made Scotty feel okay—as if Beth had just stepped out

32

and would be home soon. Her husband is on the trip with Pete."

Reid stared at the note. The paper looked rumpled, and he figured it was an all-purpose note, one Beth had written at some point to reuse whenever she went out. Plenty of people did that in towns like Black Hall, where they thought they could trust their neighbors. But anyone could have stuck it to the door—not necessarily Beth. The killer could have put it there.

"I have to notify Pete, Kate," Reid said. "Do you have his cell number?"

She scrolled through her phone's contact list and gave it to him.

Instead of writing it down on his pad, he programmed it directly into his phone. He would make the call shortly.

"What's the name of the boat?" he asked.

"*Huntress*," Kate said.

"Thanks," Reid said.

"What if I could have saved her?" Kate asked. Her green eyes glittered with tears, her face marked with despair. "She was my sister, my little sister. We were so close. Why wasn't I here for her? How could I have let this happen? It's the second time." She grabbed his hand, squeezing it tight. Electricity ran up his arm, into his heart.

"You're talking about the gallery? When you were kids?"

33

"No." She gave him a sharp look as if shocked he'd say that. Then she shook her head.

"Second time for what, then?" he asked.

"I wasn't there for her. And something terrible happened."

"What was the first?" he asked.

She didn't respond, just pulled her hand back a second time. Back then, in the basement, all emotion had seemingly drained from her—she had turned completely blank. Now she crackled with rage and grief. He noticed other differences and comparisons. Physical details: she was five six, slightly taller than she had been at sixteen. Her dark-brown hair was tied back in a ponytail, just as it had been that day long ago. Light freckles still dusted her cheeks. She was dressed in jeans and a sleeveless shirt, and her tan arms were toned and showing a serious devotion to working out. Right now, she seemed barely able to hold herself up. Reid fought back the urge to comfort her.

"I'm going to ask you to give your statement to Detective Miano," he said, pointing toward his partner. Jennifer stood next to a pot of white geraniums with her pad open, talking to Officer Hawley. "I'll send her over to talk to you, and then we'll make sure you get home."

"I have to tell Sam," Kate said. "Before the news gets out."

"Won't her father do that?"

34

"We don't know where he is, do we?" Kate asked.

"No," he said.

"You have no idea how much I hate him," she said.

"Tell me." He stared at her hard and waited to hear how aware she had been of Pete's secret life.

But she shook her head and turned away from him. He gestured for Miano to come over, then glanced back at Kate. *What if I could have saved Beth?* she had asked. *How could I have let this happen?* Maybe they were just aimless questions, but the second in particular implied power over the situation, as if she believed she could have stopped the murder.

Reid wondered how she thought she might have done that, what the relationship between the sisters had become. Had those hours when they'd been tied up in the gallery basement pulled them closer or driven them apart? Did they have any choice, controlling the course their lives took, or had they been programmed, even ruined, from the moment the intruder entered the gallery?

It had certainly controlled him. Standing close to Kate now, he felt his hands shaking and jammed them into his pockets so she wouldn't see. The Woodward sisters' pain was his white whale, his torment.

You have no idea how much I hate him, she had said about her brother-in-law. He actually

35

did have an idea about that. Keeping an eye on the Woodward sisters meant he saw what the other people in their lives were up to. He felt uncomfortable, most likely knowing more about her sister's marriage than Kate did.

"Did Beth and Pete have a good marriage?" he asked, keeping his tone steady because he knew the ugly answer.

"No," she said flatly.

"Were there other people involved?"

"On his part—yes," she said.

He waited for her to say the name *Nicola,* but she began to cry softly, burying her face in her hands.

The muffled sound of a ringing phone came from inside the house. He hesitated, hating to leave her in tears. Then he turned away, so she wouldn't pick up on his fixation on her and her sister and their shared history. What had happened in that basement had happened to him too. He walked toward the front door, wondering what was the first time she'd let something bad happen.

It was time to go see Beth.

3

The forensics team had arrived and was ready to start processing the scene, but Reid wanted to enter the room first. He grabbed a pair of disposable gloves from a box on the sidewalk and snapped them on. The house smelled stale, as if no fresh air had entered in days. When he reached the top of the stairs and opened the bedroom door, he felt the blast of cold and tasted the sweet stench of decomposition.

He stood back, gazing at Beth. From this angle, looking at her from behind, he could almost imagine she was sleeping: her reddish-gold hair spread across the pillow, the curve of her hip, and the languid way her arm covered her eyes to block the morning light. But as he moved closer, the illusion was shattered.

Approaching the edge of the bed, he nearly tripped on the bloodstained marble owl. He circled around to the other side.

He saw that Beth's skull had been cracked behind her ear, the wound deep and red with fine slivers of bone stuck in the dark blood. A bruise of ligature marks encircled her throat. There were impressions of lace; a torn bra and panties lay on the floor. He stared at them: evidence of a sex crime?

Her swollen tongue jutted between clenched teeth, and the whites of her clouded eyes were full of red-and-purple pinpoint dots, petechial hemorrhages indicating strangulation. Dry, almost invisible whitish crust had formed around her lips and run down her chin, and Reid knew the medical examiner would find amylase-rich saliva. Her legs were bruised.

"You were so young," he said out loud.

He wasn't talking to the teenage Beth he'd rescued all those years ago but to the thirty-something-year-old Beth who lay on the bed before him. He stared into her cloudy eyes as if she were looking back at him. He heard the air conditioner chugging so hard it rattled in the window frame. Instinctively, he knew Beth hadn't turned it on—her killer had.

Whenever he drove by this house—not as often as he patrolled Kate's loft, but at least once a week—he noticed that the windows were always wide open. The curtains might be rippling in the breeze; he'd hear voices from inside, or music coming from the daughter's room, or the TV on in Pete's study. Beth liked fresh air. Kate did too. Reid figured the preference came, partly, from having been shut up in that dank cellar for nearly twenty-four hours.

The killer had left the UPS note on the door, had

turned up the AC, had wanted everyone to think Beth had been alive longer than she actually had. Reid would be checking for sex offenders in the area, but why would a rapist care about messing with the time of death?

His gut told him this was something else. The killer had needed to build in time, enough for him to establish his alibi—such as getting onto a sailboat with his buddies and heading off-shore, hundreds of miles away, where he couldn't possibly have killed his wife.

Gazing into Beth's face, Reid couldn't stop shaking. He was in the process of breaking a cardinal rule of investigation: making up his mind before reviewing all the facts. Two men who were supposed to have loved Beth—her father and now her husband—had destroyed her. Reid glanced across the room at the empty picture frame and wondered if Pete had gotten ideas from the earlier crime. He turned back to Beth.

Suspicion wasn't enough. He needed hard evidence, and he started by looking at Beth's hands. Her fingernails had been manicured recently; there were no scratches or bent or broken nails, no obvious skin or blood caught under the nail tips. Why hadn't she grabbed for him while he was strangling her? Why hadn't she scratched and slashed and tried to break his grip, to yank the ligature away from her throat, snagging some of his DNA under her nails? Perhaps she had, and Reid simply wasn't seeing it. The coroner would tell him.

Outside the bedroom, in the upstairs hall, the forensics team was getting impatient. He could hear them talking. Although he knew they would document the scene with detailed video and photographs, he removed his iPhone from his jacket pocket and took photos of Beth, the blood-stained pillowcase, and the owl. Before leaving the room, he walked to the wall where the empty picture frame hung. The gilded frame itself gave him a jolt. It brought back the past; he would know it anywhere.

On the bureau a sketch pad lay opened to a page with small ink drawings of a sailboat, a row of beach umbrellas, and an ornate antique key. There were notations beside each sketch, and he recognized Beth's handwriting from the note downstairs:

The husbands go sailing away—Pete and Nick and their pals—so Beth and Scotty and Kate and Lulu get to be beach girls for a week!

Reid pictured Pete somewhere off the coast, on a beautiful boat sailing on the deep blue sea, feeling safe and smug. The gallery president who didn't do anything. Another husband who wanted it all—just like Kate and Beth's father—and figured it was his for the taking.

He photographed the empty frame and the

page of drawings. He stood beside the bed, his gaze moving from Beth's head wound to the strangulation marks around her neck to the ripped lingerie on the floor. Had she been hit or strangled first? If it had been a rape-murder, would Beth's attacker have stolen the painting as a trophy? Again, his instinct told him that a stranger had not done this.

Reid heard the house phone ringing downstairs. He left the bedroom, and the techs entered. He hurried downstairs, and just as he got to the kitchen door, the landline stopped ringing. He imagined the call going to voice mail. He pulled out his cell phone, and, reading the house phone number printed on the telephone base, he dialed and heard Beth's voice:

Hi, you've reached the Lathrops, and we're probably out walking Popcorn, so leave your message, and we'll call you just as soon as we get back from the beach! Then BEEP.

A few seconds after he hung up, the phone rang again. Reid picked up but didn't say anything. He just held the receiver to his ear.

"Hello?" a man's voice said. "Beth? Bethie! Are you there? Why haven't you been answering? You having too much fun with the girls? I've called your cell, and you're not calling me back, and I'm going a little crazy . . ."

"Who is this?" Reid asked, although he already knew.

"Who the hell is *this?*" the voice asked.

"Detective Conor Reid of the Connecticut State Police. Who am I speaking to?"

"Pete Lathrop. Did I dial a wrong number? I'm calling my wife."

"You have the right number," Reid said.

"Where is she?"

Reid paused for a beat. "Mr. Lathrop, I am very sorry to tell you that your wife is deceased."

"Christ, no!" Pete shouted. "You're lying. You've got to be. God, Beth!" The phone clattered, as if he had dropped it.

Over the course of Reid's career, he had had occasion to play 911 tapes to juries: perpetrators phoning in supposed discoveries of their own crime scenes. You could almost always tell real from manufactured shock. Pete's reaction was so instantaneous, so canned, it came off as rehearsed.

"What is your position?" Reid asked.

"We're approaching Oak Bluffs, on Martha's Vineyard," a different voice said.

"Who's on the line?"

"Leland Ackerley. A friend of Pete's. And Beth's."

"What's the nearest Coast Guard station?" Reid asked.

"Menemsha."

"Okay, then. Go to Menemsha, and I'll meet you there," Reid said.

4

Sisters were forever. They were made from the same blood and bone. Kate remembered when she was six and Beth was five, Beth had pointed at their mother's belly and said, "We came out of the same stomach!" It was true. Since the minute Beth was born, until today, Kate had never known a moment on earth without her sister. She had always been able to feel her sister's breath in the summer breeze, hear her voice whenever their favorite songs played on the radio, hear her laughter when anything reminded her of one of their private jokes.

Kate had to tell Sam. That's what kept her going right now—the fact that Sam would need her, and Beth would want Kate to take care of her child. But even that thought was too insane—the fact that Kate had to tell Sam her mother was dead—because Beth couldn't be dead. Kate couldn't stand it if she was: this could not be true.

Pretend she's not, she said to herself. *Talk to her as if she is here. Right here with me. Sisters together forever! Right, Beth? Are you with me?*

But then Kate pictured her sister on the bed, the expression on her face—that was barely a face anymore. Beth's skull, shattered like broken glass. Kate had stared into a hole in her sister's head and seen pieces of white bone clumped in her blood.

Sam was at camp, and she didn't know. Stories like this made the news and spread fast. Kate had firsthand experience of that fact—nothing went viral faster than small-town crimes, murdered mothers. If she didn't get to Sam fast, some kid would read about it on Facebook. So she called the camp and asked that Sam be kept away from the media, and then the camp manager reminded her that cell phones and laptops and iPads weren't allowed, that Sam would hear nothing until Kate arrived.

The last time Kate had visited Sam at camp was two years ago, and Beth had been with her. Sam had just been a camper then, but now she was a junior counselor. The sisters had driven north in Kate's Porsche with the top down and the radio on. They'd traveled almost the whole way on back roads, through pine woods, past farms and wide-open meadows. Although they lived relatively near each other, they didn't get enough time together—Kate's flight schedule was intense, and Beth was so busy with Pete and Sam and running the gallery. The road trip had been just what they'd needed: nonstop stories and laughter.

Kate couldn't stop feeling the need to talk to

Beth. She wanted to tell her about Detective Reid, how he'd tried to be circumspect but had been so clumsy that Kate had no doubt he knew every detail about what had happened to them. Probably every cop in Connecticut did. Sometimes Kate could still feel the ropes around her wrists, forearms, chest, and ankles. She flexed her right hand now. She could still smell the blood, all her mother's body fluids pooling around them. She and Beth almost never spoke about those hours at the gallery—they had locked the experience in a vault, just to stay sane and move on.

Camp Orion was in Down East Maine, on an island off Roque Bluffs. Kate had thought about driving today, but it was a seven-plus-hour drive, not counting the ferry ride. She needed to get to Sam right away. And the idea of retracing the route she'd driven with Beth, with the seat empty beside her, pierced her heart clear through.

She drove to the Groton–New London Airport, where early that morning she had landed the Citation X chartered by the Higginsons. She and Tallulah Granville, her best friend since child-hood, co-owned a single-engine Piper Saratoga and kept it there. Lulu was a captain on Delta, active in the pilots' union. Normally Kate would check with her to make sure she didn't have plans to fly. Last week Lulu had been in Atlanta training on a new aircraft. Kate wasn't sure where her schedule was taking her today. The idea of having to tell her about Beth right now, when she hadn't yet seen Sam, was too excruciating to think about.

The Saratoga was high performance, an all-metal beauty with retractable landing gear and tapered wings. Kate removed the chocks from around the plane's wheels and climbed into the cockpit. She ran through the preflight check, put her headphones on, and called the tower to request clearance for takeoff.

The airplane taxied down the runway, took off like a dream, banked over Long Island Sound with a view of three states—Connecticut, Rhode Island, and New York—and began to climb into the clear blue sky.

Kate had caught a tailwind back from LA, landing less than five hours after taking off from hot Van Nuys Airport in the San Fernando Valley. Because there had been a second pilot in the cockpit, her max allowable hours today were nine instead of eight, and that would give her just about enough flying time to get to Maine and back. Rules were important in the air and every-where. Her grandmother had taught her that.

Her grandmother had also taught Kate to fly. Mathilda Harkness, even at eighty-two, had been the best pilot Kate had ever flown with. She had served in the WASP in World War II, but she'd never earned her wings.

"We knew our stuff as well as any man," she'd said on Kate's fifth lesson in a chartered Cessna. Kate was seventeen. It was the summer she should have been getting ready to go to college—she'd gotten into Sarah Lawrence—but she had deferred attending. She couldn't stop reliving those hours in the gallery's basement. Missing her mother and facing her father's legal troubles made the idea of going away to college unbearable. And Mathilda had insisted she and Beth get intense therapy for what she said was trauma—and Mathilda would have known. She'd been in the war.

"I am sure," Kate had said to her grandmother, loudly enough to be heard over the noisy single engine, "you knew your stuff *better* than the guys."

"You're right," Mathilda said. "We trained as hard as they did. Eleanor Roosevelt said we were 'a weapon waiting to be used.' Instead, they kept us off to the side, never sent us overseas. They expected us to come home from the war and take care of the men, have their children."

"But you did have a kid," Kate said. "Mom."

"Yes," Mathilda said. "But I did it without getting married, and I was damn glad she was a girl, because I wanted to raise someone strong and independent enough to know the idea this is a 'man's world' is a bunch of bullshit."

"Why did you join the WASPs?"

"I wanted to serve my country," she said. "And live up to Jacqueline Cochran."

"Who?"

"My idol," Mathilda said. "Jackie finished first in the Bendix Race of 1938, beating every man. First woman to break the sound barrier, and even till this minute, she's broken more altitude, speed, and distance records than anyone, including men. It was her idea to train women exactly like men in the air corps—the army way."

"The way you're tough on us," Kate said.

"Girls have to be dauntless," Mathilda said. "And twice as excellent. That's what I taught your mother, and it was what she was teaching you and Beth. And what I still am teaching you."

"Beth is already excellent," Kate said. "She doesn't need lessons in it." And it was true. Despite that day and night in the basement, what Kate had come to think of as *the basement hours,* her sister made high honors. While Kate's life was in shambles, her inability to start college filling her with shame, Beth stayed focused.

Still in high school, Beth had plans to attend Connecticut College, near enough to Black Hall so she could take over the gallery from the executor and start to run it as soon as possible. In the meantime, she wrote papers on the early American Impressionists—familiarizing herself with the family collection. Not only that, she volunteered at the Marsh View Nursing Home and the New London soup kitchen.

"Beth's the kindest, most generous person I know," Kate said. "Isn't that excellence?"

"It is," Mathilda said. "But who's up in the plane with me?"

"Beth is more of an on-the-ground person," Kate said. "Dad always said that about her. She's feet on the ground, and I'm head in the clouds."

"That monster," Mathilda said. "Leave it to him to sum up his daughters in such simplistic terms. But if you want to speak in clichés . . ."

Kate cringed, sorry she'd mentioned her father.

"You have to have your head in the clouds to shoot for the stars," Mathilda said. "Do you hear me, Katharine?"

"Yes," Kate said. They were flying toward the southern tip of Block Island. Soon she would make the turn over Great Salt Pond and begin to angle down toward the airport.

"You don't need to live a conventional life. You don't need to do anything people say you should do. Shoot for the stars, just like you're doing."

Kate had banked left then, starting her descent for Block. That was over twenty-three years ago, and she banked left now, descending toward the Barred Owl Airport to pick up Sam. It was a short runway, but the Saratoga could handle it.

She thought about a conventional life— Mathilda would never know how much Kate had wished she could have one. Mathilda had chosen the path she wanted—despite family pressure, she had never married, even when she had had a child. Instead she had fallen in love with Ruth, and they had lived together at Cloudlands, the big house on Sachem Hill.

Kate knew herself in terms of her career and passion for flying. Her personal life was another matter. At thirty-nine, like Mathilda, she had never married. People saw her laughing, driving, flying, and they didn't realize they were seeing a ghost. No one knew that ghosts could freeze—just like mist or vapor forming lacy crystals on windows in the winter—but Kate's spirit had turned to ice that day in the basement. It had been November, and the cellar had been damp, but all three of them jammed together, all that body heat, had given her a fever. Despite feeling scalded, Kate had been frozen, and when she had thawed, her life force, every possibility of desire, had trickled out of her.

She didn't care about owning a house in Black Hall, about tending an English country garden. She and her sister had been bequeathed many paintings by the Black Hall Impressionists, but unlike Beth, she displayed few. She didn't think about having a child and sending her to the right schools, the best camp. In her mind, she longed to be touched and held and loved, but her body refused it. Ghosts couldn't feel.

Kate had watched Beth and their two best friends—Lulu and Scotty—flirting and dating and talking endlessly about the exquisite torments of love and passion. Kate convinced them she didn't care about such things. She kept busy trying to outfly all the male pilots she knew, just as Mathilda had done in the war and beyond.

Beth had been the one to do those other things. She had met Pete when he'd visited the gallery, fallen madly in love and married him at twenty-two, had a perfect daughter. She had taken over the gallery, leaving Kate free to fly. She was great at cultivating wealthy collectors, and she assisted law enforcement agents and insurance investigators on the trail of criminals who had stolen paintings from museums and other galleries. She had become something of an expert in the psychology of art thieves—whether those who made it their careers or one-timers, like their father.

He had been behind the crime. He had needed money to fund his gambling habit. Beth's theory was that all thefts and cons were born of insatiable need and that their father's had been to restore his bank account—as much for the sake of the family as himself. Kate considered that to be bullshit. If he had had any insatiable need, it had been to keep blowing money at the casino and supporting his young mistress. The fact that his wife had died, and that she and his daughters had gone through hell, had been less important than achieving his goal.

And even after what he did, convicted and locked away for life, Beth was kind to him. She was all good. Through everything, she'd never stopped volunteering—especially at the soup kitchen and homeless shelter. She had been as excellent as anyone on this earth could be. Thinking about her sister, Kate felt her eyes blur with tears. She had to squint hard so she could see the dangerously short runway. She judged the length, determined a steep approach, maintained speed, reduced throttle, and touched down.

Mathilda would have been proud of her landing, especially through teary eyes. And that made Kate sad, because Mathilda had never felt truly proud of Beth. She had loved her. She and Ruth had enjoyed holidays at the Lathrops' house, occasionally attended openings at the gallery that Mathilda's parents had founded. Mathilda had been happy she'd lived to meet Samantha, her great-granddaughter. But she'd always felt Beth had taken the expected way, the society-approved path as a woman.

Although she'd never said it out loud, Kate knew that Mathilda hadn't truly believed that Beth had attained excellence.

But Kate believed it. She always had—her sister had been excellent in more ways than anyone knew. Anyone but Kate. Because they were sisters. Forever. Even now. Especially now. Kate climbed out of the cockpit and took a deep breath. It was time to go find her niece.

5

The state police helicopter landed at the Martha's Vineyard airport, and a police officer from West Tisbury drove Detectives Conor Reid and Jennifer Miano to Coast Guard Station Menemsha. An American flag snapped on a tall flagpole outside the USCG's big white red-roofed building on the hill above the harbor.

Reid stood on the dock, watching a forty-seven-foot boat coming through the inlet. His brother, Tom, a Coast Guard commander, had been on his cutter in Woods Hole, across Vineyard Sound, about fourteen miles away. As a courtesy to the Reid brothers, Menemsha Station had deployed one of its forty-seven-foot motor lifeboats to pick up Tom, and the vessel had met *Huntress* in Vineyard Sound to escort it to the USCG pier in Menemsha Harbor.

The Coast Guard boat docked, and Reid watched Tom and a crew member jump onto the dock to help cleat off *Huntress*'s lines. When the sloop was secure, Reid walked toward Tom. It didn't happen often enough, but because he worked in coastal towns, Reid's investigations sometimes intersected with the Coast Guard.

"Thanks for getting the husband here," Reid said, shaking his brother's hand.

"Husband, not suspect?" Tom asked.

"Remains to be seen," Reid said.

"I can't believe it's Beth Woodward," Tom said. "Shit, Conor."

"I know."

"Have you talked to her sister yet? What's her name again?"

"Kate. And yeah, I talked to her. She found the body."

"Jesus."

"What do you think of him?" Reid asked, gesturing down the dock toward Pete. "First impression."

Tom glanced over his shoulder. Pete and his friends were clustered by the stern of the boat, all talking on cell phones. "Arrogant, that's for sure," Tom said. "Just now, when they were docking, I heard him giving everyone else orders. You know—'You take the bowline; you stay in the stern.' Does he own the boat?"

"No."

"He's a dick," Tom said.

"Sounds like it," Reid said. "Can you hang around? I want to speak more after I interview him."

"Yeah. I'm off for the weekend. Heading home."

"Great, you can ride back on the chopper. Thanks for helping with this."

"No problem," Tom said.

"There's something else," Reid said. "The painting was stolen again. Cut right out of the frame."

"Which painting?" Tom asked.

"You know the one."

Tom stood there, obviously shocked. He had played a role in catching the girls' father's accomplices and, therefore, helping to bring Garth Woodward to justice. Of the several paintings stolen the night Kate, Beth, and their mother were tied up, *Moonlight* was the most valuable and the one that captivated the jury. Tom shook his head now and clapped his brother on the shoulder.

Reid walked toward *Huntress*. Jennifer Miano stood by the sleek sailboat's stern, speaking to each man and taking notes. He saw her writing down their names in her notebook. As he approached, he noticed a very tan, very blond man standing off to the side, his posture straight.

Reid recognized Pete. He'd seen him often enough over the years, and earlier that day, he had examined some framed photographs around the Lathrop bedroom. One, next to the window with the air conditioner, had shown him in a tuxedo, standing beside Beth in a black gown, surrounded by old and valuable-looking paintings. The thing that had struck Reid then was the fact that the monogrammed sterling-silver frame had been coated with frost. The air-conditioning had been that cold.

"Mr. Lathrop," he said. "We spoke on the phone. I'm Detective Reid."

"Can you take me to Beth?" Lathrop said, his voice quavering. "Right now? I've got to see her."

"Yes, very soon," Reid said.

"I have to know—what did they do to her?"

" 'They'?" Reid asked.

"Or he, whoever. You said she was murdered."

"I said she was deceased," Reid said.

"No, I distinctly heard . . . never mind. Just, can we go? Please."

That had been a big slip on Pete Lathrop's part, Reid thought. It would be helpful to use in court. He wished Miano had heard the exchange. Seeing the empty frame with the canvas cut out, it would have been normal to assume Beth's murder was part of an art theft, possibly connected to the old crime, to what the Woodward girls' father had done.

Reid thought it was more complicated than that. Based on Pete's callousness toward Beth in other areas of his life—his infidelity and general lack of respect—Reid could not help believing that the missing painting was part of a staged scene. The connection to the earlier crime might have been Pete adding psychological torture, wanting to remind Beth of what had happened before.

The torn underwear, though: that was a new

element. A stranger had broken in, raped, and murdered her? No, Reid didn't believe it.

The medical examiner had made a very preliminary estimation. He had told Reid that, based on Beth's body temperature and the fact it was still in rigor, it appeared that Beth had died a full day after Pete had left on the sailing trip. But there were other factors to take into account to gauge the time of death, starting with the piles of dog shit. Popcorn hadn't been walked in days. There were five copies of the *Day*, New London's newspaper, in and around the delivery tube by the road.

Once an autopsy was performed and they were able to determine her last meal, the time of death could be narrowed down even more. The bruises between her legs indicated sexual assault; if she had been raped, there would be semen or at least traces of fluid.

And now—Pete, on this hot summer day, was wearing shorts and a long-sleeved shirt.

No, Reid thought again—not a stranger.

"Why are you dressed so warmly?" Reid asked, pointing at the shirt.

"It's sun protection, special fabric. My wife bought it for me so I wouldn't burn."

"Would you please roll up your sleeves and show me your arms?"

Pete recoiled. "What? Are you kidding? I need to get home."

Reid didn't lift his gaze from the cuffs, buttoned tight around Pete's wrists. Strangulation victims often fought to get the ligature from around their necks, raking their killer's skin in the process. He recalled how Beth's hands had appeared to be unharmed, her fingernails unbroken, but he hoped that his initial assessment was wrong and that she had scratched her killer.

"Is there a problem with showing me your arms?" Reid asked.

"Yes," Pete said, glaring. "I'm not going to stand here and be treated like a criminal when you can ask *anyone* how much I loved my wife."

"Okay," Reid said, nodding. "Fair enough. You don't want to show me—that's your decision."

"Can I please leave?" Pete asked.

"Yes," Reid said. "We're going to fly you back to Connecticut on the state police helicopter."

"Thank you."

"And we're going to talk," Reid said.

"Good, because I want you to tell me everything, every detail. My mind's going crazy," Pete said, a tremor in his voice.

"Well, I'll tell you one thing right now."

"What?"

Reid stared into Pete's pale-blue eyes. The expression on his face was tense, as if he'd been practicing how to set his jaw.

"I think you killed your wife," Reid said.

6

Tom felt gravity pulling him down as the helicopter lifted straight up. Conor and Pete Lathrop were across the aisle in two seats facing each other. Conor had arranged it so Pete was sitting backward. Tom looked out the window at the ocean below. They flew over the Elizabeth Islands—Naushon, Pasque, Nashawena, and Cuttyhunk.

"You comfortable?" Conor asked Pete.

"No. I'm not freaking comfortable," Pete said. "How could you think that I could have done anything to Beth?"

"We'll get to that," Conor said.

"Should I have a lawyer?"

"That is absolutely your right," Conor said.

"*Right,*" Pete said. "What a joke. You haven't even *read* me my rights."

"That's because you're not under arrest. This is just a courtesy ride."

"But you just accused me of murdering her!"

"Was she giving you grief about your girlfriend?" Conor asked.

"You have no idea about Beth and me. We loved each other one hundred percent. We were devoted to each other."

"I bet she loved the fact you have someone else."

Tom watched the burning intensity in his brother's face, the cold fear in Pete's.

"You're going to arrest me because I had an affair?"

"I wonder how Nicola would feel to hear you calling it an *affair*. Doesn't she think it's a whole lot more than that? Didn't Beth? But no, I'm not going to arrest you."

Pete's eyes widened as he took that in. He looked surprised, then relieved: a pinched smile, as if he was getting away with something. His eyes were pale, more gray than blue, the color of spit. Tom glanced at Conor. His younger brother was staring at Pete with laser focus.

Tom loved when he and Conor crossed paths on a case. Two, including this one, were related to the Woodward family. Twenty-three years ago, when Tom was a USCG lieutenant and Conor was in his first year as a Connecticut state trooper, the shoreline had been rocked by the violence and brutality of what had happened to Helen, Kate, and Beth at their family's fancy art gallery in Black Hall. The fact that their husband and father had paid people to commit the crime had made it all the more horrific.

Conor was new to the Connecticut State Police after a stint as a town cop. Tom was a relatively seasoned Coast Guard officer after four years at the Academy and six years climbing the ranks. The crime scene swarmed with town and state cops, but very quickly the FBI took control of the case. The Coast Guard never would have gotten involved if, the same night as the gallery heist, Tom's vessel hadn't performed what had seemed to be a relatively random boarding operation.

It was a Monday in mid-November, just before dusk. The sea off Montauk was dark and calm, the sky the color of a black pearl. Most of the New England yachts going south for the winter had left weeks earlier. Winter in the north Atlantic was nothing to mess with, and decent skippers knew that.

Tom was aboard *Nehantic*, a 270-foot cutter. Just a week before they'd had a successful narcotics operation and were still riding high from it. With a USCG helicopter hovering overhead, they had tracked a narco-sub, a semisubmersible reported to be stuffed with fifteen tons of cocaine. *Nehantic* had gone to battle stations, deployed two raid boats, and gotten to the sub just in time to catch the crew preparing to scuttle. They'd arrested six smugglers and confiscated the coke and a cache of weapons before the vessel sank, and they'd become cartel-busting heroes in the media.

Then it was back to regular patrol. With a lull in November's often stormy weather and no reports of smugglers, they had a run of easy days.

Cruising off Montauk Point, Tom stood on the foredeck looking west and saw the orange line of sunset just above the horizon. When he turned east, the sky was darkening from slate gray into night, and for just a moment, he thought he glimpsed the silhouette of a large sailboat.

He raised the binoculars to his eyes. There it was again—backlit by the loom of Block Island. It was completely dark, no running lights. The mast was bare, no sails hoisted. He had a good look and estimated the boat's length at sixty feet overall with a graceful shear and an elegant waterline. At first, he thought the boat was becalmed, but after a few seconds, he saw that it was underway, motoring at a slow speed.

Seconds after spotting the sailboat, he lost sight of it. The vessel passed Block Island into the open ocean, and with no light behind it, the silhouette dissolved. Although the last three days had been calm, a gale was forecast, and by dawn the Atlantic would be roaring.

Glasses held to his eyes, Tom radioed Luis Santiago, the deck watch officer, up on the bridge.

"Twenty degrees off the port bow," Tom said. "A sailboat running south-southeast without lights. I had her but I lost her."

"I got her on radar. A smuggler or just a goddamn idiot?" Luis asked.

"Going south is the wrong direction for smuggling drugs," Tom said.

"Then check box number two. A goddamned idiot who missed the September exodus. His voyage to Saint Barts or wherever will have to wait. We're going to ruin his night."

Nehantic sped toward the invisible boat and minutes later approached what appeared to be a ghost ship. The yacht glided across the glassy sea, its wake white and rippling in the floodlights of the cutter. Its transom was illuminated, and Tom read the name and port: *Rembrandt*, Newport, Rhode Island. The cockpit was empty, but the boat steamed along, obviously on autopilot.

"Yacht *Rembrandt*!" Luis said, his voice booming out the speaker. He didn't have time to say anything else—two heads poked out of the companionway, and a man and woman scrambled up on deck.

"Hello!" the man called. "We're fine! Everything's okay."

"Running lights," Luis said.

"Oh, shit," the man said. "Sorry—it got dark so fast we didn't even notice. Flip them on, will you, Sally?"

And the yacht's running lights—white masthead and stern lights, the red port and green starboard lights—came on. That should have been enough. Maybe a citation for ignoring rules of the road. It might have been stupid to be heading south in November, but it wasn't illegal.

But in the spotlight's glare, Tom spotted

65

firearms, and not just any: just behind the nav station were two AK-47 assault rifles. They looked like the Chinese Norinco Type 56s they'd taken off the narco-sub a week before. The man glanced at Tom, noticed his line of vision, and inched toward the wheel, moving toward the guns. Tom drew his sidearm and pointed it at the captain and Sally.

"Hands up!" he said.

"You're making a mistake," the man said. "We're heading south for the winter, and we . . ."

"Hands up!" Tom shouted. The man and Sally complied. The entire *Nehantic* crew had responded. Several crew members were standing along the port rail, weapons drawn and pointed at the two people aboard *Rembrandt*; others were hurrying down to the deck where Tom stood. A call was made to headquarters—a request for air-and-sea backup. The raid boat was readied and lowered. Tom led the boarding party.

They handcuffed and searched the two people on board *Rembrandt*—Joshua Anderson and his wife, Sally. Both had Glock 9s in hip holsters hidden beneath their red fleece jackets. The hands of both suspects were covered with deep scratches. Tom took photos of their hands to show that with the blood already coagulating and scabbing, the injuries couldn't have been caused during the arrest.

The boarding team secured the weapons.

The yacht was a Nautor Swan, one of the most luxurious and seaworthy production sailboats made. Tom heard Joshua babbling about pirates, how you can't be too careful these days, how the Glocks and Chinese AKs were for self-defense, how the rules of the high seas were different, how boat invasions were just as deadly and prevalent as home invasions.

Tom scrambled down into the cabin. At first he thought the gold-framed museum-looking paintings on *Rembrandt*'s walnut-paneled walls were just part of the Swan's decor. He spotted a thin edge of metal between two of the walnut panels and leaned closer to examine it. He wondered if it was a hinge, so he ran his hands over the wall, pressing as he went, and a door opened. Inside the secret compartment were at least ten more paintings in heavy gold frames and several canvases that looked as if they'd been sliced out of their frames.

He pulled out one of the framed paintings and propped it up on the chart table. It depicted a night scene of beauty and mystery. A large stone house was bathed in gauzy silver light. The moon glinted through dark-green leaves and illuminated a young girl dancing in the yard. The painting conveyed passion and urgency. The lower left corner was signed *B. Morrison*. Tom looked on the back of the painting. The canvas was protected by a sheet of brown paper. A yellowed card taped to the paper gave the painting's title and other information: *Moonlight* by Benjamin Morrison, 1906.

Ever since the Isabella Stewart Gardner Museum in Boston had been robbed in the early-morning hours of March 1990, New England law enforcement officers and military had been on the lookout for over a dozen stolen works of art. Rumors had flown—they'd been stolen by the Irish mob to pay for guns; or a gang of drug dealers had ordered them stolen as ransom to have their leaders released from prison; or the old favorite ORDIAMITB theory: *One Rich Dude in a Mansion in the Bahamas* who wanted to keep the paintings in a locked room for only him to see.

One of the most important missing paintings was *The Storm on the Sea of Galilee* by Rembrandt van Rijn. Could *Rembrandt*, the name of the yacht, be a play on that? Tom wouldn't know a Rembrandt from a Picasso, but *Moonlight* looked like it belonged in a museum, and the idea occurred to him. He told his theory to his commanding officer, and he figured that if there was anything to it—if the paintings had come from the Gardner—the FBI would take it from there.

But the source of the paintings was much more local. It hadn't hit the news yet, but they had been stolen from the Harkness-Woodward Gallery earlier that day. And Tom's brother had been first on the scene.

Glancing across the chopper, Tom knew that case had inaugurated Conor's career and got him promoted to the Major Crime Squad. Conor was gripped by that long-ago case. He rarely talked about it, but Tom had seen a change in him after he'd rescued the sisters. He began drinking too much, and when Tom called him on it, Conor said he couldn't sleep, that he figured scotch was better than sleeping pills. Eventually Conor had cut way back on the booze, but he'd never returned to the easygoing way he'd had before.

Tom knew Conor would never forget what he had seen in that basement, and right now Tom felt uneasy, wondering whether it could be clouding his judgment about Pete. He could read his brother's mind, see the gears turning, and knew that Conor 100 percent wanted Pete for Beth's murder.

There were overlaps, and Tom saw that it made logical sense to think that Pete could have been inspired by his father-in-law's crime: twenty-three years earlier a husband, although a hundred miles away, had set in motion a violent act that had caused his wife's death.

Garth Woodward's wife had died during the course of the crime, so the charge had been raised to felony murder. Some believed it hadn't been an accident at all—that Garth had wanted

Helen killed, had ordered the Andersons to make sure the gag was so tight she would choke, so he could collect insurance not only on the paintings but on her life.

Is that what Pete wanted too? To collect the insurance on Beth? Tom forgot to worry that Conor was rushing to judgment and watched his brother stare at his suspect with the unrelenting attention of a hungry panther tracking its prey.

Tom smiled at Pete Lathrop.

You're in for it, he thought.

7

It was hard to believe that just that morning, Kate had found her sister's body. Every minute that ticked by took her farther away from Beth yet made the realization she was gone even more horrifying. Flying to Maine and back, trying to find anything halfway comforting to say to Sam, had filled the hours with heartbreak.

The kettle whistled, and Kate poured boiling water into Mathilda's Blue Willow teapot. The scent of Earl Grey, Beth's favorite tea, nearly knocked her over. Sam was wrapped in a blanket, watching TV. Kate had told her to keep the news turned off, but Sam wanted to see everything. Kate heard the somber voice of a newscaster broadcasting from outside her sister's home at 45 Church Street, Black Hall.

Kate lived on the top floor of an 1833 warehouse on Bank Street in New London. Although gentrifying, the maritime neighborhood was still rugged. Bars had always lined the street, but now cafés and a hair salon had moved in. The sturdy granite Custom House with its Doric columns, now the New London Maritime Society's museum, was next door.

The terrible day had turned to night. Late-afternoon summer light had blazed through sky-lights and tall windows, and now there was darkness. The Thames River, with all its boat traffic, flowed by. Train tracks ran along the river-bank. Two Orient Point ferries passed each other near the New London Harbor Light, exchanging short horn blasts—everything reminding Kate that time was passing, more time without Beth.

Telling Sam about Beth had been unthinkable, a nightmare; Sam was still in shock. Now it was time to tell Lulu. The four of them—Kate and Lulu, Beth and Scotty—had been best friends forever, and Kate owed it to Lulu to make sure she heard it from her—no one else. But all her calls went straight to voice mail.

Scotty had not simply called but had been waiting at the airport when Kate had landed after getting Sam: a tearful, grieving welcoming committee of one. Kate hung back while Scotty went straight to Sam. She embraced her tightly—the way Beth would have. Sam actually put her head on Scotty's shoulder for a minute—after all, Scotty's daughter Isabel was Sam's best friend, and Scotty was practically a second mother to Sam.

"Have you talked to Lulu?" Kate had asked Scotty when they'd met at the airport.

"I can't reach her," Scotty had said. "It's weird and so not Lulu. She always answers her phone."

Now Kate could barely breathe. Lulu didn't inspire worry. She was the most independent woman Kate knew, other than herself. But her skin felt charged with the knowledge that the worst could happen, as it had to Beth. She needed Lulu to call so she could know Lulu was okay.

She leaned against the kitchen counter for a minute, pulling herself together, then loaded a tray with the teapot, cups, and a plate of oatmeal cookies.

"Tea," Kate said, setting the tray on a low table in front of Sam. Popcorn lay on the floor at her feet, tongue out and eyes friendly. His tail thumped.

"Look, it's our house," Sam said, gesturing at the TV. "There you are, Popcorn." The screen showed the dog on a red leash, a police officer leading him into the back of a patrol car. Popcorn had been at the Black Hall station until Kate and Sam had picked him up on the way home.

"Turn it off," Kate said.

"They keep showing pictures of us," Sam said. "Me, Mom, and Dad. Mostly Mom. Where did they even get those pictures?"

"Not from me," Kate said.

"Some rancid so-called friend probably sold them. Now, look, here comes the body bag again. That's the other thing they keep running, the medical examiners carrying her out of the house."

"Why are you watching that?"

"Because I want to know and see *everything* that happened to her," Sam said.

Kate tried to grab the remote, but Sam held it out of reach. At least she'd muted the sound. Kate poured two cups of tea. Sam was sixteen, long legged, and beautiful, a brilliant student getting ready to look at colleges. But right then, curled up on the sofa, she seemed like a tiny girl. Her lower lip wobbled, but she didn't cry. She had always been stoic. Kate took her bike riding one time when she was six. She skidded on sand and fell off, scraping her elbows. *I'm brave,* Sam had said. *Shake it off, don't cry.* And she hadn't until they'd returned home, and the minute she had seen Beth, she'd thrown herself into her arms, sobbing. Only with her mother could she let her feelings out.

Kate's phone buzzed, and she glanced at the screen. The state police had flown Pete back to Connecticut from the Vineyard, and he had just been to the morgue. Now he wanted to pick up Sam.

"It's your dad," she said, showing her the message.

"I just want to stay here," Sam said. "I can't talk to him yet."

Kate stared at her niece. She could think of many reasons why Sam might be mad at her father; she just wasn't sure how much Sam knew about the issues between him and Beth.

"Can you tell me why?" Kate asked.

"It's too hard," Sam said.

"I know, honey. We're all so sad. But he's your dad. You need to see each other."

"Not yet," Sam said.

"Sam, you're each other's family."

"Stop!" Sam said, her voice rising.

"Listen, Sam. You need each other."

"You're the one who's not listening. I don't want to talk about it anymore!"

Kate felt shocked by Sam's fury.

"Okay," she said, trying to sound calm.

Sam took a deep breath. She gave Kate a quick glance.

"Thanks," Sam said, holding Kate's gaze for a few seconds. Kate felt her wanting to say more, but then Sam looked away.

"There's one thing we can't put off," Kate said. "The detective wants to talk to you too. I spoke to him on the phone, and he's coming over."

"I am not ready to talk to anyone," Sam said.

"I know the feeling," Kate said. It was 8:00 p.m., barely twelve hours since she had found Beth.

"So don't let him in."

"Sam, he has to interview us," Kate said. "It's important."

"Nothing's important anymore," Sam said. "Not without Mom."

Kate closed her eyes. How would a world without Beth make sense for either of them?

"I could have stopped it," Sam whispered.

"No," Kate said. "Don't think that."

She sat beside Sam on the gray tweed couch. She thought back to when she and Beth were the girls whose mother had died in an art robbery gone wrong. The cops had asked them countless questions. The details of what they'd been through blurred together. Every time Kate told the story, it seemed a little less real. The experience began to feel like a dream, something she had made up. Because how was such a thing possible in life? To be tied to your mother and sister, the knots so tight you couldn't slip free? To have to just sit there, listening to your mother choking and feeling her body going limp and tilting over, unable to move and save her life?

"You couldn't have stopped anything. It's not your fault—not one bit," Kate said to Sam.

"Doesn't feel that way," Sam said. "If I hadn't been at camp . . ."

"Then you might have gotten hurt too."

Sam tipped her head back, gazing up at Kate. Her eyes were pale blue, like her father's, and she had Mathilda's dark hair, like Kate. But she had Beth's full lips, her heartbreaking smile.

"Killed, you mean," Sam said.

"Yes," Kate said.

"You know what I hated?" Sam asked.

"What?"

"Seeing Mrs. Waterston at the airport," Sam

said, her voice breaking. "She was Mom's best friend. What's she going to do without her?"

Kate's heart cracked. She watched tears leaking from Sam's eyes. It was as if her niece couldn't cry for her own pain but only while imagining someone else's. And she wasn't wrong about Scotty: Kate knew something was bothering Scotty, and her only true confidant was Beth. Scotty had put on weight, and she constantly berated herself for letting herself go. Sometimes she smelled like wine a little too early in the day. Whatever Scotty was going through, she could share it with Beth.

The buzzer rang. For a second Kate thought it might be Lulu. After running to the door, Kate checked the image on the video monitor: Conor Reid stood at the entrance to her building. She pushed the intercom button. "Yes?" she asked.

"Hello, Kate," he said, staring straight into the camera. "May I come up to speak with Samantha?"

She hesitated, glanced over at her disheveled niece, watched Sam slash tears from her eyes.

"It's the detective. I'm really sorry, Sam. But we need to talk to him," she said, waiting for a response.

"I'll do it for Mom," Sam said finally.

Kate punched in a series of numbers. Because she had once been held against her will, she had bought the best biometric security system available. The voice-recognition software measured her particular patterns—the velocity of air expelled from her lungs and across her larynx. She could have said anything, and depending on her mood, her words could get very colorful. But mindful of Sam on the sofa, she quoted a line from a favorite poem: *Turning and turning in the widening gyre, the falcon cannot hear the falconer* . . .

The lock tumblers whirred and clicked, and she heard the downstairs door open.

"What's that you just said?" Sam asked, curious in spite of herself.

"It's from 'The Second Coming' by William Butler Yeats," she said. "Mathilda taught it to me."

Sam nodded, and Kate half smiled, glad to provide a momentary distraction. Sam had always been fascinated with her aunt's ever-changing alarm system, had loved watching Kate offer her left eye to the iris-reading camera or stare at the screen so the software could recognize her face.

Kate opened the loft door, and Popcorn came loping over to stand by her side, tail wagging. They both watched Reid climb the stairs. His blue blazer looked as if it had been balled up in the back seat of his car; it had been a long day.

"Hello, Kate," he said.

"Hello, Detective Reid," she said.

"Conor's fine," he said.

She nodded. "Thanks," she said.

"Hello, Popcorn," he said, petting the dog, whose tail was going faster than ever. "We made friends at the house."

"Popcorn makes friends with everyone," Sam said.

Both Kate and the detective turned to look at her. Kate closed the door and watched Conor cross the loft, offer his hand to shake Sam's.

"Samantha," he said. "I am very sorry about your mother."

Sam's mouth twisted, and her chin wobbled. She looked back at the TV screen.

"I'm in charge of investigating what happened. I'm going to do my best to find out who did this to her."

"It doesn't matter who did it," Sam said.

"I think it matters a lot," he said. He sat down in the brown leather chair opposite her, leaning forward with arms folded on his knees, looking directly into her eyes.

"She's gone," Sam said. Tears pooled but didn't spill over.

"I know," he said, letting the silence last. Then, "How are you?"

She shrugged.

"Have you seen your dad yet?"

"No," she said. "He wanted to, but . . ."

Kate watched her close her eyes tight, pull

79

herself together. She also noticed Conor hanging on her words.

"Who is that?" Sam asked instead of completing her answer, pointing at the screen.

"That's Officer Peggy McCabe. She's with the Black Hall Police Department, and she and her partner were first on the scene. Your aunt called the police when your mother didn't answer the door."

"You found Mom?" Sam asked, head snapping to look at Kate.

"Yes," Kate said.

"You didn't tell me," Sam said.

Kate touched her shoulder lightly. As much as she loved her niece, she felt confused and hesitant, not knowing just what to say or when. She hadn't wanted to volunteer anything without having a sense of what Sam was ready to hear.

"You mentioned that Popcorn is friendly with everyone," he said.

"Yes, as you can tell."

"Does that mean he doesn't bark when a stranger comes to the door?"

"Sometimes he does," she said. "But more in a curious way. He's not exactly a watchdog."

"Your aunt has a very good security system," he said.

"I know," Sam said, glancing at Kate. "Fancier than the one at the gallery. We tease her."

"What about the one you have at home? Does

your family always use it or sometimes leave it off?"

"Depends on who's coming and going. We usually have it on."

"Usually but not always?"

Sam gave him a long look. "Always at night. And Mom would have had it set the whole time since she was there alone."

Kate sat at the end of the sofa next to Sam.

"But it wasn't on," Kate said. "We broke in through the sliding door, and the alarm didn't go off."

"Would she have let a stranger into the house?" Conor asked.

"Never," Kate and Sam said at the same time.

"She was nervous," Sam said. "Because of what happened when she was a kid. At the gallery."

"Did she talk about that?" he asked.

"Not a lot," Sam said. "But she taught me to be careful. It sucked big-time, the worst nightmare, what happened to her and Aunt Kate and their mother. Also, the art collection—it's valuable. She didn't even want to keep the paintings in the house."

"What do you mean?" he asked.

"Well, because robbers would want them. She thought they would be safer in the gallery— and that we would be safer, too, because the art wouldn't be a magnet for criminals," Sam said.

"So why were they in your house? If she didn't think they should be there?"

"My brother-in-law overruled her," Kate said, remembering how she'd tried to get Beth to stand up for herself, insist on what she wanted.

"One of the paintings was cut out of its frame," Conor said. "In the bedroom."

"Really? Which one?" Kate asked.

"I was hoping you could tell me."

"I didn't notice anything in that room," she said. "Except Beth."

"Of course," Conor said.

"Obviously Mom was right, then," Sam said, her mouth twisting. "About the paintings being safer at the gallery."

"Because one was cut from the frame?" Conor asked.

"Not just this time. What I meant was, a painting almost got stolen last year." She paused. "Exactly a year ago—around the time I went to camp last summer."

Kate felt stunned. Beth hadn't said a word about it. How could she have kept something so critical from her?

"Your mom never told me," she said, trying to keep her voice steady.

"You were probably flying. She had Mrs. Waterston for things like that," Sam said.

"Things like what?" Kate asked, unable to believe what she was hearing.

"I don't know," Sam said. "The stuff that happens at home. You're an important pilot. Mom and Mrs. Waterston had lots of time on the beach to talk about problems. Besides, the painting thing wound up being a lot of worry for nothing."

Kate was reeling and couldn't speak.

"Sam, I didn't see any police reports about a painting stolen from your house last year," the detective said.

"Because we didn't report it," she said.

"Why?" Kate asked.

Sam frowned and shrugged. "It just wasn't a big deal."

"Sam! It absolutely was—is—a big deal. Tell me . . ."

"I said *almost* stolen," Sam said, her voice rising and face reddening. "It was really bizarre. It turned out the robbers left it behind—they must have gotten spooked or something. We just didn't find it for a while. Mom found it shoved into the hall closet, behind the rain boots and umbrellas. She hung it right back up in their bedroom."

Kate felt pins and needles in her face and hands. *It couldn't be.*

"Which wall?" Conor asked.

"The one near the window, next to the bookshelves."

"Who was the artist?" he asked.

"Ben Morrison," Sam said.

"And the name of the painting?"

Kate closed her eyes. Her entire body felt ice cold.

Of all the Black Hall Impressionists, Kate and Beth loved most the work of Ben Morrison. His love of nature flowed from his brush, and she believed his romantic and tragic vision of love was based on the heartbreak and betrayal he'd suffered. His most famous painting hung in the Wadsworth Atheneum. It showed a young woman on the moonlit lawn of a stone house, dancing alone in a moment of private abandon.

Kate's family owned a similar painting by Morrison—it depicted the exact same scene, smaller by half, and somehow infused with even greater longing, a sense of the woman's unmistakable desire. Many art historians considered the canvas superior to the one at the Atheneum. It had already been stolen once, by Joshua and Sally Anderson the night Kate and Beth's mother had died. It had been returned to the family after the couple's arrest. And since Beth's marriage to Pete, it had hung alone, illuminated by a spotlight, on the east wall of their bedroom.

"The name of the painting?" the detective asked again.

Kate's heart seized. She knew even before Sam said it.

"Moonlight," Sam said.

It was happening again, Kate thought. Someone else she loved had been killed over that same painting.

8

After Sam got tired, Reid didn't want to push her for more answers. He thanked her for her help, and Kate walked him to the door. She checked her phone, not for the first time since he'd arrived, as if impatient for a call. Popcorn shimmied against Kate's side, and she grabbed his red leash and clipped it to his collar.

"I'll walk you out," she said.

He watched her go through the routine of disarming and rearming the alarm. At the top of the stairs, she spoke quietly into a microphone, and the only words he heard clearly were *autumn garage*.

"What did you just say?" he asked, keeping up as she and Popcorn ran downstairs.

"It's a quote from *Franny and Zooey*," she said. At the front door, she turned to see if he knew what she was talking about.

"No idea what that is," he said.

"A book by J. D. Salinger," she said. "Beth's favorite. And mine. Sibling love."

From her tone, he realized he'd failed some test. It was also clear that as much as he thought he knew about her, Kate's inner life was a mystery.

They walked outside. The temperature had dropped, and fog was creeping in, ghostly in the streetlights. Salt air blew off the harbor, smelling of Long Island Sound, the river, diesel fuel, and beer from the bar next door. Kate cut down a deserted alley that led toward the empty wharf.

"What a paradox," he said.

She gave him a quizzical glance.

"For someone who has the most sophisticated private security setup I've ever seen, you like to live dangerously," he said. "This is a pretty crime-ridden stretch."

"I've got some moves," she said, giving a slight smile. "No one's going to bother me. And I've got Popcorn."

"Right," he said. "The great watchdog."

"Don't insult my buddy," she said as Popcorn lifted his leg to pee on a pile of trash.

They slipped through a break in an anchor fence to get closer to the river. The black water rippled yellow-orange from garish lights on the other side. General Dynamics—better known as Electric Boat or "EB" to locals—manufactured submarines for the navy and was lit up like a small city. The dark conning towers of two subs rose high above their docks and the river's surface.

"My brother and I used to think this exact spot would be the best place for Russian spies," he said.

"Beth and I thought that too," she said. "Our parents would bring us and our friends to New London for Sail Fest, and we'd walk along the pier eating clam chowder and lobster rolls, looking over at EB and imagining how many of the tourists supposedly taking pictures of the tall ships were actually spies snapping shots of the nuclear subs." Then, "You have a brother?"

"Yes, Tom," Reid said, glad for the chance to tell her.

"Older or younger?"

"He's older," Reid said.

"Like me," Kate said. "Are you close?"

"We are," he said, meeting her eyes. "Were you and Beth?"

"Our whole lives. We thought we had such a happy childhood till . . ." She trailed off.

"You lost both your parents," he said.

"In different ways," she said. "Our mother died, yes. Beth stayed in touch with my father after he went to prison. I never saw him again. Or took his calls."

"You know, my brother found the paintings," he said.

She stopped to face him.

He nodded. "Tom was on the Coast Guard ship that boarded *Rembrandt*. The Andersons had their running lights off—trying to slip offshore without being seen. Tom was on deck and spotted them. And when he went aboard, he found the artwork stashed in a hidden compartment. The first painting he pulled out was *Moonlight*."

"Please thank him for me," she said, her voice catching. "Now it's gone again. And so is my sister."

They walked in silence while Popcorn explored the oily pilings of a ruined dock. A tugboat chuffed past. The sound of I-95 traffic crossing the Gold Star Memorial Bridge, although half a mile away, was unending white noise, but Reid and Kate were close enough for him to hear her phone buzz. She reached into her pocket, looked at the screen, and put it back.

"Waiting for a call?" he asked.

"Yeah," she said. "A close friend. I want to be the one to tell her about Beth."

"That wasn't the friend?"

She shook her head. "People I haven't talked to in ages are coming out of the woodwork. They've heard; they're leaving messages. I don't want to speak to them."

"No," he said. "I get it."

"I hope I can help Sam," Kate said, "half as well as my grandmother helped me."

"Will she live with you?" he asked.

Kate glanced up, surprise on her face. "No, with Pete, of course."

"Oh, right," Reid said.

"Why wouldn't she?" Kate asked, stopping.

Reid didn't answer. He stared into her green

eyes, trying to read them. And he felt her trying to read him back. He had made up his mind about Pete right away and was doing his best to fight his bias. Was Kate's reaction a sign that she trusted Pete enough to want Sam to stay with him?

"You think he did it?" she asked.

"What did you mean, early today, when you said you could have stopped it from happening?" he asked, avoiding her question.

"Now I'm a suspect?" she asked. "Me and Pete together? You're an idiot." She started to walk away.

Reid took a deep breath and knew he had to be careful with what he said. He didn't want to lead her. "Tell me what you mean," he said.

"I wouldn't go to the corner with Pete. The only reason I even speak to him is for Beth and Sam's sake."

"Earlier you said you hate him. Can you explain why?"

"You're the detective. Haven't you uncovered all the dirt?"

"The investigation is just beginning," he said.

"Well then, start with Nicola Corliss," Kate said.

"Okay," Reid said, keeping his voice calm. He didn't want to let on how much he already knew, had known all along, and he needed to listen as dispassionately as possible to everything she had to say.

"She is—or was, till Beth fired her—a gallery employee. An assistant curator. Beth and I hired her straight out of grad school at Bard. She wrote her master's thesis on Childe Hassam's flag paintings, but her great artist love is, you guessed it, Benjamin Morrison. Those are the reasons we chose her from among the other applicants."

"Why did Beth fire her?"

"Because even more than Morrison, she loved Pete. And he loved—or loves—her right back. My sister is so smart and wonderful, but she re-created just about every mistake my mom made. She married a guy just like my dad, who cheated with a grad student, broke her heart."

"How long had Pete been having the affair?"

"He kept ending it. It was over; then it wasn't; then it was. Beth tried to believe him for as long as she could. But she was over it—done."

"How did Nicola react to Pete's stopping and starting back up?" he asked.

"Why?" Kate said, stopping dead, turning to face him. "You're not saying *she* could have done it?"

"No. I'm just trying to get the full picture," Reid said, envisioning the murder scene, staged to look like a rape. Kate had seen it too. She seemed mostly focused on the lies Pete had been telling Beth, but could she imagine Nicola doing it? "But tell me how she reacted to Pete saying he planned to stay with Beth."

"I'm sure she wasn't happy," Kate said. "But we weren't exactly confidants."

Reid nodded. "You say Beth was done. She was going to leave him?"

She did not answer the question. She just stared into the swirling black water. "Look, even though he broke Beth's heart, he didn't kill her."

"What makes you so sure?"

"He was out in the Atlantic Ocean with five other guys. Besides, you heard what Sam said about *Moonlight*. Whoever took it last year probably came back to steal it right this time." She looked at him. "Only this time, he took everything Beth had. You saw what he did to her, the lace around her neck, right? Was she raped?"

"We don't know yet."

"Well, even my dad didn't arrange for the Andersons to sexually assault my mother. To do that to her, to us. But considering what my father did, I do realize that supposed loved ones can do terrible things. But I can't imagine Pete, regardless of what a creep he is, hiring someone to do that to Beth."

They were silent for a moment, Reid wondering exactly how to put it—whether to tell her he thought Pete had killed her himself before he left. He had caught some attitude from Tom earlier that day after the helicopter had landed. When Pete had refused to be interviewed, saying he needed to see his daughter before he did anything else, Reid and Tom had stood by the helipad, watching him walk away.

Reid had looked at Tom and opened his mouth to speak. He'd been about to say, *Guilty as hell,* but Tom had shaken his head.

"Don't go there yet," Tom said. "Let it play out."

"Tom, I know this guy."

"No, you don't. And you don't even know the sisters—you just think you do."

"He's a liar and a cheater, and if you saw Beth . . ."

"You want to be taken off the case before you even get started? Keep your head down and do your job," Tom said sharply, being an asshole older brother.

Now Sam had confirmed she and Pete hadn't seen each other yet. So much for the concerned father. Walking along the waterfront, Reid glanced at Kate.

"I don't believe he had it done," Reid said slowly.

"Oh, because you think I did it?"

"No," Reid said. "Not at all."

A ferry slid by, lights rippling on the black water.

"Remember, outside Beth's house, I mentioned I let something bad happen to her before?" she asked.

"Yes," Reid said.

"It was about Nicola."

"What happened?" Reid asked.

"Beth was determined to confront her and Pete—she called to tell me, when I was about to fly a family to Paris. I told her to wait till I got home, and I'd go with her. Beth couldn't find any of Nicola's contact info at the gallery—Pete had gotten rid of any trace of her. But Beth called the gallery's accountant and told him to look at Nicola's tax form. It had her address on it—my grandmother's house."

"You didn't know where Nicola was staying?" Reid asked carefully, because he did know. Once he had realized Pete had a girlfriend, he had started watching him more often and had followed him to Cloudlands.

"I had no idea at the time—neither did Beth. She and I own the property. We sometimes rent it out to the Black Hall Art Academy—in the past they've used it for their acting president, or sometimes an important visiting professor. Pete handles a lot of Beth's business matters. She put him in charge of renting the house."

"She trusted him?" he asked skeptically.

"In that regard, yes," Kate said. "The house seemed a safe job to give him—if it was leased at all, it was to someone in the art world. He made it seem the Academy had taken it again, but instead he put Nicola in there—he paid the rent from a bank account Beth didn't know he had."

"But she found out."

"Yes, like I said, through Nicola's tax form. While I was flying to Paris, she went to Mathilda's house and let herself in. And she caught them in bed. And that's a sight that burned in her brain, but it wasn't the worst."

Here it came, Reid thought. Kate knew. He made himself ask: "What was the worst?"

"Pete's baby. The son he had with Nicola was sleeping in the cradle next to them. The cradle that Beth and I had slept in when we were babies. The one she had planned to bring home for Matthew."

Reid watched her without expression, not wanting to show his emotions—they overwhelmed him, thinking of what Beth must have gone through in that instant and what Kate must be feeling now. Pete's relationship with Nicola was a major reason Reid had instantly suspected him. But Reid wondered: Would he have killed Matthew, his own baby, as well?

"Beth had no idea?" he asked.

"That he had a kid with her? No. She didn't even know Nicola was pregnant. She thought it was just an affair."

Reid stared into the distance, trying to imagine how Beth had felt, finding out that way.

"That's what I would have liked to protect her from," Kate said. "Having to see that by herself. See it at *all*. I should have been there with

96

her." She paused a moment. "She got pregnant right after that. She hadn't been planning on having another child, but I think . . . she needed Matthew."

"Because Pete and Nicola had a baby?"

"Because my sister had so much love inside her. She needed someone else to give it to." Kate wiped tears from her eyes. "If you think I helped him kill my sister . . ."

"Kate, I don't think you did," Reid said. "I *know* you didn't."

"Good. Thank you."

He nodded.

"Will you get whoever it was?" she asked.

"I will," he said.

"It had to be whoever stole *Moonlight* last year," she said. "Right? He came back for more. Don't you think?"

Reid's mouth was dry. He knew exactly what he shouldn't say and said it anyway. "If you think your brother-in-law staged an art theft, then yeah."

"Pete? He hired someone? You checked his bank account?"

"He didn't hire anyone."

"So how did he do it? He swam from Nantucket to Black Hall?" she asked. "Wouldn't the guys have missed him?"

"He killed her before he left," he said.

"He couldn't have," she said.

His heart was thumping. Yes, he'd thought it was Pete from the beginning, especially knowing about Nicola, but the evidence he was seeing—including Sam saying she hadn't seen her father—made his conviction even stronger.

"I think he left that note on the door for the UPS driver," he said. "So no one would be suspicious if she didn't answer."

"It was in her handwriting!"

"Yes," Reid said. "She wrote it herself. But she did it before—I don't know when, but Pete saved the note to use when he killed her. To make it look as if she was alive longer than she was."

"But he's been gone for days—if he killed her—I mean, the forensics people can tell when. I know from my mother—they can tell to the hour."

"You were in the room," he said. "It was a refrigerator."

"It's been incredibly hot all month," Kate said. "Beth's pregnancy made her really sensitive to the heat—I know she loved fresh air, the sea breeze, but she turned on the AC so she could sleep."

"No, Pete did that," Reid said. "He sealed the windows and turned the air conditioner as high as it would go to affect her body temperature and trick the medical examiner. He planned this carefully, Kate."

"You act like you know for sure. But how can

you? Did you actually *see* him do it? Watch him kill my sister?"

"I wish I had," Reid said. With all the times he had passed the house, followed Pete, observed Beth, why hadn't he been there that day? The thought of it made him sick. "My job is to figure how he did it and to prove it. And I will."

She stared at him, her eyes bright.

"You told me to call you Conor before," she said.

"Yes, I did," he said, watching the wild emotion in her face.

"So, catch him, Conor," she said.

He nodded—a promise. He wanted to keep walking with her, to say more, but she abruptly turned. It was time for her to get back to Sam, so together they walked to her front door, and Reid watched until she and Popcorn went inside, until he heard the bolts slide into place.

He drove ten minutes home to Silver Bay. It had been a long day. When he pulled into the driveway of the white 1853 saltbox he had owned for fifteen years, he unloaded his surf rod, leaned it beside the back door, and entered the kitchen. The house felt stuffy from being closed up all day, so he opened a few windows and let the breeze cool things off. He brewed a single cup of coffee and took it into his home office.

He regarded the far wall above his desk. He had kept clippings of former cases and tacked them up to remind him of his purpose in life. There were articles about crimes that had been solved, others that hadn't. His dad had been a cop, and he used to say, "Keep your eye on the ball." To Reid, that meant remember the victim. Catch the bad guy.

Reid leaned back in his desk chair, coffee mug in hand. One of the biggest headlines on his wall had appeared in the *Day* twenty-three years ago: "Gallery Owner Implicated in Wife's Death."

The facts were simple and ugly. Garth Woodward, the girls' father, had had a gambling problem. He'd liked the roulette table at Foxwoods. He had also fallen in love with Francesca Conti, a young woman getting her PhD at Yale's Department of the History of Art. To cover his debts and pay for a love nest in Wooster Square, he decided to stage a robbery at the Harkness-Woodward Gallery so that paintings could be stolen. He could double profit from both black-market resale and a large insurance payout.

He met Joshua and Sally Anderson at Art Basel when they tried to sell him what he quickly recognized as a forged Hassam. A criminal recognizes criminals. He hired them for the job.

Reid was certain Garth had not planned for his daughters to be at the gallery that day, but he was equally sure that he had known his wife would be. The plan had been to tie Helen up, but since Kate and Beth had stopped by on their way home from school that cold November afternoon, the Andersons determined that they had to be dealt with too.

Joshua shoved Helen and her daughters into the basement. He and Sally bound them together with nylon rope, shoved gags into their mouths. Whether they expected Helen to choke and die was beside the point.

At ten the next morning, Wade and Paula Banks—collectors and regular customers of the gallery—arrived from Greenwich for a meeting with Helen and Garth. They knew the Woodwards would never forget an appointment, and when they saw Helen's car parked out front, and she did not answer the door, they became concerned and called the police.

Reid was the resident trooper and arrived within five minutes. He circled the gallery, brushing aside thick rhododendron branches to look into windows. There was a cellar hatchway in the back of the building, and he heard thumping coming from inside. He broke the lock and entered the basement.

He discovered the three of them—Helen, Kate, and Beth, still tied together, back to back. Kate was banging her feet as hard as she could, splattering fluids that had drained from their mother's body, pooled around them. Beth was screaming through the fabric tied around her mouth. Helen was slumped over; blood had dried black on the gag and her chin, had run onto the concrete floor and coagulated. She had urinated and lost control of her bowels. By the fact that she had gone into rigor, Reid knew that she had been dead for hours. Her face was gray-blue, her eyes opaque.

His hands shook as he cut the family loose. He tried to help Beth stand, but she wouldn't let go of her mother. Kate was pure white, her lips blue, in shock, backing away as if she wanted to melt into the wall.

Garth Woodward arrived minutes later. He had been on an ostensible art-buying trip to New York and had come straight to the gallery, instead of going home first, for the meeting with the collectors. The minute he ran down the stairs he cried out—either genuinely stunned to see that Helen was dead, or a great actor. Woodward had started pacing, holding his head, while Beth had cradled her mother's cold body, and Kate had stood with her back pressed to the basement wall, staring into nothing, completely silent.

Twenty-three years later, Reid still saw Kate pressed against the cellar wall nearly nightly in his dreams. His training as a police officer had prepared him for all kinds of crime scenes. He had seen fatal accidents on I-95 and country roads, had been to houses on domestic violence calls and tended to victims with black eyes and broken bones, had had guns pulled on him twice—once on a domestic call, another at a beach bar where he had gone to break up a fight. The husband had dropped his shotgun; the drunk had held on to his pistol. Reid had shot the drunk. He had blown a hole in his chest. It hadn't affected him the way Beth's reedy screams and Kate's blank stare had.

Seeing what had happened to the Woodward sisters had changed him. He had taken in their pain through his skin. He was from a close family. He loved his parents and brother. The idea of having his mother die beside him, unable to help her, filled him with despair and rage, things he could imagine the Woodward girls feeling. Especially Kate. Her silence that day, the way her hand had felt like ice, had sliced his heart.

After the art was recovered, Francesca had been interviewed by the state's attorney, and she had willingly provided evidence against Garth. Although she had not known his plan, her testimony about their town house and his trips to the casinos had made his motive clear.

The Andersons had taken plea deals and testified in court, each sentenced to twenty-five years in prison. Garth Woodward had gone to prison for life without the possibility of parole. Beth eventually had gotten married and had Sam, and Kate had taken to the sky.

Reid's coping mechanism was wood carving. He had a workbench set up at the far end of his office. Narrow drawers held his knives, chisels, and adzes. Blocks of butternut, basswood, and aspen were stacked high. A few of his favorite pieces were displayed on shelves above the bench. They included a pair of mallards, a loon, a kingfisher, a striped bass, and, carved from cottonwood—the palest wood he had been able to find—an albino whale.

Just like Moby Dick.

He sat at his desk now, drinking coffee. What if he was wrong about Pete, if he went down the wrong track and didn't get Beth's killer? Maybe Tom was right, and Reid's feelings were blinding him. He took out a yellow legal pad and made two columns. The first was for names of suspects, the second for possible motives.

In the first column he wrote *Pete.* Under it he wrote *Nicola.* Under that he wrote *Stranger.*

Then he crossed out *Nicola* and *Stranger.*

He exhaled and took out his cell phone. He had programmed Pete's number in after the call to the Lathrops' landline, and he dialed it now. He didn't really expect an answer, just wanted to leave a message, and was taken aback when Pete picked up.

"Hello?" Pete said.

"Pete. This is Detective Reid."

"Oh," Pete said. "I was just going to call you."

"Really, what about?"

"Well, I was pretty upset earlier. I'm sure you can understand. I wanted to tell you I'm ready to talk whenever you are. We've got to find who did this."

Reid hid his surprise. He had expected to chase Pete. On the other hand, it was smart of Pete to seem to cooperate. "Great, that's what I was calling about," he said. "To schedule a time."

"I'll come tomorrow," Pete said. "Can we make it afternoon? We have to make funeral plans in the morning."

"Afternoon is fine," Reid said. "Will you be bringing your lawyer?"

"Why would I need one? I'm innocent."

I didn't ask if you were innocent, Reid thought. "Okay, tomorrow. Three o'clock?" he asked, thinking of the alibi witnesses he planned to interview first.

"Fine," Pete said.

"By the way," Reid said, "how is your daughter?"

Pete let out a long exhale. "Not good. As you can imagine."

Reid gave him the address to the Eastern District Major Crime Squad office. When they hung up, he sat down at his desk and started making notes about the day. After a few minutes, he paused and stared up at the yellowing twenty-three-year-old article on the wall.

Pete hadn't exactly lied and said he had seen his daughter. But he hadn't said he hadn't, either.

9

The call came in the middle of the night. At 2:11 a.m. Kate fumbled for the phone next to her bed, saw the caller ID.

"Hello?" she said. "Lu?"

But the connection was bad, crackling on the line, as if Lulu was somewhere without cell reception. Kate said, "Hello, hello? Can you hear me? I can't hear you. Are you there?" Then she disconnected. She waited a few moments, staring at the screen, waiting for it to ring again. But instead she got a notification that a voice mail message had dropped in. She listened to it.

"It can't be true," Lulu's recorded voice said, thick with tears. "Tell me it isn't, Kate. I've had my phone off all day. I'm in Tokyo on a ridiculous long haul, and I just got your texts, and then Scotty called. She told me. Not Beth, Katy; not our Beth," Lulu said, and then her voice broke. "I love you so much. I am with you, Kate." Her best friend's sobs brought on Kate's, and she lay in bed clutching her phone, tears running down her cheeks, swallowing the sounds of weeping so Sam—fast asleep, she hoped—wouldn't hear. She dialed Lulu back, but again—voice mail. It frustrated her, but she listened to the message again, and eventually she dropped the phone on her pillow and drifted into troubled sleep.

Hours later, Kate didn't want to get up. She couldn't bear to face a sunny day that Beth would not see. Her heart skipped, skipped, skipped again, couldn't find its rhythm. Her sister wasn't in the world. How could she go on if she couldn't feel her sister's living, breathing presence? She replayed the detective's words, how he'd said Pete had killed Beth. In the light of day, that seemed impossible. Didn't it?

At least she had heard from Lulu.

Popcorn had slept on the floor beside Sam, but now he was bouncing up and down next to Kate, paws on the mattress, down on the floor, his tongue giving her cheek one big wet slurp.

"Okay," she said. "I know. Time to go out."

Kate was wearing a gray T-shirt and white cotton pajama bottoms printed with blue starfish, and she didn't even pull on a robe when she walked Popcorn down the stairs and onto the street. The sun was rising above the buildings across the river. The beauty of it hurt her heart.

Popcorn was probably disappointed by the short walk, but Kate had things she had to do. He dragged, climbing the stairs to the loft. Kate stood at the kitchen counter, staring at the Cuisinart coffee maker as if she'd never seen it before. She went through the motions of spooning French roast into the basket, measuring the right amount of water. She heard and smelled it dripping into the pot, then walked away without drinking any.

She dressed in jeans, thought better of it, and changed into navy-blue slacks and a white blouse. She walked to her sleeping niece and stood looking down. This would be her first full day without her mother.

"Sam," Kate said. "Time to get up."

"Runnggh," Sam said into the pillow.

Kate touched her shoulder, and Sam opened her eyes and moaned at the light. "Just a little longer," she said.

"Not this morning," Kate said. "We're doing this for your mother."

They had to make funeral arrangements. Eventually the medical examiner would release Beth's body, and they had to be ready. Sam forced herself up. She walked into the bathroom, and Kate heard the shower start. When Sam came into the kitchen wearing a white dress printed with red cherries, Kate handed her a cup of coffee.

"You're not going to tell me this is inappropriate?" Sam asked, touching her skirt.

"You want me to?"

"Well, Dad will."

"That might be true," Kate said.

"Mom gave it to me before I left for camp. This year's summer dress."

Kate nodded. She knew, because she'd been with Beth just three weeks ago when she'd bought it at a boutique in Watch Hill, after a barefoot walk along Napatree Point's tide line and lunch at the Olympia Tearoom. Their mother had always gotten them each one special dress per summer, and Beth had kept the tradition going. They had sat at their sidewalk table on Bay Street, drinking fresh-squeezed limeade, and toasted their mother.

"We'll keep it up," Kate said now. "A new dress every June."

"No more," Sam said. "Not with Mom gone."

Kate opened her mouth to say she'd carry it on, buy next summer's dress, but the words caught in her throat. It wouldn't be the same, an aunt trying to do what Sam's mother had always done.

"We should leave," Kate said. "Your dad wants us there by 10:00."

"I'm afraid to see him," Sam said.

"Why?" Kate said.

"Because it's just him and me now. Our family is too small. We were always supposed to be three, and she's not here anymore."

Kate searched for something to say, but every word seemed trite.

Sam turned away and rinsed out her coffee cup. Kate tried to see if she was crying, but when Sam turned around, her eyes were dry, and she walked out to the car as if hypnotized. If she was upset

110

that Pete hadn't asked her to come home, hadn't seen her yet, she hadn't shown it.

The Bryer Funeral Home was a pale-gray Victorian house with white shutters, located improbably, and too beautifully, on the southern bank of Black Hall's twisting Pequot River. Marsh grass rippled in the light breeze, and when Kate slammed her car door, she flushed a great blue heron, ungainly wings unfolding as it flew around the bend into deeper shadows. The last time Kate had been here, it had been for their mother. She and Beth had come together.

Pete had already arrived. Kate waited for Sam, but she was busy texting and said she'd meet them inside. Kate walked in the front door into a parlor that seemed designed for a tea party, with maroon velvet chesterfield sofas, burled yellow birch tables, a rosewood sideboard with crystal candlesticks at either end. The paintings on the walls were of cows and gardens, purchased from the gallery a generation ago by the first Edward Bryer—the current owner's grandfather.

Kate thought of Mathilda, who had once owned these paintings, and she tried to feel her presence. It would have given her strength, steadied her. But before she could channel her grandmother, she felt a hand on her shoulder.

"Kate, why did this terrible thing happen?"

She turned around, came face to face with Pete. He hugged her in his typical stiff-armed clamp.

She felt him pat her back in a there-there way, and she stepped back. She sought signs of grief in his pale eyes. His mouth was set, as if holding back emotion, or pretending to. Her blood was pumping hard. She thought about what Reid had said about him last night. Even without his suspicions, she was ready to explode with rage.

"Where's Sam?" he asked.

"In the car. Coming in a minute."

"I should go to her," he said, staring at the door but not moving.

"I don't know what to say to you," she said through clenched teeth.

"What do you mean? We've both lost her. We all have."

"You hypocrite," she said, her voice shaking. "You liar."

"If you're talking about Nicola," he said, "I get it. I'm a shit. But that was between me and Beth. She forgave me; I'm sure she told you. We were working things out." His voice caught. "Now we won't have the chance."

She stared as his watery blue eyes filled with fake tears. She thought of the pain he'd put Beth through, cheating on her.

"Why would I believe anything you say?" she asked. "All you ever did was lie to my sister."

"Don't make me feel worse than I do."

"Why did you have to go away?" Kate asked. "Leave for a week when she wasn't feeling well?"

112

"Why did *you?*"

"I was working, not on vacation."

"Look, I don't like your tone, Kate. She was my wife. Not only am I dealing with her death, such a *horrific* death, but I'm going crazy over the fact she was probably raped."

"It leaves you free to be with Nicola," she said.

"Nicola had nothing to do with me and Beth!"

"Right. As if anyone believes that," she said. And what if Reid was right? It would mean Pete had killed not only Beth but also Matthew.

"Hello, Kate, Pete," Eddie Bryer said, entering the parlor in his black suit, hands folded across his chest.

Kate felt jarred at the sound of his voice, pulled away from her dark thoughts about Pete. Eddie belonged to the same beach club as her family, and she'd seen him swimming with his kids, showing them how to crack shells on Lobster Night. Kate was used to seeing him in a bathing suit, not looking like a mortician. His father had handled her mother's funeral.

"Hi, Eddie," she said.

"Words can't express how devastated Barb and I are. We loved Beth; we just can't believe this really happened," he said.

Kate took his hand. His eyes were leaking; he sniffled loudly. He was their family friend, not just a funeral director.

"Thank you," Pete said. "We're all in shock."

And at that moment, Sam walked through the door. She saw her father, and Kate swore she hesitated before walking over to give him a hug. Pete grabbed her in a hard hug, whispering in her ear. He started to cry, and the sobs rose and fell. Sam stepped back, and the look on her face was blank, skeptical.

"Oh, Sam," he said. "Sweetheart, your mother. God, I loved her so much. What am I—what are we—going to do without her?"

That set him off again. His crying sounded the way someone thought grief should sound, and Kate didn't see any actual tears.

Eddie walked them into his office, arranged three plush red-leather chairs across from his desk. Sam sat in the middle.

"These are very hard decisions, I know," Eddie said, his voice still unsteady as he fanned brochures on the mahogany surface. "Now, Kate, I know the family plot in the Heronwood Cemetery has space reserved for you and Beth and your families . . ."

"*Reserved?*" Sam asked. "You mean you've already made plans to put us in the ground? Like a dinner reservation?"

Kate put her hand on Sam's arm. She knew how weird it must seem to a kid—just as it had to her and Beth. Facing death young took hold and made you into someone else. "It's okay, Sam.

Your mom and I talked a long time ago—we both said we wanted to be cremated."

"Whether that's true or not, Kate—it's up to *me* to say," Pete said sharply.

"Of course," Kate said, kindly for Sam's sake, breathing deeply to keep her heart rate down and to keep from saying what she really felt: that he didn't deserve the right to make any decisions about Beth.

"As it happens, Kate is correct," Pete said. "Beth will be cremated, per her wishes, her ashes interred with her mother's and Mathilda's. Eddie, I want to purchase the best urn you have."

"Okay, Pete. Count on it," Eddie said. His eyes were red. He shifted in his seat, making an obvious effort to control his emotions.

"Fine," Pete said. He checked his watch. Kate's pulse started racing again. If he had killed Beth, it was obscene that he would be here, picking out a container to hold what was left of her. She watched his eyes flick at the time, knowing he had somewhere else to be, and she turned away so Sam wouldn't see how furious she felt.

"Thank you, Eddie," Kate said. "Excuse me, will you?" She left the office, Pete and Eddie murmuring behind her, and walked out of the building.

A slight breeze ruffled the tall green marsh grass. Two egrets stalked along the opposite bank, gleaming white, their long yellow bills pointing downward, ready to spear silver fish. She breathed the fresh air and tried to feel less furious, for Sam's sake.

She started the car to get the AC running and checked her phone for a message from Lulu—nothing. But there was a text from Scotty—no words, just four red hearts. She watched Sam and Pete emerge from the funeral home. They stood close to each other, obviously arguing. She had opened the car door and started over when they came toward her.

"Kate," Pete said. "I think it will be very traumatic for Sam to return to the house where the tragedy happened."

"Where Mom was murdered," Sam said. "Just say it."

"The point is," he said, "I don't think you should be staying there right now."

"It's home," Sam said. "It's where I live."

Kate almost smiled. Contrary Sam: just last night she hadn't even wanted to talk to her father.

"Of course," he said. "But for the time being. Just for a while. Don't you agree, Kate? That it would be better for Sam to stay with you for now?"

Kate remembered the smell of the house. How even before she had approached Beth on the bed, some ancient part of her brain had registered her sister's death. Even now, a day later, she tasted decay in the back of her throat. She wondered how long that smell would stick to the house. She didn't want Sam to know it. And she didn't want Sam staying with him. Because, if she hadn't wanted to believe it before, seeing Pete cry his crocodile tears was convincing her that he really had killed Beth.

"Sam, please come back with me. I'd love it if you did," Kate said.

"Do I even have a choice?" Sam asked.

"For now, no," Pete said. "Let the adults make the decisions. You're in good hands with your aunt."

"Okay, fine," Sam said, sounding annoyed to comply, just like she had at ten, when Beth would make her eat broccoli or tell her she had to stop reading under the covers and get to sleep.

"I'm really glad," Kate said.

"I want to go to Isabel's for the afternoon, though. We're just going to hang out," Sam said.

"That's a good idea," Pete said. "I'll drop you off."

"No," Sam said while texting. "Rebecca's meeting me at the soccer field. She'll drive me over."

"Stay close to your friends during this time. Kate, can you pick her up when she calls later? I have some things I have to take care of."

"Yes," Kate said. Pete's words, "during this time," rang in her ears. During this time when your mother is dead for the rest of your life, during this time when you realize nothing will ever be the same.

"I'm going now," Sam said, her voice catching as she wrapped her arms around herself. "I hate this place. I want to get out of here."

"Just text when you're ready to come home," Kate said.

Sam gave her a sharp glance. "It's not really home," she said. "Where I live, lived, with Mom. That's home."

"I know," Kate said.

Sam headed down School Lane to meet Rebecca, and Pete got into his black Mercedes S560. Kate hung back while he drove out of the parking lot. Then she put her car in gear. She stayed a quarter mile behind Pete's car as he headed north along the river.

Kate didn't know where he planned to go, but she was going to follow him and find out.

10

Sam slouched in the front seat of Rebecca Dwyer's rust-pocked VW Bug as they headed toward Hubbard's Point, the most magical beach in Connecticut. Driving along the main road, you'd never even know it existed—there were no signs. But once you went under the train trestle, everything changed: the real world slipped away. The security guard leaned toward the car window to ask whom Rebecca and Sam were visiting.

"The Waterstons," Rebecca said.

"Isabel!" Sam said, leaning across Rebecca. "And her sister Julie, too, that cute little unicorn. You know her, right? We're all going to build sandcastles and live happily ever after."

The guard smiled and shrugged and made a notation on his clipboard. He waved them in, and Rebecca drove down the narrow beach road.

"Why did you act like that?" Rebecca asked.

"Like what?"

"I don't know, sarcastic. Kind of rude," Rebecca said.

"I'm sorry," Sam said, her throat tight. Coming to Hubbard's Point, no matter what was going on in her life, had always made her feel happy and safe. But right now, entering this haven of sun and sea, she felt as horrible and dead inside as she had since Kate had given her the news.

"It's okay," Rebecca said, giving her a concerned look.

"You know what that funeral jerk said? That they had a place *reserved.* Her spot in the ground. Like at a death hotel."

"That's horrible," Rebecca said.

"It is," Sam said, closing her eyes. She had the feeling she might fall off the world. Everything felt dangerous; she wasn't sure her skin could hold her bones and blood and heart inside.

"Do you want to go home?" Rebecca asked.

Sam shook her head. Hubbard's Point and the Waterston family were her second home. "I just really, really hope Isabel has some weed."

"Sam," Rebecca said, sounding helpless. "I know this is a terrible time. But you got weird last year, and, well, your mom hadn't even . . ."

"Been murdered yet," Sam said. It was true. Rebecca was a very straight arrow and didn't smoke or drink, but she was right. Sam didn't used to do those things either. She used to take honors classes. She had been chosen as one of only ten students in Connecticut to take a special Saturday seminar in stage design at the Eugene O'Neill Theater Center in Waterford. Her mother had been so proud—a subspecialty of the gallery were paintings of opera sets by Dr. Elemer Nagy, artistic director at Hartford's Hartt School of Music decades ago. They were perfect, delicate watercolors of productions such as *The Princess and the Vagabond*, and Sam had loved them since she was a little girl.

But things in her family were going downhill fast, and so was Sam. She had stomachaches too many Saturdays, so she dropped out of the O'Neill seminar. Her straight As plunged to B minus, then dropped more, and it was clear she had to leave the honors program.

Her family pretended they didn't know what was wrong, but she couldn't believe they hadn't figured it out. Her mother took her first to Dr. Alonzo, her pediatrician, then to a gastroenterologist at Yale-New Haven—but all her tests came back showing she was totally healthy.

Sam wanted to tell them to skip the tests. Her parents had tried protecting her from the truth for months, but try hiding a seriously deep, dark secret from your teenage daughter—it's a colossal waste of time.

Her dad was cheating with Nicola, from the gallery. As soon as it started, Sam felt a storm cloud settle over her house. She began listening at doors, and when her father left his computer on, she read his email. The truth was right there in front of her face: gushy notes to Nicola, sometimes complaining about Sam's mom. Having a dad who lied, who wanted to be with another woman instead of staying home with his wife and daughter, sucked in a way that made Sam literally sick, to the point she couldn't concentrate on schoolwork. Or anything.

Sam listened to her parents whisper and fight in their bedroom with the door closed. She wanted to hear every single detail and pretend it wasn't happening, both at the same time. One day they walked out of their room, stone faced, and caught her standing in the hallway.

"I know," she said.

"What do you know?" her father asked.

Sam looked at her mother. From the stricken look in her eyes, Sam could see her mother understood. Her mom had a sixth sense when it came to Sam.

"Why did you bother dragging me to all those doctors?" Sam asked.

"Because of your stomachaches," her father said. "And the fact you're failing in school."

"You can tell him the real reason for that, Sam," her mother said softly.

Sam wanted to, but she couldn't bring herself to say the words. Her mother said them for her.

"It's you," her mother said.

"I know about Nicola, Dad," Sam whispered.

Her father didn't hug her or apologize to her mom or anything else. He just stood there as if he had frozen. Sam waited for him to say something. His mouth started to form words, but no sound came out. The tension in that hallway was so intense Sam couldn't take it anymore. She ran out of the house and didn't stop until she got to Hubbard's Point, across the sandy parking lot and right into Isabel's arms.

After that, her parents didn't even bother to hide their fights. The night her father's son, Tyler, was born was one of the worst of her life. Sam and her dad were in the den watching *Vice Principals* on HBO. They were on the couch, feet up on the big footstool, eating ice cream and laughing at who could be the biggest jerk at the school. It felt good, almost normal, as if they were still a real family. But then her mother walked into the room, holding up her dad's cell phone.

"You left it in the kitchen," she said.

"Yeah, we're watching the show. Come sit with us," he said.

"You have a text," she said, handing the phone to him. Sam leaned over to read the screen.

Nicola had texted: My water just broke.

That was that. Her father didn't say a word, didn't kiss her goodbye, just left the house. He didn't return for two days, and when he did, he didn't mention Tyler. Sam had to find out the details, the fact that she now had a half brother, by hearing her mother talk on the phone to Isabel's mom.

So partying began to make more sense than studying. Isabel was into it too. She had had some family stuff she hadn't wanted to talk about, but Sam had been able to tell by the way their moms had whispered on the beach that they had had dark secrets in common.

"Be all right," Rebecca said.

Sam looked over at Rebecca, her big brown eyes, blonde hair falling in ringlets to her shoulders, her mouth quivering as if she was about to cry.

Rebecca wanted to be really close to Sam, but it was impossible, as long as Sam had Isabel. Sam and Isabel had been friends forever, since before the beginning. Their mothers had sat together on the beach when they had been pregnant, the two about-to-be moms in a tight friendship knot that included Kate and Lulu—both non-mom types. But even so, the four of them were blood-sister close. They even had a name for their friendship—the Compass Rose. Four directions on the compass.

"I just want to help you," Rebecca said.

"Thanks," Sam said, forcing a smile. But she knew: no one could help. She had thought her family was one way, and it had turned out to be another. Sam knew why her mother had gotten pregnant when things were so bad with her dad, even without being told. Matthew was going to be *hers,* just the way Tyler was *his*. Sam hated to even think this about her mother, but it was almost as if she was having a baby out of spite.

They parked along the stone wall next to the boat basin and walked up to the Waterstons' front porch. Isabel's parents were abnormally normal. They had cookouts and went waterskiing. They played Scrabble and Mad Libs. Their life didn't revolve around nineteenth-century art, acquisitions and sales, provenance, pretending to be happy while one of them was fucking the assistant, having babies all over the place.

Mrs. Waterston was the sweetest, just like Sam's mom; that hug at the airport had melted Sam's heart, reminded her of how her mom had always hugged—full blast. The only thing was, sometimes she could be a little judgmental. Like, watching the news, she always remarked about how stupid people were, or how they deserved what they got because of their own bad actions. But she never said things like that about their circle.

"Well, we can't all be perfect like you, Scotty," Mr. Waterston had said once. Sam had cringed, because she'd seen the hurt cross Mrs. Waterston's face.

She really was Sam's second-favorite mom in the world. Sam glanced around for her—she craved another one of those hugs.

Isabel was waiting on the front porch. She stood when she saw Sam coming, and they ran together and held each other. Isabel was Sam's soul sister, and Sam knew instantly that she instantly got it.

"Oh, Sam," Isabel whispered. "Nothing, nothing could be worse. I am so sorry."

"Thanks, Izz."

"My mom's falling apart over it," Isabel said.

Sam drew back and saw the sadness on Isabel's face.

"Where is she?" Sam asked.

"At the beach, and my dad's at work," Isabel said. She imitated putting a joint to her lips, and Sam felt her heart ease a little. That was the gift of having someone truly understand and know what would help. Isabel reached into her pocket. Sam flicked her lighter.

"Don't do that. It's bad," Julie said from under a wicker table.

"I didn't know you were there," Sam said, crouching down, lifting the flowered cloth to see seven-year-old Julie. Blonde and pale, she wore glasses with blue frames that slipped down her freckled nose. She had an audio processing disability that wasn't immediately obvious, but kids in school picked up on it and bullied her.

Julie wouldn't meet Sam's gaze at first, but then she stole a glance, blinked, and looked away again. It was hard for her, even though Sam had known her since birth. She was severely shy, always hovering just out of sight. When she did talk, it tended to be disjointed and blunt.

"Your mother died," Julie said.

"Yes," Sam said.

"You are sad."

"Very."

Julie nodded, still looking away.

"Mommy said the bad man hurt her," Julie said.

"Yes, someone did."

"Weird and bad," Julie said.

"Enough, okay, Julie?" Isabel asked.

"Don't smoke," Julie said.

"You tell, and you're in trouble," Isabel said.

Julie scooted back out of sight. Sam let the edge of the tablecloth drop. Then she stood up and filled her lungs with smoke until they burned, and she knew that Julie, through whatever circuits her mind worked, was right. "Weird and bad," Sam said out loud as she exhaled the smoke.

11

Kate followed Pete up the river road, in no danger of being seen. Once he left Bryer Funeral Home, passed the library, and headed north, she knew exactly where he was going. A dump truck from Pawlik Construction, loaded with trap rock, rumbled between her car and Pete's, belching black exhaust. The countryside was beautiful—rolling hills overlooking the Connecticut River and Sill Cove—the same landscape painted by the Black Hall Colony artists. But development was rampant—lots clear-cut, three-hundred-year-old trees felled, and acres of wildlife habitat destroyed for ugly six-thousand-square-foot houses.

Cloudlands, Mathilda's property, was high on Sachem Hill. The stately white house had been built in 1745 by Judge Thomas Ludlow in the midst of one hundred acres of forest and meadows sloping down to a tidal inlet. Kate watched Pete drive between the tall stone pillars that marked the beginning of the mile-long private road.

Instead of going in that way, she turned left down an untended dirt trail that belonged to the property and skirted the cove out of sight of the driveway and house. The family used to come here to swim and canoe and have picnics. She parked where the pebble-strewn road dead-ended in a thatch of marsh grass.

At the sound of an engine, she turned around and saw a black Dodge Charger bouncing over the ruts. It stopped behind her Porsche, and she recognized Conor's unmarked state police vehicle.

"What are you doing?" he asked, getting out.

"I own this place, I told you. My grandmother's," she said.

"I know that, but why are you here now? You're following Pete?"

"You're following *me?*"

"No, him. But you got in the middle. I saw you all at the funeral home."

"Yes, we were there," she said.

"What are these steps?" he asked, pointing at the steep stairs carved into the granite ledge, shaded by tall pines, half overgrown by myrtle and poison ivy, green with moss.

"They lead to the house," she said, looking up. "We used to come down here to swim and canoe and have picnics. They're a shortcut, and if we hurry, we'll beat Pete."

She took the steps two at a time, and although it was a hot day and Conor was wearing a jacket and tie, he kept up without losing his breath. So she went faster. Something drove her to practically run the 473 steps—she and Beth had counted once—to the clearing behind the house.

They stayed in the shadows of what the family called Mathilda's Forest. The clay tennis court was sprouting weeds, and the deep stone swimming pool was dry. But Harold Maxwell, the gardener, still came once a week, and the blue hydrangeas were as dazzling as ever. Black-eyed Susans, pink and white phlox, and bee balm grew tall along the stone wall circling the house. Kate had refused to allow the big center chimney to be capped—both Beth and Pete had argued that squirrels could get inside, but Kate had prevailed—and a family of endangered chimney swifts wheeled through the blue sky above the roof.

"Why are you following him?" Conor asked.

"Because of what you said last night."

"You think you're going to catch him with evidence?" he asked.

"I just thought . . . if I could see how he acted when he didn't know people were watching, I would know." She looked down at her feet for a few seconds. "Last night, after I talked to you, and this morning, seeing him at the funeral home, I was sure it's him. But I don't want it to be. For Sam. No matter how I feel about him, Pete's her dad."

"Look, you have to let me do this," Conor said. "He's coming in for questioning later. There's a whole process, so why don't you—"

"Leave?" she asked. "No chance."

Conor squinted at her, then looked up at the house. "How are we supposed to see him from here?"

Without answering, Kate led him behind a tall hedge into a boxwood labyrinth. Once they reached the innermost path, they came to a weathered wooden door. The hinges squeaked, and the door opened into a damp cellar.

"You're allowed to do this, right?" Kate asked, glancing over her shoulder. "You won't get in trouble for not having a warrant?"

"I'm with the owner," he said, smiling at her. They took a few steps inside. There was a light switch at the far end of the house, but this part of the basement was pitch dark. She knew every step of this house, could have found her way blindfolded, but Conor swore as he stumbled into her. She grabbed his hand to steady him.

"Where are we?" he asked.

"A cellar Pete knows nothing about."

"Why doesn't he?"

"Well, there's another, one we actually use. It has a wine cellar, a storage room, the furnace, all the water pipes—normal house things. But this was dug during the Revolutionary War, a staging point to fight the British. It was a hiding place, in case of attack."

"Cool history," Conor said as she pulled her hand away.

"We found cannonballs once."

They walked through the darkness. A few times they heard claws scrabbling on the rock walls.

"Monsters," she said.

"Field mice," he said.

"You're right. My grandmother always had a cat, and he brought us little furry gifts nearly every night."

At the far end of the passageway, Kate flipped the light switch to illuminate a single bulb, swinging from a cord overhead. She carefully and quietly unlatched a door, wincing when it creaked open. They climbed the narrow spiral staircase.

As children, she and Beth had played here, pretending to be spies hiding from the redcoats. The stairs led up three flights to a tiny room, originally built for escape from enemy soldiers, accessible from the main house by a secret door that only Mathilda and the girls knew about. A peephole gave onto the library.

She and Conor looked down. There was Pete. He'd obviously just walked in and was puttering around, putting his wallet and car keys on the desk. He disappeared, and Kate heard him in the kitchen. It was just past noon. He returned with a sandwich on one of Mathilda's blue-and-white Canton plates.

Now he sat in the chair, pointing the remote toward the TV, wolfing down his lunch. This

133

had always been a room for Mathilda's vast collection of books, including works of fiction, art, Connecticut history, and aviation. Pete gave every impression of being alone. There were no sounds coming from within the house. Not Nicola calling a greeting, not the baby laughing or crying.

That surprised Kate. Pete had claimed he and Beth had been working it out, but she had never really believed that. He had always been out for himself. He had moved Nicola and Tyler into this house and destroyed his marriage to Beth in the process. Kate had been dreading seeing them here today.

But it was just Pete, sitting in an ugly brown leather recliner that Mathilda would have thrown down the cliff before allowing in her house. He had obviously brought it here, moved it right in. Kate watched him flipping through television channels. The quiet made Kate all the more aware of Conor squeezed so close beside her, their arms pressed together.

"Where's Nicola?" Conor whispered.

"And the baby?" Kate whispered back.

12

After leaving Cloudlands, Reid drove to the boatyard where *Huntress* had been taken for repairs after sustaining damage on the trip. Nick Waterston had been the friend in charge of the charter, and he was overseeing the work. He had agreed to meet there. Reid wanted to nail down some details of the voyage before he questioned Pete.

The harbor glittered under a cloudless blue sky. There was a good breeze, and sailboats rocked at their moorings. Reid drove around the large shed filled with boats needing work, past a pile of masts and tangled rigging, and parked facing the wharf. He spotted Waterston on the deck of a sleek sailboat tied to the dock. Reid recognized it as *Huntress*.

The afternoon was hot, but Reid pulled on his suit jacket and headed over. Nick unclipped a section of the lifeline encircling the boat's deck, and Reid stepped aboard. The two men shook hands.

"It's so terrible," Nick said. "We cannot get it through our heads. It's broken my wife's heart. She's devastated."

"Your wife is Scotty?" Reid asked.

Nick nodded. "Yeah. Best friends with Kate and Beth, especially Beth—they were closer in age—since they were kids. Inseparable. I loved Beth too. She was practically family to us."

"Was Pete also like family?" Reid asked.

"Right," Nick said, barking out a laugh. "By the way, I told Scotty I was meeting you here, and she's coming by. I know you want to talk to her as well, and we thought it would be easier."

"That's great," Reid said. "Why did you laugh when I asked if Pete was family?"

"Because he's a pompous ass, and no one can stand him."

That got Reid's attention. "But you went on a weeklong sailing trip with him."

"Yeah, well, he's a friend of Lee's—Lee Ackerley—and he chipped in on the charter. Believe me, if it were up to me . . ."

"Okay," Reid said. "Why don't you tell me about the trip?"

"Great weather, incredible breeze. The first night, we cruised around Nantucket. Pete was distracted, though. He kept saying he was worried about Beth—her pregnancy hadn't been easy. I told him Scotty was there, even though Kate and Lulu—their other friend—were away. My wife would do anything for Beth."

"How did he act worried?"

"Calling her constantly. Making a big deal about

the fact she wasn't picking up. Totally distracted."

"Distracted in what way?"

"Yeah. The reason the boat's here now. Pete took a turn at the wheel, and when he rounded Sankaty Head, he was so busy checking his cell phone he missed the buoy and steered straight over the east end of Davis South Shoal—shallow and dangerous, and every sailor knows it. He dinged the keel, and it's going to cost a few grand to get fixed." Nick paused.

"How did the crew react?"

"Pissed off, but you couldn't help being concerned. The guy was definitely off his game. From then on, it was all, 'You okay, Pete? You doing all right?' He loved the attention. It's like he got what he wanted."

"You saying you think he was acting worried and distracted on purpose?"

"I have no idea. With Pete it could be anything. He's got this intellectual superiority, so he thinks the rules are different for him. He'd probably think it was beneath him to look at a chart. He's a member of Mensa. You know what that is?"

"Tell me."

"The genius club. For people who have super-high IQs, to quote Pete. He'll be very happy to tell you about it."

"So, take me through more of the trip," Reid said.

"Well, at one point I had the wheel. Up ahead

a whale surfaced and spouted, then another—it was a pod of humpback whales swimming by. Just beautiful. But we wanted to get back to port for dinner, and I was making time. Pete told me to bear off."

"Bear off? What's that?"

"It means fall off the wind. Stop going so fast. Pete was on the rail with his camera out, as he had been practically the whole voyage. He said he wanted to get a picture for Beth, that she's whale-crazy."

"What's unusual about that?"

Nick snorted. "Pete never cared about taking a picture for Beth in his life. A photo of whales, fine. But then he wanted us to go in a completely different direction to get a shot of a three-masted schooner. Then a flock of gulls. Then a guy catching stripers. It was like he wanted us to notice how much he wanted to do for Beth."

"What did he wear on the trip?"

"Jeans. Long-sleeved shirt. And it was hotter than fuck."

Reid nodded. It was what he'd hoped to hear.

"Did you ever see him with his shirt off, or a T-shirt—anything like that?" Reid asked.

"Nope. And to each his own, but all night in the cabin he kept complaining that he needed to sleep next to the fan; he was dying of the heat. Typical Pete—stealing all the oxygen from any situation."

"Got any pictures of the trip?"

"No, and Detective Miano asked that as soon as we docked up in Menemsha. Last thing I want is to have my cell phone out when I'm on vacation."

"I get that," Reid said.

"You know, I couldn't blame Beth for not picking up when he called," Nick said. "Pretty much everyone knew about the gallery assistant. Nicola. You've heard about her?"

"Yes. Was it serious?"

"Pete never talked to me about it."

At the sound of tires crunching on gravel, Reid glanced toward the parking area. A blue Volvo wagon pulled in next to his sedan, and a blonde woman wearing a pink sundress stepped out. She was carrying an old-fashioned picnic basket covered with a checked cloth.

"Hello, hello," she called. She wore flip-flops encrusted with blue jewellike crystals, and when she stepped aboard, she handed Nick the basket and kissed him.

"Detective Reid, this is my wife, Scotty," Nick said.

"I am so happy to meet you," Scotty said, shaking his hand, then holding it with both of hers. Her big eyes instantly dampened with tears. "You have to solve this, tell us who killed our Beth."

"Yes, Mrs. Waterston."

"Call me Scotty," she said.

He nodded. "We were just talking about Nicola," he said.

"Lovely Nicola," she said, grimacing.

"Do you know her?"

"We all do. She was the sweet little gallery assistant. Beth hired her! Well, and Kate too. We thought she was just darling, and so smart, and so helpful. Till she helped herself to Pete."

"Was Pete intending to leave Beth for her?"

"At one point, yes," Scotty said. "Beth was devastated. But after she got pregnant, it seemed that Pete really wanted to fix the marriage, make things better."

"And Beth, did she want to fix it too?"

Scotty paused. A blush spread up from her neck, and her eyes filled again. "She wanted to, but it was hard. She'd been so hurt by what he did. How could she trust him after that? Trust between a couple is everything." Her eyes darted to her husband, and Reid wondered if there had been adultery in the Waterston marriage too.

"How did Pete take her reluctance?"

"He didn't like it, of course. Pete is the kind of person who thinks he can control everyone. He has this Svengali-like personality. Very controlling, bends you to his will. At first, for years, Beth went along with it. She just wanted to make him happy. But after he got together with Nicola and their son was born— she saw the light. She got much more assertive, and that did not thrill Pete, to put it mildly."

"How do you mean?"

"Oh, he got very sarcastic. All passive-aggressive, saying she was turning into her grandmother. Mathilda was extremely independent, did not believe in needing a man for anything."

"Was Pete ever violent toward Beth?" Reid asked.

Scotty narrowed her lips and looked away. She started to speak, then shook her head and sighed. "I don't know. I have my suspicions, but Beth never said for sure."

"What were your suspicions?"

She shook her head hard, thinned her lips, and looked away. "If only I had stayed with her."

"When?" Reid asked.

"Well, that morning. I popped by very early—she called me. She was upset about something with Pete, and I headed over to just be with her. She was out in the yard. There was a flat of impatiens—she always felt better when she could work in the garden. I helped her do some planting before the sun got up too high. She was affected by the heat."

"The day we left?" Nick asked.

"Yes, darling. You didn't notice I was gone?" she asked with a teasing tsk, tsk.

"Guess it was when I was out for my run?"

"Yes," she said. Then, to Reid with an edge to

her voice, "He runs every day. It's how he keeps his boyish figure."

"So, you helped her plant. What did she want to talk to you about?" Reid asked.

"She was upset about Nicola. Pete was on the phone with her."

"That morning?"

"Yes. He always tried to hide it from Beth, but she could hear him talking in the study. Just so thoughtless—cruel, really. Beth pregnant and him about to leave, and he spends what should have been time together with his wife on the phone with his mistress instead."

"Did they fight?"

"I don't know about that day," Scotty said, "but I assume so. Beth wasn't happy, that's for sure."

"What happened after you gardened?"

"She got tired and wanted to go inside. And, I suppose, have it out with Pete. I hurried home to see Nick off. And I was there when Pete and Lee showed up an hour later—to pick Nick up."

"But you went back to Beth's? I heard about you finding the UPS note."

"I did," Scotty said. "Around eleven, I brought blueberry muffins to cheer her up. Beth had been so down, about Pete's affair, and even the baby . . ."

"Tyler?" Reid asked.

"No, Matthew. She felt so sad because of the situation with his father."

142

"Because she was planning to leave Pete?" Reid asked.

Scotty nodded. "Her family was destroyed. He opened the door to real hell when he started seeing Nicola."

Reid nodded. "I'd like to go back to a question I raised a few minutes ago. When I asked if Pete was ever violent toward Beth, I felt you wanting to say something. Can you tell me?"

Scotty thinned her lips tighter this time. She looked away, and for a moment Reid thought she was going to change the subject again, to avoid answering. Instead she sighed and stared him straight in the eye.

"One time she had bruises on her upper arms," she said, "as if someone had shaken her. Another time she met me for coffee, and she was wearing makeup—and that just wasn't Beth. She'd use lipstick, eyeliner if she was going out at night, but she was one of those old-school New England fresh-faced women who'd probably never even touched foundation before that day. I asked her what she was trying to cover up." Scotty lowered her eyes and stayed silent for a few seconds.

"And what did she say?" Reid asked.

"Her exact words were, 'Some things just have to stay a mystery,' " Scotty said, her voice husky. She wiped tears from her cheeks. "She couldn't even bring herself to tell me. She protected him, kept it to herself. But I knew he'd hit her."

"You never told me that," Nick said.

"Girl talk, sweetheart," Scotty said. "We keep each other's secrets." She took the red-and-white checkered napkin off the picnic basket and pulled out a bottle of white wine.

"Isn't it a little early?" Nick asked.

"The sun's over the yardarm somewhere," Scotty said. "My best friend was murdered. I think I can be forgiven for having a libation. Detective Reid?" She held out a glass toward him.

"That's okay," he said.

"Hey, Detective," Nick said. "Lee's the one you should really talk to. He's probably closer to Pete than anyone."

"He's on my list," Reid said. In fact, he was meeting him next.

"He's a real nice guy," Nick said. "He builds these amazing musical instruments."

Reid nodded. He knew that from the initial background he and Miano had done on the sailing companions.

"Works of art," Scotty said, taking a big drink of wine. Nick glared at her.

"He might have been the last one, besides Pete, to see Beth alive," Scotty said.

"When?"

"The day we left to go sailing," Nick said. "Lee picked him up. Then they came to our house to get me. Pete gave Beth a call from our kitchen, right, Scotty?"

"Uh-huh," she said, having more wine.

"We were right there. We heard him talking to her. I don't like the guy, but that's why I know he couldn't have done it," Nick said. "He was with us. He talked to Beth right there in our house, while we were all standing around. I heard him say he loved her. Then we drove to the boat, and he was never out of our sight after that."

"Never, not once?"

"No. And once we sailed away, we never hit the mainland. Out to Nantucket, that was always our plan. He couldn't have gotten back here, killed Beth, and snuck onto the boat without us knowing."

There were flights off the islands and back again, Reid thought. It could be done. Or maybe the friends were protecting him, the way Beth had for so long. But the steam was going out of his theory: unless everyone was lying, Pete had not had the chance to be alone with Beth after Leland had picked him up.

"Is there anyone you can think of who might have wanted to hurt Beth?" he asked.

"No," Nick said. "She was a sweetheart. Everyone who knew her loved her."

"A stranger," Scotty said, her voice thick. "Someone who broke in. It had to be. No one we know would do something like that." She paused. "And in that way."

"In what way?" Reid asked. Had news about

the sexual element leaked out? Had Kate told her?

Scotty turned pale and started to cry. "Just so heartless. She was pregnant! Oh God, Matthew!"

Nick put his arm around her shoulder.

"Are you searching for him?" Scotty asked, sobbing. "I mean, God forbid he does it again."

"We are investigating every lead," Reid said and thanked them for their time.

As he drove away, he thought about the Waterstons. They seemed like a long-married couple, comfortable with each other. Scotty seemed very maternal and kind, obviously devastated over Beth's murder. Was something else driving her emotions? Reid's instinct told him there was some kind of trouble in paradise. Scotty had made that crack about trust between couples and Nick running every day; did he have something to hide? Was that why Scotty drank wine so early?

You never knew what went on behind a family's closed doors. Even in pretty, affluent, seemingly picture-perfect Black Hall, people could be hiding ugly truths. Heading toward a local restaurant to meet the next witness, he mulled over what Scotty had said: "We keep each other's secrets."

Reid wondered what other secrets of Beth's she was keeping.

13

While he drove to meet Leland Ackerley, Reid considered the issue that had been bothering him since seeing Tom yesterday: that he had an ax to grind with Pete Lathrop. Tom had been right to question his objectivity. Caring about the sisters, keeping an eye on them, had given him too much information about Pete and the way he had treated Beth.

Now, considering the way the time line was shaping up, and Pete having had no obvious opportunity, Reid had to rethink his theory. He wasn't supposed to be emotionally involved in his cases, but he couldn't help the fact he had a pit in his stomach: if not Pete, who? He really needed to hear from the forensic examiner and find out whether Beth had been raped. Maybe there really was a stranger.

Still, he had to rule Pete out. Of all the crew, he was most interested in interviewing Leland Ackerley. The other guys were casual acquaintances of Pete's, but according to Miano, who had taken an initial statement from Ackerley on the dock in Menemsha, he had known Pete the longest and had actually attended school with him.

Reid had arranged to meet him at the Bee & Thistle, a Black Hall restaurant halfway between New York and Boston. Ackerley was traveling from his studio in Tribeca to Boston to meet with someone at the Boston Symphony Orchestra. Arriving ten minutes early, Reid parked in the curved driveway in the shade of a massive oak tree and then googled Ackerley's name.

Leland Ackerley owned a small company that built high-end stringed instruments, which, as Scotty Waterston had just said, were works of art themselves. His work was so sought after there was a seven-year waiting list. He had supplied acoustic guitars to James Taylor and Mary Chapin Carpenter, mandolins to top bluegrass artists, a cello to Yo-Yo Ma, and a violin for a soloist with the London Philharmonic, among others. He played guitar and occasionally sat in with the clients whose instruments he built.

It was clear that Ackerley was a top businessman as well as a talented musician. After reading some articles, Reid formed the opinion that he was serious and accomplished, two things Pete Lathrop was not.

Ackerley arrived right on time. Reid watched him park a vintage black Jaguar E-type and get out. He was tall with dark hair pulled back into a ponytail. He wore black Ray-Ban sunglasses that he removed as he entered the restaurant. Reid followed him in.

"Thanks for coming," Reid said, meeting up with him in the bar area. They shook hands and sat at a table next to the window.

"Well, I want to help, any way I can," Ackerley said. "Beth was a good friend."

"You knew her a long time?"

"Through Pete, yes. I was in their wedding."

The waitress came over, and both men ordered iced tea.

"You went to high school with him?" Reid asked.

"Boarding school in Rhode Island. Saint George's."

"You've stayed close all this time?"

Ackerley paused. "Yes," he said.

But to Reid, he didn't sound convincing. Reid waited.

"I wouldn't say *close*," Ackerley said. "We're very different. But for the most part we've stayed in touch since then."

"I've heard that you're the reason Pete was invited along on the sailing trip."

"Well, that's true." Ackerley stared out the window for a second. "It sounds terrible to say, but I feel sorry for him. Or I did . . . till recently."

"Why?"

"Back in school, he wanted so badly to fit in. He tried really hard, and the harder he tried, the more certain guys smelled blood in the water. They'd mention lower school at Collegiate when

149

they knew Pete was ashamed of going to parish school in Providence. Someone would mention an upcoming vacation skiing in Chile or sailing in Antigua, knowing Pete was going to spend his washing floors at a gym."

"You were one of those guys, mean to him?"

Ackerley shook his head. "I liked the way Pete hung in there. He didn't quit. Some people bet he wouldn't come back after the first Thanksgiving break, but there he was. I respected him for that. He tries really hard at whatever he does. My family invited him sailing with us one winter vacation, and everyone liked him. He turned out to be a great sailor."

"And you've kept it up all these years?"

"Yes," Ackerley said. "A bunch of us get together to go out every summer, and I make sure he's invited."

"This year's trip—you picked him up at his house?"

Ackerley nodded. "I left the city early, drove straight to his house, and we went on from there."

"And you saw Beth?"

Ackerley frowned, staring down at the table. The waitress delivered their iced teas. He took a long gulp and swirled the ice in the glass for a few seconds before looking at Reid.

"No, I didn't see her."

"Okay."

"But she called goodbye from upstairs," Ackerley said.

"Did Pete go up after that?" Reid asked. Now he wondered how long it would take for Pete to smash Beth's head in, strangle her with her panties. Could he have cut *Moonlight* from its frame then too? How long before Ackerley would get impatient? And wouldn't he hear sounds of a struggle? It seemed like a stretch.

"No, he did not go up after that," Ackerley said. "He said he had already kissed her goodbye. He was ready to get on the road."

"Got it. Was he ever out of your sight? Even for a few minutes?"

"Not once."

"Let's go back to Beth calling down from upstairs," Reid said. "What did she say?"

Ackerley looked out the window again, then finished his iced tea. The waitress returned with a refill. Reid hadn't touched his. He sat there staring at Ackerley, who seemed involved in some sort of internal debate. Reid waited for him to speak.

"I wouldn't lie for him," Ackerley said.

That got Reid's adrenaline going. He watched Ackerley fidget with his spoon. "Did he ask you to?"

"Look, as I sit here right now, I believe I heard her voice. But . . . I didn't remember that right away. After we knew she died, I mean. We were

151

rushing out of the house, like I said; Pete was so anxious to get going. And—I never would have thought it would be the last time. I wouldn't have necessarily registered it."

"Okay," Reid said, nodding. "That makes sense. You were in a hurry."

"Yeah, we were."

"So," Reid said, keeping his voice steady. "If you didn't remember or register hearing Beth right away, how did that change?"

"Pete keeps reminding me she called down the stairs."

"Reminding you," Reid said, and now his heart was beating out of his chest. "So it might not have happened? He's coaching you to alter your recollection?"

"I didn't say that."

"Why didn't she come downstairs, by the way?"

"Beth was in bed. She had edema in her legs."

"Complications from the pregnancy," Reid said.

"Exactly. So it makes total sense she wouldn't come down to see us off. Pete said she wanted to get outside, back into the garden. She had been out earlier and gotten overheated. The day was so hot and muggy."

That jibed with what Scotty had said.

"So Pete talked her out of it—he was afraid

she'd get heatstroke. And that's why she stayed in bed, didn't come downstairs to see us off. But she did call down."

"And what did she say?" Reid repeated.

" 'Have a great trip, Lee! Love you, Pete!' " Ackerley said.

"Did you hear that or not?" Reid asked.

"Pretty sure," Ackerley said.

"Okay," Reid said. "What about on the boat?"

"He was worried about her. We all understood— it didn't seem strange or out of character. He's a caring guy. He had messed up his marriage, and he was trying to put it back together."

"What about his clothes?" Reid asked.

"His *clothes?*"

"What was he wearing on board?"

Ackerley gazed outside, into the branches of the big oak tree as if trying to remember. "I didn't really notice."

"Long sleeves, short sleeves?"

"I have no idea," Ackerley said. Then, "Wait, hang on." He pulled his cell phone out of his pocket and began scrolling through.

"What have you got there?" Reid asked.

"I know, the other detective said you wanted our photos, but I didn't have any of Pete then. Someone texted this to me late last night—a guy we ran into on Nantucket. His band was going to be playing at the Chicken Box. I made his guitar, and he wanted us to come by for a set, but we

153

were taking off. He wanted a shot of me playing the guitar."

Ackerley handed Reid the phone, and Reid examined the photo. The men were lined up on the ferry's deck, with Leland Ackerley holding the guitar, everyone smiling. The sun was bright, glinting off the water. Everyone but Pete was in T-shirts. Pete wore that same long-sleeved sun protection shirt he had had on when Reid had met him at Menemsha.

"Looks like Pete was cold," Reid said carefully.

"Well, there was a breeze—it can get chilly, especially if you've had too much sun."

"I wonder why he was the only one," Reid said.

"I don't know," Ackerley said.

"Did you notice scratches on his arms? The backs of his hands? At any time did he go swimming—did you see him with his shirt off? Scratches on his neck?"

"No," Ackerley said. "Not at all." He paused. "Look, I know what you're getting at. I didn't see any scratches. He's innocent. Why aren't you looking for the person who stole that painting? The moon one? That's who you should be after."

"We're following all leads," Reid said.

"I mean, don't you know what happened to Beth when she was young? All for that painting?"

"Yes," Reid said. "We're aware." He paused for a few seconds. "Did you know he and Beth were having problems?"

"Of course," Ackerley said. "Pete told me."

"At the beginning, when I asked if you were close, you said you felt sorry for him. And you added *until recently*. What happened recently?"

"Maybe I didn't put it right," Ackerley said. "In fact, maybe I should have started feeling even sorrier for him. He screwed things up with Beth."

Reid waited for him to go on.

"Nicola, the affair. Then having a kid with her. Jesus."

"So, you're saying it was hard on Pete?"

"Of course. He fell in love. He's a middle-aged idiot who fell for a grad student. And he ruined his marriage." Ackerley shook his head. "He couldn't get out of his own way, just kept compounding his mistakes."

Reid wanted him to say more about the mistakes, but Ackerley pushed back his chair and stood up. He pulled his sunglasses from his pocket and put them on, signaling that the interview was over.

"I have to get going," he said. "Good luck finding who did it."

Reid paid the bill and walked outside, caught up with Ackerley as he was unlocking the Jag.

"Listen," Ackerley said. "Pete felt really bad about hurting Beth and Sam, wrecking the marriage, but it wasn't all his fault."

"In what way?" Reid asked.

"I loved Beth. But she never gave Pete any

credit. He might not have grown up in the art world, but he caught on right away. He's a member of Mensa, you know?"

"I've heard," Reid said, trying not to roll his eyes.

"Well, he could have run that gallery like a real business instead of, to be honest, a family hobby. That's all it was to Beth. A way of showcasing her family's collection. She was all about coddling artists, not making money. Not turning a profit."

"How did she coddle artists?"

"You know, they're all so sensitive. A little crazy. Suffer for their art, you know? Pete would see her turning herself inside out, paying them more than their paintings were worth. Getting taken advantage of. She'd send them to the doctor if they were sick, including therapy in at least one case. She even paid for a sculptor to have a root canal. She'd get too involved with them."

"Is that what Pete told you?"

"Well, yes," Ackerley said, his brow furrowed. "But it was pretty obvious to anyone who knew her. She got more wrapped up in the artists than she was in her husband. Poor Pete."

Reid looked at Ackerley's troubled expression. Whether Pete was the killer or not, he was a manipulator. Guys like him wanted the world to feel sorry for them.

"Thanks for your time," Reid said, handing him

his card. "If you think of anything, don't hesitate to call. And please text me that photo."

"Yeah," Ackerley said. He started the car. The engine gave a throaty roar as he pulled out of the parking lot. Within twenty seconds, Reid's phone buzzed: Ackerley had texted the photo.

Reid drove up the I-95 entrance ramp, merging onto the highway and hitting normal summer-in-Southeastern-Connecticut traffic. As soon as he could, he sped up to eighty miles per hour and headed toward his office to meet Pete. He knew a lot more about him than he had at their first encounter, on the dock in Menemsha. He wasn't sure what it added up to, but it made him all the more interested to hear what Pete would have to say.

14

"I want to take a polygraph," Pete said the instant Reid walked into the lobby of the Major Crime Squad's offices in Walboro. He was wearing pressed khaki pants and, as always, a long-sleeved shirt. He looked perpetually suntanned and windblown.

"You do?" Reid asked, surprised by the statement.

"Yes, absolutely," Pete said. "Put this to rest so you can start looking for the person who really killed Beth."

"Why don't we go in here and talk about it," Reid said, gesturing for Pete to follow him down the wide corridor, into an interview room.

Pete took a seat at the table. Reid told him to wait there, then walked into the control room next door to make sure the camera and microphone were turned on. Then he went to his office, picked up the accordion file in which he kept his case notes. He glanced into Miano's office. She wasn't in there, so he texted her:

Lathrop's here for his interview. You coming?

Still at the ME's. Talk later.

OK

She had told him she planned to stop by the medical examiner's lab in Meriden because she wanted to push the coroner, Dr. Humberto Garcia, to speed up the autopsy, especially the DNA results.

Reid grabbed a notebook and two bottles of water. When he returned to the interrogation room, Pete was sitting very still, exactly as when he'd left, looking unperturbed. Reid always left suspects alone in here for a while before starting the interview. They almost invariably got nervous; it wasn't unusual to return and find someone in a cold sweat, or pacing the floor, or asking to use the bathroom. But Pete seemed as comfortable as a man sitting on his own back deck in a summer breeze.

"Pete, before we start, I want to establish that you are here voluntarily, and you are not under arrest. You're free to leave at any time," Reid said, sitting across the table from him.

"Thank you," Pete said.

Reid handed him a bottle of water. Pete didn't open it. He let it sit on the table in front of him.

"So, Pete. Even though you're not under arrest, I'm going to read you your rights. You have the

right to remain silent. Anything you say can and will be used against you in a court of law. You have the right to an attorney. If you cannot afford an attorney, one will be provided for you. With these rights in mind, do you wish to speak to me?"

"Yes, I do."

"Okay, then. Are you comfortable? Do you want anything besides water to drink? A Coke?"

"Now you're being nice to me?" Pete asked. "What happened to 'I know you killed your wife'?"

"Did you kill her?" Reid asked.

"No, I definitely did not. And I sincerely hope you will schedule that polygraph right away, so you can get on with the *right* kind of investigation."

Reid took note: the first two *ly* words. He'd found that suspects who turned out to be guilty tended to use adverbs, thinking they were being more convincing. He also noticed the way Pete emphasized "the *right* kind of investigation," marking his territory as a genius and the smartest person in the room. Reid would use that.

"Yes, I will contact our polygraph examiner, and we will get you in right away."

"Today?"

"It might take a little longer."

"Well, I am tempted not to waste either of our time by answering questions twice," Pete said.

He opened the bottle of water but didn't drin from it.

"The more you can tell me, the more helpful it will be," Reid said. He placed the notebook on the table and took a pen from his pocket. "So, since you and I are here now, why don't we start with a very simple question. When did you last see Beth?"

Pete sighed. "It's burned in my brain. The morning I left to go sailing with my friends. She'd gone back to bed, not feeling great. To the point I genuinely considered canceling the trip."

"About what time?"

"Around 8:00."

Reid jotted down the time. "She'd already been outside gardening, is that right?" he asked, thinking of Scotty Waterston's account.

Pete frowned. "Maybe. I guess so. She liked to garden before the sun got too strong."

"But you don't remember?"

"No."

"That seems odd to me. The last morning of your wife's life, and you don't remember whether she was out in the garden, planting flowers to make your house look pretty?" *Especially since Scotty had been over.* Could Pete really have missed that?

Pete glared at him. "You want me to make up something I don't remember?" he asked.

Like you tried to coach Leland Ackerley to do? Reid thought but didn't say.

"What made you decide not to cancel the trip?" he asked instead.

"Beth. She insisted I go. It was an annual thing with the guys. She knew I enjoyed it."

"But you could have decided not to."

"I loved my wife. But I'll be honest. We needed a break. We'd both talked about it."

Reid's goal was to be objective, but *I'll be honest* was an indication of guilt, right up there with *ly* words.

"When you say you 'talked about it,' what do you mean?" Reid asked.

Pete narrowed his eyes. "I'm sure you know about Nicola and Tyler."

Reid nodded slowly. Often suspects threw out a fact, seemed willing to discuss something difficult or embarrassing. In fact, coming in for questioning at all was frequently wanting to learn what the police knew.

"I'd like to know more," Reid said.

"Well, feel free to talk to Nicola. She's expecting it. She'll tell you the same thing I will: we all got along. Beth wasn't thrilled at first—not at all. I could have handled it better, I admit. But Beth was a grown-up. She knows people make mistakes."

"So having an affair with Nicola was a mistake?" Reid asked.

"Twisting my words," Pete said with a sarcastic smile, shaking a finger at him.

"Was I doing that? Hmm," Reid said.

"If you would simply stick to the facts as I am presenting them to you, if you actually listened to me, you would do better—you'd rule me out and solve the case faster, because you'd start looking in other places." He grabbed the water bottle and drank.

Reid was silent, watching Pete's body language change. The finger shaking, the fact he straightened his posture and rewarded himself with a long drink of water. If the interview was a chess game to Pete, he felt he was winning.

"Let's go back to the last time you saw Beth," Reid said. He pretended to consult his notes. "Around 8:00 a.m. What was she doing?"

"I told you, she was in bed."

"Did she have breakfast?"

"Yeah. We had it together," Pete said.

"What did you eat?"

"Scrambled eggs. Cantaloupe and blueberries."

"Okay, so she's back in bed by 8:00. What about you; what were you doing?"

"I was getting ready to leave . . ."

"Packing?"

"I had *already* packed. I sat on the edge of the bed, told her she should call me if she didn't feel better, or for any other reason. Then I told her I loved her and kissed her goodbye."

"Why don't you remember if she was gardening?" Reid asked, hammering the point.

Pete sat there drumming his fingers on the table and frowning, as if deciding what to say next.

"I was Skyping with Nicola. Okay?"

Reid could just imagine how that had gone over with Beth. No wonder she'd wanted to get outside, needed her friend Scotty for support.

"Did you and Beth fight about it?" Reid asked.

"Absolutely not."

"Any physical altercation at all?"

"No."

"Pete, will you roll up your sleeves and show me your arms?"

"Jesus Christ."

"Is that a yes or a no?"

"It's an intrusion," Pete said. "It's a complete insult. I've already told you—there was no *altercation.*"

"Then why have you been wearing long sleeves, on the boat trip and every time I've seen you, in the middle of the summer?"

"I believe I recall telling you that these are sunproof shirts—bought for me by Beth. I had a couple of skin cancers removed last year, and she wanted me to be careful so I didn't get more."

"So then, what's the problem with letting me see? You said you wanted to clear things up so the investigation can progress. One of the surest ways is to show me your arms. And pull down

165

the collar so I can see your neck and chest," Reid said.

"It makes me sick that you're treating me this way. Like a common criminal," Pete said. "I've just lost my *wife.*"

"You going to show me or not?"

Pete let out what started as a sigh but turned into a guttural groan. His face turned red, and his gray-blue eyes narrowed. He stood up fast, unbuttoned his left cuff, and pulled so hard on the right that he ripped the button off. Reid saw him go from controlled to rage in two seconds, and that told him a lot.

Composing himself, Pete rolled both sleeves up to his elbows and displayed his arms. Without touching him, Reid examined the backs of his hands and arms and saw no scratches.

"Other side, please," Reid said.

Pete rolled his arms and showed him the pale insides of his wrists and arms. Two long scratches, nearly healed, ran the length of his left forearm, from his wrist to the crook of his elbow. Reid leaned closer.

"Those are from thorns. I helped Beth prune the rose bushes in June," Pete offered, even though Reid hadn't asked.

The scratches were pink and looked as if the scabs had healed. Could they have happened in June, possibly over a month ago? He would take a photo.

"Will you take off the shirt, please?" Reid asked.

Pete complied. Under his blue sun-protection shirt, he wore a gray T-shirt that said *Harvard* in red. As far as Reid knew, Pete hadn't gone there, but he would save the question for later. He examined both outside and inside Pete's upper arms—no signs of a struggle.

"Would you mind removing your *Harvard* shirt?" Reid asked.

"I was in Cambridge for a seminar, in case you're wondering," Pete said.

Reid could almost feel Pete wanting to tell him he got an A; the statement served as a delay technique. Pete stood still, making no move to take off the shirt. Reid's pulse kicked up a notch. He knew there was something Pete didn't want him to see. Pete was in a bind. He had complied with the outer shirt; if he failed to take this one off, he'd be indicating some sort of guilt.

"Mr. Lathrop?" Reid asked.

Again—the face reddening, growling groan, and in one quick motion, Pete whipped off his shirt. He stood facing Reid, breathing heavily. There was one nick, about an inch long and mostly healed, on the skin over his left collarbone.

Reid examined it. "From the rose bushes," Pete said.

Other than that single mark, the front of his body was clear.

Reid walked behind him. Pete's back was another story.

There were four deeply scored scratches, scabbed with dry blood, on his left scapula. There was just enough space between them to indicate they were made by fingernails. On the back of his upper right arm, the deltoid muscle, there was a bite wound. It looked severe. The area was a dark-red oval with small yellow beads of dried pus tracing the clearly delineated upper and lower teeth impressions.

"Looks like you had quite an infection back here," Reid said.

"Nothing serious," Pete said.

"Did you see a doctor?"

"No need."

"How did you get these injuries?" Reid asked, holding himself back from adding, *Rose bushes?*

"Are you kidding me?" Pete asked. "It's called sex."

That could be true, but to Reid they looked like defensive wounds. He unlocked the cabinet behind him and removed a camera. His heart was banging hard. He pictured Beth, naked and lying on the bed. He saw the bruises around her neck, the gash in her head embedded with bone chips. He held the camera and checked both the battery and the date stamp.

"I'm going to photograph the wounds now if you don't object," he said.

Pete didn't say anything, so Reid took the photos.

"Will you give a DNA sample?" Reid asked.

"Of course," Pete said.

"Let me call the lab tech," Reid said. "We'll get your DNA, and you can be on your way."

"Don't forget the polygraph," Pete said.

"We'll get that scheduled for you, Pete," Reid said.

But an hour later, after Pete had left the building and before the polygraph examiner had returned Reid's call, Reid heard from Mackenzie Green, a well-known defense attorney from New Haven, who said that from then on he would be representing Peter Lathrop, and that all future Connecticut State Police inquiries should be directed to his office.

And that Pete would not be taking a polygraph.

PART II

15

July 22

Six days after Beth's funeral, the hot weather continued, the air heavy and holding the constant promise of afternoon thunderstorms to cool things off. But the sky never seemed to break; it held the moisture and turned it to steam. Rolling white clouds would form and dissipate without ever raining.

Nicola Corliss had grown up on the first floor of a two-family house behind Mickey's Pub in Groton, Connecticut. Her mother, Jean, still lived there, and Nicola had temporarily moved back in. While her son slept in his portable crib, Nicola sat at one end of the sofa, her mother at the other. The window air conditioner rattled, failing to cool the room, but Nicola shivered. She doubted she would ever look at a window air conditioner again and not think of Beth.

A docudrama about the royal family played on TV. Nicola glanced over at her mother, who was raptly watching a reenactment of Harry proposing to Meghan Markle. Her mother loved any show that featured English accents.

When Nicola was young, her mother had told

her stories about the girl whose mother sold violets in the snow to send her to Oxford. The girl grew up to study in the Bodleian Libraries, live in Magdalen College, and dine in the fourteenth-century Old Kitchen Bar. The girl wasn't a princess like some of her classmates, but she had her own family tartan, and she was the smartest girl at the university.

From the beginning, Nicola got the point: education would get her out of the neighborhood. Her mother hadn't sold violets in the snow, but she'd trained as a pipe fitter and worked at Electric Boat. Building submarines for the US Navy, she worked third shift so she could take Nicola to school and be there when she got home.

They were Catholic and went to Mass every Sunday. Most kids from the parish attended Saint Mary's from kindergarten through high school, but Jean had sent Nicola to the Williams School, a private day school across the river in New London, on the campus of Connecticut College. It cost a fortune, but she said it was worth it— and when Nicola began to hang out at the Lyman Allyn Museum, also on campus, she was all the more gratified.

Some parents would have wanted their children to gravitate toward business, engineering, science—subjects likely to lead to lucrative jobs— but not Jean. She had always believed that arts and humanities were the way to a good life. The people Nicola would meet, the enrichment of mind and soul, were what she wanted for her daughter. What she would have liked for herself.

She rode Nicola hard to make sure she got the grades for acceptance at Yale and every other college she applied to. After four years at Yale and graduate school at Bard's Center for Curatorial Studies, Nicola was ready for launch. She had had the drive, the desire to learn, a curious mind that had led her in fascinating directions.

Yet here they were, two women with big visions, spending a summer day watching trashy television. Tyler sighed in his crib right beside Nicola and turned toward her, as if he could hear the sound of her breathing. Dreaming, his tiny fists tightly clenched, he shadowboxed the air. Nicola thought she would melt from love.

"Is he hungry?" her mother asked.

"No, just sleeping," she said.

"Should we take him down to the beach?" her mother asked.

"It's too hot." Nicola glanced at the window. Her mother usually kept the thin white curtains open, but this morning Nicola had pulled them closed. Detective Reid had shown up yesterday. His questions had led Nicola to think about things she wanted to keep buried, and now they were all she could think about.

The detective had knocked on the door, asked if Nicola would be willing to talk to him.

"Does she need a lawyer?" her mother had asked.

"No, not unless she wants one. That's certainly her right," he had said.

"I'm fine, Mom," Nicola said, because she knew she was innocent. The irony was, when Pete had called her after being interviewed by the detective, she had told him he *had* to get a lawyer, that he should have done it before talking. And fortunately he had been able to retain Mac Green, a legend in Connecticut.

She turned to Detective Reid. "Ask whatever you want."

They sat in the living room. Her mother perched on the footstool beside her like a Drala warrior, a protector deity in the Tibetan art Nicola had studied at Yale.

"When is the last time you saw Beth Lathrop?" the detective asked.

"I'm not sure. I can't remember exactly," Nicola said. She'd never been good at lying, and she tried to keep her face inexpressive.

"Well, in general. This summer?"

"Spring, probably."

"Before the baby was born?"

"It's hard to remember—it's been a blur, you know? Taking care of an infant?" she said, practically babbling so he wouldn't ask any more.

"I see," he said.

"Do you have children?" her mother asked.

"Uh, no," he said.

"Well," her mother said with a small laugh. "You can't possibly imagine what it's like. Especially caring for a baby *alone.* It's hard to keep track of anything but formula and diapers."

"I'm sure you're right," he said. He smiled and turned his attention back to Nicola. "I thought Pete would be helping more. By the way, I thought you two had moved into Beth's grandmother's house."

"I wouldn't say 'moved in,' " Nicola said. "We stay there sometimes."

"But you're here. Is there a reason you're not living together right now?"

"I'm not sure that's any of your business," Nicola said.

"Tell him, Nicola," her mother said.

Nicola shot her a furious look. *Shut up,* she thought. *Don't go there; don't say anything.*

"Nicola, what happened?" the detective asked.

"The name of the game is *fear,*" her mother said.

"Of what? Did he threaten you?" the detective asked. "Or hurt you?"

"For God's sake!" Nicola said, jumping out of her seat. "I'm not going to say anything bad about Pete, all right? There's nothing *to* say! He's completely devastated—his wife was murdered, and I moved out as soon as I heard. It felt like the right thing to do, to let him be with Sam and grieve, okay? And I need that too." She choked up, thinking of Beth. "I loved her."

"Oh, darling," her mother said, standing up to hug her. Nicola sobbed on her shoulder. She heard the detective rising from his chair. She glanced over and saw him place his card on the front table.

"Please call me anytime, Miss Corliss," he had said, and he had let himself out.

Nicola couldn't stop crying after he left. She had so many feelings boiling inside: sorrow, confusion, guilt, and the most terrible yearning to go back in time and make everything be okay. She lay down on the couch and closed her eyes for ten minutes, but she couldn't relax. She turned on her side, facing the front window and thinking about looking out.

"I suppose you're hoping he's back," her mother said, watching her.

"Mom, stop," Nicola said. But she knew Pete had been there early that morning, willing her to see him and come outside, return to him. Despite what she had told Detective Reid about leaving Mathilda's house to give Pete time to be with Sam, there were additional complicated reasons that she was afraid to admit, even to herself.

Jean went to the window, pulled the curtains wide open. From the way her shoulders stiffened,

Nicola knew that Pete's car was idling across the street. Jean stared him down.

"Mom, stop looking out."

"No, I don't think so," Jean said, folding her arms and glaring across the street. "He must have watched the detective arrive and leave so he'd know when to station himself right back here in your face."

Nicola knew her mother wanted Pete to see her angry expression, to feel her displeasure. It was more than that: Jean hated Pete. At first, she'd been so proud that Nicola was working at the prestigious Lathrop Gallery, but her pride hadn't lasted. She blamed Pete for wooing Nicola, getting her pregnant, diverting her from her high-achieving path, stealing her chance for excellence. Pete hadn't introduced her to his mother, and Nicola thought it was because Mrs. Lathrop would feel the same way about her—that she had ruined Pete's life.

Nicola was still a Catholic girl at heart, and she knew that adultery was a sin. She wouldn't trade having Tyler for anything, but she felt guilty for so much of what she'd done. She believed she would have to pay for it, somehow.

"Pete wants us to work it out," Nicola said.

"Well, I hope you don't want that."

"That's why he's here . . . ," Nicola said.

Her mother didn't turn around. Nicola was glad, because she didn't want to see the shame and disappointment in her mother's eyes. Nicola had fallen in love with a married man and had had his baby. In her mother's view, Nicola had ruined her life as well as Beth's and her family's.

Her mother would never understand how Pete had helped her feel like part of an alien world, how he had taken her under his wing and assured her she belonged, that she was as good as all the rich people who bought art. He had come from a working-class background just like Nicola's, and it was as if he sensed every insecurity she had. He gave her what she needed—a level of acceptance and under-standing—even before she knew she needed it. He was a magician who could read her mind. He had made her feel adored.

"He's Tyler's father," Nicola said.

"Women have raised children alone before," her mother said, tapping her own chest. "Case in point."

"I know, and I'm so lucky I had you. But Dad left—he didn't give you a choice. Pete's right here. We just have to get through this. It will get better."

"Through *this?*" her mother asked, finally turning from the window. "His wife's murder? The fact he's a suspect? And that you are?"

"I'm not!"

"You're not stupid; I know that," her mother said. "But in this case, you are being a fool. It was written all over that detective's face. He thinks he killed her for you. To be with you. He might think you planned it together."

"That's crazy! I never would! And Pete wouldn't either—and he didn't! Mom, you don't know the art market—the painting that was stolen is extraordinary. I can't even imagine trying to set a price for it. That's the motive—an art thief killed Beth for *Moonlight*. And it's not the first time it's been stolen—or caused a death." She said it with conviction, precisely as if she really believed it.

"You're being naive," her mother said. "You'd rather believe in a cursed painting than see the truth. Your boyfriend killed his wife."

"You don't know what you're saying. This is a terrible time for Pete. To lose Beth this way. He's beside himself," Nicola said. Tyler stirred in his crib, waking up. She lifted him out and nuzzled his head.

"What I understand is that it's terrible for *Beth*. And her daughter and the baby. And her sister."

"Mom, I know. I'm heartbroken. Pete is too!"

Her mother was tall and strong, her hands callused and rough from her job. She had sharp cheekbones and a long straight nose she'd inherited from her French Canadian father and English mother. Her long dark hair had a single wide white streak on the left side that had been there as long as Nicola could remember. She was the crème brûlée of mothers: hard shell on the outside, total mush on the inside.

"You sound very sympathetic to Pete," Jean said.

"Of course."

"Then what are you doing here?" Jean asked in a flat tone.

"I . . . we . . ."

"I know you had a fight. I realize there's stress," her mother said. "But some women get through that without running home to their mothers. Honey, I know you're scared. You are scared to death. I don't know what he did to you—put the fear of God into you, I can tell. Did he hit you? Knock you down?"

"No, Mom, he never would; I swear."

"Did he confess to you?"

"I told you, no!"

"Nicola, I know my daughter. I can tell when you're lying. And when you're terrified. I think you know he did it. Either he told you, or deep down inside, you just feel it."

"You are so wrong," Nicola said. She tried to sound as if she was outraged at her mother's ideas. She told herself the man she loved could never have killed anyone—but she stayed awake as long as possible every night because every time she fell asleep, she dreamed of seeing Pete with his hands around Beth's neck.

She kept trying to tell herself dreams meant

nothing. She was probably reacting to his anger, the intensity of it right after Tyler was born. Pete had still been officially living at home with Beth and Sam but spending every possible moment with Nicola and their son. He would apologize, telling her he loved her, he loved Tyler—if only she would quit nagging him to leave Beth. If only she would keep the baby quiet when he visited so he could think. He was a brilliant man, and changing diapers was beneath him.

So to keep him happy, she had tried so hard to push aside her wish that they could be a real family, living together during these first days and weeks of Tyler's life. She loved taking care of their baby. She wanted Pete to love him as much as she did. It killed her that Pete didn't share in the joy, that he seemed about to explode in rage whenever she asked him to feed or change or even walk Tyler until he fell asleep. So she had stopped asking.

What had happened to the girl from Bard? That strong, funny, sexy, smart, sure-of-herself person named Nicola? How could someone so dynamic have turned into a mouse? She was positive that if she ever met her old self, she'd be scared of her.

But she wasn't scared of Pete—she told herself that over and over. The pressure of the police investigation was getting to him, because he wanted them to go after the person who had invaded their home and killed Beth instead of wasting their energy on him. Not because he had anything to hide.

Well, almost anything. Nicola thought about what she'd seen Pete stash in the boarded-up dumbwaiter in the upstairs hall, above the kitchen in Cloudlands. Murderers kept trophies, didn't they? Is that what Pete was doing? She bit her lip hard, trying to block the image from her mind.

It didn't work.

It had absolutely devastated her to see him doing that, and that's when she had left. She had driven straight home to her mother. But she had to admit to herself: even before Beth's murder, she had started to wonder whether he could hurt her and Tyler.

She told herself now that she was being crazy. He hadn't killed his wife and unborn baby. He wasn't keeping trophies. His current moods were related to helplessness over the ridiculously misguided investigation. He needed Nicola as much as she needed him. He had always told her she brought light into his life. Her fear was so misplaced.

She sighed and rose to her feet.

"What are you doing?" her mother asked.

"Going home with Pete," she said.

"Please, no," her mother said. "Listen to your gut. I know you, sweetheart. You came here because you're terrified."

"That is not true. I just had to . . ."

"What?"

"Let him get through the funeral. Beth's cremation. But now it's over, and it's time for us to go home."

She went into her old bedroom, packed up Tyler's diaper bag and her backpack with the few things she'd brought with her, and kissed her mother goodbye. Jean didn't say a word. Carrying Tyler, Nicola walked out the front door.

Pete grinned through the windshield, his blond hair tousled, his pale gray-blue eyes shining with expectation and happiness. He got out of the car, opened the back door, took Tyler and buckled him into his car seat. He turned to Nicola, wrapped her in his arms, rocked her as they stood right there on the sidewalk. She knew her mother was watching.

"It will be better," he whispered into her ear. "I promise. I love you so much."

"I love you too," she whispered, closing her eyes. Just before she did, she spotted a big black car parked down the street. Was it the detective, watching her? Were she and Pete about to be arrested? Or maybe it was just a car service, waiting to drive one of the neighbors somewhere. She didn't know what to think anymore. She closed her eyes so tight she saw stars.

16

Kate flew through the cerulean sky, holding the controls steady as the Citation X hit turbulence over New York. She looked down at towering cumulonimbus clouds threatening thunderstorms on the ground. The jet bucked. Charlie MacDougal, her copilot, had white knuckles. Kate didn't often say it out loud, but she loved rough weather. She did her best to steer above or around it for the passengers' sakes, but when it was unavoidable, she rode through it and felt exhilarated, the way she imagined ocean racing sailors welcomed high winds and big seas and the chance to perform to the max.

She began her descent, and the clear blue gave way to dark gray. Clouds boiled around the jet, but she'd left the thunderheads over Fairfield County. No lightning in eastern Connecticut, just rain and the first storm gusts blowing in. After one stomach-dropping bump, she touched down at Groton–New London.

"That was special," Charlie said.

Kate laughed. Taxiing from the runway to the terminal, she was surprised to see Conor's car parked outside the anchor fence, windshield wipers going. They hadn't made plans to meet. The ground crew rolled stairs to the port side, and Jenny, the flight attendant, opened the jet door. Kate adjusted her uniform jacket, tucked stray tendrils of hair up into her French twist, and exited the cockpit.

Jeremy and Peyton Pratt were regulars. He was a Hollywood producer, and she was a documentary director. They owned houses in Watch Hill, Rhode Island, and Brentwood, California, and they chartered jets at least twice a month, always requesting Kate as their captain.

"I'm sorry about the bumpy ride," she said, greeting them in the cabin. It was lined with cream leather seats and polished exotic woods, a haven for the rich customers who flew Intrepid.

"Well, you can't control the weather," Jeremy said.

"Kate, do you have a minute?" Peyton asked.

"Sure, what is it?"

"Kate. I've known you a long time. I can only imagine what you're going through, losing your sister. I'll cut right to the chase. I want to make a documentary of her case."

Kate paused, taken aback. "Thank you, Peyton, but no. We don't need to relive this."

"I understand," Peyton said. "The whole thing must bring back the trauma of when you were young." She paused, waiting for Kate's reaction.

"Being tied up all night. Your mother's death—oh my God."

Kate stared at her, stone faced.

"For Beth to have survived that experience and then to die in such a violent way. I just can't tell you how affected I feel. This will not be a sensational, ripped-from-the-headlines, crime-of-the-week production."

"Kate, Peyton knows what she is doing," Jeremy said. "She will have your family's interest at heart."

"It will be an in-depth study of Beth," Peyton said. "The fact she ran the very gallery where the defining moment of her life occurred: the trauma in the basement."

"The defining moment?" Kate asked, thinking of all the shimmering, beautiful moments of Beth's life. Love had defined her, not tragedy.

"Can we schedule an on-camera interview?" Peyton asked.

"No," Kate said. It was all she could manage. She couldn't even fake a smile as she turned her back. She heard the Pratts mutter as they gathered their belongings. She barely made it to the head before throwing up.

Her body remembered everything from those hours when the Andersons had tied them up in the basement. Retching over the toilet, she could feel her chafed wrists, bound to Beth's and their mother's. The weight of their mother's body, slumping over, pulling at the ropes. Beth stiff, shaking uncontrollably and leaning into Kate for as much comfort as she could give.

Beth had spoken gibberish through the cotton gag.

"Beth, I'm here," Kate had tried to say, choking on the cloth they'd stuffed into her mouth behind the strip of duct tape. She struggled like a madwoman to get free, but the harder she pulled, the tighter the ropes felt. She had known her mother was unconscious, but as time went by, her body grew cold, and the unthinkable hit Kate: her mother was dead. Yanking violently, she knocked her mother's body over on her side so that both she and Beth were trapped beneath her. Beth screamed behind the gag. Kate had stroked Beth's wrist with her thumb, trying to signal her to calm down, to stop fighting. She had been terrified that Beth would choke too.

"Hey, Kate."

In the plane on the tarmac, she heard Conor's voice now. He'd climbed the gangway and stood in the cabin. She washed her mouth out with water, spit into the sink, wiped her lips. Glancing in the mirror, she saw her eyes red rimmed and wet with tears she hadn't even realized she'd cried. Stepping into the cabin, she saw him standing there, watching her.

"Are you okay?" he asked.

She started to nod yes, but instead she shook

her head no. He put his arm around her, sat beside her on the wide leather sofa along the starboard bulkhead.

"Those passengers who just got off? The woman wants to make a documentary of my 'sister's case,'" Kate said. "Is that how you see her—as a 'case'?"

"No, I see her as Beth."

Kate took a deep breath, felt herself relax a little at that. Conor's arm tightened around her shoulders.

"They come out of the woodwork at a time like this," Conor said. "They all want to be first, get the exclusive."

"Have they called you?"

"Yes. The answer is always 'no comment.'"

"Thank you," she said.

"They're all important to me, every murder victim, but this one even more so."

"Why?"

He paused and reddened. She sensed him trying to find the words. "Because it feels personal."

She wanted him to say more. Personal because Beth reminded him of someone? His wife, his sister? As she stared into his eyes, the tiniest spider threads of memory began to spin and weave together. She felt the rope around her wrists, scraping the skin raw. Someone had untied her.

"It was you, wasn't it?" she asked in a low voice.

191

"Me?"

"Who found us in the basement. Who rescued me and Beth."

He nodded.

She felt torn in half. She wanted to hold him, press her body against him as hard she could, and she also wanted to turn away, to stop seeing his eyes and remembering the way he had looked at her that day.

She cleared her throat. "There's no way I can thank you . . . ," she began.

"Don't, Kate. You don't have to."

"Yeah, I do," she said.

"I just want you to be okay," he said. "I know how hard this is, going through this kind of loss again. I don't want to push you."

"Push me?"

"I came here to ask if you'll go with me to the gallery," he said.

She shivered, closed her eyes, and opened them again. "Why?" she asked.

"Just looking for leads, anything that will help the investigation. I'd need your permission no matter what, but I'd rather have you with me. You can help me see if anything's off, different than it should be. But if it's too much . . ."

Kate steadied herself. "Of course I'll go with you," she said. "I'll meet you there."

"Thanks, Kate," he said.

They walked off the plane together and drove

away in separate cars. She went straight to h
loft to walk and feed Popcorn. After he ate, l
looked at her with big expectant eyes. She kne\
he wasn't hungry anymore; he was waiting fo
Beth to come back. She hugged him for a lon
minute. Then she changed out of her uniform; pu
on blue jeans, a crisp white T-shirt, and brown
suede ankle boots; and headed into Black Hall.

The gallery was halfway down Main Street,
between the firehouse and the white Christopher
Wren–inspired church that had been the subject of so many Impressionist paintings. She
directed Conor to park in the gallery's driveway.
The Victorian house had once belonged to Lydia
Stewart Smith, the benefactor who had founded
the town's library, and had been impeccably
restored with a bequest from Mathilda.

The house turned gallery had been an almost
enchanted sanctuary during her mother's lifetime,
a place where Kate and Beth had spent rainy days
and gotten lost in stories created by the paintings.
Kate had loved the house as a child, but when she
entered it now, it felt like a tomb. It reminded her
of crime and unbearable loss.

She unlocked the front door. The space was very
much as it had been in her grandmother's day:
wide-plank pine floors, eight-over-eight windows, white walls hung sparely, each with one
or two large-scale, gilded-framed, nineteenth-
century paintings. A fireplace with a white

marble mantel hadn't been used in recent years.

Upstairs was a second gallery space. There the walls were packed tightly with small paintings, drawings, and etchings, floor to ceiling, salon style, the way art was hung in Gertrude Stein's home at 27 rue de Fleurus. The arrangement had inspired Mathilda during a visit to the house in Paris immediately after the war.

Beth and Pete shared an 1875 mahogany partners desk, flush against the back wall. One of Beth's sweaters hung over the back of her chair. Kate's fingers trailed over the soft blue wool. She felt vertigo imagining how recently Beth had sat here. Her sister's work surface contained stacks of books and monographs.

Across the desk's tooled green leather surface, Pete's work area was laid out with invoices and letters. His chair had been neatly pushed in. She wondered what it had been like for Beth to spend her days sitting opposite the husband who had betrayed her.

"What are you hoping to find here?" she asked.

"Mainly the missing canvas," he said. "*Moonlight.*"

"So, you still think Pete did it?"

"He's my strongest suspect."

"You think he'd put it in the gallery? Isn't that a little obvious?"

"Pete thinks he's smart, right?"

"That's for sure," Kate said.

"Well, I believe he'd hide it in plain sight. Rolled up with other canvases, hanging on the wall, anywhere. And he would laugh at everyone for not figuring it out."

Kate nodded. They started at opposite sides of the room, taking down every frame, looking behind the paintings. Conor lifted the antique rugs, checked the umbrella stand, went through the upright compartments in the third-floor storage room. He moved slowly, taking his time, meticulously gazing at the art.

"Could someone have painted over the original painting, to hide it?" he asked.

"Pentimento," Kate said. "Theoretically, yes. But I can't imagine Pete would have that done with a picture that valuable."

" 'Have that done'?" Conor asked, jumping on the phrase.

"Pete's not an artist. He would have had to hire someone."

"Well, he must know a lot of painters. What about Nicola?"

"She's an art historian, not an artist. She wouldn't be able to pull it off."

"Then someone else?"

"Who's going to desecrate *Moonlight*, then not come forward after hearing Beth was murdered?"

"You'd be surprised what people do," Conor said.

Kate couldn't disagree with him. She thought

of her father. Her gaze was pulled to the basement door. When she dreamed about what had happened to her family down those stairs, she always saw her mother and father dissolving away. They had turned into memories.

She drifted away from Conor back to the partners desk and sat in her sister's chair. Beth's absence felt as real and solid as the furniture. It was an actual, physical force. Her sister had been flesh and blood and kindness and humor—and now she was gone. Now Beth was a memory too.

Kate stared at the top book in a tall pile, a volume about the flag paintings of Childe Hassam. Beth had flagged many pages with yellow Post-its, each covered with her neat handwriting. Kate read: *Hassam was the only major American Impressionist to paint the home front during World War I. Between 1916 and 1919, he produced his flag series, over thirty paintings of flag-draped Fifth Avenue. Stars and Stripes/ British Union Jack/French Tricolor—celebration of the allies, Armistice. Exhibition—next July 4th? Dedicated to Mathilda? Discuss with Katy.*

Kate moaned softly, her shoulders curved forward. She felt actual pain, seeing her name in her sister's handwriting. Childe Hassam and his World War I paintings had been a favorite subject of Mathilda's. She had been moved by his patriotic dedication, the way it had emboldened his primary colors and broken brushwork. It was incredibly poignant to think of a gallery show to honor their grandmother.

Kate's heart broke to know that Beth had wanted to talk to her about the exhibit and that she would never have the chance. She was glad Mathilda wasn't here anymore. She would never have to bear what had happened to Beth.

She began opening drawers. Each one seemed to contain a gift from her to Beth. Whenever she traveled, she always picked up souvenirs, the tackier the better, and brought them home for her sister. She'd found a slot machine key fob from Las Vegas, a teddy bear wearing a straw hat from Miami, an Eiffel Tower–shaped pen from Paris, a beer stein pencil holder from Munich. She reached into the drawer for the small box she'd bought at Liberty in London last April. Covered with deep-red William Morris print cotton, it was an uncharacteristically serious present, something she'd thought Beth might actually use, instead of only making her laugh.

She took the top off and looked inside. It seemed empty. She and Beth had always loved boxes and bags with hiding places, a legacy of their grandmother. She pried open the silk-covered rectangular false bottom that had made the box irresistible to her and was shocked to the core by what she saw.

There was a key, a slip of paper with a phone number, and a small beautiful charcoal drawing of a nude woman. The subject of the drawing stood looking out a window, completely unself-conscious, hair cascading over her shoulders and full breasts. The artist had signed it *JH.*

The woman in the drawing was Beth. Kate could hardly breathe. The artist had captured her sister's beauty, gentleness, and spirit. There was such intimacy in the work—who had drawn it? Who had Beth posed for?

Kate glanced across the room. Conor was standing by a tall bookcase, looking through coffee table–sized art books, apparently waiting for *Moonlight* to fall out from between the pages. She knew she should show him the box's contents, but she couldn't, not before she knew more about her sister's secrets. When she was sure he wasn't watching, she slipped the drawing, key, and paper into her jacket pocket and pretended to keep searching her sister's side of the desk.

17

Sam's phone rang. She looked at the screen—
it was her dad, and the sight of his name made
her stomach flip. She wanted to kill the call, but
finally she answered.

"Hello," she said, forcing her voice to remain
flat.

"Sammy," he said. "How's my girl?"

She did not reply because anything she would
say would come out in a scream.

"Not so great?" he asked. "Me neither, honey.
It's just unbelievable. God, I miss your mother.
I just want to see her again. You doing okay at
Kate's?"

"Fine," she said.

"You sound mad," he said.

"Dad, what do you think?"

"At me?" he asked.

Her blood simmered, nice and low and constant, just like lava in a volcano before it blew.
She fought not to.

"I didn't say that," she said.

"Well, you sound it. I'm suffering just like you,
missing her, and . . ."

"You miss *Mom?*" she asked, the simmer

starting to really bubble. "Because it honestly didn't seem that way when she was alive."

"Sam! Don't you talk to me that way. I am devastated about your mother. Beyond that—I am destroyed. You can't even imagine. We were trying to fix everything. The new baby, all of us together."

"But you're still with *her*, aren't you?" Sam asked. "You're with them right now, Nicola and Tyler, right?"

Silence on the line. She could hear her father breathing—wait, was he turning on the tears? "Dad?" she asked.

"Mom is gone," he said. "I'm your dad, Sam. I am here for you. That's all that matters to me right now." Then he started to babble. *Here come the waterworks without the water.*

Sam held the phone away from her ear because if she had to listen to her father faux weep, she would start to scream.

"Dad, please stop," she said, her voice shaking.

"I wish I could, honey," he said. "I'm so sorry to upset you." She heard him trying to swallow a sob. She really couldn't take it.

"It's okay," she said.

"Let me come pick you up," he said.

"You don't sound great to drive. It's okay if you get me later," she said.

"Oh, Sammy. Thanks for understanding. Things

are just really hard right now," he said. "They'll get better."

How the fuck? Sam wanted to ask. But instead she just blew a kiss into the phone and said goodbye.

After hanging up, she closed her eyes. She didn't like the way he always brought pity out in her. She hated herself for thinking that sometimes he faked crying. Her mother had always said what a rough life he had had. Born without money, always wanting it, his father dying young, his mother working just to put food on the table. Sam had never really understood how bad it was.

But now that her mother had died young, she did.

18

They'll get better? Had he really just said that to Sam? Her mother had been murdered.

Pete was waiting to hear back from his lawyer. Everyone said Mac Green was one of the top defense attorneys in Connecticut, but Pete found him incredibly annoying. He didn't have the courtesy to return Pete's calls in a timely manner. In fact, if Nicola hadn't insisted Pete engage a lawyer, and if Lee Ackerley hadn't asked around and gotten a referral to Mac, Pete would have been happy handling the situation on his own.

One thing Pete hated was someone telling him what to do and how to do it. Mac was an old-school, old-boy, white-haired Yalie who had rules for his clients. One was no taking a lie detector test, no matter what. Pete stared at his phone, pissed off that it wasn't ringing. As soon as Mac deigned to call, he was going to hear *Pete's* rules. He had a few of his own.

Beth had died angry at him, and she had had every right to feel that way. Waiting gave him too much time to think, and his mind kept racing through all the things he could have done differently, starting with letting Nicola stay in Beth's grandmother's house. It had been a horrible, disrespectful thing to do. His mother would be even more ashamed of him if she knew—at least Beth had left that detail out when she had called to tell her about the affair with Nicola. She had run straight to his mother, knowing that would hurt him more than anything.

Maybe he deserved it. He literally could not bear to think about what he had put Beth through. And Nicola, too, for that matter. Nicola had loved being at Cloudlands at first, but even that had changed. He couldn't believe she had actually taken Tyler home to her mother's. What a slap in the face that had been. It had made him feel he didn't matter. That she could leave so easily, even though she had returned, was disturbing. He wouldn't forget it.

Lately, she kept saying she wished she could feel clean again. She had had an affair with him while he was married, gotten pregnant, and had his child. Now it seemed she wanted to go back to the easy piety of her days as a Catholic girl. Obeying God and the capital C Church was easier than existing in moral ambiguity and let her feel as if she was a good girl. Pete, a lapsed Catholic himself, knew that guilt had been drummed into her from the start.

There was so much about Nicola he understood. They had similar backgrounds. He had sensed her nervousness when she had first started working at the gallery—although she was brilliant and beautiful, it was daunting to be around all that old money. He knew because he had felt it himself. His mother had worked her fingers to the bone to send him to private school, but the kids at Saint George's—Episcopal, of course, the high-class religion—would ask him how the other half lived. They'd meant from the wrong side of the tracks. His mother would have been furious if she'd known how they'd treated him.

He had shown Nicola compassion, knowing it would move her. He had a special gift for knowing what women needed—not just wanted. She began to find ways to be near him at the gallery. At first, she was just scholarly and pretty, and then she was scholarly and sexy. It wasn't that she changed the way she dressed—she wore a near uniform, slim black pants and a white silk blouse, sometimes with a black blazer. It was more a shift in attitude. They gravitated toward each other.

Beth never would have believed this, but Pete had grappled with his desires for a long time before giving in to Nicola. He enjoyed the act of seduction, getting someone to want him. He craved knowing a woman felt passion for him, but acting on his own was another story.

He had been a good husband. He had had plenty of opportunities too. Women would stop by the gallery, divorced women from town or visiting their summer places, pretending to look at art but so obviously lonely, seeking what everyone wanted: someone to love.

Sometimes the women would pretend to consider buying a painting; occasionally they would actually do so. At openings, when there was wine, they would stand a little too close, link arms with him to lead him across the gallery and ask about the provenance of this Hassam, that Morrison.

The affair with Nicola began in the least romantic of places—down in the gallery basement, damp from the water table, recent rains, and shades of the Woodward family horrors. Pete had been framing a little jewel of a painting by Malcolm Grant, a lesser-known Black Hall artist. It was a tiny oil of a frozen stream at dawn, bright with breaking light.

He stood at the workbench, measuring segments of wood. A harsh overhead lamp illuminated particles of sawdust in the air. Nicola walked over to him. He could picture the painting as if it were in front of him right now, he could feel the sawdust stinging his eyes, but he couldn't remember the words she said. Suddenly his mouth found hers, her arms were around his neck, and he swept all the framing materials and that valuable little picture aside, lifted her onto the table, his cheek against hers.

Six months later, six months of passion, they were in the basement again.

"I'm going to . . . ," she said.

"Going to what?"

"Have your baby. Love you."

"I love you to death," he said, putting his hand on her belly, already starting to get slightly round. He knew he should be upset—they hadn't planned on her getting pregnant, and when Beth found out it was going to be hell for everyone. But he had never felt love like this, so pure and true.

"I want to be with you forever," she said.

Her words filled him with such emotion. "I want that too," he whispered.

"Just one little problem. You're married to someone else," she said.

He hadn't liked her saying that. It made her sound callous, and he knew she wasn't. She cared about Beth. That was what caused them exquisite pain—they both had Beth on the mind, but their desire was so great it overrode their consciences. Too often the institution of marriage became one of convenience and habit; he and Beth had let that happen. He would have to extricate himself as kindly as possible—take care of Beth and Sam. He would not fall into habit, into the mundane, when he and Nicola were finally able to marry. He wouldn't make the same mistake again with her.

"Besides, we don't have a choice," she said. He had removed his hand, but now she placed it back on her belly, as if he needed reminding. Every time he touched her he felt emotional.

"I want this so much," he said.

"Tell me."

"A life with you."

"Yes," she said, her voice beautifully warm and sweet. "We will be so good together. I'll make you so happy, Pete."

"You already do."

"I want to wake up next to you every day. Live as a family. I know I shouldn't ask you for that, and I won't. Not now. When you're ready, you'll tell me, won't you?"

Instead of answering, he had made love to her, right there on the workbench in the gallery basement.

But as time went on, he felt how tense she had gotten, how worried about their future. At the very beginning, when they'd first found out she was pregnant, she had said she didn't expect him to leave his wife, that she understood Beth and Sam were his family, and that she and their baby would be fine. She was an independent woman, a grown-up. She had gotten into this with her eyes wide open.

And she had been amazing, self-sufficient, and accomplished, a winner of academic prizes, the author of an important and widely circulated monograph on Benjamin Morrison. Someone Pete would have been proud to be with.

But midway through the pregnancy, everything changed. She had become needy, even nagging. Whispering "I want to wake up next to you every day" had given way to constant tears and whining, "When, when, when?"

By the time she gave birth, he had watched her confidence drain away, witnessed this gorgeous, brilliant woman transform into someone who couldn't completely lose the baby weight, who smelled like Tyler's spit-up, who would rather read parenting magazines than keep up with trends in curation and advances in her work as a conservator.

The seduction had been lovely, but the pressures were ruining his life. All he had ever wanted was to do justice to the sacrifices his mom had made for him to get ahead. He wanted to make people, especially her, proud of him. Beth had given him so much. She represented stability, prestige, the life he had worked for. They had a wonderful daughter together. They were known and respected in the art world.

But once he fell in love with Nicola, she was all he could think about. Before her, he'd had a hard time really understanding love—it had felt more like an ambition, a responsibility, than an all-consuming feeling. He was all set to leave Beth for her until his lovely, crafty wife outsmarted him: right after Tyler was born, Beth gave him the news.

That *she* was going to have a baby too.

To Pete, the pregnancies were a one-two punch.

The sick irony was, Beth no longer wanted him; even though she was pregnant, she had asked for the separation. He had never seen her like this, the way she had been in the months before her death. She had become almost brash, standing up for herself, even when it was at his expense— like when she'd called his mother and told her everything.

Back when they'd first met, he had sensed her vulnerability—she was only twenty-two, a recent college graduate, running the family gallery, dealing with the horrible way she had lost her mother. She needed a man who would be everything to her—to heal her pain, to be her family, to make up for what her father had done. Pete's instincts about Beth, about women, had been dead on.

He thanked his mother for that.

His mom was a saint—there was no other way to look at it. Pete remembered how the kitchen light would be on past midnight, his mother studying at the Formica table. Pete had to find a way to make her life easier.

She had not been able to afford a new computer on her own, but even though Pete was only in eighth grade, he had saved from his after-school job cleaning up at a downtown gym, given her money to help buy it. His brothers and sisters could not be bothered, and his mother had rewarded him for it. "Here comes my jewel," she'd say when he'd go into the kitchen for his nightly glass of milk. Nothing had made him feel better than the sound of her fingers clicking on the keyboard, doing her schoolwork.

And now, thanks to Beth, his mother knew about Nicola and Tyler. He had never wanted to disappoint his mother, a devout Catholic who despised anyone who committed adultery, never mind getting divorced. This woman who had given the best years of her life so Pete could succeed.

It was a struggle. Nicola had wanted a future for them. Beth had tired of him. She had not been able to hide it, and he hadn't been able to keep pretending that their lives had been great—that what had gone on between them privately matched up to how they had looked from the outside: the perfect Black Hall couple with the elegant art gallery and big house and lovely, brilliant daughter.

He'd made a fucking mess of everything. And now he couldn't go back and fix it, not at all. It was too late.

He couldn't stop thinking of his and Beth's last minutes together. He had hugged and kissed her, told her how much he loved her. He had told her he was worried about her health, wondering if he should leave on the sailing trip at all. He had begged her to rest, to stay cool and out of the sun, not worry about the garden, keep her feet elevated, stay in bed as much as she could while he was gone. He ran through these thoughts over and over, until he could feel them happening again. *Hugged, kissed, I love you, worried, you need to rest, Beth, keep your feet up, stay in bed . . .*

"Oh, Beth," he said out loud now. Almost as if she could still hear him.

And he felt pierced by guilt because her death had made everything so much easier. Even though his love for Nicola was draining away, at least he didn't have to deal with two demanding women.

One was really enough.

Sometimes he wondered, though, whether the wrong woman had died.

Finally, the phone rang—"Green, Green, and Wolcott Attorneys-at-Law" popped up on the screen.

"Mac!" he said in his most jovial way. "Finally, we speak."

"Sorry, Pete, I was in court all morning. What's up?"

"I really need to know when you're scheduling my polygraph."

Silence on the line, then Mac's low voice. "We discussed that. I strongly advise against it."

"Right, you don't like your clients taking them.

But guess what, Mac? I don't know about your other clients, but I'm innocent. I need to prove that as soon as possible so Reid and the rest of them start looking for the actual murderer."

"Pete," Mac began.

"I have to insist on this," Pete said. "If you don't want to represent me anymore, fine. I'll do it on my own."

After they hung up, Pete felt pleased by the way he had stood up to the big, fancy WASP-y lawyer. Mac relented and was going to accompany Pete to the examiner's office. As Pete had known he would. No lawyer would want to lose a client like Pete. And Pete would nail the exam, just as he had every test he had ever taken. He was a member of Mensa; he doubted very much that Mac could say the same.

Closing his eyes, he ran through the last moments again:

Hugged, kissed, I love you, worried, you need to rest, Beth, keep your feet up, stay in bed . . .

19

"Should we go school shopping?" Kate asked.

Sam lay on the sofa, texting. Morning light streamed through the loft's tall windows, bouncing off the red brick wall, casting a blush on Sam's face. She didn't look up. "I need to get my phone fixed," she said.

"That one seems to be working fine," Kate said. "Considering you're always on it."

"I dropped it, and the screen cracked," Sam said. She stopped, raised her thumb, and showed Kate the beads of blood.

"Why are you typing on broken glass?" Kate asked, nudging Sam's legs over and sitting at the other end of the sofa.

"I don't know," Sam said.

"We'll get you a new one," Kate said.

Sam shook her head. "I just need a new screen. I'm keeping the phone. Mom gave it to me."

It was a warm day, but Sam had wrapped a blanket around herself. Kate tucked it more tightly around her legs, not looking into her eyes. She understood. There was a plastic water bottle in the back of her car that Beth had left there one day in July. They had gone to the arboretum at

Connecticut College, to walk through the trees and sit in the shade, and Beth had drunk from the bottle. Kate kept hearing it rattle around, hollow and dull, under the driver's seat, but she wouldn't throw it out.

"Let me see the screen," Kate said. Sam handed her the phone. It had a rose-gold case. Beth had thought it pretty and that Sam would like it. She'd driven to the Apple Store at Providence Place and bought it the first day the new iPhone had come out. It had a good camera with tele-photo enhancements, and Beth had hoped Sam would start taking pictures. She had never stopped encouraging Sam's interest in art—any form would do, from photography to watercolors to the dry and more scholarly pursuit of studying other artists' work.

"To answer your question," Sam said, "I don't need school things."

"I thought all kids did."

Sam shook her head again. "I don't want anything new."

"No?"

"I don't want anything that Mom hasn't seen. Hasn't touched. If I got new shoes, she'd never know about them. Or a new jacket. She'd never be able to tell me she liked it, or didn't like it, or button it up for me the first time I wore it. She still did that, you know. It was so funny; I'm old now, but when I got my winter coat last year, she did all the buttons for me before I walked out the door to get the bus."

"You're not old now. You're just sixteen. You were always hers, and you still are. Her little one."

"Yeah, I know."

Kate's chest tightened. She wanted to do and say the right thing. She had always been an on-the-sidelines aunt. She'd loved this girl from the minute she first met her as a tiny, red-faced infant in the hospital, the third to hold her after Beth and Pete. But Kate lived the life of a pilot, more at home in the sky than on earth. She had avoided relationships and commitment since she was sixteen. So how could she, right now, be everything Sam needed?

"What should we do today?" Kate asked. "Besides get your phone fixed?"

"I was thinking," Sam said slowly, "that I should go home."

That stopped Kate in her tracks. She pressed her lips together, gathering her thoughts. She wondered if Sam knew that Pete was basically living at Mathilda's. Kate planned to kick him and Nicola out, but she'd been too absorbed in Sam and racking her brain to figure out where the funny little key she'd found in Beth's drawer fit.

"I want you here," Kate said. "Does it seem I don't?"

"You've been great," Sam said, giving her a

crooked smile. "Even though I know you'd probably rather be flying places with Lulu, whatever."

"There's time for that, but right now I'm concentrating on you," Kate said.

"You're a lesbian like Mathilda was, right? In love with Lulu—it's obvious. Why won't you come out?"

"I'm not," Kate said, not completely surprised by Sam's assessment but knowing the truth would be too hard to explain.

"In this day and age, is it seriously so hard for you to be honest about yourself?" Sam asked. "You're allowed to be who you are! Do I have to be the one to tell you that? Didn't your grandmother and Ruth show you?"

"Sam," Kate said, wanting to shut the questions down.

"Okay, whatever," Sam said, grabbing her phone back, frowning with little lines of hurt furrowing her brow. Despite the splintered screen, she gave it all her attention and resumed her swift double-thumb typing.

Kate knew that Sam would have liked her to confide in her. To have an adult moment, a grown-up aunt-and-niece moment in which Kate told her what she never told anyone. And Kate was pretty sure her niece expected to hear Kate say that, yes, she was a lesbian. She might have been surprised to hear that Kate wasn't anything. She felt wild, bottomless love for Lulu.

218

And for Beth and Sam, too, for Scotty. But since that day in the basement, she had never felt romantic love, not even slightly. Parts of her heart and body had shut down during the hours of imprisonment.

Before that, her mother had called her boy crazy. She knew only one way to fall in love—madly—and it had started in first grade. Every school year she would be entranced, fascinated, in love with one particular boy. Billy in first grade, Dennis in second, Palmer in third, Patrick in eighth, all the way up to Michael when she was a sophomore.

She would dream about them when she was really young, turn bright red if they spoke to her. She couldn't wait for her first kiss, and it happened when she was fourteen and went with Patrick Reilly to a beach movie. Whatever was playing, they didn't bother to watch. They walked to the end of the beach and skipped stones into the dark water. She found the flattest, most perfect scaler. When she handed it to him, he pulled her close. The kiss was fire, and she melted through the soles of her feet right into the sand.

Patrick was her boyfriend until sophomore year when his family moved to New Hampshire. Kate had cried for a month. Then Michael asked her to frostbite with him. Frostbiting was sailing in winter regattas when the water was cold, sometimes crackling with ice. They would bundle up in dry suits, sail even if it was snowing, both of them so competitive they'd put the rail under and sometimes capsize.

The crash boat would rescue them, and one of Kate's favorite parts of the race would be warming up with Michael in front of the fire at the yacht club. They would sit close to each other on the sofa, arms touching, drinking hot chocolate and plotting how they would annihilate the competition the following Sunday. One time he reached for her hand. The next week she scooted across the sofa and put her head on his shoulder. From then on, they began losing regattas because they'd rather be kissing than racing.

Frostbite season ended, then came the spring series, and by summer they had figured out how to balance making out with high-performance sailing. They were sixteen, and Kate had started fantasizing about the next step. She and Michael were in love. Every time they were together, they went a little further. They would lie together, holding each other, and she would imagine what it would be like with their clothes off, and the thoughts would start to take over and keep her from being able to think of anything else.

Then she didn't have to imagine anymore. She lost her virginity in Michael's bedroom while his parents were at work. His body was hot and gave her a fever. She literally got delirious, her head spinning so hard when he touched her breasts and between her legs, when he entered her, that she couldn't breathe and wasn't sure whether she was awake or dreaming. She hadn't known bodies could do that.

Lulu had been jealous. She had never told Kate how she felt about her, but Kate knew. The way Lulu would always sit really close, the back of her hand accidentally-on-purpose brushing Kate's, gazing at her as if she was *hers*—as if she could see into Kate's soul like no one else.

The thing was, Kate knew it was true, and she felt the same way. The feeling was so intense it sometimes made Kate uncomfortable, especially when it stirred up her dreams. The day after such dreams, Kate would flaunt Michael to Lulu. She'd tell her about the things they did and those they wanted to do. Lulu would never smile during those talks.

Michael and Kate were each other's first. They climbed into his bed whenever they could. He used condoms, and then she got her doctor to give her the pill. Supposedly she had to wait a full cycle before the birth control would kick in, and it was so hard to wait to feel what it would be like without anything, even that thin layer, between them.

She kept her eye on the calendar, ready for the day, but then the basement happened.

It was as if her virginity returned, clamped

down on every single bit of her. She couldn't let herself remember how being with Michael had felt. She began to doubt they had ever even had sex. It was easier to pretend they hadn't than to miss him, miss the feeling of his hands on her skin. Her heart and body had never come back to life after that. There was no more longing, no more wishing. There was nothing to wish for.

Michael kept telling her he loved her, trying to hold her and kiss her, begging her to tell him what he'd done wrong. It was only August, months away from frostbite season, but she was frozen solid. Instead of telling him it wasn't his fault, that she had changed because of what she had been through, she stopped speaking to him. She refused to go to the phone when he called her at Mathilda's.

She didn't start school that September. Whenever possible, she slept all day. Eventually Mathilda eased her out of bed and drove her to a hospital in Massachusetts, south of Boston. There were other depressed girls and lots of psychiatrists, psychologists, art therapists, music therapists, psychiatric nurses dispensing meds, taking the girls on long walks in the fresh air along trails through a forest of birches and sugar maples and the falling leaves of October, but nothing made Kate come back to life.

By the time she was well enough to return to Black Hall High School, Michael had started going out with someone else. He tried to talk to Kate once, but she pretended not to see him. The truth was, she saw the hurt on his face and hated herself for putting it there. When boys asked her out, she said she had a boyfriend in New Hampshire. Lulu and Scotty embraced her and Beth, nurtured them through that school year.

Beth had survived and somehow started to heal.

Kate had died, but she had kept it to herself.

Staring at Sam, she wondered whether she would recoil from or be intrigued by the way her aunt felt or didn't feel. Kate knew she was an oddity among the passionate Harkness-Woodward women.

"I really do want to go home," Sam said, typing even faster.

"Well," Kate said.

"Today," Sam said. "I need to be with Dad. And with Mom. Because if she's anywhere, she's there. I know she is. It won't matter that I can't see her. She'll be there, at home. I want to sleep in my own bed on the sheets she put on it. And go into Matthew's room and put up the mobile I made for him."

"Okay then," Kate said.

She stood, clipped the leash on Popcorn, and went down to the street. She had to call Pete and tell him to get himself home. She had to tell him his days at Mathilda's were over, she was kicking him and Nicola out, and that he'd better keep Nicola away from Sam. He'd better.

Her emotions weighed on her, made her feel leaden, but she told herself that with Sam gone, at least she'd be able to spend more time figuring out who'd done the drawing of Beth, to find the lock that fit the key.

20

Lulu Granville was back from Asia. She had actually requested a series of trips starting in Tokyo that kept her as far away from the people she loved most in the world, and she felt completely guilty for it. Thoughts of what she had missed sliced her like knives, especially Beth's funeral.

Being present for Kate should have mattered more than anything, but Lulu had been too selfish. She needed time to pull herself together, to grow a shell too thick for Kate to see through. She hated herself for doing it, but the idea of seeing Kate, talking about Beth—not just her death, but the secret she'd told Lulu—was unbearable.

For many years, Lulu had been a nomad, sharing apartments with other pilots. She loved moving around, seeing the world, and because she was single, she had had the luxury of changing her base whenever she wanted. At various times she had flown out of New York, Boston, Los Angeles, and Atlanta. Her last share, five years ago in Greenwich Village, had been a nightmare, so she had transferred down to Atlanta and bought a cozy Victorian bungalow in Grant Park.

Because shoreline Connecticut would always be her true home, she rented a guest house close to where she had grown up, on Black Hall's Main Street. The point was to stay close to Kate. Beth and Scotty too.

But she'd chosen to be as far away as possible, just when Kate needed her most. Now that she felt centered enough to handle it, she was back in Connecticut.

She spent the morning at Hubbard's Point beach, swimming to clear her head. Long Island Sound was blue and calm. She swam out to the raft, then around the big rock, slicing through the water with long, sure strokes. She felt streamlined as a jet in her sleek red tank suit, long hair drifting out behind her. She had left the roped-off swimming area, swam along the far side of the breakwater, heading for Little Beach. A couple in kayaks slid by, calling hello. A jerk in a Grady-White shouted that she'd better be careful; she'd get run over.

If Kate were here, they'd laugh. They'd never kept inside the lines their whole lives. Of the four best friends, she and Kate were the fearless ones. The foursome had called themselves the Compass Rose in high school, each representing a different point on the compass but swearing they'd stay together for life because they needed each other to find their way and stay on course.

Lulu was west—after the great aviator Beryl

Markham's *West with the Night*; Scotty was east because she was *so* East Coast, in love with the comforts and conventions of life in their small town; Beth was south, her personality as warm as the sea breezes off South Carolina, as sweet as magnolias; Kate was, of course, north—at times distant and chilly, but brighter than anyone, a blazing aurora, the northern lights over the Arctic tundra.

After her mother's death, Kate had stopped seeing Michael. Her protective shell kept everyone away but Lulu, Beth, and Scotty. High school kids said she was cold, but Lulu knew she was the opposite—so warmhearted, she shut down after the nightmare, knowing what her mother had suffered. She had never recovered the part of her that had been lost that day. She refused to allow herself physical, or even emotional, pleasure.

Lulu's heart was pumping, her eyes stung from salt water, and her muscles released the tension that had built up since her arrival in Connecticut. The idea of seeing Kate was both thrilling and unbearable. The Compass Rose hadn't exactly stayed intact. Although the four of them had remained friends, their closeness over the years had dissolved. Even Kate's and Beth's. Lulu and Kate had stuck together tighter than the others.

She swam over the rocky bottom, climbing out at Little Beach and scraping her thigh on barnacles. She shook salt water off her dark-blonde hair, staring at graffiti on the granite boulders. This was a nature sanctuary. When she and the rest of the Compass Rose were young, they had respect for the beauty here. They cleaned up beach litter, would never have dreamed of desecrating the rocks with spray paint like this: a black-and-red bull's-eye, splotches of bright blue and yellow flowers, a Jet Ski. Some idiot had actually painted *Hubbard's Point is Great!* It made her feel sick.

She wiped the blood off her thigh as she walked through the oak-and-black-walnut-spiced woods, along the twisting path back to Hubbard's Point. The graffiti made her want to never come back here again. Hubbard's Point people had used Little Beach for decades, although it was private and a nature preserve. Now they'd damaged it. She felt like building a fence across the path.

It was a hot August day. The sand—though not as crowded as July—was still covered with low chairs, striped umbrellas, beach blankets. Scotty sat below the tide line, her chair so close to the edge that small waves licked her toes. She waved Lulu over. Lulu gave her a long hug, then sat in the wet sand beside her.

"It's awful," Scotty said.

Lulu's mind was still on the graffiti, but then reality slammed back.

"Beth," Lulu said.

"We just can't believe it. It's all beyond. Nick

was on the boat with Pete when he got the news. He had to call and tell me! That's how I found out. Lulu, I thought I would die too. I'm still in shock over it; we all are."

"How is Kate?"

"You haven't seen her yet?" Scotty asked.

"I'm going to today." The words kicked Lulu's heart rate up. She started to stand, brushing sand off, noticing the blood from her scraped thigh had pretty much stopped. The cuts weren't deep, but they stung.

"That's good, Lulu. She's such a tough girl, but she needs us."

"I know. I'm heading to meet her now."

"I wish I could be with you two, but I have to volunteer in New London. Beth got me started working at the soup kitchen once a week, and today's my day. I did it for her, and I don't know, I guess I'll keep at it for now."

"Does Jed still go there?" Lulu asked.

"I haven't seen him since Beth died," Scotty said.

"So no one has talked to him?"

"Well, I haven't," Scotty said, her voice sounding surprisingly sharp.

Lulu was about to ask her what was bothering her, but Scotty gasped. "Oh God, no," Scotty said. "I can't believe it. Don't turn around."

Lulu immediately turned her head and saw Pete walking down the hot sand from the sea-wall toward the tide line. He carried two chairs, a beach bag, and an umbrella. Nicola walked beside him, holding a baby in a pale-blue sun hat.

"What gall, what absolute nerve of him to parade around with her," Scotty said.

"That's not new," Lulu said. "He hasn't exactly been discreet."

"I know, but have some decency, so soon after your wife's been murdered."

"I guess there's no point in hiding now," Lulu said and stared: Pete was tan, his hair sun bleached, his hibiscus-printed board shorts salt-water faded. He frowned with concentration as he worked the aluminum umbrella stand into the sand, set up the chairs, shook out and arranged the blanket. Lulu's stomach clenched because she recognized it: a Hudson Bay blanket from L.L.Bean. She knew where Pete had found it.

She and Kate had pulled it from Mathilda's linen closet back when they were in high school, taken it camping and beaching. White with black, yellow, red, and green stripes at one end—the white had yellowed over the years and with outdoor use.

"They're still living at Cloudlands?" Lulu asked.

"Yup," Scotty said. "So far Sam hasn't wanted to go home, so that's his excuse."

"I can't see Kate letting them stay at Mathilda's much longer."

"Why Beth did, I'll never know," Scotty said.

Pete held the baby while Nicola settled herself on the blanket. She smiled as she reached up to take her son. Pete's face was impassive—or was that still a frown, the wrinkles in his brow, his set mouth? Nicola bent her head to free her left breast, and Pete draped a towel over her shoulder as she began to feed the baby.

"Jesus," Scotty said, turning away.

"Seriously, you have a problem with that?"

"Of course not. I'm just thinking of Beth and Matthew."

Lulu squeezed her eyes tight. She pictured Beth, heard her soft voice. *Can you keep a secret?* When she opened her eyes, she looked at her hand, saw the small scar. It reminded her of the last time she saw Beth. A huge shiver ran through her body.

"What's wrong?" Scotty asked.

"It's just all so sad," Lulu said, giving her a hug. "I've got to go see Kate."

"Don't leave me alone with those two right there."

"Just look the other way," Lulu said. And she stood behind Scotty's chair and swiveled it, the aluminum rungs digging through the sand, so it was facing away from Pete and his new family.

"Thanks," Scotty said, but she moved her chair back to where it had been. "Look at him. Flaunting his other family. People are saying

231

he killed her to be with them. I just can't bear thinking about it."

Lulu didn't reply. It was all too depressing. When she got to her green Range Rover in the sandy parking lot, she pulled a white cotton sundress over her damp bathing suit and drove out of Hubbard's Point. She pictured Pete and Nicola on the beach. He was a creep; there was no doubt about it.

But Beth hadn't been a saint either.

21

Kate had arranged to meet Lulu at Cloudlands. Mathilda's 120-acre property ranged across two hilltops in the lower Connecticut River Valley, with views of Essex and the estuary, down to the two lighthouses at Saybrook Point, then across Long Island Sound to Orient Point. Late golden light filled the haze, made the river shimmer like a blue mirage.

Mathilda had loved follies—little secret places built of stone, set all around her property. Kate sat in her favorite now, the crenellated tower of a small stone hideaway built in homage to Gillette Castle up the river. She opened the heavy manila envelope she'd brought to show Lulu and withdrew the small key she'd found in Beth's desk. She had tried it everywhere she could think of, but it was such an unusual size it didn't fit any lock. Right now, in the tower, she stared at a weathered wooden door. It was only waist high, and she remembered looking inside as a little girl—Mathilda had kept some garden supplies in there. She tried Beth's key now but no luck.

When she looked up, she saw Lulu walking

across the wide lawn. Kate saw in her the sixteen-year-old girl she used to be, carefree in that white dress, in the way she waved and started to run when she spotted Kate.

"Finally," Kate said when Lulu had climbed the stairs.

"I'm sorry," Lulu said, squeezing beside her on the narrow bench, throwing her arms around Kate, kissing her forehead, both cheeks. "There's no excuse for taking so long."

"You're right; there isn't," Kate said. "You were in *Tokyo?*"

"And Beijing, and . . ."

"But you couldn't make it back for Beth's *funeral?*"

"Katy, I hate myself," Lulu said. "But I literally couldn't show up. I was so afraid."

"Of what?"

"You?"

Kate was stunned. "What are you talking about?"

"I just couldn't bear to see you. It's the most unbearable thing, you losing Beth. I couldn't face you, Kate. I was too scared . . . of this."

"But I've needed you," Kate said. She rarely cried except, for some reason, with Lulu. She tried to blink back a million burning tears, but they poured down her face.

"Our girl, our South," Lulu said.

"Lulu, I saw her. I'm the one who found her,"

Kate said. "She was broken, Lu. Her head was cracked. Her neck . . ."

"Oh, Kate," Lulu said, holding her tighter.

"My little sister," Kate said. "Her beautiful eyes were so cloudy, staring into nothing. The last thing she saw was someone killing her."

"This is what I was so scared of," Lulu whispered, stroking her hair. "Not being able to face what I know you've been through. Why did you have to find her? Of everyone, why did it have to be you? I don't want it in your mind, that sight of her. I want you to remember her alive and happy, our girl . . ."

"I'm so glad it was me," Kate said. "It was as if . . . I was taking care of her, for the last time. Being with her. Not turning away. I had to see her, Lulu. It would have been ten times worse if I hadn't. She was so alone at the end. And she lay there all that time, by herself in that cold room, and no one knew. I had to be the one to find her."

"I should have been here," Lulu said.

Kate pushed herself away to dry her tears. She nodded. "Yeah, you should have. I know what you said, but I still don't get why you weren't. Not really." She waited for Lulu to reply, but Lulu just stared down at her feet, shaking her head.

Kate's gaze fell upon Lulu's leg, crisscrossed with thin bloody lines.

"What happened?" Kate asked.

"I had an incident at Little Beach. Barnacles." Lulu paused. "Have you been through the path lately?"

"No," Kate said.

"Kids sprayed paint all over the rocks," Lulu said, the awkward non sequitur hovering between them.

Kate closed her eyes. The last time she'd been there was with Beth. This past June they had walked to Little Beach, along the water's edge at dusk, looking for moonstones. The pebbles had glistened in the wet sand, opalescent in late-day amber light, lighting their path like tiny fallen moons.

"Are you okay?" Lulu asked, watching Kate, bringing her back to the present.

"I'm kicking Pete and Nicola out today. The locksmith is coming."

"Can you imagine what Mathilda would say if she knew Pete was here? After what he's put Beth and Sam through?" Lulu asked.

"She'd be apoplectic. Beth should have made them leave the minute she found out they were here."

Lulu looked away, seeming to think about it. "Maybe she had other things on her mind."

Of course Beth had had plenty on her mind, but the way Lulu said it made Kate feel uneasy. "What do you mean?" she asked.

Lulu didn't reply.

"Well, my theory is it made her feel strong," Kate said. "Like she had the power. Knowing she could get rid of them at any time."

"She had a lot going on," Lulu said.

"Yes, the pregnancy, running the gallery . . ."

"Et cetera," Lulu said.

Kate gave her a sharp glance. "*Et cetera?* Is there something you want to tell me?"

"No. I'm just upset. Who's going to run the gallery now?" Lulu asked.

"Maybe I'll have to."

"What about your job? Uh, you're a pilot."

"I know. Maybe I can do both."

Lulu gave her a skeptical look. "They're both kind of full time, aren't they?"

"I'm not ready to think about this," Kate said.

"You can hire someone to run the gallery. As long as you don't sell it. You have to keep it in the family. I still think of it as Mathilda's."

It touched Kate how loyal Lulu was to Mathilda. Mathilda had influenced both of them to become pilots. Lulu had gone up with Kate and Mathilda many times. But Lulu was right: the gallery had always been and would always be Mathilda's. It bore the stamp of her style and personality, a home for the art of the Black Hall Colony.

"Beth was planning an exhibit around Hassam's World War I flag paintings. It would have been an homage to Mathilda. She really loved that series."

"Well, she was a veteran, a patriot."

"She always told us that Hassam had wanted to volunteer to go to Europe and record the war. I think she wished a Black Hall artist had done that for her war."

Her war. World War II, when she'd learned to fly. As Kate and Lulu headed across the lawn to meet the locksmith, Kate thought of the Harkness-Woodward women, how they had been shaped by their grandmother's bravery. She'd withstood bullets and bombs and being demeaned by men in power. There must have been times when she had been so afraid, but she'd never talked about it to Kate. Maybe she had to Ruth. Kate thought about how even the strongest women could feel fear. The idea of Beth's last hour filled her mind.

"She must have been terrified," Kate said.

"Mathilda?"

Kate shook her head. "Beth. At the end, when he was strangling her, knowing that she was going to die. That she'd lose the baby. And whatever led up to that moment when . . ." She couldn't finish the sentence. "Do you think about it?"

"Of course," Lulu said, staring into space. "All the time." Her mouth and jaw were tense, set, as if holding back words.

"What is it?" Kate asked.

"Look, there's the locksmith," Lulu said.

Their feet crunched over white gravel and crushed clamshells as they approached the maroon van. It was painted with a gold lock and key. The locksmith was young and lanky, with a long dark ponytail covered by a red bandana. Kate showed him the doors with locks she wanted changed. Seven altogether, all around the first floor of the big house. When he was done, he wanted payment in cash. Kate had gone to the ATM and was prepared.

She and Lulu went into the kitchen and grabbed big black plastic garbage bags. Going through the bedrooms, they filled them with Pete's and Nicola's things. Kate stared at Tyler's toys and clothes and couldn't bring herself to touch them.

They piled the trash bags next to the driveway. Kate made Earl Grey tea, and out of a sense of reclaiming Mathilda's house, served it in Limoges cups she had loved as a child—the translucent white porcelain delicately painted with butterflies, tiny roses, forget-me-nots, and ladybugs. She tucked the large manila envelope under her arm and carried the tray out the side door.

They sat on the side porch, the ceiling painted the palest shade of sky blue. The Compass Rose had had many tea parties in this exact spot. Mathilda had taught them to brew loose Darjeeling the way she had learned in

England, when she had been stationed north of London during the war. Once the leaves had steeped enough, Kate poured the tea, and Lulu added extra sugar to hers.

"I want to show you something," Kate said after they'd finished the first cup.

Lulu watched her reach into the envelope and pause. Kate felt torn—Lulu was her best friend and had loved Beth as much as anyone. But revealing her sister's secret felt like a betrayal.

"What is it?" Lulu asked.

"I found these hidden in Beth's desk," Kate said. "She obviously didn't intend for anyone to see them. I wouldn't show them to anyone, even you, but I need help, to figure out what they mean."

She handed Lulu the key, laid the drawing on the white wicker table. Kate stared at the signature, JH. The nude figure study was beautiful, showed Beth's soft curves, her wavy hair falling loosely over her shoulders, the gentle heaviness of her breasts and slightly rounded belly.

"She's pregnant here," Lulu said, leaning closer. "But not very far along."

"I thought that too," Kate said, noticing that Lulu didn't express surprise. It wasn't the fact Beth had posed without clothes—when they were young, living in an art town, they'd all picked up a hundred dollars per session as models for the Black Hall Art Academy's figure-drawing classes. It had been no big deal—a prestigious college, their family's art lineage, their grandmother's blessing. But Beth's pregnancy meant she had posed for this within the last year, and that's what Kate found surprising.

"It's formal but also romantic," Lulu said. "It doesn't feel impersonal."

"Who is JH?" Kate asked. "I can't think of anyone with those initials."

Lulu didn't reply. She lowered her gaze from the drawing to the squat, almost square key. She lifted it up, bounced it in her hand as if judging its weight.

"Heavy little thing," she said.

"Too small for a door, too wide for a safe-deposit box."

"American doors, maybe. But it reminds me of a Paris door key," Lulu said. "They're shaped just like this. Don't you remember?"

It was true, and Kate did remember. For her high school graduation, Mathilda had taken her, Beth, Lulu, and Scotty to Paris. They'd flown Air France from JFK at night, and while Mathilda and Ruth had sat in first class, the Compass Rose had occupied the first four seats in coach. Kate had loved the feeling of lift, the surge of big engines, the knowledge they were flying over the Atlantic, into the sunrise.

In Paris, they stayed in a large apartment in a Belle Époque mansion in the seventh arrondisse-

241

ment, on rue de Varenne. The house was owned by Hubert and Karine Millet, friends of Mathilda and Ruth. The Millets had gone to Greece for the summer. Hidden from the street by high stone walls, it had an interior courtyard with a stone fountain and was filled with Renoir paintings and gilded Louis Quinze chairs that Mathilda warned them were antique and priceless and not to be sat upon.

The graduation trip was a whirlwind of museums—the Louvre, the Musée d'Orsay, Centre Pompidou, Cluny, Musée Jacquemart-André, and Kate's favorite, the exquisitely intimate Marmottan. Mathilda rented a car, and they drove out of town to visit Claude Monet's home and gardens at Giverny and the port town of Honfleur, the site of so many Impressionist paintings. The vacation was centered on art.

They visited the Normandy landing beaches and stood on the cliff looking across the English Channel, imagining the boatloads of Allied forces ready to storm the beaches. Ruth took Mathilda's hand. Instead of facing out to sea, they looked up at the sky where the Eighth Air Force bomb groups and fighters had provided tactical air support on D-Day.

Mostly they stayed in Paris. The Musée Rodin was a few doors down from their house. They had wandered for hours among its marble sculptures, orderly rose gardens, and reflecting pool, greeting the ghost of one of Mathilda's most revered artists, Camille Claudel, Auguste Rodin's model and thrown-away lover.

Lulu was absolutely right—the key to the Millets' tall front door had been exactly like the one Kate had found in Beth's drawer.

"Maybe Beth saved it," Lulu said, fingers closing around the key. "From our trip. Maybe Mathilda gave it to her."

"But Mathilda would have left it with the concierge—she wouldn't have taken it home with her."

"Then where's it from?" Lulu asked.

"I have no idea," Kate said, but a dream formed in her mind—one in which Beth could have been happy and still alive. A hideaway, someplace she went with the artist who did the drawing. Somewhere she could have escaped Pete and everything he had put her through.

Kate took the key from Lulu. The metal was warm from Lulu's hand. Beth had held the key too. She had treasured it enough to hide it in the small box along with the drawing someone had done of her. The two objects radiated love. Through them Kate felt her sister's passion.

"Who can this be?" she asked again, pointing at the signature on the drawing. "JH?"

Once again, Lulu didn't reply. In the distance, they heard a car shifting gears as it climbed the hill, tires rumbling over gravel. Through a row of cypress trees, Kate spotted Pete's big Mercedes sedan entering the turnaround.

"Here we go," Lulu said. "In honor of Mathilda, bombs away." Had she invoked Mathilda's name as a way of distracting Kate from the fact that she didn't want to answer her question about JH?

Kate put the key and drawing back into the envelope and headed toward the front of the house.

"Goddamn it!" Pete bellowed as he raced around tearing open the trash bags.

Pete's reaction should have gratified Kate, but she was still mesmerized by the unfamiliar sense of desire—not truly hers but borrowed from her sister. The abstraction of passion filled her mind. Then it ran across her skin, a river of it. It made her shiver, and she wanted the feeling to last, to be hers, no one else's.

Maybe the key wasn't to a house where Beth had already been but to one she had planned to go. A place where she could have been in love.

But with whom?

22

Nicola had spotted Lulu on the beach, but they had avoided actually encountering each other. That was impossible here at the house. Lulu and Kate stood in the shade of an ancient copper beech tree, watching Pete ripping open the garbage bags.

"You're only going to have to pack them again," Kate said.

"This is uncalled for," Pete said, sounding outraged.

"I don't think so. I want you out. This wasn't your house to move into."

"Beth knew about it," he said. "I'm not saying she was happy about the situation . . ." He glanced at Nicola. She had gotten out of the car with Tyler and was standing off to the side. She felt mortified to be there, facing Kate this way. "But she let them stay here."

Them, Nicola thought. *Not us.*

"She was so caring," Pete said. "She wanted the baby to have a good place to live until I could find somewhere else."

"She had her own baby to think about," Kate said.

"Your other son," Lulu said.

"Please, stop," Nicola said. The mention of Matthew made her go weak in the knees. "We'll leave."

"Hey, you stop," Pete said loudly, practically yelling, scowling at her. "I'm dealing with this."

Nicola flinched, and Kate saw. Nicola felt shame, having Kate hear him talk to her that way. Kate drifted closer to her and Tyler. She moved like a sleepwalker, close enough so Nicola could feel her warm breath on her forehead. She was staring down at Tyler. Nicola's arms tightened around him. She felt Kate's eyes casting a spell on him. Nicola shivered, thinking of Maleficent, but Kate's expression was gentle.

"My sister's baby didn't get to be born," Kate said.

"Kate, I am so sorry about Beth," Nicola said, the first chance she'd had to say it, or even see Kate.

Kate didn't raise her gaze from Tyler.

"Could I hold him?" Kate asked.

Nicola felt shocked by the request, but her instinct was to reach out, hand her baby to Kate. Pete came over and stood between them, blocking her. But Nicola stepped around him. Dark-red light stippled through the leaves of the copper beech, tiny flames from the sky. Nicola heard Pete swear as she put Tyler into Kate's arms.

Kate held Tyler awkwardly, a woman unaccustomed to holding an infant. Tyler had been asleep, but he stirred, opened his eyes wide, looking into a stranger's face. Nicola's arms tensed, ready to grab him back.

"I wish I could have held my nephew," Kate murmured.

"I'm so sorry," Nicola said again. Kate looked up, and for a long moment their eyes met and held. Kate's were red rimmed, filled with emotion—rage, sorrow? No, it was anguish; Nicola recognized that now. She felt it herself, for Beth. Kate started to hand Tyler back to her, but Pete grabbed him. It startled Tyler, and he began to fuss.

"Let's go," Pete said, facing Nicola. "We'll check into a hotel. Something temporary."

"I've changed my mind," Kate said. She stared at Pete with hatred. And then, as if she wanted to say the one thing that would hurt him most, "Nicola and Tyler can stay here. Not you."

"They're my family," Pete said. "Where they go, I go."

"Sam's your family too," Kate said. "She needs to be at home."

"I thought she was staying with you," he said. "I thought you had poisoned her against me."

"Beth wouldn't want me to do that. The last thing I want is for Sam to live with you. But

247

you're her father, and Beth would want you to take care of her. Sam wants that too. It's already done, Pete. I dropped her off this morning. She's waiting for you."

Nicola felt wild inside, hearing this exchange. Thinking about Beth, about Sam, about the mess she had helped create. What had she been thinking, that she and Pete and Tyler could ever have a normal life after this?

"Kate's right," Nicola said, forcing her voice to stay calm. "Sam needs her home and her father. But I don't think Tyler and I should stay here, Kate."

"Really? Where are you going to go? Nowhere near Sam, that's for sure," Kate said.

Nicola panicked. Kate was right; she had nowhere to go. She couldn't return to live with her mother and face all that criticism of Pete, the constant litany of how her mother believed he had murdered Beth.

"So," Kate said. "I assume you'll stay."

Pete looked at Nicola with that intense expression that scared her. It was pure rage, and it contained a warning.

He wanted her to say she would go with him, let him check her into that hotel, but she stepped back to let him know she would accept Kate's invitation and stay here.

"Thank you, Kate," Nicola said, trying not to sound meek. "I would like to stay."

Kate put the key in her hand. Nicola's fingers closed around it. Something made her look straight at Pete, and despite the hateful fury in his face, she didn't look away.

23

After everyone left, Nicola put Tyler down for his nap and wandered through the house. It was so big the signal from the baby monitor wouldn't carry from one floor to the other. She felt feverish. It might have been a slight sunburn, from the hour they'd spent on the beach, or it could be the heat of extreme pressure, a coal in her chest.

The house didn't have air-conditioning, but even on a muggy day such as this, it didn't need it. The windows were open, and a fresh Long Island Sound breeze blew up the cliff from the estuary, circulating through the hallways and rooms. She thought of the lengths to which museums went to make sure galleries were temperature and humidity controlled to within a degree or a bar, but Mathilda's collection filled the walls, and the trained conservator in Nicola saw no problems at all.

A dumbwaiter ran between the upstairs and downstairs kitchens. Nicola felt its presence as if it were alive and calling to her, reminding her of what Pete had hidden there. She resisted its pull and walked into her favorite room—the library.

The walls were papered in a color between rose and brick.

A marble fireplace, laid with logs, dominated one walnut-paneled wall. Chest-high overflowing bookcases lined two more, and the fourth had French doors. Hung with thick draperies of expensive fabric, Clarence House's Tibet pattern—playful striped tigers in shades of cinnabar, sage green, and pale citron—the doors overlooked the boxwood hedge maze; stone garden ornaments, including gigantic spheres from an eighteenth-century Irish castle; and a lawn sloping into various crags and valleys down toward the river. The effect was both exotic and very New England. This was how the upper class lived. Nicola had never felt more like a girl from the sketchy side of Groton.

Small paintings by Willard Metcalf, Matilda Browne, Benjamin Morrison, William Merritt Chase, Henry Ward Ranger, and William Chadwick filled the walls above the bookcases; Childe Hassam's *Fifth Avenue in December* hung above the mantel. It depicted New York at twilight under snow. The avenue was quiet; the day's traffic had ceased. The sky seemed heavy yet charged, as if a blizzard had just passed. The painting's electric quality came from the American and French flags flying from every building. The tableau was patriotic, but Nicola felt it warned that joy would be misplaced—World War I had ended, but the world remained uneasy. The blizzard could circle around, and another war was coming.

The baby monitor crackled. It was Tyler fussing. Nicola left the library and walked up the wide center stairs. She looked into the room where she and Pete had slept. Their son lay peacefully in the white cradle. He was quiet, deep in slumber; he must have been dreaming.

Why had Kate allowed Nicola to stay? Why had she accepted? She knew Pete had been furious by the way Kate had treated him. Perhaps, in a way, she was glad. He had swept her off her feet, but then he'd seemed not to have the foggiest idea of what to do about it. And it had made him angry.

The smart, ambitious woman he'd fallen in love with had slipped under the weight of his dark moods. She didn't like who she was becoming—quick to please him just to stop his anger, less likely to listen to herself than to him. Accepting Kate's invitation had felt delicious, a reclamation of who she wanted to be, just as her rebellions against her mother had always helped her draw the line between their strong personalities.

Nicola knew Detective Reid thought Pete had killed Beth, and most of the time Nicola fought that theory. She told herself that if she really believed it, she'd know physically; she'd be constitutionally unable to stay with him. So why, as her mother had asked, had she moved back home for those days in July? And why had she decided to stay here at Mathilda's instead of letting him create another temporary nest for them at a hotel?

The dumbwaiter was still exerting its gravitational force. She walked to the end of the second-floor hall, entered the small upstairs kitchen. Unused now, it must have been useful for household staff. It had a gas stove, old-fashioned icebox, and a cupboard full of Spode china with an inordinate number of eggcups. Perhaps the Harkness family, and whoever had lived here before them, had enjoyed breakfast in bed.

Three days after Beth's murder, Nicola had watched Pete enter this room with a canvas bag and a large claw hammer. When she heard the sound of nails being wrenched from the wall, she stood quietly in the hall, watching him. The dumbwaiter had been boarded up, and he removed the plywood. There in the opening was a small rectangular wooden box that could be raised or lowered between kitchens by a rope and pulleys.

When he reached into the canvas bag, her pulse began to race because she knew what was coming out—it was going to be *Moonlight*, the stolen Morrison cut out of its frame, and it was going to prove to her that Pete had killed Beth.

But it wasn't the painting. One by one, Pete removed toys from the bag. They were for a baby boy: a stuffed blue bunny, a blue teddy bear, a striped ball, a turquoise plastic teething ring. They weren't Tyler's. Pete glanced over his shoulder and saw Nicola. His eyes were blank. He showed no hint of emotion—the chill made Nicola want to cry out.

He stared at her for a full minute. Then he turned back to what he was doing. She watched him tug on the ropes to lower the box full of what had to have been Matthew's things, bought perhaps by Beth in anticipation of his birth, into the dark shaft. When he had begun to nail the boards back over the door, the hammer blows echoing down the hall, she had walked away. They hadn't spoken about it then or since.

He had completely replaced the wood covering the dumbwaiter, and she stared at it now. She could see the nailheads, the steel bright silver, polished by the recent hammer strikes. They glinted, calling attention to themselves. Through the baby monitor in her pocket, she heard Tyler waking up. She turned and walked down the hall to lift her son from the cradle and feed him.

24

Reid's desk at the Major Crime Squad over-
flowed with photos of the Beth Lathrop crime
scene, the report from the coroner, and a binder
filled with transcribed interviews with witnesses.
He cleared space and leaned on his elbows, a
cup of coffee by his side, to read the autopsies of
Beth and her baby, Matthew.

The coroner had ruled that Beth had died of
asphyxia by strangulation. She had received
blunt force trauma to the head, the contours of
the skull fracture consistent with being struck by
the marble owl. But her death had been caused
by someone using his hands, thumbs crushing
Beth's larynx.

The details of murder, the small ones, were
the most piercing. Beth's fingernails had been
lacquered pearl white, her toenails hot pink. A
rainbow had been painted on the nail of her left
index finger, the colorful lines slightly wobbly
as if she had done it herself. She had dressed to
please someone, most likely her killer, in sexy
underwear, and he had torn off her bra and panties,
wrapped the lacy waistband so tightly around her
throat that it had left deep, purple-red impressions.

The coroner had examined her hair and finger-nails, the orifices of her body, and the surface of her skin. Trace evidence had been collected—including hair, fibers, dirt, and soil—and analyzed. There had been no DNA found under her fingernails—the head injury had disabled her to an unknown extent and could have prevented her from fighting back.

Reid thought of the deep scratches on Pete's back. They hadn't been made by Beth. Dental impressions had been taken of her mouth; the deep bite marks on Pete's shoulder were not a match either.

No semen had been found during the course of the autopsy.

She had been covered with bruises, as if she had been battered around the head and shoulders and the forearms, perhaps during a struggle before the killer had landed the head wound. Her legs had also been bruised, including her thighs.

Full-color autopsy photos revealed U-shaped bruises on her shoulders and chest where her killer had knelt while choking her. Her blood had settled in postmortem lividity on her left side. Although she had died on her back, the killer had posed her facing the window. Perhaps that was the position she had slept in, and he had known it. The medical examiner would testify to clear-cut classic signs of strangulation—fractured

hyoid bone, petechial hemorrhages in her eyes—
if the killer was ever brought to trial.

Some sadistic murderers choked their victims
to the point of death, then released the ligature
and brought them back to consciousness, giving
them hope of life, repeating the sequence over
and over. Reid didn't believe Beth's killer had
done that. The sureness of the marks showed
that once he had started, he'd worked hard and
steadily to bring about death.

It had taken minutes for Beth to die. The killer
had administered a devastating blow to her
head. Then he had used his hands, and then he
had twisted the ligature around her neck. Beth's
adrenaline would have been pumping. The
coroner had questioned whether she had fully
lost consciousness after the head wound. To
some extent, she would have felt terror and the
atavistic instinct of fight or flight. She would
have had ringing in her ears, vertigo, cyanosis,
drastic weakening of her muscles. She had bled
from her nose and ears. The salt of her tears had
crystalized on her eyelashes. Her hands would
have involuntarily clenched. She would have
been aware of the baby struggling inside her.

One or more seizures would have occurred. Her
heart would have continued beating for several
minutes. At or before the moment of death, she
would have lost control of her bladder and bowels.

Reid turned to the section on Matthew. He had

died from lack of oxygen. He would have lived slightly longer than Beth. His heart would have continued circulating oxygenated blood for over a minute after his mother stopped breathing.

At six months, Matthew had been considered viable—if delivered, he could have lived on his own. That meant that by killing Beth, the suspect had committed double, or capital, murder. In the years before Connecticut's death penalty statute had been repealed, the murderer, if convicted, could have been sentenced to death by lethal injection.

Reid looked through the file for information on Matthew's DNA. He was surprised not to find it. Dr. Garcia, the state medical examiner, was very thorough. Reid would have expected to find a paternity test here. Not that there was any question about Pete being the father, but still, for the sake of trial, if and when it came to that, Reid liked having every base covered. It was the kind of detail a defense lawyer like Mac Green could attack.

He picked up the phone and rang the ME's office. Sally Driscoll, Dr. Garcia's assistant, answered.

"Hey, Sally. It's Conor Reid."

"How're you doing, Conor?"

"Everything's good. I'm just looking at the Beth Lathrop autopsy, and I don't see paternity results for the child."

"Huh, let me check," she said.

Reid hung on the line, receiver pressed to his ear. His coffee had gotten cold, but he drank it anyway. He heard music playing through the line, as if Sally had a radio on at her desk.

"Conor, did you request a paternity test?" she asked.

The question was a punch in the gut. "No," he said. "But I never do—I always assume it's protocol."

"Dr. Garcia said you didn't make the request, so he didn't perform one," Sally said. The music had been turned down, and her tone had become more formal. Reid pictured Humberto Garcia in the same room, perhaps glaring at her in his famous, heavy-browed way.

"Okay, thanks, Sally," Reid said and hung up. He tapped a pen on the page of Matthew's autopsy conclusions and thought about it. A test would have been pro forma, would have been nice to have one, but they didn't need it. Not really, anyway. But the lack of it made Reid's stomach churn—it was his fault for not specifying.

Reid didn't want to leave Kate without answers. He had driven past her loft last night, seen the windows lit up and warm against the dark. The last few days, he'd gone to the Groton–New London Airport, where she kept her Piper Saratoga, and watched planes take off and land. He told himself it was meditative, a way to clear his mind and let ideas about the case come in sideways.

Now, sitting at his desk, Reid considered the lack of DNA and believed that indicated a staged, rather than authentic, sexual assault. *Sideways,* he told himself. He still wanted Pete for the murder, but he was determined to stop focusing on any one suspect and not rule anyone out.

The bedroom had been full of fingerprints: Beth's, Pete's, and Sam's, of course, but also Kate's, Lulu's, Scotty's, and Isabel's. There were also several made by an unknown person. Most of Beth's friends' prints had been in the seating area, where a sofa and two chairs were arranged by a fireplace, where French doors opened onto a small balcony overlooking the distant beach and sea. It would make sense for Beth and her friends to sit there, enjoying the view. But he would check on that.

He had looked at sex offenders in Southeastern Connecticut and found one of real interest.

Twenty years ago, Martin B. Harris had been an astronomy professor at a community college in Baxbury. He had been married with two children. There had been a string of home invasions in the suburbs around the school. The crimes were violent, sexual in nature, but not always rape. The victims were white women ranging in age from eighteen to thirty-eight. The attacks always occurred early in the day, mostly during the summer. They took place in the woman's house, on her own bed, and the scene was always strewn with lingerie—some owned by the victim, but most of the racier pieces brought by the perpetrator. DNA was everywhere, but it didn't match anything the police had on file.

Harris was arrested on a fluke. A witness had seen a blue Toyota driving away from the scene of one of the attacks, and she reported that it had a Baxbury Community College parking sticker on the bumper. Investigators scoured the college parking lots and found plenty of blue Toyotas. The owners were painstakingly cleared. But during one interview, a student reported that he sometimes parked his car next to his astronomy professor's, and he noticed Dr. Harris almost always had a Frederick's of Hollywood bag in his back seat.

The police arrested him in his classroom. They had warrants for his home, office, and vehicle and found trophies taken from every home he had entered. His DNA matched. He had a penchant for black lace underwear and always brought some to his crime scenes, in case his victims had other taste.

He'd accepted a plea deal for fifteen years. His wife had divorced him and taken the kids. The college had fired him.

Reid read through Harris's parole records

and saw he had been released from prison two years ago and was living in a residence hotel in Silver Bay—one town over from Black Hall. He checked in with his parole officer once a week and was subject to unannounced drop-ins.

Reid called Robin Warren, Harris's parole officer, to give her a heads-up that he'd be stopping by Osprey House to question Harris.

"Thank you for letting me know," she said. "May I ask, why is he of interest to you?"

"The Beth Lathrop case," he said.

"Oh, yes," she said. "That was a terrible thing."

"So you know the details?"

"Those that have been made public, of course," she said.

"Did you think of Harris?"

She paused for a long moment. Reid had worked with her before, found her to be thoughtful and thorough, an excellent officer studying for a master's in psychology. She had lived in Zimbabwe as a child, and her accent was elegant and formal.

"I saw similarities with Mr. Harris's past crimes," she said. "But no, I did not think of him in relation to this case."

"Why's that?"

"He willingly undergoes anti-recidivism treatment. He takes two testosterone-suppressing drugs, and he goes to therapy once a week."

"What kind of therapy?" Reid asked, feeling

weary. Psychological, and even drug, treatment for sex offenders was controversial at best.

"I hear that tone in your voice," she said with a hint of amusement. "Police officers are not inclined to believe it works. But it does. His doctor works with him on imaginal desensitization."

"Right," Reid said. "Get those dirty pictures out of his mind."

"And thoughts. And desires to act."

"What about actual pictures? Does he like pornography? And how hard is it for him to stay away from Victoria's Secret?"

"Possession of any of those items would constitute a parole violation. And he would return to Ainsworth," she said.

The prison where Harris had been incarcerated.

Warren asked if it was okay if she was present when he interviewed Harris, and he said sure. He grabbed his jacket from the hook behind his office door. The drive took twenty minutes, including a stop at a drive-through Dunkin' Donuts for coffee and a plain cruller. He burned his mouth on the coffee and scarfed down the cruller just before pulling up to Osprey House.

The big, sprawling yellow Victorian building had a wide porch and a large cupola, and a hundred years ago, it had been a resort hotel. Now it was the land of broken toys: people whose luck had run out, who were trying to hide from a spouse or the law, who were trying to kick drugs or wanted an anonymous place to take them, who had lost their driver's licenses and enjoyed the fact that cheap booze was just a two-minute walk away, whose income didn't cover anything nicer than a tiny bedroom with a microwave and a shared bath down the hall.

"Hey, Paul." Reid waved to the manager sitting in the front office behind bulletproof glass. They had met on many occasions. Quite a few of Reid's frequent flyers—people who often seemed to wind up in trouble with the law—found their way to Osprey House.

"What's up, Conor?" Paul O'Rourke asked, coming out to shake his hand. He was in his mid-fifties, with white hair and a bristly mustache, bright eyes, and a ready smile. Reid knew that his job was hard and that he was as much a bouncer and social worker as hotel manager.

"I've come to see Martin Harris," Reid said.

"Ahh," Paul said, glancing at the clock on the wall. "Considering it's not yet 4:00 p.m., you should find him at least semicoherent."

"Enjoys a drink?"

Paul nodded.

"Does he get belligerent?"

"Braggadocio after he's had a few—you know, how he used to be a professor, and he'll fight anyone who says he wasn't. To look at him now, you'd never believe he was. But mostly he keeps to himself."

"Has there ever been an incident? A woman complaining about him?"

Paul shook his head. "No. We're aware he's on the SOR, but we've never had a problem with him." He pointed at the stairway. "Room 408."

Reid walked up four flights. He wasn't surprised that Paul would keep track of residents on the sex offender registry. The stairwell smelled antiseptic, trying to cover stale cigarette smoke and ancient vomit. Every few weeks the morgue was called here to remove a body—mostly overdoses, some accidental and some suicides. The walls were soaked with the sadness of lonely people drinking themselves to death in their small rooms.

When he got to the top floor—the fourth—Reid walked slowly down the dark hall. Music and talk radio came from behind closed doors. There were eight rooms, two bathrooms. He heard a shower running. Room 408 was at the end on the right. Reid listened for a moment. Silence.

He rapped loudly. Music and talk radio in the other rooms stopped. There was something about a loud knock that announced a cop.

"Mr. Harris!" he said, knocking again.

After a moment, the door inched open. A short, stout bald man peeked out. He looked bleary eyed and was in a white-ribbed undershirt and baggy, faded blue boxers. He stank of last night's vodka.

"Yes?" he asked. "May I help you?"

"I'm Detective Conor Reid. Are you Martin Harris?" Reid asked.

"I am," he said, rubbing his eyes as if trying to wake himself up.

Reid heard footsteps on the stairs and turned to see Robin Warren entering the hallway. She was about forty, dressed in a stylish off-white suit and matching heels. She wore her long dark hair braided around the crown of her head. She and Reid nodded to each other.

"Robin, what's this about?" Harris asked.

"I'd like to ask you some questions about Beth Lathrop," Reid said.

Harris had a strong, instantaneous reaction. He gasped, covered his mouth with his hand.

"I read about that," he said.

"Did you know her?" Reid asked, all his senses activated as he watched the emotions cross Harris's face.

"No, I just felt sorry for her. And her family. Who would do that? Kill her and the baby?"

"Did you ever want to kill one of your victims?" Reid asked.

"Oh my God, no!" he said.

"Do you mind if we step into your room?" Reid asked. "And look around?"

"That's fine," he said, glancing at Warren. "But you're not supposed to search, right, Robin?"

"He can, if there is reasonable suspicion," Robin Warren said in a kind voice.

Reid stood in the room, barely big enough for a twin bed, bureau, closet, and microwave set on a countertop. The walls were blank except for a few postcards tacked above his bed. The wastebasket was half-full of empty nip bottles. Cans and cartons of chili, mac and cheese, and tuna, classic food pantry/soup kitchen fare, were stored on top of the microwave.

Piles of books covered the floor—Reid glanced and saw titles by Carl Sagan and textbooks about stars and planets; self-help books titled *Take Charge of Your Life NOW*; *The Past Was Never Your Friend*; *Say Hello to the Present (Your Greatest Gift)*; *Turn Those Inner Demons into Angels!*; and, most surprisingly, three novels by Danielle Steel.

"What are your 'inner demons'?" Reid asked.

"Normal ones!" Harris says. "Everyone has them."

"Okay," Reid said. So far he was just standing there, turning in a tight circle, seeing what was obvious to the naked eye. He hadn't opened a drawer or the closet door.

"I am very upset about this," Harris said. "I haven't done anything. Ask Robin! So how can you possibly say there's 'reasonable suspicion'?"

Reid leaned close to look at the postcards above Harris's pillow. There were five, all tourist shots of towns in Connecticut. Vineyards in Stonington, docks in Mystic, the ferry in Hadlyme, and Main Street in Black Hall.

The shot of Black Hall showed the big white church and the Lathrop Gallery.

"You like Black Hall?" Reid asked, lightning shooting down his spine.

"I like all those towns," Harris said, sounding nervous. "They're beautiful. They have dark skies, perfect for seeing stars. Places I would like to live, buy a good telescope, and get back to my profession, when I get off parole." He paused as if waiting for a question that never came, then clarified. "Astronomy. That is my profession."

"Been to the Lathrop Gallery?" Reid asked.

"No, never."

"I asked if you knew Beth Lathrop," Reid said.

"And I said no!"

"How about her husband? Pete Lathrop?"

"No!"

Reid straightened up. "Well, Mr. Harris," he said. "This is what they call *reasonable suspicion.* I'm going to call for some Silver Bay police officers to take you to the station. And then we're going to search your room."

"Robin," Harris wailed.

"Just do what he says," she said sternly.

"I need a drink before I go," Harris said, sounding on the verge of tears.

"That will have to wait," Reid said, snapping

on latex gloves, staring at the postcard of the gallery, his heart beating faster, knowing he was about to see what Harris had hidden in his drawers and what was written on the back of the postcard.

25

There were often late-afternoon thunderstorms at summer's end, but today's weather looked clear and fine for the flight to Cleveland. Kate stood on the tarmac, greeting David Stewart, a regular client, who had a board meeting. An elderly man with sharp blue eyes and a full head of white hair, he and his wife summered on Fishers Island.

"Hello, David," she said, and they shook hands.

"Kate, I haven't had a chance before now to tell you we're so sorry about your sister. Lainie and I are heartbroken."

"Thank you," she said.

"She was an extraordinary woman."

"You knew Beth?" Kate asked, surprised.

"Yes, she and Lainie both volunteered on Thursdays at the New London soup kitchen."

"Beth loved doing that."

"She cared about the people so much. Lainie always said so. It didn't matter who they were, where they came from. Drug addict or the artist down on his luck—she treated them the same way."

"Well, she was known for helping artists," Kate said.

"Yes, a true philanthropist. We really appreciated her recommending one fellow to teach art to our grandkids."

"Who's that?" she asked.

"Very talented young man. Beth introduced him to Lainie, knowing that we love art and that we'd enjoy helping him out—but it turns out, he's done so much more for us than we have for him. As a matter of fact, he's heading out to the island again today. Third time now. The kids love Jed."

"Jed?" Kate asked. "I don't think I know him."

"Oh, I thought you might. Beth told Lainie she was considering a show for him at the gallery. He was at the soup kitchen too."

"A volunteer?"

"No, a client. He takes his meals there. Lainie says he's a brilliant artist, graduated from the Black Hall Art Academy, but is rather down on his luck. Literally a starving artist. She says he's a master at line drawings. She's already bought two of his drawings, to help him out."

Drawings. Kate's heart skittered. She pictured the nude, the signature, first initial *J*.

"David, do you know Jed's last name?" Kate asked.

"Hilliard, I believe. Yes, that's it. Jed Hilliard."

Kate was rocked by a full-body tremor. *JH.*

David took his seat, and Kate entered the cockpit. She heard Jenny offer him coffee. She and Charlie ran through the rest of their preflight checks. Kate had to pull herself together. Had the mystery of the drawing been solved?

Her hands were shaking. She knew she shouldn't fly.

"Charlie, you want to take the controls today?"

"Sure," he said, sounding happy. She rarely gave him the chance.

He called the tower, and they were cleared for takeoff. Charlie began to taxi to the runway. He released the brake, but Kate barely noticed. Her thoughts raced: Beth at the soup kitchen, JH drawing her nude. The plane accelerated at roughly the same rate as her heart, gaining speed along five thousand feet of asphalt into liftoff. Charlie banked left over Fishers Island Sound, giving David a good look at the island, then turned west.

The Citation X was a fast jet, powered by large Rolls-Royce engines, flying a mile in six seconds. They landed in Cleveland less than two hours after takeoff. The crew had four free hours before David would be ready to fly home. Sometimes they hung out together, but Kate left them in the airport; all she could think about was Jed Hilliard.

She texted Lulu:

I figured out who JH is. CALL ME.

Then Scotty:

Did you know Beth had a friend named
Jed?

Kate pulled the envelope from her shoulder
bag and looked at the drawing again. It was
undeniably a fine piece of work, but she didn't
care about that. Now that she knew the name of
the artist, she looked for signs of what Beth had
been feeling. Had it been a romantic relationship? She stared at Beth's pregnant belly—could
everyone be wrong about Pete being the baby's
father? No, it wasn't possible. Her sister would
never have cheated. She would have talked to
Kate if she even had feelings for someone else.

She needed to feel close to Beth, so she took a
cab to the Cleveland Museum of Art. Imposing
and graceful, presiding over the Wade Oval,
the neoclassical white marble building soothed
her upon sight. She had been here before, on
past trips with David, and although she usually
liked to visit the current exhibitions, today she
went straight to an old favorite in the permanent
collection.

A painting from Claude Monet's *Water Lilies*
series occupied an entire wall of the East Wing's
Impressionism gallery. She took a seat on the
wide bench and stared at it. It had been painted
at Giverny, during the last years of Monet's

life, when he'd stayed home creating massive paintings, triptychs of his beloved lily pond. Viewing this panel brought back the trip to France.

It brought back Beth. Her breathing slowed as she stared at the painting.

The October before the gallery incident, their parents had taken the girls to New York. They stayed at the Stanhope Hotel, across the street from the Metropolitan Museum and Central Park. While their parents met with a collector on Park Avenue, Kate and Beth went to the park. Kate skateboarded from the Obelisk down to Conservatory Water and around Bethesda Fountain while Beth ran along with her.

"Let's go to the Met," Beth said after an hour. "I'm cold."

Kate was wearing a red wool hat and a navy-blue down jacket. Beth wore a camel-hair coat, but even so, Kate took off her jacket to put around her sister's shoulders.

"Now *you'll* be cold," Beth said.

"Let's head down to Poet's Walk. You love the statues."

"No, the museum," Beth said.

"Aren't you tired of art?" Kate said. "We have that at home. We're in New York—do you really want to look at more paintings?"

Beth smiled.

Orange and yellow leaves carpeted the ground.

The graceful statue *Angel of the Waters* rose from a pedestal in the circular pool, above the park benches and lake. Kate wanted to stay outside, watch people, and get a hot pretzel, but she couldn't say no to her little sister.

Half an hour later, they were standing in front of a Renoir, a mother with two daughters in blue dresses. Kate had had to check her skateboard at the front door.

Kate shook her head, staring at the Renoir. "Impressionism is too pretty. It's too easy. Let's go look at Kandinsky."

Beth had given her a look as if she had felt sorry for her. "Haven't you ever listened to Mathilda? The Impressionists changed everything. The way they created light out of paint. One brushstroke, and it's a red hat. Just like yours."

"Yeah, well," Kate had said.

Now, looking at the large canvas of Monet's *Water Lilies*, Kate thought of how much Beth had loved this series—and Kate had to admit she did too. Their feelings about art had changed after their mother's death. Kate had almost instantly needed the comfort and familiarity, warmth and light of Impressionism—not French but American, the work her family had collected. Beth, in contrast, had decided that art had caused their mother's death, and she never wanted to think about it again.

That hadn't lasted long. Soon after their

mother's death, the two sisters had switched paths. Beth had become devoted to the idea of working at the gallery. She had lost herself in scholarship and paintings. To Kate, art was a pleasure to be abandoned, like everything else.

Had Beth met Jed Hilliard at the Academy or in New London? His talent was unmistakable. Kate ached, wondering why Beth had never said a word about him, at least to her. Had she talked about him to Lulu? Was that why Lulu had acted so strange when Kate had shown her the drawing? She checked her phone—neither Lulu nor Scotty had texted back.

Kate stared at *Water Lilies*, getting lost in the wash of subtle color and shadows, passing the time until David's meeting was finished, till they could fly home to Connecticut, until she could learn more about what Jed Hilliard had meant to her sister.

26

Sam had never thought of a house as being alive, as having a soul. She had lived at 45 Church Street since the day her parents had brought her home from the hospital. She had never much thought about it. She had taken for granted the walls, the windows, the floors, the rooms, the way her mother had decorated, the way the kitchen was bright in the morning, the bird feeders just outside the bay window. Plaster and paint and wood and a chimney. That was a house.

Now that she'd returned from her aunt's loft, she realized that she'd been wrong all along. Her house had been alive. It had hummed with life. It had been singing and dancing. It had been cooking meals and planning for holidays, and when holidays came, it had been full of the season. At Thanksgiving it had crackled with roasting turkey, and for Christmas, it had smelled of evergreen, cookies, and wood fires, and it had sounded like *The Nutcracker Suite*.

Sitting in the kitchen, Sam realized that the life in her house was gone. It wasn't a dead thing, exactly. It still had electricity and running water, the stove worked, the coffee maker could still brew, the refrigerator kept food cold. But the house had become a phantom. It was no longer living and breathing, surrounding the family and making them feel safe. It wafted along, an untethered spirit, drained of everything it once had been.

Even Popcorn felt the lifelessness. Instead of romping around, wanting to play, he lay in a patch of sunlight on the kitchen floor, looking out the sliding glass door at a squirrel chattering and hiding acorns in the yard. He wasn't even barking at it.

The sun caught a glinting something in the door's track. Sam went over to see what it was—a small sliver of glass. She held it in her palm. No one had told her the actual details, the moment by moment of that day when they'd found her mother, but she had watched the TV news showing clips of the house from every possible exterior angle. She knew that her aunt and the police had smashed the door to get inside. Her father must have gotten the pane replaced at some point, but this little piece of glass from the old one remained.

Sitting at the kitchen table, she held the sliver of glass as if it were as precious as a diamond. She angled it into a shaft of sunlight, tilted it back and forth, refracting rainbows onto the ceiling. She touched it to the inside of her arm. Oh, it was so tempting. She burned to write *I miss my mom* in her skin, to watch dark red bubbles of blood quiver and spill. Cutting had worked in the past, purged the pain like nothing else.

She had smoked weed that morning, after her father had left the house. Getting stoned had seemed like a good idea, but it had messed her up, made her feel as if she was on the outside looking in. Her mind kept flashing little nuggets of self-pity: *You are the daughter of a murdered mother. You will never see your mother again. Your father would rather be with his mistress and kid than with you.*

Leaving Kate's, she had intended to come here and hang the mobile. She had made it for Matthew in June. She and her mom had gone to the Whaling City Shelter in New London. There were a lot of women and kids there, and Sam's volunteer job was to do art projects with the kids.

Her mom's friend Jed helped out too—he was the real deal, an itinerant artist who'd never had a day job, who was willing to do grunt work and eat at the soup kitchen to keep his freedom, to paint and live the creative life. He'd helped her and some of the younger kids do a whole series of watercolors of birds—the kind that came to the feeders her mom always filled, backyard birds that might have seemed ordinary but were incredibly beautiful.

The day Sam made Matthew's mobile, she

painted downy woodpeckers, goldfinches, cardinals, starlings, and white-breasted nuthatches on both sides of the thick watercolor paper her mom had donated to the shelter. Then she cut out the birds, glued two narrow slats of wood together at the center so they formed a cross, and strung the watercolor birds from the cross in a way that allowed them to balance and twirl.

It wasn't exactly Alexander Calder, but she was proud of her mobile.

"Your brother is going to love this," Jed said, holding it overhead and watching the birds move on air currents, almost as if they were flying.

"I'll be in college by the time he's old enough to know who I am," Sam said.

"That's not true. He already knows who you are," her mother said. "He can hear your voice right now. You're already teaching him."

"Teaching him what?" Sam asked. Her grades had slid since the whole thing with her dad and Nicola the Gallerina, with the fact she *already* had a baby brother—one she never even wanted to know. Tyler.

"Teaching Matthew about birds and nature, about staying strong and getting through hard times the best you can," her mother said.

"I wouldn't say I'm doing great at that."

"She said 'the best you can,'" Jed said. "And that counts. Take it from someone who knows."

On the way home in the car that day, Sam

glanced over at her mother. They weren't the type of mother-daughters who had deep talks. They were close but in ways that did not involve talking about problems. Except for the occasional comment, her mom kept quiet about their family mess. Questions had been building up. Sam wasn't sure why, but having Jed be so kind made it seem okay to ask.

"Why do you stay with Dad?" Sam asked. Most kids wished their parents wouldn't get divorced. She couldn't say that she was crazy about the idea, but on the other hand, it troubled her that her mother would put up with her dad's bullshit.

"We're a family," her mother said slowly.

"But he's demeaning you," Sam said. "Flaunting Nicola."

"She's nothing," her mother said. "I actually feel sorry for her."

"How can you?"

"She has to be pretty insecure to do what she did. Fall in love with someone else's husband."

"She had a baby so now you have to?"

"It bothers you?"

Sam shrugged.

Her mother was quiet, maybe deciding how much Sam could handle.

"Sam, I know how much we will love this boy," her mother said. "I have you, and soon we'll have Matthew." She paused, glancing over, then back at the road. "When I first got married,

I thought I needed someone to take care of me. Even though I was smart, educated, knew how to run a business—my family business—I had gone through a lot. With my mother, all that. You know."

"Yeah."

"Your dad came into my life, saw what I needed—someone who understood, who could take care of me. Fill a big hole in my life. He convinced me he could do that, and I wanted to believe him."

"Did you ever love him?"

"Of course. So much. But things changed along the way. Just because I married him doesn't mean I'm not enough on my own. I had stopped knowing that. It took the garbage with Nicola to really figure it out. I hope you know that about yourself, that you are perfect on your own. You have to make yourself whole—no one else can."

"I know," Sam said.

"Good," her mother said.

"I'm not sure Dad believes it about you, though," Sam said.

"That's been the problem," her mother had said.

Now, sitting alone in the kitchen with the piece of broken glass, Sam thought how much everything had changed. The world was upside down. She only wished her parents *had* gotten divorced—maybe her mother would still be alive.

It didn't go deep, but it allowed a flower of blood to bloom. A trumpet blossom, bright and red. Cutting had always given her relief, and she needed that right now—to release the pent-up tension and grief. But the first cut did nothing, so she tried again. She stared at the blood, saw the red feeder clustered with the hummingbirds her mother had so mystically called from their hiding places, and she missed her mother so much she began to scream.

Loud, loud, louder, deep in the cellar where no one could hear, screaming as if the house were falling down around her, because the person she loved most in the world had died, was gone forever, would never feed the birds again, would never hug Sam again. Screaming because the world had ended.

And what did that mean? The thought scared her, as if she could believe her father would rather kill her mom than go through a divorce.

"He didn't kill her," Sam said out loud.

She counted the reasons why: she was pregnant, he loved her and Sam, he could never hurt his family that way—having an affair was one thing, but actually planning and murdering her—no way. But deep down, Sam couldn't help thinking of what her mother had been skirting around that day driving home from the shelter. Her father hadn't liked her getting strong.

A light breeze came through the open windows. She stared out at the garden. Without her mom to tend it, the flowers looked dry and weedy. The bird feeders were empty. The sight of those birdless feeders made Sam feel almost as bad as anything.

She started to throw the little piece of glass away, but instead she tucked it into an antique brass bowl her mother always filled with pine cones in the fall. Then she went into the garage, took the lid off the large galvanized bucket. It was full to the brim with #2 sunflower seed— the mix her mother had bought at the Audubon shop in Madison. She lugged the bucket outside, then went back into the garage for smaller pails of thistle seed, peanuts, and safflower seed. Suet could wait till winter.

The feeders were long tubes that hung from

four curved arms on a decorative wrought-iron pole. A large cylindrical baffle halfway up the pole deterred raccoons and squirrels from climbing up. Across the yard, a house-shaped feeder swung from a branch in a big red oak tree. It had a flat platform that nonperching birds like cardinals could use. Sam took her time, carefully filling each feeder to the brim.

When she was finished, she went to sit on the stone wall and wait for the birds to discover their food was back. Sam's heart expanded a little. It had been so small and tight for weeks. Looking at those empty feeders had made it shrink even more. But just then, she felt some blood flowing around her body, back into her heart. Just a little, not a lot. Filling the feeders was like bringing something back to life.

She couldn't do that for her mother, couldn't even do it for their house. But at least she could do it for the birds. At least that. She caught sight of the clear red feeder, its base shaped like a flower. How could she have forgotten the hummingbirds? It was always magical to see the tiny birds hover, dip in for a taste, dart away, faster than bees. They were attracted to red; her mother planted columbine and trumpet vines for them, and she also kept their feeder full.

Standing on tiptoes, Sam removed the scarlet flower from the suction cups sticking it to the window over the kitchen sink. She went back into

the kitchen and opened the refrigerator. Inside was a crystal pitcher filled with sugar syrup. Her mother made it fresh every week. Sam started to pour, then noticed a ridge of frosted sugar around the rim.

The syrup was a few weeks old now. Was it still okay? Maybe Sam could make some more. It had to be simple, but why had she never watched her mother do it? She was pretty sure she had to cook it, or perhaps she could just stir the sugar and water together. That was when it hit her—this was the last hummingbird syrup her mother would ever make.

Sam placed the pitcher back in the refrigerator. She closed the door and left the red flower feeder in the sink. Her heart shrank again—she felt it close up, tight and hard. She thought of the glass sliver. She grabbed it from the brass bowl and headed into the basement, making sure to close the door behind her.

Summer silent, the furnace hulked in the corner. Her dad had a workshop filled with his tools. Sam walked to the far end, toward the laundry room with the washer and dryer, some wooden dryer racks, and a wicker basket of single socks. Her mother had decorated the whitewashed concrete walls with pictures Sam had drawn in elementary school, photographs she had taken more recently.

Sam held the tiny glass shard and made one long, shallow slit on the inside of her left wrist.

27

The New London soup kitchen was located in the parish house of Saint Ignatius Loyola Church at the foot of Bank Street. The Whaling City Shelter was right around the corner. Kate had had to fly to Los Angeles twice in the last week, but today was the first of four days off. The church and shelter were a five-minute walk from her loft. She'd passed them countless times, seeing clients and residents lined up around the block, waiting for a hot meal or a safe bed. Just before lunch, she headed over.

Although Beth had volunteered at both for many years, Kate had never stopped in. Sometimes when Beth was working in town, if Kate wasn't flying, the sisters would meet at the Witchfire Teahouse on the water side of Bank Street, a place where they could drink Darjeeling and Beth could have her tarot cards read.

Kate passed it now. The storefront was painted violet, the sign dark pink with swirling black letters. Purple taffeta curtained the windows, intended by the owner to create an air of mystery for people who wanted to believe.

"An occult thrill for the suburban set," Kate

had said one snowy afternoon last winter, when they were seated inside on a shabby amber velvet love seat, the space lit by candles and Victorian lamps with fringed silk shades.

"It's not that," Beth said. "It's just fun. Thessaly!" She tried to catch the owner's eye.

"Thessaly?" Kate asked, her tone translating into, *How contrived.*

"It's the name of the thousand-year-old witch in Neil Gaiman's *The Sandman.* She adopted it."

"Okay then," Kate said. "She knows how to play the part."

Tall and thin, too young for the long silver hair that Kate was sure was a wig, *Thessaly* wore a crocheted black dress, black lace-up boots, and big glasses with round black frames.

"If you don't like it here, why don't we meet somewhere else?" Beth asked. "You make me feel like an idiot."

"What are you talking about?" Kate asked.

"You're so technical, scientific. You don't have faith; you don't believe in anything except instruments and gauges, and I respect that. I never tell you to lighten up, to be more spiritual. But you condescend to me. I can tell you think I'm a fool."

"I do not!"

"Yeah, you do. If I asked Thessaly to read my cards, you'd sit there with a smirk on your face just like you did when I told you her name."

Kate stared at Beth and knew she was right. She did think the whole Witchfire vibe was bogus, that Thessaly knew how to appeal to bored women who wished they had more in their lives.

"And all your comments about the 'suburban set.' What was it you said last week? 'Housewives having their fortunes told and looking for love.'"

"I wasn't even talking about you!"

"Well, I'm a housewife."

"Who runs an art gallery!"

"But what was the crack about looking for love?"

"I don't know. I was kidding around."

"You make it sound as if you think I want to have an affair. Looking for love, and truly, what's so wrong about that?" She narrowed her eyes at Kate as if challenging her.

"Actually, I think I said, 'Looking for love *advice.*'"

"No, you didn't. You said *love.*"

"I don't remember. I'm sorry," Kate said.

"I get belittled enough at home."

"Pete?" Kate asked. She wanted to Pete bash, to defuse the discomfort.

"Let's not talk about it," Beth said. Then, with a sharp gaze, "Maybe *you* should look for love. It might help you understand what the rest of us go through."

When Thessaly came over, she refilled their

teapot with hot water, but Beth didn't ask her to throw the tarot. That was the last time the sisters had met here. Beth had never suggested it again, and they'd started going to Dutch's Tavern, more Kate's style, for red wine and burgers. Now, passing the teahouse and looking back on the odd conversation, Kate wondered if Beth had wanted to tell her about the man who had so lovingly captured her beauty and soul in that charcoal drawing. Jed.

Lunch was underway at Saint Ignatius. Two women stood behind a long counter, serving what looked like Thanksgiving dinner: turkey with gravy, mashed potatoes, and peas. But it was August in Connecticut, so there was also corn on the cob.

The clientele ranged in age from teenage to elderly. They lined up with trays, carrying their meals to long folding tables set up in two rows. The room had basketball hoops at either end, as well as five easels folded in the corner. It obviously had multiple uses, from dining room to gymnasium to art studio. Was this where Beth and Sam had worked with people on art projects? Kate looked around, scanning all the men's faces, wondering which one was JH.

"Hey! Kate!"

She turned to see Scotty emerging from the kitchen, carrying a tray of sliced tomatoes and basil.

"I forgot you worked here," Kate said.

"Beth got me started."

"Did you grow those?" Kate asked, looking at the ripe, red slices.

"Yes, but the basil is Beth's. I stopped at her garden to pick some on my way over. She always did things to make the meals special. People here loved her. They miss her." She gestured at a bulletin board across the room on the wall. A photo of Beth in her gray shirt and white cap, her arms around two beaming women, had been tacked to the board. Beneath it was a banner that said FOREVER LOVED. It was covered with signatures.

"Everyone who comes in is invited to sign it," Scotty said. "They all do."

Kate drifted over to look at the names. Scotty put the tray down on the serving station and followed her. Kate read every name, but she didn't find what she was looking for.

"What brings you here?" Scotty asked.

"I was hoping to see a friend of Beth's. In fact, I sent you a text about him—didn't you get it?"

Kate turned to see Scotty hovering nervously behind her. A few tendrils of blonde hair fell from her cap. She had a very slight tan and faint lines around her brown eyes. They had been friends for a lifetime, and Kate knew those eyes so well. They were full of remorse.

"Sorry, I thought I replied," Scotty said.

"Who's Jed Hilliard?" Kate asked.

Scotty blushed and looked away.

"Both you and Lulu knew, didn't you?"

"Beth would have told you eventually," Scotty said. "She was afraid you wouldn't approve."

"Of course I would have," Kate said. "Anything that made her happy." But their last conversation at Witchfire, the defensive tone in Beth's voice, echoed in her mind: *You think I want to have an affair.*

"Is he here now?"

"No," Scotty said. "He hasn't been back once since she died."

It felt like a blow. Kate had thought if she could meet him today, ask him about Beth and the drawing, she might find some peace. She'd wanted to hear that he'd loved Beth and she'd loved him, that life had become happier for her. "Were they together?"

"Not like that! They were just good friends," Scotty said, but Kate wasn't sure she could believe her.

"Was he Matthew's father?"

"Oh, come on, Kate! Why would you even ask that?"

"Do you know where he lives?" Kate asked.

"For a long time, he was a handyman at the Academy, and they gave him a room in the attic. Then he was living here in New London—on

State Street, in that building they're converting into artists' studios."

"Is he there now?" Kate asked.

"I don't know," Scotty said. "If he was, I can't imagine why he wouldn't be showing up for food."

"She met him at the Academy? When he was working there?" Kate asked.

Scotty bit her lip. Her eyelids fluttered in a way that brought a sinking to Kate's heart. She could read sorrow in her old friend's eyes.

"No," Scotty said. "He never even knew Black Hall until Beth brought him there."

"Then how?"

"She met him at the prison, when she was visiting your father. He was there at the same time."

"Working there?" Kate asked, her stomach churning to think of her father being connected in any way. "Volunteering?"

"An inmate," Scotty said.

Kate let that sink in. "What did he do?"

"He got caught selling marijuana. She said your father would talk to him. They had art in common."

Kate couldn't speak. Beth had stayed in touch with their father all along, and even though Kate half knew she had visited him, Beth had under-stood that Kate hadn't wanted to hear anything about him. She had cut him out of her life the day she'd learned the part he'd played in those twenty-two hours. Beth had regularly gone to the prison, and she'd met a man there, and now she was dead. Kate felt sick. Her sister had had a secret life, and it had involved her father and another convict.

Maybe Pete wasn't the killer after all.

"Thanks, Scotty," she said.

"Kate . . ."

Kate gave her old friend a quick hug, then walked out of the room. The spicy, pungent scent of basil from Beth's garden hung in the air. She smelled it when she walked out onto the street, into the bright sun, and all the way home to her loft, and her eyes burned with tears as she thought of all the things her sister had never told her.

28

Reid's search of Martin Harris's room at Osprey House four days earlier hadn't turned up anything of interest, but that of the shared bathroom at the end of the hall had. The walls were lined with blue tiles probably as old as the two-hundred-year-old hotel itself—some of them cracked, pieces missing, caulk chipped away. The housekeeper obviously tried to keep it clean, but the mildew created by years of seaside fog and the steam of thousands of showers made it a losing battle.

The floor was covered with yellowed linoleum. Reid noticed how the corner under the sink was curled up, so he pulled on the edge and found a cache of porn. Whole magazines wouldn't fit, so pages had been torn out and slid under the loose floor. Reid called for a team to process the scene.

The pages came from different kinds of publications, from soft- to hard-core porn, suggestive photos of celebrities and models ripped from mainstream magazines, and even photos of models in pajamas and bathing suits ripped from the J. Jill and Sundance catalogs. Among the stash were images of naked women tied up, bound with their own underwear, gagged and blindfolded.

Because the bathroom was shared by all eight rooms on the fourth floor, and residents from the other three floors could use it as well, Reid couldn't immediately link the pages to Harris. The state police lab found twenty-two different sets of fingerprints—the Osprey House version of a dirty magazine being passed around a camp cabin—and one was Harris's.

Harris had not been sent back to Ainsworth, the state's highest-security prison, but he was being held at Avery, the local jail on the road between Silver Bay and Black Hall, used to hold prisoners waiting for trial, usually on lesser offenses. Reid had checked his alibi for Beth's last day; Harris claimed to have been drinking with some Osprey House buddies in the first-floor TV room. Three of them confirmed it, but all three admitted to having passed out drunk, so how good were their stories?

"This isn't looking good for you," Reid said, sitting opposite Harris and Lisa Lewiston, his attorney.

"I didn't do anything," Harris said.

"Mr. Harris," Lewiston said, her hand on his arm.

"I need to tell him," Harris said. "So he understands. And I'm going to." He gave his lawyer a stern look. He hadn't had a drink in the four days since he'd left Osprey House and been held at Avery, and his eyes looked clearer. His voice had an echo of the authority it might have had when he was still a professor.

"I'm listening," Reid said.

"Those were not my pictures," Harris said.

"But your fingerprints were on them."

"I know." Harris took a deep breath. "I can't help what other people do. There are plenty of guys not on parole at Osprey House, and they can buy whatever magazines they want and keep them in their rooms."

"But not you."

"Right. But not everyone can afford to buy magazines, so when people are finished with theirs, they share. Doris, the housekeeper, wouldn't allow things like that lying around, so guys tear out the pages they like and hide them in the bathrooms."

"Where you found them."

"Yes," Harris said. "I didn't know what it was at first. I saw the corners of some papers sticking out from under the linoleum, and I pulled them out. Detective Reid, I was shocked."

"I bet."

"No, I mean, really. I haven't looked at pornography in twenty years. Since I was arrested. With all the treatment I've been through, honestly, it makes me sick."

Honestly. Reid kept a straight face.

"So that's what happened. I saw the pictures, and I put them right back. It was only that one time. I should have reported it to Robin, or even Paul downstairs, but I just wanted nothing to do with it. Wanted to wipe the whole thing from my mind."

"Mr. Harris, do you think you're in jail because of those pictures?"

"Yes," he said, looking confused.

"They're just the reason we can put you in jail. But the real trouble is, you had that postcard of the art gallery in Black Hall. You know, the one Beth Lathrop's family owns."

"I told you I just like pretty towns."

"Yes, you did tell me that," Reid said. He opened his briefcase and took out the postcard in a cellophane wrapper. He felt confident but on edge. What Harris had to tell him would make or break the theory that had been growing stronger. "But I'm wondering why you wrote the names Beth, Judy, Alissa, Gennifer, Rose, and Faith on the back? And at the top of the card, the names Pete and Martin?"

Reid stared at Harris as the blood drained from his face. He pushed the postcard, picture side down, across the table.

"That is your handwriting, isn't it?" Reid asked.

"Hmm," Harris said.

"Is that a yes?" Reid asked.

"Uh, yes." The professorial authority had gone from his voice.

"So why do you have Beth's name at the top of that list?"

"No reason."

"Those others are the names of the women you were convicted of sexually assaulting, right? Judith Lane, Alissa Fratelli, Gennifer Mornay . . ."

"It's a coincidence," he said.

"So, you sexually assaulted every woman on that list except Beth Lathrop?"

Harris nodded, looking miserable.

"We'll come back to that in a minute," Reid said. "I see that you've put these two men's names at the top, and you've written them in bolder ink. Like you must have really pressed down, to make the names nice and strong. Read me the names, will you?"

Harris coughed. He looked away, then back at the postcard. "Martin and Pete," he said finally.

"Martin and Pete," Reid said. "Martin . . . that's you, right?"

"Yeah."

"So what about Pete? Who's he?"

"I guess it's Pete Lathrop."

"You guess? Or you know? Considering you wrote it."

"I know," he said. "It's Pete Lathrop."

"But I thought you said you don't know him,"

Reid said, watching for even a blink that might give him away.

"That's true. I don't."

"Never met him?"

Harris shook his head.

"So what is Pete Lathrop's name doing on this list you made of the women you assaulted?"

"Except Beth," Harris interjected. "I did not assault her. We need to be clear on that."

"Well, let's say we are. Still, what is Pete's name doing here?"

Martin Harris glanced at his lawyer. A little color had returned to his face, two pink patches on his round cheeks. His eyes were full of anxiety.

"I advise you not to answer," Lewiston said.

"But otherwise he'll think . . . ," Harris whispered. "And it will be worse."

Lewiston shrugged. "I've given you my advice."

Harris seemed to make up his mind. He sat taller, folded his hands on the table in front of him.

"I wanted to help you solve the crime," he said, staring into Reid's eyes.

Reid tried not to show his disbelief.

"And how would you help me?" Reid asked.

"Unfortunately, from my past behavior, I know too much about people who do . . . things to women. Such as those that were done to Beth."

Beth. Reid controlled his breathing. He had been careful about what was reported in the case. The department had held back certain details of the crime scene, including the fact that lace impressions had been left by the force of strangulation.

"What things were done to her?" Reid asked.

The pink patches on Harris's cheeks were turning red. *Temperature rising: he's getting excited,* Reid thought.

"Horrible things. Rape things," he said.

"Like what?"

"Being stripped. The strangling with hands. Hands all over her body, then around her neck."

Reid watched Harris's hands unconsciously flexing and unflexing, making an oval as if wrapping around a throat.

"Did you do these 'rape things'?" Reid asked, chilled as he watched Harris's hands tighten and release.

"Not to Beth."

"Did you see someone else do them to Beth?"

He hesitated, started to say something, then changed his mind and shook his head.

"It seems to me like you did," Reid said.

"Not really."

"Not really? But sort of?"

He sighed. "I dreamed about it," he said. "My treatment is working; it is, truly. But I can't help what I dream."

Truly. "Of course you can't," Reid said. "So, what did you dream?"

"I saw Pete doing it to her," Harris said. "She was on the bed. So beautiful and dainty, wearing her nightie. Pregnant. And how lovely a woman is at that time. There is a glow—I've seen it many times. My own wife . . ."

Did you want to strangle your own wife too? Reid wondered, watching sweat break out on his forehead.

"Right. So you dreamed of Beth on her bed."

"And Pete, her strong husband, standing over her, very serious."

Wives are dainty and lovely; husbands are strong and serious, Reid thought.

"What did Pete do?"

"Well, he hit her, of course. That's what the bruises are from. And he did this," Harris said, mimicking strangulation with his hands, consciously this time. "Then he would have taken her panties, which he would have removed after he hit her—I left that out—and then he would have wrapped it around her throat, and, well, you can imagine."

Reid watched him in silence. During the course of most of Martin Harris's sexual assaults, he did use ligatures. He would start to choke his victim, then stop just as she was about to pass out. He always wore a mask. He'd never strangled a woman to death; he had always stopped short.

"I really can't imagine, Martin," Reid said. "You need to tell me exactly what you're talking about."

"Well, after he wrapped her panties around her throat, he would pull them tight. And then, eventually, she would die."

"That's what you saw Pete do?"

"In my dream, not real life! Wasn't I being clear?" Harris asked.

"Not entirely," Reid said. "What did her panties look like?"

"Black. Lacy edge." As he said the words, Harris tickled his own neck, then made a finger slash, as if cutting his throat. He shivered and tried to hold back a smile. "They matched her bra."

Reid pictured the crime scene as if he were there right now. Beth on her side; that bruised lace-imprinted line around her neck; her black panties and bra, the French lace torn to shreds, lying on the floor.

No one who had not been in that room, or read the police reports, knew those details. Reid's heart was slamming in his chest, and his mouth was dry.

"You were there," Reid said.

"No! I told you. I just dreamed about it!"

Reid picked up the postcard and looked at the way Harris had written Pete's name next to his own, almost like doodling the name of a crush.

Reid knew that criminals, especially those with paraphilic disorders, loved to communicate with each other, relive their crimes and share fantasies.

"I'm really curious about why you wrote Pete's name right next to yours. I know you say you dreamed about him, but to me it seems like more than that, Martin. To me it seems as if you and Pete did something together. Or maybe he told you about what *he* did."

"Yes!" Harris said, looking almost triumphant, as if Reid finally got it. "That's exactly it! In the dream he told me. He showed me! I saw it all! That's what I mean by wanting to help you solve the crime. That's why I put his name and Beth's with the list of, you know."

"The women you assaulted," Reid said in a calm voice.

"Well, yes. Because even though I don't do that anymore, have no desire whatsoever to do that again, I understand people who do. That's why I dreamed of Pete. I don't want to sound like I admire him—honestly, I don't. But I can get right into his skin and feel how he hurt his wife and then killed her."

Honestly.

"Let's get a written statement on that," Reid said.

"So you believe me?" Harris said.

Reid stared at him. He believed that Martin Harris had either killed Beth or spoken to the killer, who had given him very specific details. He saw the hopefulness in Harris's eyes. Reid was happy to dash it.

"The problem, Martin, is that I don't believe in dreams," Reid said. And he left the interview room, the Black Hall postcard in his hand.

29

Her phone buzzed, and Kate glanced at the screen. It was Lulu, calling for the third time since Kate had left the soup kitchen. Scotty had obviously raised the alarm. Again, Kate let it go to voice mail. In the midday sun, she walked from downtown New London past Fort Trumbull to Pequot Avenue.

Nothing revealed a person's character like the poetics of loss. Beth's death had revealed the dark sides of people she'd loved and trusted. Kate had felt guilty for not telling Lulu about the sketch, but the way she and Scotty had known everything and kept Beth's secret felt like a much worse betrayal. Even deeper than that, Beth herself had chosen to keep it from Kate.

When Kate got to Monte Cristo Cottage, the boyhood home of Eugene O'Neill, she slowed down. The Victorian house was up a slight rise from the street, and she sat on the wall along the sidewalk and faced the harbor. There was barely a breeze; two boats with sails futilely raised motored toward the Sound, looking for wind. She felt a presence behind her—not a person, but the cottage itself. O'Neill's father had been an actor, the house named for his most famous role, the Count of Monte Cristo. It had been the setting for O'Neill's play *Long Day's Journey into Night*.

When Kate was a senior in high school, Mathilda had taken her and Beth to see the brilliant production in New York at the Plymouth Theater, with Vanessa Redgrave and Brian Dennehy starring as Mary and James Tyrone, Philip Seymour Hoffman as Jamie, and Robert Sean Leonard as Edmund—O'Neill's autobiographical character.

The play had hit Kate hard. It was about a Connecticut family so full of love for each other yet tormented with addiction and sinking with secrets. Mary was a morphine addict, James a liar, Jamie an alcoholic, Edmund dying of consumption. She'd thought of her own family, of how happy she had thought they were. In some ways, they were completely different from the Tyrones. Her family didn't suffer from addiction or alcoholism. No one had a fatal disease. Instead of two sons, there were two daughters.

Her father had not been a drunk, but he had been a liar and a cheat. He had acted the role of good husband and father but was actually a different person entirely.

When they saw the play, her mother had been dead barely a year. It was only in retrospect, after her mother's death and father's imprisonment, after Beth's retreat from closeness, and after

Kate's own heart became concretized, that she realized how her father's secrets had destroyed them. He had had a private life unknown to the family.

He was so charming. Even Kate was charmed by him, only back then she had called it love. She had adored her dad—he could do no wrong. Even though he stayed out lots of nights, and her mother seemed upset about it, Kate figured he deserved to have fun. He worked hard at the gallery that had belonged to her mother and grandmother, built it into an even more successful business because of all the collectors he befriended. Everyone wanted him to like them.

He loved to gamble. Even on family vacations, they would often go to places that had casinos— like the trip to Monte Carlo the summer Kate was thirteen. The excuse had been to visit the Jean Cocteau murals in Villefranche-sur-Mer, to stay in Saint Paul de Vence, the medieval village above Nice, and to dine at La Colombe d'Or. Legend had it that artists had paid for their meals with paintings. The walls were hung with art by Matisse, Léger, Picasso, Chagall. But the way her father had driven them back to the auberge; kissed them all good night, saying it was "for luck"; and left for the rest of the night, Kate knew he was speeding back to the casino.

"What's he doing there?" Kate asked her mother.

"He enjoys games," her mother said.

"What kind of games?" Kate asked.

Her mother laughed. "Why don't you ask him that?"

So Kate did when he returned late the next morning. "Why would you rather play roulette than stay at the hotel with us?"

Her father chuckled. "Wait till you're older. You'll see James Bond movies and get it." Then, just as the rest of the family was heading to Èze for lunch, he went to bed to sleep through the day.

One late night during school vacation, *Dr. No* was on TV, and Kate made Lulu stay over and watch it with her. James was playing baccarat at a casino. He wore a dinner jacket and looked handsome, just like her father. Kate tried to imagine what her father had been trying to say, but to her, hanging out in a casino seemed boring.

Living in Connecticut, temptation was close for him—Foxwoods and Mohegan Sun casinos were not far from Black Hall. But instead of just being away from dinner till dawn, he had started not coming home for days at a time. One day he came home just before she left for school. He hugged her, and she smelled perfume. She was only fifteen at the time, but she knew right then that he was having an affair.

She wanted to tell Beth, but Kate took her position as older sister seriously and had to protect her. She watched her mother, to see how she reacted. For the longest time, her mother seemed fine. But once in a while, her father would talk on the phone in a low voice, then leave the house. Kate would see her mother hitting redial after her father left.

Kate figured her mother must have smelled the perfume too.

Walking down Pequot Avenue, Kate had intended to keep going to the lighthouse. But when she stopped to sit on the wall outside Monte Cristo Cottage, she realized this was where she had wanted to come all along. She needed to visit this house, to feel Eugene O'Neill's spirit and bring back a moment in her life when she had sat with Beth and Mathilda in the theater, when a certain truth about her father had clicked in her mind.

Her phone rang again. This time she answered without even looking at the screen.

"You didn't even text me back. You couldn't bring yourself to tell me," Kate said.

"You have no idea how much I wanted to," Lulu said.

"But Beth made you promise not to?"

"No, she never said that. I can't even figure it out, why I didn't. At first I thought that, yes— that if she'd wanted you to know, she'd have told you herself."

"Am I that terrible?" she asked. "That judgmental?"

Lulu studiously avoided answering the question. "Kate, I want to see you. We need to talk in person."

Kate's jaw was so tight she could barely speak.

"Where is Jed Hilliard now?" she finally asked.

"I don't know."

"If you had to guess."

"Kate, we weren't friends. I only met him once—accidentally."

"Where?"

"On the Block Island Ferry. It was late last winter; the boat was practically empty. I had a few days off and was heading out to clear my head. I spotted Beth standing on deck—I was in the cabin; it was so cold. I remember there was ice on the lines, and it was starting to snow. I was so surprised to see her there at all—I started to go outside, when a guy walked up to her, handed her a cup of something hot—coffee, I guess. I tried to hang back, but she saw me, so I couldn't avoid going over to talk. She introduced him as an artist friend, said they were going to go to Mohegan Bluffs to take photos of the cliffs in the snow so they could paint the scene later."

"Maybe they were just friends."

"I saw him kiss her when he handed her the cup," Lulu said. "It was a real kiss."

Kate stared out at the water, picturing her sister

on the ferry, kissing a stranger. So Scotty had been wrong—they were more than just friends. And the baby? Could he have been Jed's? She closed her eyes and tried to imagine how Beth must have felt. It must have been exciting. She must have been happy. Kate kept the small fat key in her pocket, and her hand closed around it now.

"Whose baby was it?" Kate asked.

"Where are you?" Lulu asked.

"New London."

"At home?"

"On Pequot."

"Stay there," Lulu said. "I'm coming to get you."

30

Kate had already decided what to do next. When Lulu picked her up, Kate asked her to drive her home. She needed to be behind the wheel of her own car, regain a feeling of power and control. "I need to get my car," she said.

"To go where?" Lulu asked.

"Ainsworth."

"Holy shit."

"You can come if you want."

So Lulu parked her Range Rover in Kate's spot behind the loft building, and they took off in Kate's Porsche. Kate had sworn she would never see her father again, but he was going to explain this to her—how he'd introduced Beth to a fellow inmate. Kate drove north on Route 9, following directions to the Ainsworth Correctional Institute.

"Why are we doing this?" Lulu asked. "I should be buying you martinis at the Ocean House and begging you to forgive me and understand why I didn't tell you."

"Yes, you should. But I want to find Jed."

"Tell the detective. He'll find him."

"I plan to," Kate said. "But this part's on me. I

want to know if my father introduced Beth to her killer. Do you think Jed did it, not Pete?"

"Well, he wasn't happy with her."

"What are you talking about?"

Lulu exhaled hard. "She was married. He wanted her not to be. They fought about it."

"Was he the father?" Kate asked.

"I'd say it's a distinct possibility."

"Did you *ask* her?"

"She didn't tell me everything, Kate."

"And she didn't tell me *anything*."

"What the hell are we doing?" Lulu said. "Get the detective on this so you don't have to see your father for the first time since . . ."

"He paid to have us tied up in the cellar," Kate said, finishing the sentence.

Lulu had a point. Kate was so good at blocking out feelings she'd made herself dead from the brain down. This was tricky. Her father, her dad. She had loved him like crazy when she was little. They used to go on expeditions in the backyard, with him carrying her on his shoulders. They'd see their shadow cast by the house lights.

"A two-headed giant," he'd say.

"Don't scare me," she'd say.

"Never," he'd say. "What are we?"

"Sweethearts and partners," she'd reply.

"That's right," he'd say, bouncing her up and down, tossing her up to the stars and catching her as she fell.

She sped along, the Connecticut River on their right, through Hartford. She and her father used to go to the Wadsworth Atheneum, and she felt her old daughterly love flooding back. She had been close to her father. Whenever they had stopped at the Atheneum, they had visited Andrew Wyeth's *Chambered Nautilus*, a painting of a young girl in her gauze-canopied bed, looking out the window with unbridled longing, a luminous seashell on the hope chest at the foot of the bed.

"Why do you think it's a hope chest?" her father had asked one time.

Kate stared, reddening as if he had caught her having a fantasy. "Because the girl wants to get married," she said quietly.

"That's her greatest wish?" he asked.

Kate stared at the painting, haunting in shades of white, wheat, and gray. The girl in the bed reminded her of herself: thin with long brown hair, filled with constant yearning. She could never have expressed that to her father or anyone. No one thought of her as a girl in bed; she was an athlete, always on a tennis court, a sailboat, or skis. She laughed; she didn't moon. At least those were the things she showed the world.

"Kate?" her father prodded. He stood beside her, tall and lean, the handsomest man she knew. He wore a navy-and-black houndstooth jacket from Allen Collins, gray flannels, and loafers without socks. He had a narrow face with a crooked nose and deeply sensitive hazel eyes always ready to smile. His hair was short and full, brown with white starting to come in. *Silver threads among the gold,* he would joke.

"Her fondest wish is to get out of the bed and run," Kate said. "And do something exciting."

"That's my girl," he said. "You still think it's a hope chest?"

"It's a blanket chest. For when the nights get cold. When it's winter."

"That's what I think too," he said.

They always had lunch at the Hartford Club, with its brick facade and arched windows, just across Prospect Street from the Atheneum. He seemed proud to show her off—she'd wear a dress, and he'd ask people if they didn't think she had long legs like a thoroughbred. She had often been conscious of thinking she had been lucky to be there alone with him, that he'd taken her and not their mother or Beth, but it had made her feel guilty at the same time.

Speeding past the Colt Armory with its dark-blue star-dazzled dome and the ghosts of makers of firearms, she couldn't help glancing at the Hartford skyline, trying in a split second to locate the museum and the club. Memories flooded into her just like the dam her dad had told her about that had broken in 1936, nearly washed away Hartford and his parents' home, drowned an aunt he'd never meet. He had grown up with the family's legacy and fear and hatred of that flood and all it had taken.

"We're getting closer," Kate said to Lulu.

"Are you okay?" Lulu asked.

"Yes."

"Because it seems like you might not be. In fact, how could you be? It's a big deal seeing him."

As she listened to Lulu's words, Kate's heart began to harden again. To purposely do without someone you loved was a big deal. But so was setting in motion a crime that would destroy his family.

She took one of the last exits before the Massachusetts border. The maximum-security prison was set back from a main road, down a long driveway. Two rows of tall anchor fences topped with triple coils of razor wire surrounded the premises. The visitors' parking lot was clearly marked. It was crowded, but Kate noticed a steady stream of people, mostly women, leaving the building, getting into their cars. Kate imagined them visiting husbands, boyfriends, sons, fathers—all incarcerated just like her father.

"I don't know how to do this," Kate said, staring at the brick building. "The procedures. I should have called to see about visiting hours."

"I'm sure they'll tell you when you get to the door," Lulu said. "Are you nervous?"

Kate nodded.

Lulu hugged her hard. "I'll wait in the car," she said. "Take your time."

Kate walked down a sidewalk, past a sign:

NO WEAPONS
NO CELL PHONES
MODEST DRESS

Despite the number of people leaving, there was a line, again mostly women, many holding grocery bags. One by one they went through metal detectors. Correctional officers stood talking to each other while watching the visitors enter.

"Who are you visiting?" a guard at the desk asked Kate.

"Garth Woodward," she said.

"Your name?"

"Kate Woodward," she said, watching him scan a computer screen. "Why?"

"You have to be on his visitors list."

"I'm not," she said.

"Then you can't visit till you are."

Kate wanted to argue with him, but she knew there was no point. Frustrated, she turned to go.

"Wait," the guard said. "Katharine Woodward?"

"Yes."

"You're on here." He handed her a pass and directed her to Garth's cellblock.

She swallowed hard, walking through the metal

detector. She hadn't visited, written, or called for twenty-three years, but he'd kept her name on his list. She and the other women walked through a series of metal doors, one clanging shut behind them before the next opened. Correctional officers inspected the grocery bags, riffling through them. Kate heard potato chips crunch and break as one guard pawed through a woman's bag roughly.

"Hey," the woman said. "Don't bust them."

"What's the difference? He's going to eat them anyway."

The woman turned to Kate, anger in her eyes.

"No respect here, none."

"No talking!" a different guard barked.

It took thirty minutes to get from the prison's front entrance to the last metal door.

A massive guard stood in the middle of the corridor, making the women go around him. He had the neck of a bodybuilder and the gut of a lazy slob. His brown hair was slicked back, his complexion sallow. He watched the women pass with half-lidded eyes, like a frog waiting to lap up a fly. His left thumb was hooked into his belt, his fingers dangling down the front of his pants.

The visiting room was full. Prisoners in bright-yellow uniforms sat facing their visitors across long tables that reminded Kate of the soup kitchen. Many of the men had tattooed arms and necks. Kate wondered what they had done to land here. She felt sick at the idea of a criminal from Ainsworth worming his way into Beth's life.

Guards were stationed around the room, keeping watch. The door guard had followed the women in. Kate could barely breathe. She looked at all the faces, wondering if she'd even recognize her father. She thought maybe he was still in his cell, but in the half hour since she'd signed in, she saw the guards had gotten him.

He saw her approach and stood.

She held back a gasp. He was old. Her tall, handsome father was stooped and gray. His skin was pale; he had a white scar on his forehead. But he was beaming, his smile at the sight of her as delighted as ever. When she got close, she had to hold herself back from crashing into him with a hug.

"I never thought you'd come," he said.

"Neither did I," she said.

They stood facing each other for a minute, till a guard approached them and gestured to keep a distance apart, sit down on opposite sides of the table. Kate tried to keep her face from crumpling, but it was a losing battle. She felt like a little kid whose heart had been broken. She stared into her father's hazel eyes, saw all the love and pride he'd always felt for her, thought of all the years he'd stolen from them.

"My name was on your list," she said.

"I know, Katy. I never gave up hoping."

"You probably should have," she said.

"But I didn't."

She looked at his hands. Gnarled and veined, they were flat on the table, as if he wanted to reach across and take hers, reassure her like he used to when she was a little girl, let her know that everything would be all right. He'd been the best father ever, until he wasn't.

"What happened to your forehead?" she asked.

"A fight," he said. "Years ago, when I first arrived."

"You fight in here?" she asked harshly.

"No," he said. "I got beaten for what I did to you and Beth. People here don't like fathers hurting their children."

She braced herself, her whole body shaking, remembering the ropes around her wrists, the weight of her mother's body.

"Do you know about Beth?" she asked.

"Yes, Kate," he said, the smile completely gone. The moment rocked her. The horror of Beth's death hit her again, seeing the grief in her father's eyes.

"Murdered," she said. "Just like Mom."

"Who did it?" her father asked. "Her husband? I want to kill him, Kate. If he gets caught and winds up here, I will."

"Your mind goes straight to that?" she asked. "That's not how most people think."

"It's how fathers think," he said.

She took that in and imagined how he must feel, trapped in here, unable to be with the family, to have protected any of them—to have put them in such danger. She had loved him so much. She wondered how he had lived through the last twenty-three years, knowing what he'd done to his daughters, to his wife.

"Tell me—do they think it's Pete?" he asked.

"No one has been arrested."

"I know, but you two were so close, and you have the best instincts. I don't believe you don't know—whether it's been proven or not, you know in your gut. No one knew Beth better than you."

"Actually, I think you knew her better."

Her father sat back. She'd shocked him. "That's not true," he said.

"We weren't close anymore. We haven't been since the day Mom died."

"Don't say that."

"It changed everything between us. We were never the same after that," Kate said. She delivered the words like blows. She saw the pain in his face and didn't care that she was being cruel.

"She talked about you every time she came here," he said. "She told me about your job, all the famous people you flew, the places you visited. You always brought her presents. She told me about dinners you two had and what a great aunt you are to Samantha. How you and Lulu are still best friends. No, Katy, you're wrong in what you're telling me. She adored you as much as ever."

Kate looked down. She hadn't said that she and Beth didn't love each other deeply. In fact, she thought they'd loved each other even more as time went on. But they'd been blocked by the trauma, a force field created by the violence of that day, impermeable to words. Each of them occupied her own dark solitude; feelings could break through, but language couldn't.

"I don't know if it was Pete," Kate said, thinking of what Lulu had said.

"Then who?"

"Who is Jed Hilliard?"

"Jed?" her father asked, looking confused. "The kid who was here?"

"Kid?" Kate asked.

"Well, to me. Thirty, thirty-one, something like that last time I saw him. The artist."

"Yes, an artist."

"Why? What does he have to do with Beth?"

"She met him here."

"Yes, but they barely knew each other. He's a good artist; he has a fine eye. I told him if I still had the gallery, I'd give him a show."

"Is that why you introduced them? So she could exhibit his work?"

Her father paused. His gaze sharpened, a

terrifying look entered his eyes, and for the first time she saw the deep change in him—not just age, but the darkness of life in prison.

"No. Definitely not. But I was proud of her," he said. "I was being a big shot, letting him know I used to be someone, that my daughter was a star in the art world. Are you saying *he* killed her?"

"I don't know. I didn't even know his name until this week. Where is he?"

"He's not from Connecticut. He got arrested here, a pot conviction; that's why they sent him to Ainsworth. When he was released, the plan was for him to go back to Warwick, Rhode Island. That's where he lived before, where his family lives. He had to return there; that would have been his parole arrangement."

"Warwick's not far from New London. Where did he get caught?"

"The shoreline somewhere." Her father nodded slowly. "Maybe New London, I'm thinking. Maybe it was. But still, Beth lived in Black Hall—that's a world away from drugs and the back streets."

"She volunteered in New London; didn't she tell you?"

"She sure did. I was proud of her."

"And Jed wound up at her soup kitchen. They became friends," Kate said, watching for his reaction.

"She appreciated talent, and he was a master of the line," he said, frowning slightly. "He had a touch of Matisse in him."

"I've seen his work," she said.

"You did? What did you think?"

"I think he caused her problems," Kate said.

"What problems? What did he do?"

"Worked at getting close to her. Complicated her life," Kate said.

"He wasn't a user, Kate. I know a little about people in here, after all that time, and I didn't get that from him at all. Beth had good sense, and if she liked him, it was because he is a decent person. And I'm sure she saw his talent. Like I did. In fact . . ." He stopped himself.

"In fact what?" she asked.

"Well, he missed nature in here. It ripped him apart. He was always sketching rivers, hills, trees. When he was getting out, I told him he should draw the gardens at the Ledges."

The Ledges was an abandoned estate a few miles north of Mathilda's house, also on the Connecticut River. Years ago, a nonprofit group had restored and operated it as a state park. There was a sunken garden full of lavender and old roses. Concerts and plays had been held in an amphitheater beside the rock ledge sloping into Long Island Sound. Many Sunday nights, her family had gone there to picnic and fly kites and listen to Mozart or bluegrass, see performances

331

of Gilbert and Sullivan and once a production of *Henry V*. But there were financial misdeeds on the part of the nonprofit's board, and the Ledges went untended. Kate didn't tell her father that the mansion had fallen into ruin, the gardens now overtaken by weeds and tall grass.

"Jed was never violent," her father said, a ravaged tone in his voice. "He was peaceful. I worried about him in here. He wasn't tough enough. I can't believe he would have . . . that he could have attacked anyone. He was always one of the ones who needed to go home, who didn't belong in this place. But I swear to God, if he fucking hurt her . . ."

"How *did* you find out she died?" Kate asked.

"Scotty Breen told me," he said, using Scotty's maiden name. "She called. It was the worst day of my life. The second worst."

"Those two days are connected," she said.

"I don't dare ask you to forgive me," he said. "I don't even want you to. I don't deserve it."

Kate knew she should get the words out. This was her chance. Everyone always said forgiveness is not forgetting, that the act is as full of grace for the forgiver as the forgiven. This would not hurt her. She gazed at the old man across from her. She knew that she would never see him again, and she also knew she could never absolve him.

"It's okay," he said, as if he knew her struggle.

Kate pushed her chair back, ready to go, the words caught in her throat.

"Kate," he said. "Thank you for coming."

She nodded.

"You haven't called me Dad," he said.

She knew she hadn't. She had told herself, long ago, that she no longer had a father. Gazing into his hazel eyes now, she went back a thousand years, was jumping up and down, wanting him to put her on his shoulders so they could be a two-headed giant.

What are we? he used to ask.

Sweethearts and partners, she would reply.

She turned to leave. Some of the women she'd come in with were still at the tables; others were on their way to the door. She glanced over her shoulder. Her father hadn't taken his eyes off her. A guard approached him, ready to escort him back to his cell.

"Dad," she called.

"Katy," he said.

"What are we?" she asked.

He beamed, exactly the way he had when she'd first walked in, the way he had when she was a child. She walked fast, past the frog-eyed door guard, leaving the visiting room before she could hear her father answer.

31

Kate's hands felt light on the wheel, as if she were made of air. Driving south, past all the landmarks that had reminded her of her father, felt different now. He wasn't just a specter from the past. He existed. The memories changed character as she sped through Hartford. They weren't as poignant, she thought. But that was wrong—seeing him in prison, in his jumpsuit, with the scar on his forehead, made them more so.

"He's never getting out," Kate said out loud. They were miles from the prison, but she hadn't spoken till now.

"What was it like?" Lulu asked.

"Like walking through the steel-doored gates and ten circles of hell. These poor women bringing bags of snacks to locked-up men—in line, no talking, marching through the doors, guards watching everything. The guards," she said, remembering the look on that one's face. "They wanted something; I don't know. For a prisoner to act up, to catch a visitor with contraband."

"You were in there a long time."

"It took forever to get to the visiting area."

"And you saw him."

"Yeah," Kate said.

"Is he . . . how is he?"

"He's old. He's sorry about everything."

"What did he say?"

Kate shook her head. She didn't want to talk about her father anymore. Every detail of the visit reverberated. The stoop of his shoulders, his old familiar smile, the sound of his voice. She wanted to hold on to the moments, keep them to herself. If she spoke about them, they would become conversation and dissipate. They wouldn't belong to her anymore.

Lulu sensed it and looked out the side window. They sped out of the cities, south toward the shore. Once past Middletown, the landscape became wooded. The day had been long, and shadows from trees and rock cliffs lengthened across the pavement. Although the day was hot, summer was drawing to an end. The sun had noticeably shifted its place in the sky, the angle of the light lower, moving toward the equinox.

"You know what we should do?" Lulu asked just before they hit the Baldwin Bridge over the Connecticut River. "We should swim."

Kate had imagined dropping Lulu off at her car in New London, heading to the Ledges to sit in the tangled garden and wait for Jed Hilliard to show up. Or maybe he would be there already, sketching weeds and wildflowers, waiting for the moon to rise. More likely, it was only a place her father had mentioned to him in passing, no meaning at all. Maybe Jed had never even been there.

"You're right," she said to Lulu. "A swim. But what about bathing suits?"

"What about them?" Lulu asked.

They laughed, and Kate drove them down to Hubbard's Point. They told the summer cop by the train trestle they were visiting Scotty Waterston. The tide was high, the sandy parking lot damp. It had been built on a wetland, cleared of spartina and its thickly woven root system. The salt water followed its eternal path and still rose through the sand beneath a thin layer of gravel and broken shells.

Bypassing the main beach, scattered with late-day beachgoers, they walked to the western end and climbed the steep hill to take the path to the deserted haven known as Little Beach. The crescent strand was backed by a coastal forest of pines, white oaks, and black walnut trees. Beyond the woods was the Great Marsh, fed by Seven Mile River.

The sun had just dipped behind the trees, and the beach was shadowed. There wasn't a person in sight. Kate and Lulu dropped their clothes and walked into the water. The Sound was cool, but Kate didn't hesitate. It had always been a point of pride that while others stood at the edge, getting used to the temperature, she dove right in and accepted the shock.

She swam straight out, underwater, eyes wide open. At high tide the rocks were far below, and she saw tendrils of sargassum weed drifting upward in the current. When her lungs were bursting, she crashed up through the surface and took deep breaths. Lulu was swimming toward the breakwater. Kate stayed where she was, treading water, facing shore.

Blinking, her eyes cleared, she caught sight of the graffiti Lulu had mentioned—sayings, initials, and patterns. She felt disgusted by the desecration and turned around to look out to sea.

Across the Sound, two ferries heading in opposite directions passed each other. Sunset gave the white boats a pink cast, turned the water's surface lavender. Skinny-dipping at Little Beach was one of summer's great pleasures and always had been.

She, Beth, Lulu, and Scotty had started doing it when they were in their teens. It had seemed grown-up and forbidden, and it had always appealed to her rule-breaking side. She felt the water on her body, but it wasn't at all sensuous, and she wondered if it was for other people. She knew she was missing something but didn't dwell on it.

For Kate, the best part of swimming without clothes was freedom. She was part of the ocean.

It came close to the abandon she felt while flying. As her arms and legs moved water around her and kept her afloat, she started to let go of the claustrophobia of being at the prison, the unexpected sorrow she'd felt for her father. The rush of Long Island Sound's waves hitting the shore took away the clang of the doors.

"Ahhh," Lulu said, sidestroking in from the breakwater.

"This was the right idea," Kate said.

"I figured you needed it. I know I did."

They swam to shallow water, walked onto the beach, and slipped back into their clothes. The fabric stuck to their damp skin, but it quickly dried in the cool twilight breeze. They sat on the hard-packed sand. With the sun down, flies had stopped buzzing around clumps of seaweed along the tide line. She listened to the waves slapping the shore. Above, the first stars had started to appear in the violet sky.

The Compass Rose had sat here a million times. They had skinny-dipped, picnicked, searched for moonstones and sea glass. In the last blue light, Kate and Beth would walk along the damp sand at the very edge, watching for the moonstones' glimmer. They would fill their pockets with the tiny, perfectly smooth ovals of feldspar. Kate always intended to make jewelry with them, but they were so beautiful by themselves, she kept them in a glass jar instead. They never gleamed as magically at home, though. It was never the same as seeing them in the sand, brushed by waves, collecting them with her sister.

"Are you still mad at me?" Lulu asked.

"About what?"

"Not telling you about Beth and Jed."

In the peace of the moment, Kate had almost forgotten.

"No. More at myself."

"Why?"

"Because I'm obviously a hard-assed, judgmental witch, or Beth would have told me herself. Or you would have, or Scotty," Kate said, half hoping Lulu would say she was wrong.

"What did your father say about him?" Lulu asked. The question instead of a direct response confirmed Kate's statement and pierced her heart.

"He had no idea that Jed and Beth were involved. He introduced her to him, though."

"Did he know where Jed might be?"

"Some vague ideas, but not really. Just that he's from Rhode Island and is a talented artist, but I already knew that part."

The sound of voices, excited and raucous, came from the direction of the path. It was dark now and hard to see, but Kate could tell it was kids. They were too far away to recognize, but Kate heard the clink of bottles as if they were drinking a toast. Then rattles that sounded as if they were all shaking maracas.

"Spray paint," Lulu said, jumping up. "Hey, stop!" she called as she and Kate started toward the group.

The kids scattered, but Kate ran toward one and grabbed her arm. In the starlight, Kate locked eyes with her niece.

"Sam," she said.

Sam didn't reply. She lowered her gaze. In her right hand, she held a paint can. In her other, she gripped a half-empty bottle of Heineken. Lulu had cornered Isabel Waterston, and they came toward Kate and Sam.

"You did this?" Kate asked, pointing at the rocks.

Still no answer from Sam.

"It's art—better than bare rocks," Isabel said, slurring her words.

"Okay, you've been drinking, no point in talking about it. Come on; we're going home," Kate said, glancing at Sam, feeling both angry and scared, not knowing quite how to handle her being drunk.

The four of them walked through the path. Kate had been here so often she had no problem making her way in the dark, but for the sake of the girls, she turned on the light on her iPhone. When they got back to Hubbard's Point, they headed toward a cottage on the boat basin.

Scotty, Nick, and Julie were sitting on the screened porch. Nick was reading, and Scotty and Julie were playing Scrabble. At the sight of

Isabel, Scotty and Nick stood. Julie bolted into the house. Kate noticed she'd stopped in the living room, crept back to peek around the door.

"They were graffitiing the rocks," Kate said, looking straight at Sam, worried out of her mind at what was going on with her.

"Along with a few others who ran away," Lulu said. "Nice friends, leaving Sam and Isabel to take the blame. It was as if they weren't even there. Disappearing friends."

"We shoulda run too," Isabel said, letting out a long burp.

"Where did you get the booze?" Nick asked. "Who bought it for you? You tell me, Isabel, right now."

"They took it from here!" Julie called, still hiding around the corner. "Beer from the garage!"

"Sisters don't tell on sisters!" Isabel said.

"That was always Kate and Beth's code," Lulu said.

Julie stared at her. "Why did you say that?"

"Well, because they are sisters too," Lulu said.

"Not now," Julie said. "The thing before. The disappearing friends. Talking to the air, no one there. It was bad and sad, your mother died, and . . ."

"Look how you've upset Julie," Scotty snapped at Isabel. She put her hands on Julie's shoulders and led her into the house, closing the door behind her. For a second, Kate thought she wanted to stop Julie from saying more. But when Scotty came out, she kept railing at Isabel.

"For God's sake, do you know what you've done?" Scotty demanded.

"Scotty," Nick said, "take it down a notch. We'll deal with it."

"Don't shush me!" Scotty said, slapping his hand. "She's drunk. She's made a mockery of our family, acting this way. I'm ashamed."

"Mom, sorry," Isabel said.

"You should be. I'm disgusted!" Her voice was shaking, and her face was red. She turned to Kate, pulled her and Lulu away from Nick and the kids. "Hey, did that cop ask you about tea parties in Beth's room?"

"What?" Kate asked. She had expected Scotty would want to talk about how to handle the girls and felt shocked by the change of course.

"Yeah, he asked me," Lulu said. "He's just ruling out fingerprints. He found all of ours in her room."

"I found it offensive," Scotty said, looking at Kate. "Didn't you?"

"I'm sure he didn't mean anything by it," Kate said, feeling off balance, still thinking about Sam and Isabel.

"We were all best friends," Lulu said. "Her room does have the best view in the house, and we did sometimes drink tea there."

"Especially in the winter . . . ," Kate said,

343

remembering. "It was so cozy by her fireplace. She loved that."

"Well I think it was outrageous," Scotty said. "He made me feel like we went creeping through there after she died, to pick at her jewelry or something! I really feel like saying something to his superior. Find Beth's killer—arrest Pete, if that's who it is! They're just wasting all our time."

"Well, the investigation takes time," Lulu said.

"They're doing the best they can," Kate said.

Scotty exhaled, eyes red with tears, sputtering as if she was the only person who really loved Beth, who wanted to see her killer brought to justice. Then she took a deep breath and hugged Kate. "I'm so sorry for overreacting. I'm just a wreck. Thanks for getting Isabel home. We'll talk tomorrow, okay?"

"Okay," Kate said, exchanging a *wow, that was intense* glance with Lulu. She said goodbye to Nick, gave Isabel a quick kiss. She had wanted a minute alone with Scotty—to get a mother's advice on how to deal with the girls' drinking and defacing the rocks—but Scotty was clearly not in a place to give it.

She, Lulu, and Sam walked to the parking lot. Sam seemed steady, as if the alcohol hadn't affected her as much as it had Isabel. They drove to Pete and Beth's house, but there were no lights on.

"Where's your father?" Kate asked.

"Three guesses, and if one of them is *with Nicola,* you're right," Sam said.

"He went to Mathilda's?" Kate asked, upset at the idea of Nicola letting him be there after Kate had gone out on a limb for her.

"Yeah, I think so."

"Then you're coming home with me," she said, trying to contain her out-of-control feelings. On the way to New London, they didn't talk at all. Lulu tuned the radio to a nineties station with Smashing Pumpkins singing "1979." I-95 was crowded, and they hit a traffic jam that lasted from Niantic through Waterford.

Back on Bank Street, Lulu stopped before getting into her Range Rover. Kate watched her press her forehead against Sam's.

"Don't do that again," Lulu said. "Any of it. You have to take care of yourself and be strong. And I don't want you making your aunt worry."

"Sorry," Sam mumbled.

Lulu and Kate hugged.

"What was that with Scotty?" Lulu whispered.

"I was going to ask you the same thing," Kate said.

"She's drinking more than ever. Is it Beth? Her way of dealing with losing her?"

"I guess," Kate said. "Or maybe something with Nick?"

"All of the above," Lulu said. "Remind me never to get married."

"If you'll remind me."

"Later."

"Yep, later for sure."

Lulu got into her Range Rover and drove away. Kate disarmed the alarm, and she and Sam climbed the stairs.

"Sam," she said. "How many times have you done it? Painted those things on the rocks?"

"A couple," Sam said.

"You and your friends ruined something wonderful. Don't you care about that?"

Sam shrugged. Kate gritted her teeth. How much of a cry for help was this, and what could Kate do about it?

"Your mother loved Little Beach," Kate said. "How do you think she'd feel about what you did?"

Sam swallowed hard, looking away, as if she couldn't meet Kate's eyes.

"Call your father and tell him you're staying with me tonight," Kate said when they'd entered the loft. Popcorn came bounding over, barking to be fed and taken out.

"Can we clean it up?" Sam asked, watching Kate clip the leash onto Popcorn's collar.

Kate looked at her.

"The paint?" Sam asked. "Can we try to get it off the rocks?"

"I don't know if it will come off. I don't know if the chemicals it would take would be bad for the sea."

"Can we try?" Sam asked, her voice breaking. "For Mom?"

Kate stood still for a minute. If defacing the rocks had been Sam's way of getting attention, then maybe this was the way she had to ask for help.

"Yes, we can do that," Kate said. She put her arms around her niece, felt her shoulders shaking. "Come on now, call your dad so he'll know where you are."

"He won't care," Sam said.

"He will."

"He won't, and it doesn't matter. Nothing does."

"Sam, yes it does. I promise," Kate said.

"I want my mom," Sam said, her voice thinning out and rising to a shriek.

"Oh, Sam," Kate said, dropping Popcorn's leash and pulling her niece close.

"I want my mom," Sam wailed. And she started to pull her own hair, scratch her own face, and even though Kate was grabbing her, holding her, trying to soothe her, Sam wouldn't stop.

32

The brothers had been trying to get together, but until now, Reid hadn't been able to break away from the case. He met Tom at the Y-Knot, a seedy, beer-sloshed bar, mostly frequented by sailors and fishermen, on the waterfront near the New London train station. They sat on red vinyl barstools and drank Jameson neat, just as their father had done. He had been in the navy, stationed across the river in Groton, then a cop in New London, where the brothers had grown up.

"So, fill me in," Tom said.

"I thought we had it, right from the beginning," Reid said.

"I know you did," Tom said. "I was worried you narrowed in on Pete too soon."

"Yeah, you let me know," Reid said. "But I was positive—everything lined up: not just another woman, but he had a kid with her. He thinks he's a genius, and the fact he turned up the AC—I mean it's not the most original thing, but it takes some research."

"Okay, then with the evidence you have now, you still think it's him?"

"Trick question."

Tom grinned. "Lay it on me."

Reid took a drink. He ran through the autopsy results, the witnesses he'd questioned, the fact he was having a forensic accountant go through Pete and Beth's finances, and the most recent development: Martin Harris.

"Icing on the cake," Tom said. "A perv living at the Osprey House."

"Yeah," Reid said. "I'm not sure where he fits, but he fits. His parole officer is convinced his testosterone-blocking drugs have changed his life—"

"I thought those guys never change," Tom said.

"Mostly true. But Harris even gave me permission to speak to his shrink, who claims he's the poster boy for chemical castration. No bad thoughts whatsoever, doesn't want to hurt women anymore, sex is nothing to him now. But he says he dreamed of seeing Pete kill Beth."

"Dreamed?"

"Yeah. It all came to him while he slept."

Tom chuckled. "He sounds like a nutjob. Could it be true, that he has some warped way of wanting to solve the case?"

"It's hard to explain," Reid said. "See, then there's the postcard. Black Hall, the Lathrop Gallery. If you saw his name doodled with Pete's, then Beth's name at the head of the list of all the women he'd attacked . . . it was like a love letter."

"To who? Pete?"

Reid drank from his scotch. "Yeah. Like, he's in love with the idea of a buddy just a few miles down the road thinking like him, acting like him." He paused, drank again. "Only the buddy takes it one step farther and actually murders his victim."

"You said there was no sign of sexual assault on Beth," Tom said.

"No fluids," Reid said. "But she had bruising all over her legs, between her thighs. No sign of penetration."

"So, does that jibe with Harris's MO?"

"The thing with Harris is undies. He loves lace. When he'd go to a house, he'd be afraid his victim wouldn't have pretty enough whatever, so he'd bring his own. He had charge accounts at Frederick's of Hollywood and Victoria's Secret. Spent twice as much at Fred, so I guess that's what he preferred."

"Classy guy," Tom said.

"Yeah, all the way. So that's where I get tripped up. I still want Pete for this, but Harris knew about the lacy underwear." He glanced at Tom. He kept details of the case very close, but he told his brother everything. He needed his help.

"And the only way he could have known . . ."

"Not the only way—but the most likely way is that he was there," Reid said. "Or whoever killed Beth told him about it. Or someone leaked info— from my squad, or the ME—it happens."

"You think there was a leak?"

Reid had been racking his brain on that one. He shrugged.

"Let's try this: Where do Harris's and Pete's lives intersect?" Tom asked.

"Dead end," Reid said. "Nothing's coming up. Harris can't hold a job—he's a drunk. Robin—his PO—is constantly on him to find work. When he's sober enough, he sometimes picks up cash by washing dishes at Black Whale or the Rusty Anchor."

"The Whale, maybe, but the Rusty Anchor's not exactly a Pete Lathrop kind of establishment," Tom said.

"Nope," Reid said, chuckling to think of preppie Pete stepping foot in the second-nastiest bar in New London, after the Y-Knot.

"So, where else?"

Reid shook his head. "The guy's not into art. He can't afford to eat—other than what he gets from church basements or the food pantry—so he's not about to show up in Black Hall. He has an education—that's true, like Pete. He taught college twenty years ago."

"Could he have met Pete back then?" Tom asked. "Same school, old friends?"

"Different schools. Harris grew up in Bridgeport and went to public school there. Pete's prep all the way. Rhode Island. And Pete was your basic gold digger. His job was landing Beth

Lathrop. At least Martin Harris had a real career. He was a college professor."

"So basically Pete and Martin are different as night and day," Tom said. "What's your gut say?"

"Harris has a perv mind and did a great job of imagining what he would do with the underwear if he'd been there," Reid said. "But I don't think he was."

Tom finished his whiskey and signaled the bartender for two more. The jukebox was playing Steve Earle, and two TVs over the bar were broadcasting baseball games—the Red Sox on one, the Mets on the other. A bunch of Coast Guard cadets were playing darts. When the drinks arrived, the two brothers clinked glasses.

Tom took a deep breath and a long drink. "Have you really looked at the evidence that it wasn't Pete?"

"I have, of course. He's got gouges down his back and a chunk of his shoulder practically bitten off, but not by Beth. Nothing under her fingernails, and her bite didn't match. He swears he's innocent and is insisting on a polygraph."

"One family, two murders," Tom said. "You're telling me your old case and your, um, fondness for the Woodward sisters hasn't given you tunnel vision?"

No one could get him going like Tom. They were close but competitive and always had been—in sports, for their father's approval, even in their choices of careers. Tom in the military, Conor in law enforcement.

"There's a connection between the cases, regardless of who killed Beth," Reid said. "Same town, same family. Violence. The wife dies. The same painting taken each time."

"*Moonlight*," Tom said. "Maybe Harris took it."

Reid drank, staring into the mirror behind the bar. "Funny," he said. "He's not into art, but he could be into the moon."

"Let me guess. Big dreams of being an astronaut?" Tom asked.

"Nope. But he probably taught those college students about the moon."

"Yeah?" Tom asked. "What'd he teach?"

"Astronomy," Reid said. "He loves the stars. Claims that's why he had those other postcards. Small Connecticut towns with night skies dark enough to see the stars."

His brother stared at him. "Well, that's it."

"What?"

"Pete's a sailor. We both saw him at Menemsha, aboard *Huntress*. They'd been out in the ocean."

"I don't follow," Reid said.

"The stars, idiot."

"Okay. They're over the ocean. And every other place," Reid said.

"Celestial navigation," Tom said. "It's old school, but a lot of yacht guys like Pete learn it.

They buy expensive sextants, find someone to teach them to shoot sun lines, steer by the stars. Makes them feel like old salts, worthy of their million-dollar yachts."

Reid's mind was racing. He wasn't a sailor himself, would have had no idea how to recognize a sextant if his brother hadn't lived his life on the sea. He could picture the heavy mahogany box his brother's sextant was stored in, the beautiful brass instrument inside, with fine optics and a half-moon-protractor-looking component, used to measure angles between the horizon and the sun, the earth, and the stars. Had anything like that been cataloged at the gallery, at the Lathrops' house?

"Your phone's ringing," Tom said, gesturing.

Reid grabbed it off the bar. He recognized Kate's number.

"Conor Reid," he said, answering. Playing it cool.

"Do you know about Jed Hilliard?" she asked.

"No," he said, drawing a blank on the name. "Why?"

"Because he's someone my sister loved. I'm beginning to wonder if Pete was even the father of her baby," she said.

Reid was stunned. He'd never even heard of him. "I'll be right over."

When he hung up, Tom nodded.

"You've got to go," he said.

"Yeah," Reid said.

Tom gestured at Reid's half-empty glass. "I got this. Next time's on you. And think about the connection."

"The stars," Reid said. And he left the bar.

33

It was nearly midnight. Tyler had a cold, and Nicola rocked him, trying to get him to sleep. She couldn't bear that he was so uncomfortable, and Pete's glower from across Mathilda's library didn't help. He wasn't supposed to be here in Mathilda's house—Kate had been very clear about that—but he'd spent at least part of every night with her and Tyler. He wanted Nicola to be grateful for it, but mostly it wore her out and made her nervous. The French doors were open to a cool breeze blowing off the river. The late-summer sounds of crickets, rustling leaves, and a distant owl came through.

"You don't have to stay," Nicola said to Pete.

"I'm waiting for him to stop crying."

"Well, he's not feeling well."

"I realize that," Pete said with exaggerated patience.

"It's normal for babies."

"It wasn't normal for Sam. Beth always seemed to know just what to do. She always got Sam to sleep through the night."

"Guess I'm not Beth."

"I guess you're not."

Things had changed so drastically. Back when Nicola was working at the gallery and she and Pete were first getting together, he spoke about all the things Beth did wrong. How she wasn't supportive of him, how she had always been distracted by gallery work, neglecting Sam. He'd complained about how she would rather catalog paintings for the next show instead of watching Sam's soccer games.

Now all he did was praise Beth. Nicola thought his current attitude reflected the real Beth, not the one he'd created to justify their affair. Nicola had loved her; she could say that honestly.

Contrary to what Pete used to say, Beth had been a great mother. Having a great mother herself, Nicola knew. Although Beth had money and could have afforded a nanny, she did everything with and for Sam. She had dreamed of a great life for Sam, and the deepest thorn in Nicola's heart was that her relationship with Pete had devastated both his wife and daughter.

"I never would have thought you could do this," Beth had said to Nicola. It was a week after the nightmare, when Beth had let herself into Mathilda's house, caught her resting in bed beside Pete, seen Tyler in the antique cradle. Beth had called Nicola, asked her to meet her at the coffee shop next to the Black Hall A&P. Nicola had been so scared, holding the car seat in which her three-week-old infant slept, approaching the booth where Beth sat, and sitting across from her.

"It just happened," Nicola said.

"Like a lightning strike, like a hurricane?"

"Don't say it like that. Don't make fun of me," Nicola said. "I never wanted to hurt you." She actually heard those movie-sappy words coming out of her mouth.

"It's not just me; it's Sam," Beth said. "I think she's known all along. That's why she's slipping in school. She knew what her father was doing, and she had to protect me."

"I care about Sam."

"Don't insult me by pretending you do," Beth said.

Nicola felt the words like a kick in the face.

"I thought the world of you. Both Kate and I did. We wanted to support you. We knew how hard you worked to get where you are, how you excelled all along the way. I wanted that for Sam. I wanted schools like the ones you went to."

"She can still have them."

"Right now she can't even show up for her stage design workshop. She has stomach pains and had to drop out. She's a wreck, and it's because of you and her father."

"I'm so sorry," Nicola said.

"What you think you have with him isn't real," Beth said.

"It is," Nicola said softly, glancing at Tyler.

The waitress came by to take Nicola's order and

refill Beth's coffee cup. Nicola shook her head, sent her away. There were maroon paper place mats on the table, and Beth moved hers closer to Nicola. She slid the salt and pepper shakers and the sugar bowl onto her place mat.

"You don't know him," Beth said. "Or maybe you do. Haven't you seen his moods?"

Nicola made sure she showed no emotion.

"This is me," Beth said, pointing at the salt, "and this is Pete." She touched the pepper. "Here is Sam," she said, holding the sugar bowl in both her hands. "No matter how I feel about him now, this is our family." She met Nicola's eyes, a sharp expression in hers. She tapped her coffee spoon, and it slid onto the floor. "And that's you. You're off the place mat. You're out of our lives."

"Not out of Pete's," Nicola said. The waitress came by to pick up the spoon and give Beth a clean one.

"You are," Beth said as the waitress left. "You just don't realize it yet. He's not capable. I'll do anything for Sam, and when it comes down to it, so will Pete." Her gaze was hard and furious, and she raised her hand as if she wanted to hit Nicola.

"Tyler needs his father too," Nicola said.

A look of deep anguish crossed Beth's face. Her whole demeanor changed. She crumpled, putting her head in her hands. Nicola wanted to reach across the table to comfort her. She started to, hand hovering above the back of Beth's head. But she had known it would make everything worse, so she had lowered her hand and touched her sleeping son instead.

Now, sitting in the cozy library with Pete, Nicola caressed their son's head again. It felt warm, but not like before. The fever was breaking. His crying had subsided, and she knew he was ready to fall asleep. The breeze had picked up, and the air was suddenly cool. Nicola wore a sage-green cashmere shawl wrapped around her shoulders. Afraid Tyler would get a chill, Nicola pulled the shawl off and tucked it around him.

"Fresh air is good for him," Pete said.

"He still has a little fever."

"You coddle him."

"Pete, you're being unreasonable."

She saw him scowl, and she waited for his anger. He hated being challenged. She thought about asking to see his back. She could wash and dress his wounds, kiss them so tenderly. It might head him off, stop him from blowing up. He opened his mouth to say something, but then his phone rang. He answered, keeping his eyes on Nicola, but then he walked out the French doors to take the call in private. When he returned, he looked angrier than ever.

"Is everything okay?" Nicola said.

"No," Pete said.

"What's wrong?"

"Sam is spending the night at Kate's. And you know why, don't you?"

Nicola shook her head.

"Because I'm here. Trying to keep you happy instead of being home with my daughter, where I belong."

"Then go," Nicola said.

"It's too late now," Pete said. "She's at her aunt's. I swear to God, if Kate keeps poisoning her against me . . ."

"No one can do that," Nicola said, staring at Pete with all the truth in the world. "Sam loves you. You're all she has left."

"Yes," Pete said, looking away from Nicola and Tyler.

34

"Hello, Kate," Reid said, meeting her and Popcorn outside her loft on Bank Street at midnight, a few blocks from where he'd just left Tom at the Y-Knot. "Jed Hilliard."

"My sister loved him," Kate said with a note of despair in her voice. Reid was a little buzzed. He focused on her face, on the lines in her forehead, and he felt her unhappiness. "And she didn't tell me."

Ah, Kate, Reid thought. Close sisters, a secret between them. That could hurt. It could break a heart.

"Who was he to her?" Reid asked.

"An artist she met. And cared about, and encouraged. And . . . fell in love with."

"And Pete found out?" Reid asked, checking another box in the motive column.

"That I don't know. Not yet, but I will find out."

"Take it easy, Kate. Tell me the details, and I'll track it all down. Where did she meet him?"

"At Ainsworth," she said. "Visiting our father. And later at the soup kitchen."

Ainsworth. Martin Harris had been incarcerated there too, and Reid wondered if Harris and Jed had known each other. Or if Harris had known Garth Woodward, for that matter.

"You're thinking something," Kate said, grabbing Reid's hand. "I can tell."

Reid held her hand tighter. The whiskey was hitting him.

"You're right; I am," he said. Could she smell the whiskey on him? Did he seem too loose? He couldn't seem to let go of her hand.

"I want to know—please tell me."

"Did you ever hear of anyone named Martin Harris? Did Beth mention him? Or your father?"

"I don't think so; why?"

"Someone from Ainsworth who might have run into Beth," Reid said, deliberately vague.

"The name doesn't sound familiar," she said. "But, Conor, she was head over heels. I think Jed might have been the reason she was going to leave Pete. Now I wonder if Matthew was Pete's baby at all. What if he was Jed's?"

Reid thought of the screwup, how he hadn't requested a paternity test during the autopsy. He swallowed hard, couldn't bring himself to tell Kate, and it seemed she hadn't yet thought of it herself. She seemed to be reeling, just coming to grips with the fact her sister had had a lover she hadn't known about.

"This might sound out of left field," he said, "but do you know if Pete is into celestial navigation?"

She seemed taken aback, thrown off course from thinking about Beth and Jed.

"Why?" she asked. "What would that have to do with the case?"

"I'm just curious."

"He was interested in it," Kate said. "Not seriously, but because of sailing, he thought it would be good to know."

"Does he have a sextant?"

"No," she said. "But I do. I need to navigate to fly. My grandmother thought it was just as important to be able to fly by the stars as it was by using instruments. I have the sextant she gave me, and I loaned it to Pete so he could practice."

"When was that?" Reid asked, his pulse quickening.

"I'm not sure exactly. Maybe a year ago? Something like that," Kate said.

Reid nodded. What if Pete had encountered Harris while studying how to steer by the stars? Maybe Harris had been his teacher. Maybe Harris had figured out Pete's crime because of something they had talked about. Pete was the bragging type. He might have felt comfortable confiding in a guy who had committed atrocious crimes against women, a guy who might admire Pete for the way he had killed his wife. Or what if Pete had used Harris to actually kill Beth?

Reid and Kate were standing on the sidewalk in the middle of New London, the ambient light

365

from apartments and bars and streetlights filling the sky, making it hard to see stars. But he looked up, and there were a few visible through the city's bright haze. He couldn't identify them, but they were there.

Reid looked into Kate's eyes. He wouldn't have done it if he hadn't just had two scotches, but he brushed her cheek with the back of his hand. Was it his imagination, or was she leaning into it? There was so much he wanted to tell her.

He raised his gaze again, looking into the sky.

"Beth and I used to look up too," Kate whispered. "And we'd make wishes."

"You did?" he asked.

"Yes. They didn't all come true, but some of them did."

"What did you wish on?" he asked.

"The stars, of course," she said.

Reid nodded. He stared into her eyes for a long time, thought of her and Beth, their wishes, their grandmother and her sextant, celestial navigation. He thought of his brother and what he had said barely twenty minutes ago.

The connection between Pete and Harris: *the stars*.

35

"Let's go for a ride," Kate said. It had been two days since Sam had seen her father, two nights since she had started staying at the loft again. Kate had given Conor Jed's name and told him what she knew. The murder was his investigation, but learning more about Beth's secret life was Kate's. Perhaps the two would intersect.

"Where will we go?" Sam asked.

"I was thinking the Ledges."

"I haven't been there in a long time," Sam said.

"Neither have I."

They climbed into Kate's Porsche. It was a tight squeeze with Popcorn crammed into the tiny back seat along with a canvas bag filled with picnic things. Kate put the top down, and they took back roads through the hills and countryside. The wind blew through Kate's and Sam's hair, and Popcorn rode with his tongue out and ears flying back in pure bliss. Passing Mathilda's gates, Kate glanced at Sam, who stared straight ahead.

A few bends in the road later, she pulled between two crumbling stone pillars. The driveway was cracked and rutted with unrepaired frost heaves. There was a parking area a quarter mile in, and as soon as the car stopped, Popcorn bounded out and ran to the edge of the field.

"Which way do you want to go?" Kate asked. The choices were up the hill toward the abandoned stone house built high on a granite ledge or down a dirt trail to the river. The formal gardens were near the house, but rose mallows grew in abundance along the swampy inlet. Her father had said he'd suggested that Jed Hilliard come here to draw flowers.

"River," Sam said.

They trekked through a meadow, silvery in sunlight. The tall grass was crisscrossed with deer trails. A gray ghost—a northern harrier— flew low over the marsh in search of prey. The amphitheater loomed on the cliff above. Kate's family had spent so many happy Sundays there, but now it was a wreck, crumbling stones taken over by weeds and vines, Connecticut's own version of ancient ruins.

"This place made Mom nervous," Sam said.

"She brought you here?"

"Yeah, sometimes, but she was always afraid of deer ticks and Lyme disease. The grass would tickle her legs, and she'd jump."

"What would she and you do?"

Sam shrugged. "Sketch, mainly. Or she'd tell me stories about how the Black Hall artists would come here over a hundred years ago, set up their easels, and paint the view. You know, there weren't enough women."

"Really?" Kate asked.

"Yep. Matilda Browne and Mary Cassatt were the only women who really made it as American Impressionists. I mean, Miss Florence ran the boarding house for artists, but she wasn't one herself. Willard Metcalf was my favorite, but he looked down on girls who came for art lessons, so now I'm not sure how I feel about him. Did you know he called girls *blots,* as in blots on the landscape?"

"I've heard that," Kate said, picturing the panel at the museum, *Poor Little Bloticelli*—a fifteen-year-old girl in her straw hat and white dress, painting at her easel. Kate had gone through the same thing at Sam's age, being disillusioned by the artists' lives and wondering if it was okay to still love their art.

They walked toward a stand of weeping willow trees, and Kate set down the canvas bag. She shook out a plaid picnic blanket, handed Sam her sandwich, and opened her own. They sat by the river, eating lunch, watching kayakers paddle along the Essex side. A fifty-five-foot boat with a catamaran hull headed slowly south, carrying tourists on a nature cruise. She glanced at Sam. If Sam had spent lots of time here with her mother, how big of a letdown must it be to come here now with her aunt?

"See that island?" Sam asked, pointing.

"Yes," Kate said. She knew it well. Growing up at her grandmother's, she'd heard all about the granite quarries worked in the early twentieth century for stone to pave New York City. Rare indigo hummingbirds were known to nest there every ten years. Most magical were the giant lotus lilies, completely unknown to the United States, that had bloomed on the island.

Mathilda had a botanist friend who had determined they had sprouted from seeds stored in the pyramids of Egypt, a thousand years BC. In the early 1800s, traders had looted the pyramids and stolen ancient racks of linen, to which the seeds had stuck. They had used the fabric to wrap ivory tusks to keep them from breaking on the voyage across the Atlantic. The ivory had been headed to a piano key manufacturer in Deep River, Connecticut. The seeds had blown off the linen, drifted downriver, and taken root on the island's shore.

"Sometimes Mom and I would paddle out to it."

"You'd bring kayaks?"

"Nope," Sam said, giving her a sly smile. "Come on."

They headed down to the water's edge, and Sam parted rushes and invasive phragmites to reveal a ten-foot wooden dinghy covered by a tattered canvas. Oars were stored beneath the peeling varnished seats. Tarnished brass oarlocks were already in their holders.

"Whose boat is this?" Kate asked.

"A friend of Mom's. We'd head out to the island to look for the flowers. Do you know about them?"

"The giant lilies?" *Flowers, a friend.* The back of Kate's neck tingled.

"Yep. Everyone said they lived here until a raging storm washed them away in 1927—but Mom thought that was wrong. She was sure a few were left, hidden under other plants or in a secret part of the quarries. We always searched. This was our island of flowers . . ."

"Flowers," Kate said. "You and your mother searched for them?"

"With her friend," Sam said.

"What friend?"

"An artist. I don't think you know him," Sam said. "He goes to the soup kitchen."

"That's where you met him?" Kate asked, trying to sound casual.

"He's poor, but he's really nice. I helped him with a couple of art workshops at the shelter. He's great with pen-and-ink and charcoal. Mom always said I could learn from him, that he kept it simple, like so many great artists."

"He'd help you search for the lilies?"

"Yeah. Apparently, he somehow met your father, who told him he should draw flowers. And

371

as horrible as your dad was in one way, Mom said no one knew more about art than he did."

"Where is your mom's friend now?" Kate asked.

"Jed? He sometimes camps on the island, but he's obviously not there now, or the dinghy would be on the other side. Come on; let's row out. I'm sure he wouldn't mind if we used it."

They pushed the wooden boat off the silty bank, and Sam gestured for Kate to sit in the stern. Sam took the middle seat and, facing Kate, began to row. Popcorn galloped into the shallows and swam alongside. The passage was short, barely two minutes from the shore. Kate was silent, questions running through her mind.

"Was your Mom close to Jed?" Kate asked.

"Eww, the way you say it."

"Well?"

"Just come out and ask!" Sam snapped. "I'm sixteen, not six. I don't know, but what if she was? After how Dad acted with Nicola? I hope she was. I hope she was happy."

Sam rowed through a narrow entrance to an inlet surrounded by rocks, and they both jumped out. Sam hauled the boat onto a strip of sand, threw the anchor high on the bank to hold it fast. Tension poured off her.

"Sam!" Kate said, watching her niece stalk away.

"I'm going to the quarry to look for the lilies," Sam said.

"Wait, I'll come with you."

But Kate had upset her, and Sam began to run. Popcorn followed her. Kate started after them, then hung back, suddenly relieved to be left alone. She walked in the opposite direction, following a deer trail through tall grass. Glacier meltwater had torn the island from the mainland, its edges matching just like a puzzle piece.

Good luck to Sam, discovering a lotus. Beth had had a romantic view of life, and Kate wasn't surprised to hear that she'd believed something rare and extinct survived here. All through their childhoods, and especially after their mother's death, Beth had lived in her imagination. Kate had chosen reality. And now, strolling across the island, she didn't believe anything could improve on the real and observable: golden grasses, pale- and dark-pink rose mallows, blue cornflowers, creamy Queen Anne's lace. *This was our island of flowers,* Sam had said.

A cluster of scrub oaks and white pine trees grew at the top of a hill. Kate followed a winding brook up the rise. She looked out, watching the brook flow past granite boulders toward the sparkling river. A pair of ospreys rode the air currents overhead. Kate used to have dreams of being a bird. She could open her window and soar into the night, winged and powerful, not needing an airplane. She never crashed in those dreams. And she never wanted to land.

The ground was covered in pine needles. She walked farther into the woods, still following the brook. It was shady and cool, and she was glad not to have the sun on her head. She felt tired and sat down, then lay on her back, looking up through branches that filtered the blue sky. She blinked at the glitter of light, lulled by the sound of the brook. Then, as if she had no choice in the matter, as if she already knew what she was going to see, she turned her head. Set ten yards back, deep within the thick trees, was a dark-green tent.

It was well camouflaged, hidden beneath pine boughs. She walked over to it. The nylon had been patched with silver duct tape. The entrance was zipped up, so she couldn't look inside. For a moment, her blood stopped. Maybe someone was sleeping inside. Not just "someone"—Jed.

"Hello?" she said quietly. "Hello?"

Her heart was racing. She looked down the trail, hoping Sam wouldn't come. She'd hear Popcorn; that was a good thing. When no one answered, she tugged the zipper upward.

The tent was tidy. A rolled-up sleeping bag was tucked into the corner. A gallon jug of water was half-empty. A tin cup, plate, and utensils had been rinsed and stacked. The small, close space smelled musty, of sweat and pine pitch. She was having a hard time connecting Beth with a guy who lived in a tent. Beth, who seemed to safeguard her comfortable life and position in the community, who dressed the part of Black Hall business owner and Sam's mom.

Another way Kate had sold her sister short.

Sticking out from beneath the bedroll was a hard-plastic envelope. She pulled it close to her, opened it. There were papers inside, and she paged through them. The shadowy light made it hard to see, but she peered at each sheet, looking for drawings.

Most were newspaper clippings, but there was one business-size white vellum envelope embossed with the Lathrop Gallery seal. It was addressed simply "Jed" in Beth's handwriting. Kate opened it, intending to read whatever her sister had written, but saw only a small, murky black-and-white photo.

It took Kate's breath away. She sat very still, staring at the photo, her hand on her heart.

When she heard voices in the distance, she replaced the plastic file, ducked out of the tent, and closed the zipper. The sounds were coming from the east side of the low hill, so she walked in that direction.

Hanging back in the woods so she wouldn't be seen, she looked down at the inlet they had rowed across. She heard Sam laughing and Popcorn yelping. "Come on, Jed!" Sam called. "Swim faster!"

"I wouldn't have to swim if someone didn't steal my boat!" a man's voice called.

Sam laughed again. She and Popcorn were hidden by the slant of the brush-covered hill, but Kate could see the man's head, glossy as a seal's back, slipping through the water. He held an orange backpack over his head with one hand, sidestroked across the channel with the other. When he reached shallow water, he stood and shook his reddish-brown hair, sending crystal droplets flying. He wore a gray T-shirt with an owl on it and knee-length tan shorts that stuck to his body.

Sam splashed him when he scrambled up the riverbank, and she gave him a hug.

"Sam, how're you doing?" he asked.

"Everything sucks," she said.

"I know," he said, still hugging her. "I know, I know. I'm so sorry."

He was tall and lanky. He pushed his hair behind his ears and ruffled his beard as if to dry it. He was in his early thirties, and Kate realized that although she hadn't known his name, she'd seen him doing odd jobs around the Academy. She started down the hill, sidestepping her way over and through loose rocks and tangled vines.

"Come look for the lilies with us!" Sam said to Jed.

Jed ignored Sam. Hearing Kate's footsteps, he turned toward her. His eyes were kind, soft brown, and held her gaze. He looked alarmed, almost afraid. She found herself wanting to reassure him, not spook him, learn everything she could.

"Hello, Jed," she said, sticking out her hand. "I'm Kate."

"I've heard a lot about you," he said, shaking her hand. His was cool from the swim.

"I've seen you at the Academy, haven't I?"

"Yes," he said. "Beth helped me get a job there."

"I thought you were based in New London."

"I was, till I got the job. I still have meals there sometimes, but living around here is closer to work."

She nodded. "That makes sense."

"So now everyone knows each other," Sam said, sounding impatient. "Can we please search for the lilies?"

Jed glanced at Kate, apprehension in his eyes, as if trying to tell whether she preferred he not join them. She wondered what he'd think if he knew that in the back pocket of her shorts was the blurry black-and-white photo, the sonogram, she had taken from his tent.

"Sure, Sam," Kate said. "Let's go."

"The thing is, I have an appointment later this afternoon," Jed said. "So I can only look for a little while."

"No prob," Sam said.

The three of them headed single file down the path toward the old quarry, Popcorn leading the way, Kate bringing up the rear. She wondered what appointment he had—she was sure Conor wouldn't let much time pass without interviewing him. Kate walked behind Jed now, stared at his back, never taking her eyes off him for a second.

36

Jed Hilliard didn't have transportation, so instead of having him come to the Major Crime Squad, Reid arranged to meet him at three o'clock at Black Hall's Paradise Drive-In. It was a popular ice cream stand, with picnic tables next to a marsh overlooking the mouth of the Connecticut River. Reid ate a mint chocolate chip cone while waiting.

Jed was a few minutes late. It worked out well; Reid was able to finish his cone. He tossed the napkin into the trash as he watched Jed approach, an orange backpack slung over his right shoulder.

He looked disheveled, but in an appealing way: maybe it was the artist in him. Despite what Reid knew about Jed's beleaguered financial circumstances, he would have a hard time seeing him with the Osprey House crowd: long hair, shaggy beard, tall with a loping stride, alert and intelligent eyes. He had a strong handshake. Reid asked if he wanted something from the snack bar, but Jed said no.

They sat at a picnic table, under a yellow-and-white-striped umbrella. Reid had his back to the sun. Jed had the disadvantage of having it in his eyes, and he squinted at Reid. The sadness in his face was unmistakable.

"I know you want to talk about Beth," Jed said.

"That's right," Reid said, waiting.

Jed seemed comfortable with the silence. He didn't rush to fill it, and he didn't fidget.

"She was the best person I ever knew," he said finally.

"I've heard that from a lot of people," Reid said.

"She loved . . . the world," Jed said. "She saw the good in people, and she took care of everyone."

"Including you?" Reid said.

"Oh yes," Jed said vigorously, as if he wasn't the least bit ashamed of it. "She believed in me. My art especially. But me as a person too. I was in prison." He looked Reid straight in the eye when he said it. "That's where I met her."

Reid had to respect him for coming right out with that—or maybe Jed had his con down pat, and being forthcoming was part of it.

"I've heard that," Reid said. "But what I've been wondering, Jed, is how did you wind up here in Black Hall? I looked up your record, and it says you're from Warwick, Rhode Island."

" 'People, places, and things,' " Jed said. "They teach us in AA to avoid slippery places, and the people we used with, and things that remind us of getting high. So I wasn't going back. Beth helped me decide that. She thought that coming here, working at the Academy, would give me a fresh start."

"Rhode Island," Reid said in a musing way, as if he hadn't heard what Jed had just said. "That's where Beth's husband is from. Did you know him there?"

Jed's lips tightened. "Hell no, I don't know him at all. And don't want to."

"But two guys from Rhode Island? The Ocean State?"

"No," Jed said and left it there. Reid took note. It was unusual to question someone who didn't overexplain.

"You're in AA?"

"Twenty-four months clean and sober."

"Good for you."

"Thanks."

"When did you and Beth begin to have an affair?" Reid asked. He meant it to sound harsh, and it must have, because Jed reacted as if he'd been punched.

"That sounds really sleazy," Jed said, shaken. "And it wasn't."

"You got her to cheat on her husband," Reid said. "How isn't that sleazy?"

"No. He had his thing going with Nicola. He had basically abandoned Beth. She was such a good person—even after he hurt her, she cared about him. But there was a breaking point. How could she go on with him after he had a kid with his girlfriend? There was no way. She had already decided to leave when she and I began to see each other."

"That's funny," Reid said. "Because I hear she and Pete decided to reconcile. That they were working it out."

Jed shook his head hard. "She would never take him back." He gave Reid a sharp, defiant look. "We were in love."

"And having a kid together?"

Jed blushed and didn't speak. Reid watched his discomfort grow. He had boxed himself into a corner.

"Jed. Beth was having a baby. Either you and she were in love and Matthew was yours, or she and Pete were getting back together and he was his. Which is it?" Reid asked. Still no reply. He watched Jed hang his head. Two fat tears plopped down on the picnic table's weathered boards.

Reid gazed at Jed's shoulders, which were shaking as he wept. The sounds were barely audible. There was a napkin dispenser on the table, but Reid made no move to pass him a napkin. A full two minutes passed before Jed looked up. His face was still wet, but he had composed himself. He reached for a napkin and blew his nose. He stared at Reid. Reid noticed he wore a silver band on the ring finger of his left hand.

"Are you going to answer my question?" Reid asked.

"This might make you think I'm trying to hide something," Jed said, speaking slowly, in a very measured and calm way. "But I am not going to discuss that part of Beth's and my life with you."

"Well, that does sound as if you're trying to hide something," Reid said.

Jed tightened his lips, gave a half shake of his head, as if to say he didn't care.

"Let me ask you this," Reid said. "When did you last see Beth?"

"Almost a week before she died," he said.

"That must have felt like a long time to be away from the woman you loved," Reid said.

"It did."

"So, what were you doing during that week?"

"I was on Fishers Island. Teaching art to my friend Lainie's grandchildren."

"Did you leave the island?"

He shook his head. "Unfortunately, no."

"Unfortunately?"

"That's what I said."

"Jed, what's that ring you're wearing? Did someone give it to you?" Reid asked.

Jed's mouth was clamped shut, as if he had finished talking and was ready to go.

"The soup kitchen," Reid said, deciding to change directions. "Where Beth volunteered and you sometimes had meals. Is there a food pantry there too?"

"Yes," Jed said.

"Did you ever meet Martin Harris there, at either place?" Reid asked.

Jed looked blank and shook his head. "No, I don't think so. Who is he?"

Reid thought Jed seemed to genuinely not recognize the name, or maybe it was just the numbness left over after crying. "Okay, Jed," he said. "Give me your friend Lainie-from-Fishers-Island's full name and contact info so I can get in touch with her."

"She'll tell you I was there the whole time," Jed said.

"Teaching art," Reid said. "Got it."

Jed pulled a sketch pad and pencil from his orange backpack and began writing out the name and phone number.

"One other thing," Reid said. "A minute ago, when I asked if you had left the island, you said, 'Unfortunately, no.' What did you mean by that?"

"If I had, I might have been able to save Beth," Jed said, tears filling his eyes again.

Reid stared at Jed and without thinking handed him a napkin. The thing was, he believed him, that he really did feel that way.

37

Scotty Waterston sat on the beach with Lulu, taking the sun full on, no umbrella, no sun hat, the lowest SPF sunscreen. She'd been careful all summer, but she wanted a Saint-Tropez tan. Hubbard's Point had tons of rules, including no drinking alcohol on the beach, but Scotty had filled water bottles with gin and tonics. Lulu sipped hers slowly, but Scotty was getting quietly, progressively drunk. The two women had pulled their beach chairs close to the water's edge, and the advancing tide sent waves to tickle their toes with sea-foam, then withdraw, then return.

"It's all too much," Scotty said.

"Yep," Lulu said.

"It's heartbreak for all of us, but you don't even have kids. I mean, Beth was our friend, but Sam is Isabel's. My daughter is a wreck." She stared across the water to where Isabel was sitting on the raft, all alone.

"It must be horrible. I remember how it was for us when we were her age, how hard to know how to be around Kate and Beth."

Scotty took a very long drink. She wished she had brought slices of fresh lime. No need to suffer. She'd have to remember for next time. "The detective is coming to interview Isabel. I made the mistake of telling him how she and Pete had read the same book, gruesome thing about a killer hiding a body in a cold room."

"God, like Beth," Lulu said.

"Poor girl; he's coming over to grill her later."

"Well, it's good of her to help the investigation."

"Sam isn't taking Isabel's calls," Scotty said. "They had that bit of trouble over at Little Beach, with the rocks."

"The graffiti," Lulu said, so harshly it felt like a slap in the face.

"I'm not trying to sugarcoat it, if that's what you think."

"Good, because what they did was horrible."

"I agree. But I get the feeling Kate is blaming Isabel for it. Has she said anything to you?"

"No. I just think she's worried about Sam."

"Well, of course!" Scotty said. "If you can't act out after your mother gets murdered, when can you?" She caught the look Lulu gave her and checked herself. Drinking always made her want to be outrageous—the worst was when she drunk-texted or posted political messages on Facebook or Twitter. The next day she'd go back and do a mad scrub, furiously deleting everything. At least Lulu was drinking too and hopefully wouldn't remember.

"This is really hard on Kate," Lulu said.

Scotty peered at her. Lulu always looked so chic. She and Kate hadn't had children. They'd kept their svelte shapes and single-woman attitudes. While Scotty wore a Hawaiian-print bathing suit with the hint of a frilled skirt to cover her thighs and built-in bra cups to keep everything from wobbling, Lulu wore a white lace halter dress over her black bikini and looked like a model from the Sundance catalog, where they were all too thin, too pretty, and far too cool.

"It's hard on *all* of us," Scotty said, staring out at Isabel. "We loved Beth too. And let's face it— she confided in us more than she did Kate. Has anyone talked to Jed, by the way? He must be destroyed."

"Kate met him," Lulu said. "She hasn't told me the details yet, but she texted that she found him."

"I can't believe I had to be the one to tell her about him. I felt so awful. And I haven't heard from her at all, as if she's blaming me. Where is he, anyway?"

"Camping somewhere," Lulu said, sipping her drink and looking away as if she wanted to evade further questions. That was so Lulu—keeping Kate mostly to herself. It had always hurt Scotty, the way the two of them were a closed society. Beth had felt that way too. Scotty felt herself burning over it.

"Sometimes you seem so superior," Scotty said. "What?"

"Yes, you and Kate. The pilots. Above it all, better than me and Beth. It hurts."

"I'm sorry; I don't mean to make you feel that way," Lulu said, sounding genuinely surprised. Was it possible she didn't know how fat and suburban and boring Scotty felt beside her?

"Well, you do," Scotty said. She realized she was slurring her words but took another long drink anyway. She was about to tip over into weepy territory, feeling sorry for herself about Beth, feeling helpless about Isabel's pain—and even Jed's. Beth hadn't treated him very well at the end.

And then there was Julie. Her beautiful little girl with schizotypal personality disorder. The name alone terrified her, but the reality was even worse. Even the literature was hurtful—people with the disorder were labeled "odd and eccentric." Julie turned inward, had never had a close friend. She didn't know how to interpret people's words and actions, so she was easily hurt and confused.

Julie had started dreaming about the murder, screaming out in her sleep.

"When I think about Sam's mommy, it hurts me a lot!" she cried while Scotty rocked her.

Scotty wanted her daughter to feel peace, to not be so scared. She felt as if Julie's fears would

388

pass as time went by, but some nights they were extreme.

"Sweetie, it was just a dream," Scotty whispered, holding her.

"Bad person, terrible bad person," Julie had said, shaking as she'd cried.

The rest of Julie's diagnosis, receptive and expressive aphasia and language processing disability, meant that she experienced life in ways both simpler and more complicated than everyone else. She got so frustrated trying to get her thoughts and feelings out.

Scotty told the pediatrician, asking if it would be appropriate to give Julie something for anxiety. The doctor had suggested taking Julie to therapy. And Scotty was more than willing to do that, but in the last few days, Julie had seemed quieter, retreating into her safe, private world.

Nick was far from helpful. He would come home from the office, throw on his shorts and Nikes, and go running for hours, sometimes until dark. He was training for the Labor Day half marathon, aiming for next year's New York City Marathon. He had told Scotty a bunch of people from work were doing it. Scotty pictured the women in his office. Everyone but her was in shape. She downed a big gulp of her drink.

"Let's take a swim," Lulu said, reaching for her hand. "It will be good for us."

"I'm looped."

"We don't have to go out far."

"That detective is coming to see Isabel later," Scotty said. "I should go up to the house and take a nap. I have the G&T flu." She paused, glancing at Lulu. "Who do you think did it?"

"Mostly I think Pete."

"Me too, but sometimes I think Jed—I mean, she met him in prison."

"I know," Lulu said.

"And he's an art person—it would make sense for him to take *Moonlight*. I'm sure he has a network; he could sell it. And we really have no idea how he took the fact Beth had cooled off, was seeing him less. I think she wanted to stop altogether."

"She did?" Lulu asked, and Scotty couldn't help feeling gratified that she knew at least some things Lulu didn't.

"She had made a mess of things—to go from perfect Beth to being pregnant and having two men in her life. It was tearing her apart. Didn't she tell you?"

Lulu shook her head. "She never talked to me about it, Scotty. You've told me more than she ever did. I only saw her with Jed that one time, on the ferry."

Scotty sighed. "He made her so happy for a while. It must have felt so nice to have someone all for herself, someone who really wanted her. Not like Pete, off with Nicola." She thought of herself and Nick. She couldn't help wondering about the women he worked with, beautiful and thin, training for the half marathon. Surreptitiously, on the side Lulu couldn't see, Scotty grabbed the roll of fat around her waist. The old commercial used to say if you could pinch more than an inch you needed to eat their cereal and get into shape. Scotty could pinch half a foot.

"I really need to get into shape," she said.

"You look great," Lulu said.

Scotty gave her a skeptical look. There was all this wise-woman BS about accepting yourself the way you were right now, not thinking about the body you had when you were twenty-five. Easy for Lulu to say it when she had a stomach as flat as a teenage boy's.

"You're beautiful," Lulu said.

Scotty didn't believe her, so she ignored her. "I hope Isabel remembers about the detective coming."

"Want me to go get her?" Lulu asked.

Scotty nodded. "That would be really nice of you."

"I need the swim anyway," Lulu said. She gave Scotty a big hug and kissed the top of her head, then went running into the water, dove in, and started swimming fast out toward Isabel on the raft. Scotty gathered her towel, beach bag, and chair and walked as steadily as she could across the hot sand, toward her house on the other side of the boat basin. She couldn't wait to close the door behind her. Emotions made her drink, and she was nothing but emotions these days.

Right now, she needed to lie down. She would hit the reset button and start fresh after her nap. She had to keep going on, but it wasn't easy. Murder didn't just take one life; it stole the essence, will, and ease from everyone it touched. It took their old lives and left them to make their way in a completely new and uncertain world.

Scotty had to find a way back to being alert and present for Julie and Isabel. Julie: hiding deep within herself. Isabel: her beautiful, troubled daughter. Scotty didn't want to be a bad influence, drinking to escape the pain. Nick had grounded Isabel after she'd come home wasted the night of the graffiti.

Maybe Scotty should ground herself.

38

In Reid's interviews with Pete and his friends, he had heard repeatedly that Pete was a member of Mensa, the high IQ society. Pete seemed determined that everyone know it, and to Reid's mind, if someone had to brag about being a member, he might not be as smart as he thought.

Mac Green had relented and decided to let Pete take the polygraph. Reid had questions, a list of them, and he was going to request an interview after the polygraph. He met Jen Miano at the crime lab.

"Are we going to arrest him today?" Miano asked.

"I'd like to," Reid said. "But we're not there yet."

"Jed is interesting."

"Yeah, but he has an alibi," Reid said. As soon as he had left Jed at the Paradise Drive-In, he'd called Lainie Stewart. She had told him that Jed had stayed in the main house with the family. His bedroom was between her grandson Terry's room and the master suite where she and David slept. He had given art lessons in the living room of their guest house, reconfigured as an art studio, and had been with the family the whole time, including meals.

Reid had then checked with the ferry operators, determined that Jed had taken the boat only twice—on his way to and from the island. He hadn't brought a car. The Stewarts had arranged for him to be driven back and forth to Black Hall. Reid had confirmed that fact with William Nelson, the owner of Admiral Limousine Service. The Stewarts were favorite longtime customers, and whenever they called, Nelson drove the passengers himself, as he had with Jed.

"Pete has an alibi too," Miano reminded Reid.

"True, but the time line works against him," Reid said.

"Jed was in love with Beth."

Reid nodded.

"Then there's the baby," Miano said.

Reid felt the breath rush out of him.

"Don't feel too bad," she said. "Who would think of a paternity test? Pete was the cheater! Not one thing made us think Beth was anything but faithful to Pete."

"Thanks," Reid said, appreciating that she was trying to make him feel better. To everyone, Beth had been an angel. Humberto Garcia, the coroner, hadn't tested Matthew's DNA, and Beth's body had been released to the family for cremation.

"What the hell was Beth Lathrop doing with a

guy like that?" Miano asked. "It doesn't track. He seems like kind of a loser."

"He's not, actually," Reid said. "I could be wrong, but he seems like a decent, stand-up guy."

"Yeah, but *homeless?*" Miano asked.

Reid remembered what Leland Ackerley had said about Beth: that she loved and nurtured artists whose talent she believed in. And how Jed had said she took care of everyone.

"Well, if she wanted to get in Pete's face," Miano said, "she couldn't have done better than choosing a homeless con. A *younger* homeless con. So much for the perfect Black Hall life."

"Only on the outside," he said.

"You know, if it turns out Jed's the father, it would make a hell of a motive for Pete," Miano said. "Jealousy over Jed *and* wanting to be rid of Beth so he could be with Nicola. Plus, the baby. Whose was it? I know, I know. The damn paternity test."

"Right," Reid said, feeling his chest constrict.

Pete and his lawyer had arrived. Mac Green had a full head of white hair, and he wore a perfectly tailored gray pinstripe suit. He had represented several of Reid's suspects over the years, and Reid had a grudging respect for him. He did a good job for his clients without resorting to dirty tricks that Reid considered the stock-in-trade of many defense attorneys.

Pete sauntered over to Reid and Miano. Like

his lawyer, he was dressed in a suit instead of his usual beach boy garb.

"Looking sharp, Pete," Reid said. "You look as if you're dressed for court."

"I want you to know how seriously I am taking this."

"This?" Reid asked. "The polygraph?"

"The fact my wife was murdered and you're wasting time harassing me instead of doing a real investigation."

"Harassing you? Correct us if we're wrong," Miano said, "but aren't you the one who pushed for this?"

"Pete, we're ready," Green called sharply, and Reid could see the lawyer wasn't happy with his client baiting the police.

"What a cocky son of a bitch," Miano said when Pete and Green stepped away. "What makes him so confident?"

Reid didn't reply. He felt nervous. She was right. Pete held himself with total assurance and an air of martyrdom, as if a great injustice was being done. Reid was looking forward to the results wiping that look off Pete's face, but something told him not to be too sure just yet.

An hour later, when it was all over, his misapprehension was confirmed. Pete passed. The examiner had paid extra attention to his answers to questions about Jed, Nicola, and Beth's last day. He told Reid and Miano there was no ambiguity: the machine had picked up no lies or signs of deception.

"Well then," Green said as he and Pete walked toward Reid and Miano. "I hope this means you'll be moving on."

"Not quite yet," Reid said. "We have a few more questions."

"I think Pete has been helpful enough for today," Green said.

"Yeah, it's true," Reid said. He smiled at Pete. "Beautiful day out there. Going to go sailing?"

"No, I have other things to do," Pete said, sounding haughty.

"Ever do any night sailing?" Reid asked. "Get away from land, look up at that canopy of stars in the sky?"

"Where's this going, Detective Reid?" Green asked.

"Just thinking of how nice it can be to get away from it all," Reid said. "I'd sure like to."

"As it happens, I do enjoy sailing at night," Pete said. "Ocean races especially—Newport to Bermuda. Out there in the Gulf Stream, bioluminescence flashing against the hull. Do you know what *bioluminescence* is?"

"Sea creatures that glow in the dark?" Miano asked.

"That's right. Very good," Pete said.

"Gee, thanks," Miano said. She glanced at Reid. "I got it right!"

"One up on me," Reid said. He saw Pete grin.

"Let's go, Pete," Green said.

"Did you ever do, that thing—I forget what it's called?" Reid asked, tapping his forehead as if he was trying to come up with the word. "You know, when you point that instrument at the sky to figure out where you are?"

"Celestial navigation," Pete said. "And that *instrument* is a sextant. Yes, I've done it. It's very mathematical. Really just angles. If you can do geometry, you can steer by the stars."

"Steer by the stars," Reid said. "I like that. Really nice way to describe it. Easier than celestial navigation! Well, enjoy the rest of your day, gentlemen."

Green shook hands with both detectives. Pete stood back, then turned to go.

"Hey, Pete," Reid said. "I almost forgot. I met your friend Martin."

"Who?" Pete asked.

"Martin Harris. You know, the astronomy expert."

"I have absolutely no idea who you're talking about," Pete said. He and Mac Green left the building. Reid wiped the gee-whiz expression off his face and narrowed his eyes as Pete walked away.

"That was genius," Miano said. "That bit about sailing at night. Steer by the stars." She punched Reid's upper arm. "Too bad he didn't admit to knowing Harris. Think he was telling the truth about that?"

"Hard to say."

"Then again, he just beat the lie detector," Miano said.

"It didn't show deception, that's for sure," Reid said.

"Come on—like any good narcissist, he doesn't register emotion the way normal people do. Cool as a cucumber."

"He never got riled," Reid said.

"Let's get a warrant for his computer, look for articles on how to outsmart the machine. He probably researched it!"

Reid stood still, thinking. He pictured Pete sitting across from the examiner, strapped to the machine. Pete had stared straight ahead, no change of affect no matter what he was asked. He'd barely blinked.

"We still have time of death going for us," Miano said. "Other than body temp, everything points to Beth having died the morning Pete left. Thank God for stomach contents."

"You're right," Reid said. The autopsy had shown that Beth's last meal had been eggs, melon, and blueberries—exactly what Pete had said they had had for breakfast before Ackerley picked him up.

"Those polygraph questions," Miano said, giving an exaggerated shiver.

"What about them?"

"The way he recounted their last minutes together. That he hugged and kissed her, that he told her he loved her, and then left."

"Shit," Reid said, suddenly getting it. "That's exactly what he *did* do."

"But if she was already dead . . ."

"Jennifer, I think you're right. He *did* research the polygraph."

"Okay . . ."

"But *before* he killed her, not afterward. It's why he's been insisting on taking the test!" Reid said, excitement building. "Because he knew that if he *actually* hugged and kissed her dead body, told her he loved her after he'd smashed her head in and strangled her, the machine wouldn't detect a lie when he told the story."

"Because he'd be telling the truth," Miano said. "But when he was directly asked if he killed Beth . . ."

"His research would have taught him how to control his breathing. He might not have been able to keep it up through the whole slate of questions, but for one, he nailed it."

Reid's heart was pumping with elation at the breakthrough.

"We've got to get his computers," Miano said. "House and gallery."

"And Nicola's," Reid said. "But I still think we won't find anything on any of those. We've got

400

to look at libraries, public places he could have gone to look it up."

"Books too," Miano said. "Check his credit cards for book orders."

Reid was beaming when he said goodbye and he and Miano went to their separate work stations to start working on the warrants. Two hours later, Miano told him he could leave early, that she'd finish the applications. She had a leave of absence coming up—she needed knee surgery for an old college soccer injury—and she knew he'd be carrying the caseload while she was gone. He thanked her and took off.

On the way home, he took a detour through the center of Black Hall.

He parked in the driveway of the Lathrop Gallery, stared at the historic building. The blinds on the tall windows were closed. The flowers in the stone planters on the front porch hadn't been watered, and the geraniums had turned brown. Without Beth to take care of the gallery, it looked abandoned. He wondered if Kate would take over.

He circled around back, tracing the steps he had taken twenty-three years ago. The rhododendrons were as thick around the hatchway door as they had been back then. He remembered what it had been like to hear Kate thumping her feet, the sound that had made him break down the door. He leaned his shoulder against the door now, remembering the force it had taken to break the lock.

If he counted the days and minutes since that day, he knew there would be very few when the Woodward sisters had not been on his mind. He stared at the windows, wondering what secrets the computers inside held. He doubted very much that Pete had left any trail on a hard drive that could be traced to him, but he had hope that they were on the right track.

A message from Kate popped up on his phone.

Can we meet? I have something to show you.

He texted back:

Where?

Kate replied:

My place.

When he got to Bank Street, he saw her sitting on the top step in front of her building. Her tan legs were streaked with salt or silt, silvery in the light, as if she'd been wading in the river. Popcorn lay on the sidewalk behind her and jumped up when Reid got out of his car.

"Let's talk out here," she said. "Sam's upstairs."

"Okay," he said, sitting beside her.

"Conor," she said. "I hate to say this, but you might be wrong about Pete."

"Why?"

"Have you talked to Jed Hilliard yet?"

"Yes," Reid said.

"Well, so have I," Kate said. "I think you'd better look at him more closely."

"We did, of course," Reid said. "But he has an alibi."

"So does Pete. He was on a sailboat, two hundred miles away."

"Jed was giving private art lessons to some kids on Fishers Island," Reid said.

"The Stewarts?" Kate asked. "I know them. I fly the family. David's the one who first mentioned Jed to me. But they're so sweet—he could fool them; he could have snuck off . . ."

"He spent the nights before Beth's death in their guest room, and he didn't return to the mainland until the day after. We have statements from David and Lainie, the ferry operators, and the driver who took Jed to the boat and back to Black Hall."

Kate paused, looked out at the harbor. She watched the *Cape Henlopen*—one of the big ferries that went out to Orient Point—back out of the dock, turn, and head south down the Thames.

"Well, I have something to show you," she said. She reached into her pocket and handed him a small, square sonogram in black and white.

"Okay . . . ," he said, waiting for her to explain.

"I took it from Jed Hilliard's tent," she said.

Reid stared at the picture.

"Look on the back," Kate said.

Reid turned it over, saw that someone had scrawled *Love, B.*

"*B* for Beth," Kate said.

"So you think . . . ," Reid began.

"Yes. Jed was the father of her baby," Kate said.

39

Sam sat on the glider, salt-rusted chains creaking as she pushed back and forth with one toe on the weathered wood floor. Isabel was braiding her hair, and Sam was savoring the closeness when a scratching sound came from under the table beside them. She nearly jumped. Julie crawled out, glanced at them, then disappeared under the faded tablecloth again.

"I see you," Sam said.

Julie giggled.

"We get it," Isabel said to her sister. "You're *so* adorable. You're the *most* precious. But guess what? Watching people and eavesdropping isn't nice."

"I do it, though," Julie said.

"No fucking kidding."

"It's okay, Julie," Sam said. "Come out and hang with us."

"I don't think so," Isabel said. Sam watched her glare at the rustling tablecloth.

"What's wrong?" Sam asked. "You okay?"

"I'll be honest," Isabel said. "Having you coddle Julie, when I just want to be supportive and understanding of *you,* makes my stomach hurt."

"I love you both; is that okay?" Sam asked.

"Thinking about the time," Julie said, her voice muffled by the tablecloth.

"What time?" Sam asked.

"Before the dying, before your mother went to heaven."

"Julie!" Isabel said.

"Yeah. I think about it too," Sam said.

Julie poked her head out. She actually met Sam's gaze and nodded.

Eye contact was really rare. Julie's face, always pale, was scrunched up with worry and looked translucent, almost bluish. She was obviously really upset, giving Sam a serious needle in her heart. Julie's so-called friends bullied her. They weren't patient, and they teased her.

Once when Sam and Isabel were at the beach with Julie, they overheard Cammie Alquist bullying her.

You don't look different, but you ARE different, hahaha, Cammie had said, and Isabel had grabbed Cammie by the back of her neck and said, *Different is better than shitty like you.* Seeing Isabel defend Julie had made Sam wish she had a sister—someone who had her back, while Sam had hers, just like her mother and Aunt Kate.

"Bad dream," Julie said.

"You had one?" Sam asked.

"She has nightmares," Isabel said. "Let's get out of here."

Sam wanted to stay and hear more of what Julie was talking about, but she could tell that Isabel had lost her patience and seemed ready to explode.

"Foley's?" Sam asked.

"Yeah."

They took the long way around, the road that looped along the marsh. They were beach girls and walked barefoot, the tar warm and soft beneath their feet.

"What's bothering Julie?" Sam asked.

"I can't tell, exactly. She's very upset about your mother, obviously," Isabel said, glancing at Sam. "But I think it has more to do with your father."

"What did he do?"

"Well, he came over to pick up my dad the day they left, and we all talked to him. Julie hears everything, and she knows he's a suspect." Again Isabel looked at Sam. "Sorry."

"Don't worry; I'm aware of it," Sam said, knowing she sounded stiff. Every time she thought of her father killing her mother, *she* wanted to die. It wasn't possible. He wasn't the greatest dad sometimes, but he would never do that. She dug her nails into the palms of her hands.

"Julie's just scared. That cop came to talk to me about the dumb book. Why my mother had to mention it to him I have no idea. It was just a thriller my mother picked up at the library book sale. I read it, and then my dad did, and I guess he gave it to your dad."

"What book?" Sam asked.

"*Meat Locker*. This restaurant owner kills his business partner and hides the body in a refrigeration unit to slow the decomposition of the body. I mean, there's more to the story than that, but that's the part the cop wanted to know about."

"I don't remember seeing it around our house," Sam said. "And you never mentioned it before."

"Well, I forgot about it," Isabel said. "Mom's the one who called the detective to tell him about it."

"Your mom?" Sam asked, shocked that Mrs. Waterston would get involved, would say anything that might implicate her dad. "How could she do that?"

"Well, she's worried about you, Sam."

"I've lost my mom, and now she wants to help them take my dad away too?" Sam asked.

"No! She just wants . . . to do what's right. For everyone. For your mother. And you too, of course. I mean, if your dad did it, it could be dangerous. Sam, don't be mad!"

Sam started walking faster, and they didn't talk the rest of the way. Foley's was a general store, set in the midst of Hubbard's Point. Only locals went, or even knew about it. It stocked basic food and supplies along with beach toys, and in the back, it had a snack bar with the best lemonade and grilled-cheese sandwiches in the world. Isabel and Sam sat at one of the old scarred oak tables. Generations of kids had carved their initials into the wood, and it was not only allowed but encouraged.

"Ha, look," Isabel said, pointing at her parents' initials: SB & NW. "Hello, hypocrites. Is this that different from graffiti?"

"Well, it's allowed here," Sam said.

"Where are your parents' initials?" Isabel asked. "You've never shown me."

"They didn't grow up in Hubbard's Point," she said. "So they're not here."

"Maybe you should carve them. To commemorate . . ."

Everything Isabel had said on the way here reverberated through Sam like seismic waves. People thought her dad had killed her mom. Did Sam think that? She told herself no. But right now, despair bubbled up and boiled over.

"To commemorate the fact that my father basically lives with someone else? And has a kid with her? I think my mother had a boyfriend too."

"Really?" Isabel asked. Sam could see it came as a shock—everyone thought her mother was pretty much a saint.

"I'm almost positive. He's this guy we knew from New London. I didn't think about it before she died, but now, looking back, she was happy when she was around him."

"That must suck, thinking that," Isabel said.

"It doesn't," Sam said. "It should, right? As Julie would say, 'It's weird; it's strange,' but for some reason, it doesn't suck. I'm just glad my mother was happy."

"You have to quote my sister?" Isabel asked.

"Come on. You know I love Julie. She's the only one who tells it straight. Everyone else is so polite and walking on eggshells around me. Not wanting to upset me. I know they talk about it when I'm not there."

"Are you grouping me in with the polite people?" Isabel asked.

"No," Sam said. "You're my best friend. But to be honest, it fucked me up to hear about the book just now, and you talking to the detective. I mean, I know he's interviewing everyone, but I still hate it."

"How do you think I felt?" Isabel asked. "Having to talk about how my best friend's dad might have killed her mom?"

And then, because she just couldn't take it anymore, Sam ran out of Foley's and left Isabel sitting there.

40

Sam returned to school just before Labor Day, and Kate took a leave of absence from Intrepid Aviation. Nearly two months after Beth's death, she began spending days at the gallery. It was just a quarter mile from Black Hall High, so she and Sam could drive together from New London.

Being at the gallery made Kate feel closer to Beth. She sat at her sister's desk, Popcorn lying at her feet. Time was passing, and still Beth's killer hadn't been caught. Conor seemed sure Jed hadn't done it. Her thoughts veered wildly between still believing it was Pete and starting to wonder if it really had been an art theft. And a sexual assault. She thought of the horribly torn underwear beside Beth's bed—and what it had been used to do to her.

It was all unthinkable. She tried to get the picture of Beth lying on her bed out of her mind, the marks around her neck, her blankly staring eyes. Her fingers trembled as she paged through a thick black ledger Beth kept of all the paintings that came through the gallery. It calmed and soothed her to think of the things Beth had always loved, had been good at. After a few minutes, she lost herself in Beth's notes.

Kate had always been informed about the most important acquisitions and sales. A few key paintings stood out; Beth had written about them, filled paragraphs with question marks and red arrows, words that were circled or boldly underlined. She'd been searching for clues, more information than the previous owners had been able—or willing—to supply. Works of art were a mystery—their meaning, provenance, and authenticity—and to study them, one had to become a detective and an academic.

Kate examined the small oil on a display easel beside Beth's desk. Beth had determined that the landscape, unsigned, was by Ben Morrison, the same artist who'd painted *Moonlight*. Could there be any significance to Beth's having had it right next to her desk?

It had been found with over fifty other paintings in the attic of a saltbox on Sill Lane. Edith Peck, a ninety-five-year-old recluse who had never married, had collected works of the American Impressionists who had painted in the Black Hall Art Colony. Morrison had lived there from 1898 to 1905. After Peck's death last December, it had come to light that she had two great-nephews in Bangor and a great-niece in Rochester, none of whom had any interest in owning the paintings.

Miss Peck's family wanted the Lathrop Gallery

to sell the paintings on consignment, but Beth had asked Kate to agree that the family purchase them outright.

Beth worked out a price, and Kate concurred. Edith Peck's family had felt it was fair, and the deal was made. Pete objected. He thought they were paying too much.

"They're not Metcalf caliber," he'd said. "We're talking about a couple of LeBlancs, a Potter, a Giddings, and a few unsigned that *might* be Morrison? What you've got is a bunch of barely-knowns."

Pete was correct about the fact that the works Miss Peck had collected—other than the possible Morrisons—were by artists not terribly sought after, but the passion of collectors had always escaped him: the thrill of discovering a new artist; the love of beauty; the deep satisfaction of owning a picture done over a hundred years ago, outdoors on local hills or riverbanks, of scenes that still existed today.

He would never comprehend the role the gallery played in creating reputations. Artists represented by the Harkness-Woodward—now Lathrop— Gallery *became* sought after. Once they secured the gallery's imprimatur, the value of their work went up substantially. Many artists who showed here later had work acquired by museums from the Farnsworth to the Metropolitan Museum of Art. Pete might have done well in another field; he would never understand that soul was more necessary to the art business than a calculator.

Kate examined the painting at hand, the one Beth had attributed to Morrison. The canvas was 8 by 12 inches. It depicted a brook in spring. The water's strong zigzag and diminishing diagonal drew the eye back and forth from the foreground into the distance. Light glinted on the surface and through pine needles, a wash of gold-green and clear pale blue. Claude Monet had said, "Nature does not stand still."

Kate was thinking of those words when she suddenly recognized the brook: it was on the island, running down the hill from where Jed had pitched his tent. She recognized the rock contours and the serpentine of water flowing toward the distant blue river. She had observed that exact scene the day she'd found the sonogram.

Was that the reason Beth had the painting propped up where she could see it at all times? Because it reminded her of Jed and the island? The painting was undeniably lovely, idealistic, and romantic. Could that pine grove by the brook be where she had conceived Matthew?

Lost in thought, Kate heard the discreet bell that rang only upstairs in the office, announcing that someone had entered the front door. She heard footfalls on the bare wood floor, and Popcorn loped downstairs to investigate. Kate's fists clenched—an involuntary reaction to the sound of footsteps in the gallery. After all these years, that sound reminded her of the day the intruders had come. The bell had rung upon their entrance as well.

"Hello," came a familiar voice.

She walked downstairs to see Conor bending down to pet Popcorn. He wore what she'd come to realize was his uniform: gray slacks, a white broadcloth shirt, a striped tie, and a rumpled blue blazer. He pushed his dark hair out of his eyes, sparkling with warmth.

"I drove by and spotted your car," he said. Then, "I'm surprised you're here."

"Why?" she asked.

"I thought you'd be flying."

"I'm taking time off," she said. "I thought I'd spend some time at the gallery. It's been neglected since Beth died."

"How does it feel to be back?"

"It's complicated—not all one thing." She paused. "It's practically my home. I've been coming here as long as I remember. A lot of memories. And some ghosts." She thought of the Morrison painting.

"Your mother."

"And Beth," Kate said. *My sister with her lover,* she thought. Had Beth chosen that spot by the brook to be with Jed because of the Morrison painting? Had she let art guide her?

There was another ghost too: the girl Kate used to be. Her gaze went to the basement door. She had walked down those stairs one person, and when she'd come back up twenty-two hours later, she'd been someone else entirely.

"Are you okay?" Conor said, taking a step closer to her.

Kate nodded. She felt light headed.

"You look pale."

Now he was inches away. She could feel waves of energy between their bodies.

Her skin tingled. She realized Conor was attracted to her. Maybe he had a hero complex, or perhaps it was the smell of her hair. Was she mistaken, or did he want to kiss her? For weeks now, she had sensed him nearby, watching her, even when he didn't let himself be seen.

She never had these instincts—she'd been frozen solid, and the ice had started to form right here in the gallery when she was sixteen. What would happen if she touched him? She tried it, just one finger at first, tracing the back of his hand. Her skin burned.

"You knew I'd be here, didn't you?" she asked.

"No," he said.

"Did you follow me?"

She watched him staring at her. Electricity tingled through her body, taunting her to collapse, to quit holding it all together, to give in to something sublime and terrible. She felt overcome with desire. Was this how Beth had felt when she'd gone to the brook with Jed?

"Yeah," he said. "I did follow you."

"Are you supposed to be doing that?" she asked.

"I was concerned," he said.

"About what?" she asked.

"About Pete. He lost face with anyone connected to the gallery; you're letting his girlfriend and son stay in your family house. He might be very angry."

"I can take care of myself," she said, but now, in contradiction to her words, the pressure of her finger on his hand was stronger; she was holding herself up, balancing with one fingertip on Conor Reid. Blood was rushing in her ears, a roaring brook, melting the ice in her body.

"I'm messed up," she said out loud.

"No, you're not."

She pulled herself away and walked across the room. She sensed him right behind her. He wasn't touching her, but she felt warmth pouring off him. Now his hand was on her shoulder. Her hair was pinned up, and he brushed a tendril aside. She was numb. Would he notice? Would the ice really melt? Did she want it to?

"Kate," he said, and his breath was warm on the back of her neck. She felt more than just a breeze, movement of air. He was going to kiss her. She felt everything he wanted, as if her own desire had become his.

She turned to accept the kiss. His lips nearly brushed hers. She bowed her head, shook it hard.

This doesn't happen to me. I don't do this, she said, but only to herself, not out loud.

She took one step away from him, then another. As she did, the longing that had rocked her a moment ago felt more like a dream; it wasn't real. The sound of the blood in her ears, the rushing brook, stopped.

She took a deep breath. She knew she had to be brave—face what had happened here twenty-three years ago, here and now, if she wanted to move on with her life. She walked to the basement door, pulled by the force of the past. She turned the knob and walked down the stairs.

In the late 1800s, the basement had had a dirt floor, but Mathilda had redone it with concrete. Despite that improvement, this was New England, and basements were often damp, so chill and a musty smell hit her when she opened the door.

"Kate, why are you going down there?" Conor asked. "You don't need those memories."

"I do," she said quietly.

She heard his footsteps on the stairs behind her. Beth had trained Popcorn well, and he didn't follow them down. Kate felt daring, entering the place of so many nightmares. The odor and the clammy feeling of her skin brought everything back to her. She had actually *desired* Conor. She wanted that feeling back, right now, but first she had to break the spell of the past. Maybe her body could be her own again.

Conor had been here that day. He had found Kate and Beth and their dead mother. Had he heard Beth whimpering, speaking gibberish, a language that she'd invented during that long night?

At the foot of the chestnut plank stairs, she turned in a circle. The basement held all the systems—furnace, hot water heater, electrical panel. One wall was covered with shelves filled with bronze and stone sculptures. There were three six-by-six-inch load-bearing support posts set into cement piers, original to the 1890 house. The edges of the cement were crumbling slightly, eaten away by time and moisture.

Kate, Beth, and their mother had been tied next to one post, the rope looped around and around, anchoring them to the building. They had tried changing positions, this way and that. They tried to saw the ropes against the rough edges. Each of them stretched as far as possible, trying to wriggle free. Kate's left side had been scraped raw. To this day, she had fine, threadlike, horizontal scars on her hip from scraping against the ragged concrete.

She walked over to the pole now, leaned against it, and stared at the floor. She pictured her mother, blood streaming from her nose, vomit from choking on the gag. Kate and Beth had struggled to get free so they could save her. The harder they'd thrashed, the deeper the ropes had cut into their wrists.

"Do you remember what it was like that day?" she asked Conor.

"Yes, everything," he said. "Do you?"

"I think so. It's hard to tell whether the memories are real or dreams. Sometimes I think I turned into a ghost that night. That I left the earth."

"You didn't," he said, reaching for her hand. "You're not a ghost. You're right here."

"I don't always feel alive," she said, staring at the way his fingers were clasped with hers. "But I want to."

After a moment she pulled her hand away and turned around. A framing workshop occupied the basement's east wall. A pegboard with hooks for tools hung above a long rustic workbench. Vises, a mortar board, and saws covered the wooden bench. The family had scoured estate sales for antique frames, often with inferior paintings still intact. The canvases, if they weren't interesting, would be cut out and discarded. Several large, ornate gilded frames leaned against the wall.

"He made himself useful at one thing," Kate said.

"Who?" Conor asked.

"Pete. Building frames."

Standing by the bench, Kate noticed a print by Thomas Nason. Beside it were four lengths of black-painted wood, corners mitered, ready to become a frame. Conor leaned over to examine a wood engraving of a Colonial house on a low hill, surrounded by pine, maple, and birch trees. Kate found it haunting; she wondered if Conor did too.

Kate remembered how Mathilda had told her Nason had etched thousands of fine lines in the block of wood to create depth and shadows. He'd then rolled the block with a thin layer of ink and printed the work. The print was painstakingly detailed, right down to the textures in pine needles and maple bark, the house's shingles, a glint of dying light in the window glass.

"Looks as if Pete was in the middle of building a frame for this one," Conor said. "It's Mathilda's house, isn't it?"

"It is," Kate said. "The artist used houses and barns and land along the Connecticut River as his subjects." Just as Ben Morrison had used the island and the brook.

"Did Nason know your grandmother?"

"Yes. She said he was the most poetic artist in America. She meant it literally. Some of his prints illustrated books by Robert Frost."

"I can't picture Pete feeling the poetry, working on this," Conor said.

"Trust me; he didn't. But Beth . . . ," Kate said.

421

"Beth, yes. She would," Conor said.

Kate nodded. "Frost was her favorite poet. His poems evoke New England, the places we grew up and loved."

And then it hit her: Frost's "West-Running Brook." Beth had always been haunted by it, the poem about contraries in love. Most brooks ran east toward the ocean; one streaming west was rare. Kate knew Beth had related the poem—with its dialogue between a couple questioning what they were to each other, whether to follow expected routes in life—to their parents' difficult love. She pictured Morrison's painting of the brook, so close to Beth's desk she could touch it. The stream that ran past Jed's tent. Beth's contrary love for him. Everything was connected.

"I'm glad we came down here," Conor said. "It helps me with Pete's state of mind."

"In what way?"

"I think this is where he formed the idea to kill Beth," Conor said, chasing away any feeling of redemption. "Working on the frames right here in the space where your mother died. Where the three of you suffered. It got him thinking. Even though your father hadn't intended Helen to die, he had made a plan to get himself out of a situation. Pete did something similar, only murder was the whole point."

"Let's go upstairs," Kate said. The cellar was

closing in on her, the damp smell filling her throat and choking her like the gag.

Turning fast, she bumped into the post where she'd been tied. The boiler was halfway between it and the stairs. She tripped on a wooden crate, kicking over bottles of chardonnay and pinot noir, served at gallery openings. One shattered, and when she looked down, she saw glass shards, red wine streaming across the floor. It was just like blood, just like her mother's.

"Kate?" Conor asked, catching her arm. "What is it?"

She didn't reply. The floor had a slight tilt, built that way in case the basement flooded, and the wine trickled downward toward a narrow drainage trench cut along the south wall. Kate followed the flow. She blinked hard, remembering a time long before the incident, before her mother died.

She and Beth had come into this basement alone. She could see her sister, nine years old, frustration in her eyes.

"You have a hiding place," Beth had said. "It's not fair; I want one too."

Set into the wall was a massive and long-unused stone fireplace and beehive oven with a heavy cast-iron door. Cut into the wall was a metal grate to allow heat to escape, and by wiggling the grate, Kate had been able to remove it and hide her treasures there: Revolutionary War–era coins, a tarnished silver spoon, a speckled black rock she was convinced was a meteorite, and three arrowheads she'd found in the rose garden alongside Mathilda's house.

"Okay, we have to find you a hiding place," Kate said, hugging Beth so she would feel better.

"Like yours," Beth said.

"Yes," Kate had said. "How about this?" She had walked over to the beehive oven, but when she had tried the cast-iron door, it had been locked. There had been a keyhole but no key.

Now, with Conor, Kate walked to the beehive oven and touched the lock. She felt hypnotized, as if the poem, the painting of the brook, the melting ice, and the old memories had put her under a spell. She reached into her pocket and pulled out the key she'd been carrying since she'd found it in the box in Beth's desk drawer.

How could she have not known until now? The heavy square key found its way into the lock, and Kate turned it. The iron door clanged open. She stood staring into the murk, at first not seeing anything.

"Beth's hiding place," she said.

Her fingers brushed spiderwebs as she reached inside. She brought forth a dusty packet of letters written on onionskin paper and tied with a blue ribbon. She held them in her hand, gazing at them as if unsure how they had gotten there. She glanced at one, saw that it was signed *J,* the same script as the signature on the small nude of Beth. All the way at the back of the oven was a brown cardboard mailing tube.

She felt Conor's eyes on her as she pulled it out. Peeking into the tube, she saw that a canvas with ragged edges had been rolled up, stored inside. She reached in with two fingers and carefully withdrew the small furled painting. It felt weightless as she carried it to the workbench, laid it flat, smoothed the sides.

She stared at the familiar nocturne. Summer leaves cast shadows on a black lawn, the filmy light from above illuminating the graceful girl twirling in front of the great stone house.

"*Moonlight*," Conor said.

41

Reid's heart was racing—this painting hadn't been stolen by art thieves. Its existence in the gallery was evidence that someone close to home had placed it here. Reid had mostly ruled Jed out. Although Harris was intelligent, or at least had been before he'd pickled himself, and capable of violence against Beth and stealing the painting, why would he hide the artwork here? It had to be Pete.

"Who had the key?" Reid asked.

Kate acted as if she hadn't heard him. She leaned over, face practically touching the painting, as if she was examining every brush-stroke.

"Beth," she said after a minute. Without looking up, she tried to hand him the key. He didn't touch it. He pulled a clear plastic evidence bag from his pocket and had her drop it in.

He felt the weight of the odd, square-shaped key. "How long have you had this?" he asked, trying not to sound frustrated.

"A few weeks. It was in Beth's desk."

"Would Pete have hidden it there?"

"No," Kate said. "He didn't even know it

existed. It was in a box I gave her, along with a sketch, beneath a false bottom. I had no idea it was there until that day I came back here with you."

"Then how did *Moonlight* get locked in here?"

"Beth. She stole it herself," Kate said in a flat voice. She sounded hypnotized.

Why would Beth steal her own painting? Pete staging a theft made sense, but not Beth. What was she trying to accomplish? Finding *Moonlight* was the most significant part of the case in weeks, and Reid knew he had to get it to the lab. But he was still overwhelmed by how Kate had acted upstairs. She'd gone into a fugue state when he'd tried to kiss her, and she'd led him down into the basement like a sleepwalker.

Standing at the workbench, thinking about the wood engraver, she'd come out of the trance. But once the bottle of wine had broken, the spell had overcome her again, and she had gone straight to the metal door and unlocked it. Had she known the painting would be there? Had she experienced a waking dream?

Did Kate's actions, like Lady Macbeth's, reveal a guilt-ridden mind? He stared at her, wondering if he'd been blind all along. He went back to that first day, at the house when she'd discovered Beth's body and asked if she was a suspect. Had she killed her sister and hidden the painting here? The thoughts rattled his bones.

428

"Kate, why would Beth steal it from herself?" he asked.

"I don't know."

"She couldn't have put it here after she died," he said.

"Then maybe before. I don't know," she said. She turned away from him, held her head in her hands, leaving him to stare at the painting. He knew that the initial examination should be done by a state police lab technician, perhaps with the help of an art conservator, but he put on latex gloves and turned it over anyway.

On the back of the canvas was a rust-colored drawing in the shape of a heart. It looked as if it had been made with blood. At the very bottom was a small smudge, barely a dot.

Kate glanced back, over her shoulder, and fixed her gaze on the heart. She stood beside him, staring down, reaching out with a trembling hand. He felt her wanting to trace the lines with her finger, but she didn't.

Perhaps the blood—he was pretty sure that's what it was—belonged to the artist who had painted *Moonlight* a century ago, but Reid didn't think so. He believed that heart was the signature of whoever had cut the canvas free just months earlier, in July, leaving the blank frame on the wall of Beth Lathrop's bedroom, within sight of her body.

42

Driving toward Mathilda's, Kate needed to clear her head.

Images from the gallery came back to her in quick bursts, starting with the brook painting and poem. She felt as if Beth had been with her, guiding her. She saw herself staring at the pole, touching the wooden surface, hearing a bottle smash, following the red liquid, feeling the heavy key in her hand, unlocking the beehive oven, hearing the creak of metal hinges.

She couldn't remember finding the painting inside, but she had definite, clear memories of seeing Conor hold it in his hands. She could see the heart-shaped scrawl of blood. It reminded her of being sixteen, when she, Beth, Lulu, and Scotty had become blood sisters, pricking their fingers with sewing needles, marking the moment in blood on the endpaper of a book in Mathilda's library.

It always happened this way after an episode. Pictures and memories filled her mind in bits and pieces, as if they had been chopped up with scissors. Dissociation was followed by an aura, cloudiness, and sickness, physiological complications of traumatic shock. Twenty-three years ago, the murky feeling could last for weeks. But more than two decades had gone by, and she had gotten better; her spirit had knit back together. She knew from experience, even though she doubted it every time, that this feeling would pass within the day.

The Porsche passed through the stone gates, tires rumbling up the long gravel drive to Mathilda's house. An allée of beech trees lined the road, their trunks tall blue shadows, September leaves still green but dry, rustling in the interlocking branches overhead. Rounding the last bend, she almost wished to see Pete's black car. She wanted a fight, to discharge the terrible, sick feeling that had been building inside, that always came when she got too close to those twenty-two hours, when her mind blacked out the worst of them and she felt the vertigo of lost time.

But Pete either wasn't here or he had hidden his car. Kate's stomach ached at the idea of seeing Nicola, and she felt it was a mistake, bad judgment, to let her and Tyler stay here. Popcorn jumped out of the convertible and went running out of sight to investigate the paths and hedges. Kate rang the doorbell; a minute later, Nicola answered.

"Kate, hello," Nicola said, taking a step backward and looking worried. "Pete's not here."

"Good, I'm glad. I'm not here to see him."

"I've been looking for a place to rent; I really have," Nicola said. "If you're here to tell me it's time to go, Tyler and I can stay with my mother in Groton."

"You've had Pete staying with you, haven't you?" Kate asked.

"He shows up sometimes."

Kate gave her a long hard stare. "And you don't have the balls to tell him to leave?"

"I'm sorry!" Nicola said.

"You should be. For yourself and for Tyler. Where is he, by the way?"

"Sleeping," she said.

"Can I see him?" Kate asked, surprising herself.

Nicola nodded. She was about five feet four inches, the same height as Beth. Following her, looking at her from behind, Kate felt a pang in her heart. She wanted her sister back. Nicola wore shorts and a white T-shirt, and she was barefoot.

Tyler slept in a blue baby seat in the shade on the wide back porch, his chin tucked onto his chest, arms at his side. His yellow onesie had an orange lion on it. Kate crouched down beside him. She closed her eyes and thought of Matthew. She leaned closer, smelled Tyler's clean baby smell of shampoo and lotion and sleep. When she opened her eyes, she saw that his had fluttered open, and he was looking straight at her.

"He doesn't know me," Kate said, leaning back. "I don't want to scare him."

"He's not scared," Nicola said. "Look, he's watching you."

Tyler's brown eyes were enormous, unblinking as he regarded Kate. He unclenched tiny fists. His fingernails were perfect half moons. Kate pictured Beth as a baby. Even though Kate had been only two, she had signed on for a lifetime of loving and protecting her sister. Her mother used to let her help give Beth a bath, stick the tabs to close her diapers. Kate would lay her finger against the baby's open hand, Beth would squeeze, and Kate would wish she'd never let go.

She had done the same with Sam, and now Tyler, letting him grab her index finger with a hard grip. She glanced up at Nicola, who was smiling. Nicola had brown eyes. Pete's were bright blue. She was glad Tyler's were brown.

Tyler began to fuss, and Nicola picked him up. A thousand birds called from the trees, and the flutter of leaves got louder. It was hurricane season, and Hilda, the latest threat, had skirted the leeward islands, on track to hit the Carolinas and spin out to sea before hitting the northeast coast. Even from so far away, there was an atmospheric disturbance right here on the Connecticut shore. Wild weather excited Kate, as it had Mathilda. The wind helped blow out the cobwebs of trauma.

"I came to ask you something," Kate said.

"Of course, anything," Nicola said, but she sounded apprehensive, as if afraid of what it would be.

"When you worked at the gallery, how often did Beth go down into the basement?"

"The basement?" Nicola asked. "Never. She wouldn't. Because of what happened to her—to you—down there. Even my first month working—while I was cataloging all the sculptures on the shelves—I did it alone. She didn't come down to supervise. I thought she would."

"She must have sometimes," Kate said. "Maybe when you didn't see her."

"I don't think so. Only I did. And Pete, to do the framing."

Kate flinched, picturing Nicola and Pete getting together in the basement while Beth worked upstairs.

Nicola chewed her lower lip, seemed to be thinking something over. She watched Kate for a minute.

"Kate, after Beth was killed, I saw Pete with baby clothes," she said finally.

"Well, you two do have a son."

"They weren't Tyler's. He threw them away. Or at least hid them."

"Where?"

"The dumbwaiter. Kate, I think they were for Matthew."

435

Kate couldn't stand to hear Matthew's name come out of Nicola's lips. "My sister bought clothes for him. So did I. Beth was ready for him to be born. He was her son. She loved him as much as you love Tyler."

"I took them out of the dumbwaiter. They're in the yellow room upstairs."

"Excuse me," Kate said quietly, barely able to contain her emotions. Her head was spinning with the idea of Pete hiding Matthew's clothes. Beth had bought them, so lovingly. She should be holding her baby now. He should be wearing the outfits she'd found for him.

Kate left Nicola standing there and walked into the house. She went upstairs, into the yellow room. Beth had stayed here when they were young. Had Nicola somehow known that? The buttery light was soft and welcoming.

Baby clothes were folded on the bed. Kate sat beside them. She looked without touching for a long time. Three onesies, striped in different bright colors. A sun hat printed with sailboats. Two blue soft terry cloth towels. A package of bibs with Winnie-the-Pooh characters on them. A blue baby blanket monogrammed *ML* that she had given Beth to hold her nephew. That had been the week before they'd died.

Seeing Matthew's things made him even more real. Kate lifted the sun hat, each onesie, the towels, the blanket, and held them to her chest, just as if she were hugging him. She thought of how she would have liked to take him flying. They would take off, bank over the Sound, and see where they lived from the air. She would teach him to fly, just as Mathilda had done for her.

After a while, she took a deep breath. Instead of leaving Matthew's things on the bed, she placed them in the top two drawers of the cherrywood bureau. It made her feel good to think that Beth had kept her clothes in the same drawers.

It felt like a secret, just for herself: keeping Matthew's things in this room where Beth had stayed. Kate was glad she would always know where to find them, the baby clothes her nephew never got to wear.

She went downstairs, into her favorite room of the house: the library. It was warm and ordered, as it had been during her grandmother's life. Tall windows admitted hazy white light that fell in patches on the wide-board pine floors, the antique Sarouk rug. The fireplace smelled faintly of smoke, hinting of fires from chilly days and cold nights when Mathilda was alive.

The bookshelves were perfectly arranged, not alphabetically or according to size, but by color. Although not an artist herself, Mathilda had appreciated the palette, and the books' spines ranged through the spectrum from scarlet to violet.

Kate went to the dark greens. She removed a book—not a first edition; the girls had been careful about that—Vasari's *The Lives of the Artists*. Kate turned to the last page, flipped it over, looked at the yellowed endpaper.

She saw the initials: *K, B, L, S,* written in blood.

They were surrounded by a heart, drawn in their own blood. Kate had been fifteen. It was a year before that day—she and Beth hadn't yet seen the worst of life, still trusted the world. She remembered pressing her fingertip to the page, swooshing the shape, squeezing an extra drop of blood to make a complete heart. Her sister and friends had done the same, tracing over the marks she had left.

"Blood sisters," they'd said, one by one, forming a circle and facing each other, pressing their palms together and clasping fingers.

"My secrets are your secrets," Beth said.

"No secrets between us," Scotty said.

"May our circle be free of secrets," Lulu said.

"Forevermore," Kate said.

"Promise, promise, promise, promise," each of them said.

And with a kiss they'd sealed the promise of sisterhood, friendship, secrets, and blood, bonds that would never break.

But there had been lies, and hurts, and secrets, and broken bonds and promises.

Kate stared at the smudged heart. This was

what she had come here to see. It looked exactly like the one drawn on the back of *Moonlight*: a blood heart, the symbol of the Compass Rose. She closed the book. Instead of putting it back on the shelf, she walked to the long mahogany table. Her family had a tradition of leaving books they wanted to return to later, but soon, stacked here instead of reshelving them. She wanted to leave this one out so she could find it again easily.

As she was about to place it on the table, the book at the top of the pile caught her attention. An exquisite volume with green paper-covered boards over a green cloth spine, the title and author's name stamped in gilt: *West-Running Brook*, by Robert Frost.

Where Beth had clearly left it, intending to read it again soon.

43

"Hey, Conor," Winifred Sibley said, walking into Reid's office. Tall and thin, with short white hair and bright-blue eyes, she gave him a huge smile, and he beamed back. She was the state's chief accountant and a Reid family friend, and he had asked her to come to the Major Crime Squad to go over the Lathrops' financials with him.

"Hi, Winnie," he said, hugging her. "I'm really glad to see you."

"And I you, as always. You've got a lot going on, kid," she said, lifting her black briefcase.

"Hope you have something good for me in there," he said.

"That depends on how you define *good,*" she said, giving him a wry smile.

"Why don't we go into the conference room? It will be more comfortable there. Can I get you a coffee?"

"Yes, please," she said.

"I remember," he said.

He went to the break room and filled two mugs. It had been a busy, frustrating week. Judge Caroline Walker granted the warrants for Pete's electronics, and the marshals executed them. They seized his computers and mobile phone. Analysts examined the hard drives, documenting his search history. Jennifer Miano had had her knee surgery; she had come through with flying colors, but it would be a long recuperation, so Reid had scoured the reports alone. And he'd found no evidence that Pete had searched for instructions on how to beat a polygraph exam.

After entering the conference room, he handed Winnie her coffee and sat down on the other side of the long walnut table. She was about Reid's dad's age, and they had met when they were both young cops. Over the years his dad had decided he was happiest patrolling the streets of New London, and Winnie had used her business degree to rise through the ranks of the state police.

"How's your brother?" Winnie asked.

"Tom's great," Reid said. "Other than giving me grief every chance he gets."

"Ah, the two Reid boys. Still the same."

Winnie started to unpack her briefcase. Reid watched her place two black vinyl three-ring binders on the table. Then she looked up and gazed at him with those clear, intelligent blue eyes.

"What, Winnie?" he asked.

"I recognized the connection right away. Beth Woodward. I know how much she and her sister

442

mean to you. I remember everything about the gallery crime—I had just gotten my master's in accounting, and I was assigned to go through the books."

"Yeah, I know," Reid said. "I remember that."

"It was a bad one. Your father was worried about you," she said. "He knew you'd carry it for a long time. And here you are again, same family."

Reid stared out the window behind Winnie, at the rolling hills, blue in the afternoon shadows. He had the feeling she wanted to reach across the desk, touch his hand.

"I'm okay," he said, steeling himself against the feelings: for how his father had cared about him, how Winnie did now.

"Anyway, let's get down to business," she said.

"The Lathrop family's financials," Reid said.

"Yes. And here's why my work is so much easier than yours. I follow the numbers. They are so nice and tidy. There's no blood, no death. They don't care who the killer is, and they don't lie."

"So what do they say?" Reid asked.

Winnie pushed the two black binders toward him. "The one on the left contains balance sheets from the Lathrop Gallery. Their earnings and losses, salaries and benefits, the purchases and sales of art going back to the year Beth married Pete. The one on the right contains Beth's trust documents."

Reid reached for the one on the right. He flipped it open and saw that Winnie had annotated each page, marked some with brightly colored Post-it notes.

"It's a complicated trust," Winnie said. "Originally set up by Mathilda Harkness."

Reid scanned the first page—there were a hundred more to go through.

"Can you boil it down for me?" he asked. "Mainly, what does Pete get and when does he get it? Half the gallery? Will he have to share it with Kate?"

"No," Winnie said. "Beth's interest in the gallery goes directly to Sam, to be overseen by Kate. That includes the real estate, the works of art and all other assets, and the business itself. Pete receives nothing."

"Nothing?"

"Beth leaves him a lump sum of money from her own investment account."

"How much?" Reid asked, riffling through the pages.

"One point five million dollars," she said.

That stopped Reid short. "Well, there's a motive," he said.

"Until you consider that Beth's entire estate is worth seventy-five million dollars. And add in the fact that Pete does not receive the money free and clear. It is in trust. And Kate is the trustee."

"So . . ."

"It will be her discretion as to how much is paid out and when."

"Still, one point five is a lot," he said.

"Conor, he would have gotten much more in a divorce. They didn't have a prenup. They have a sixteen-year-old daughter, and if he claimed he had helped Beth build the business, he could have a good case."

"Did he know what was in the will?"

"The trust," she said, correcting him. "The documents were on Beth's computer in the gallery, attached to an email from her lawyer."

"I doubt she gave Pete her password," he said.

"Her computer wasn't password protected. And our tech guys determined the trust documents were accessed after her death." Winnie paused. "Beth's Gmail account had a very easily guessed password."

"What, Sam's birthday?"

"Yes, combined with the name Popcorn and Beth and Pete's wedding anniversary."

"Can Pete contest the trust?"

"No. It's brilliantly written and quite unbreakable. Pete is out of the business, will only be able to stay in the house if Kate, as trustee, allows it, and will walk away with a sum that, from what I gather by looking at his rather extravagant expenses, will be gone in two years. Unless he receives wise investment advice."

"So this means he would have been better off . . . ," Reid said.

"With Beth alive. A divorce would have been in his interests. Not murder," Winnie said.

"There goes his financial motive," Reid said.

"I'm sorry," she said. "I have the feeling this isn't what you wanted to hear. It doesn't help your case against him."

And neither did the search of Pete's hard drives, Reid thought. Ahab's white whale had killed him in the end. That's what obsession could do. He shook his head hard, as if he could clear out the fog. Winnie was right; her work was easier: numbers didn't lie, and they didn't care.

"Eye on the ball," Reid said out loud.

"I've heard that before," Winnie said.

"Yeah. Dad always said it."

"You can do this," she said. "You're going to solve this case."

"I appreciate you thinking that," he said.

"I have no way of knowing whether Pete is your killer or not. He still might be, Conor. There are motives other than money."

"True," Reid said, but his heart wasn't in it. He didn't want to talk anymore. He felt as if he had been building his whole case on a ton of emotions and not enough evidence. The opposite of keeping his eye on the ball. His father wouldn't be proud of him, and Reid certainly wasn't proud of himself.

He hugged Winnie and walked her down the hall to the front door. Then he returned to his office and stared at his desk.

It was time to start again.

44

Kate walked Popcorn along the city waterfront while Sam did homework upstairs in the loft. Dark water swirled with reflected orange light. The rusty bulkhead and rocky shore were littered with old tires, broken pilings, the fiberglass core of a foundered boat, all exposed by the outgoing tide. Waves from the wakes of passing ferries sloshed the shore. Amid the cacophony of trains and ships, Kate sought white noise, but nothing stilled her thoughts of *Moonlight* hidden in the beehive oven, hearts of blood scrawled more than twenty years apart.

On her way back from the walk, she saw someone sitting on the steps of the Maritime Museum across the street from her loft. When she got closer, the man stood. The streetlights illuminated him, and she recognized Jed. Popcorn hustled over, wriggling with pleasure as he reached down to pet him.

"Hey, boy; hey, boy," he said. Then, looking up at Kate, "I was waiting for you."

"How did you know where I lived?" she asked.

"Beth showed me," he said. "We'd take walks after finishing up at the soup kitchen, and she'd always steer me down here. She loved you, Kate."

Kate looked up at the sky at the mention of her sister.

"I know," she said.

"She wanted to be closer to you," Jed said. "She wanted you to know about us. Every time we walked by, she hoped you'd be coming out your door, leaving the building, and that you'd see us."

"Why didn't she just bring you upstairs?"

"She was afraid of how you would react. An accidental meeting would be okay, but she thought it would be too aggressive to throw it in your face."

Kate glanced up at the tall windows of her apartment. The lights were all on; Sam was still up.

"What made you come here now?" Kate asked.

"You're the only other person in the world," he said, "who loved her as much as I did. Sam, of course, but I can't talk to her. I can't stand how much I miss her, Kate. I just want to talk about her."

"Yes, I want that too," Kate said.

"Can I buy you a tea?" Jed asked.

They walked two blocks to Witchfire Teahouse, open till midnight. Thessaly sat at a back table, reading tarot cards, not looking up when they brushed through strings of bells hanging in the entrance. They took a table, and Popcorn lay beneath it on the painted wood floor. A young waitress with a blue streak in her blonde hair and a ring in her nose took their order: a large pot of Earl Grey.

"When you said she wanted me to know about *us,*" Kate said, "what does that mean?"

"We were together," he said. "She was my person; I was hers."

She stared at him. He wasn't much older than thirty, seven or eight years younger than Beth.

"What about the fact she was married?" she asked.

"Pete didn't deserve her. He was a bastard, and she'd had enough. She stopped being able to pretend and put up with it, even for Sam's sake. She was going to leave him."

"And be with you?"

"She was already with me."

"But she was living with him."

"Presence is only part of it. Intent and feelings are what count."

He held out his left hand, showed her a ring. White gold or platinum, etched with fine markings. "She gave it to me, and I gave one to her. We designed them together. They were going to be our wedding bands, but we figured, why wait to wear them? They were our promise to each other."

Promise to each other. The same phrase had

451

run through Kate's mind just hours ago, remembering the blood sister ceremony. She leaned over the table to examine the ring's delicate engraving more closely, but the dim light made it impossible.

"Earl Grey," the waitress said, setting down the blue-and-white bone china pot and two mismatched chipped porcelain cups and saucers. She poured the tea, then took a pewter sugar bowl off another table and left it with a pitcher of milk.

"Beth wasn't wearing hers," Kate said as soon as the waitress walked away.

"She only wore it when we were together."

"Did Pete know about you?"

He frowned and looked troubled, didn't speak as he stirred sugar into his tea.

"Did he know, Jed?" she repeated.

"I'm not sure. She was going to tell him."

"Tell him what?"

"That we were in love. That she was divorcing him."

Kate sat up straighter. She thought of what Conor had said, about Pete's anger building as he realized everything he was losing.

"When?"

"Well, she planned to when we saw each other a few days before he left on the boat trip." He paused. "But I don't know if she followed through."

"Why wouldn't she let you know?"

452

"I never spoke to her again. We were together that day—at my tent, don't think it's weird, Beth was the most, I don't know, refined, elegant, whatever you want to call it, person I've ever known, but we were happy there. She could let all the bullshit go, all her unhappiness, and just be. Just be Beth. She left my tent that day, and I headed out to Fishers Island. She was supposed to talk to him, and she never called to let me know if she did."

"Why didn't you go looking for her?"

He stirred his tea, the milk swirling in the amber liquid, and was quiet for a long time. She had the feeling he was figuring out something to say. Inventing it as he went along? She waited.

"I wanted to. I felt like getting a ferry back from Fishers, going to see her. But I thought maybe he'd talked her out of it. That she'd changed her mind," he said finally. "It was up to her to tell me, and she didn't."

"Really? But you were so sure. You gave each other rings. You promised each other."

"I know that. I hate myself for doubting her. But I live in a fucking tent. She's Beth Woodward. She comes from all that. Maybe she decided she didn't want to give it up."

Kate thought, *The money is Beth's, not Pete's. He'd be the one giving it up.*

"To Beth a promise is a promise," Kate said instead. But was that true? Even after the

453

ceremony, the vows marked with blood, she and Beth hadn't stayed close. "Are you the baby's father?"

"What do you think?"

"Were you?"

"You went through my tent. I know you took the sonogram."

"A ring, a baby," Kate said. "But you didn't even go to see her when you couldn't get in touch. To find out what was wrong. What if it was a problem with the pregnancy? Especially if the baby was yours."

"Look, she wouldn't tell me, okay?"

"Whether you were Matthew's father?"

"Yeah," he said. "At first, when she found out she was pregnant, she said I was. But about a month before she died, she backed off from that. She told me it was possible Pete was."

"Did she even know?" Kate asked.

"She must have," Jed said. "Because when she and I got together, there was nothing between her and Pete. She said it had been over a year. That's why I was so sure."

He sounded miserable.

"So what happened a month before she died?" Kate asked. "To make her be unsure?"

"I don't know. Maybe there was just one time with him; maybe he forced her. I can't stand to think of either possibility. I think back six months before she died—February. That's when Matthew

454

was conceived. We were so happy; even before we found out she was pregnant, we knew we wanted to be together."

Kate thought about that. If Beth had any doubts, why had she given him the sonogram? Had something happened last summer to make her want to push Jed away?

"This must be hard on you," Kate said.

"Fuck yeah, it is. But in my mind, in my heart, I know for sure I am Matthew's father," he said. "I feel it, Kate. She told me she'd stopped being with Pete long before she and I got together. But then . . ." He trailed off, as if remembering something painful. "After a while, during the pregnancy, she began to seem so sad."

"About the baby?"

"About the whole thing. She cried a lot, and I had no idea how to help her. She said Sam would be upset—she already had to deal with her father having Tyler. She was really worried about Sam. I said I'd be Sam's stepdad; I'd do anything to help her. But she just seemed to get farther away from me."

"Did she say more about it?"

"She said she'd messed up her life, that everything was so complicated. I told her I loved her and our baby, and she could count on that—that she hadn't messed up her life, that we'd have a *great* life."

Kate heard the passion and tears in his voice.

455

She waited for him to be able to go on. "That's when she said, 'No one can count on anyone.' I was shocked—I didn't know what she meant. She told me she couldn't plan anything—being with me, staying with Pete. It was because of him— he's the one who messed her up. He treated her so badly."

"But she was so happy to be having the baby," Kate said. "She told me—I could see it in her."

"I know," Jed said. "She loved Matthew. It was the rest of her life that was making her crazy. Including me."

"You?"

"She loved me. But she felt pressured. I didn't want to put that on her, but she felt it anyway. She didn't want to keep me hanging—but she couldn't be sure she should leave Pete, upset Sam's life that way." He shook his head. "I figured she would sort things out once Sam was at camp and Pete left on his trip. I thought she'd tell me the truth, that I was the father. She wouldn't feel so caught in the middle."

"Except you didn't see her. Why, Jed? If you expected to hear the truth from her, why didn't you just go over there?"

"I told you! I was on Fishers Island. Beth arranged it, having me stay with her friends, give their grandkids drawing classes. I didn't want to go. I wanted to be there to celebrate with her after

456

she told Pete. I thought we'd be together then—for the rest of our lives."

"Did you tell her you didn't want to go to Fishers Island?"

"Of course. But she had made the effort for me, and I didn't want to turn down a paying gig. My goal is—was—to pay my own way with her. She said she needed time alone. She was drowning in everything—the responsibility for everyone's happiness, doing the right thing for Sam, for everyone she loved, and for us. I told her all I needed was her. She didn't answer." He coughed as if he was choking. Tears streamed from his eyes.

Kate felt tense, watching him. His emotion was hot, pouring off him. She felt it on her own face, scalding her cheeks.

"I had no idea what to think," he said, sounding as if he was about to explode. "Maybe she'd changed her mind about us—the guilt, the pressure, was too much for her. I'll be honest; I was pissed. Hurt, whatever." The anger seemed to leak out of him. He took a deep breath and peered at Kate. "Can you believe that? I wasted all that time feeling sorry for myself when she needed me."

Kate couldn't reply or even look at him.

"You hate me?" he asked. "Well, I hate myself. What if I'd gone earlier and could have stopped it?"

"Yeah, what if you had?"

"I would never have thought of what happened to her. That he could do what he did to her." His voice broke again. "Kill her."

"Did Pete think the baby was yours?" Kate asked. She felt sick, thinking of what he might have done to Beth if he had.

"I have no idea."

"You just said you were pissed. You could have refused to go to Fishers Island. You must have known there would be fireworks if Beth gave him that kind of news."

"You have no idea how guilty I feel about that. I think about it every day. What did she tell him; how did he react? What was that last day of life for her? I drive myself crazy thinking about it. Nothing you say can make me feel worse than I do already."

"I'm sorry," she said, her throat tight, knowing how much time *she* spent thinking about Beth's last day too.

He stood up, started to leave. Her hand shot out and grabbed his wrist.

"Don't go," she said. "Jed, I'm just so glad my sister was loved. That she was happy with you. I believe you when you say that."

"She was. We both were."

"The drawing you did of her—it was beautiful. I could tell, just by looking at it, that you adored her."

"That's the word I would use too," he said.

"Can I ask you—how did you decide where to pitch your tent?"

"Beth," he said. "She took me to the island to draw flowers, but then she showed me that spot up the hill. It was private, under the pines, and she loved the sound of the brook."

The brook.

Kate looked at his face, still streaked with tears. He had a faraway gaze in his eyes, as if everything he cared about was distant. What did it feel like to adore someone and to be loved this way?

"Can I see your ring?" she asked.

He pulled it off his finger, placed it in her palm. The metal felt warm.

"You designed it, you said?" she asked.

"We both did. The hearts were hers, the words were mine. Same line on both rings. My idea. I wanted the line to be about her, for her, and I needed it next to my skin."

Kate held the ring to the flickering Edison bulb in the brass sconce on the wall. The line was engraved in tiny script, but she knew it well.

"It's from a poem she used to read to me," Jed said.

Kate closed her eyes and couldn't speak. The words were from "West-Running Brook." Beth and Jed were each other's north, and the brook ran west.

"Pete thought—lots of people did—that Beth

was settled, that what you saw with her was what you got, a lady who lived in a big house and dealt with high-priced art and rich collectors. She was so much more than that. She wanted to give it all up for me, go everywhere, feel everything."

Kate was silent, thinking of the poem: *contraries in love.*

"She wouldn't have given Sam up," she said after a moment.

"No. Never. She would have fought him for Sam—we both would have."

Kate turned the ring to see the other markings. The hearts were Beth's, Jed had said. Under each were three dots.

"Ellipses? To be continued?" she asked.

"No. Those are drops of blood."

Kate's pulse quickened. She pictured the scrawled hearts on the back of the canvas and on the last page of Vasari's *The Lives of the Artists*, the book at Mathilda's house.

"Blood hearts," she said.

"Yes," he said, sounding surprised. "That's what she called them."

"Did you ever see *Moonlight*? The painting?"

"She told me about it. How it was stolen during that time, when they tied you up and your mother died."

"You never saw the back of it, the unpainted side? What was drawn there?"

"No," he said. "She never even showed me the

460

canvas. Why are you asking about the back?"

"No reason," Kate said, still staring at the hearts on the ring. "I was just wondering." Then, "Where did she keep her ring?"

Jed reached into his pocket, pulled it out, placed it on the table.

It was beautiful, smaller than Jed's. Beth had worn it. Kate picked it up. She closed her eyes and felt her sister's passion. She turned it over and over in her hand, but Jed reached over and took it from her before she could slip it onto her own finger.

45

The first Saturday after school started, Kate went to the hardware store and bought an eco-friendly gel that wouldn't leach into the sea. She filled a bag with safety goggles and gloves. She and Sam met Lulu, Scotty, and Isabel at Little Beach, and they scrubbed the boulders, removing the graffitied paint from the granite and quartz. After a while, Lulu, Scotty, and Kate left Sam and Isabel to finish the job and sat on a beach blanket to supervise. Julie walked the tide line, looking for sea glass.

September skies were bluer than August, the sea cleaner, less churned up by boat traffic. A good breeze blew the tops off low waves, sent beach grass skittering and tracing circles on the hard sand. Kate had always loved this time of year, when vacations were over and she and her friends had the beach to themselves. Even over here, this hidden, private place felt more isolated. People weren't likely to come through the path.

Kate walked down to the water's edge, picked up a piece of tide-scoured driftwood. Bleached silver by salt and sun, bark scraped off, it was a foot long, the thin, sharp tip of a broken branch.

When she returned to the blanket, Scotty was on the phone with Nick, and Lulu was lying on her back, face to the sun.

Waiting for Scotty to finish her call, Kate looked at her right index finger. For nearly a year after that day in Mathilda's library, when they were teenagers, there had been a fine scar on the pad, from where she had pricked it, coaxed blood to bubble out. The mark had long since disappeared. When Scotty hung up, she shaded her eyes to look at Kate. So did Lulu.

After smoothing a patch of sand beside the beach blanket, Kate used the branch to write the letters *K, B, L, S.* She encircled them with a heart.

"Do you remember?" she asked.

"Blood sisters," Lulu said. "We wrote in the book."

"A long time ago," Scotty said.

"Time wasn't supposed to matter," Kate said.

"And it didn't," Lulu said, holding out her hand, grabbing Kate's. "Not to me."

"Feeling sentimental?" Scotty asked.

"More like confused," Kate said.

"About what?" Lulu asked.

"My sister's secrets," Kate said.

"Which we helped her to keep," Lulu said.

"Are you blaming us?" Scotty asked.

"We promised never to keep secrets from each other," Kate said.

"Beth and I were fourteen," Scotty said. "You

two were fifteen. We didn't even know, really, what secrets meant. Look at them." She nodded toward Sam and Isabel. "They think they're so grown up, but they're babies."

"I think we knew exactly what secrets were," Kate said slowly, "when we were young. How powerful they are, how they can hurt. I think we've forgotten as we've grown up. At least Beth and I did. She was my sister, and I had no idea about her real life."

"Jed?" Lulu asked.

Kate nodded. "She was leaving Pete for him. She wanted to marry him. I didn't even know he existed."

"Kate," Scotty said. "I don't mean this in any sort of cruel way . . ."

"Nice way to start your thought," Lulu said dryly.

"Take it as you will. But Beth was in love. Head over heels, madly in love. Feeling that way lends itself to secrets—makes it more delicious, maybe. However, it was never all one thing. There were some issues . . . she couldn't make up her mind about. And, Kate, she was being sensitive to you."

"How?" Kate asked.

"Well, love isn't your thing. That kind of love, anyway."

"Scotty, is that vodka in your water bottle?" Lulu asked.

"She's right," Kate said.

"You loved Beth, you love Sam, you love us," Lulu said.

"That's not the same as *in love,*" Scotty said.

"Will you please shut up?" Lulu asked.

"I meant it in a good way, truly," Scotty said. "When you think of the fucking nightmare it can be, finding the right person, and even *afterward*—all Nick seems to do these days is run and train. He's clearly trying to escape something; I only hope it isn't me—ha. I really am sorry if it came out wrong, Katy."

"It's okay," Kate said, giving her friends a big smile, reassuring them that she was fine, not offended. "But, Scotty, what couldn't she make up her mind about?"

Scotty frowned for a second before speaking. "Well, um," she began.

Kate had a sudden, shocking feeling she was trying to get her story straight. "Just tell me. Don't be afraid of hurting my feelings."

"Okay. It was just the pregnancy. You can't even imagine what it's like if you haven't been . . . Sorry, but it's like, expectant-mom brain. Hard to make decisions."

"Like whether to stay with Pete?" Lulu asked.

"Like that," Scotty said.

"What did she say about it?" Kate asked.

"She was under a lot of pressure," Scotty said. "She felt she had to make everyone happy."

That's what Jed said, Kate thought.

"To the point it completely messed with her moral compass," Scotty continued.

"Her *moral compass?*" Lulu asked with complete incredulity in her voice. "She was an amazing, complicated woman."

"Yes, she was," Scotty said. "She taught me so much. Even at the soup kitchen. She didn't just serve the meals. She sat down with everyone, wanted to hear about their lives. She was interested. And I've gotten that way too. I don't just go there so I can be all church lady and say, 'Oh, I'm such a good person.' I look forward to it. Getting to know new friends. People who got in trouble but are trying to turn their lives around."

"I had no idea you were so involved," Kate said.

"Well, like I said, Beth taught me. The ones who knew her miss her terribly. They want to know what's happening with her case, and I do my best to fill them in and let them get their feelings out. You just wouldn't believe the emotion. It's a completely different perspective than you get in stuffy old Black Hall."

Kate smiled at Scotty. She could hear an echo of Beth's compassion in her words. Lulu stretched on the blanket, September sunbathing. Scotty squeezed Kate's hand, mouthed *Love you,* then peered at her phone's screen, scrolling through Facebook.

Love. Kate thought of the words *in love.* Love, in love, love, in love. Such different states of being, of feeling. An image came to her mind—a man and a woman standing in an art gallery, close enough to kiss each other. She remembered that moment of feeling desire. The memory of Conor came with an emotion too strong to bear, so she pushed it away.

While the girls continued to scrub the garish paint off the granite boulder, as the muted soft browns and grays emerged again, streaks of pearl-white quartz, Kate walked farther down the beach. She pictured her sister and Scotty at the soup kitchen; it sounded as if Beth was guiding Scotty still.

Just before Kate got to the next rock outcropping, she stopped. She cleared a patch of seaweed from the tide line and used her driftwood branch to write in the sand. Crouching down, she wrote her sister's name. She wrote her own. She drew two hearts, two drops of blood. She drew a full moon and squiggled a path of light on the waves. She drew stairs leading to a basement. She drew stick figures of one woman and two girls tied together, heads bowed. She enclosed the entire tableau in a heart.

46

Scotty stared at Kate, halfway down the beach, and wondered what she would have thought to know Beth had considered doing something drastic about the baby. Beth hadn't actually put it into words, but she'd expressed such misgivings. She'd been just a few weeks along, fighting morning sickness at the soup kitchen. Scotty had hustled her outside, away from the lunch line and the smells of roast chicken and sweet potatoes.

"How am I going to do this?" Beth had asked. "I can't handle it."

"You're just upset," Scotty had said. "Not thinking clearly, understandably."

"Scotty, I'm so worried. I'm terrified about what's going to happen, how it's going to affect Sam, our whole family. God, what a mess I've made of everything."

"A new little baby to love," Scotty said. "How is that a mess?"

"Pete? Jed?" Beth said.

"It's not about them," Scotty said.

"Well, actually it is," Beth said. "And what about Sam? I feel as if we've already failed her—

she's going downhill. You see it when she's with Isabel, don't you?"

"She's holding her own," Scotty said. She'd grabbed some saltines from the condiment table, and she ripped open the cellophane and handed Beth a cracker. Beth leaned against the church wall and took tiny nibbles.

"I don't think she is," Beth said.

"Frankly, Beth, I don't see how that enters the equation. Look at my family! We were per-fect—we thought we were—Nick, me, and our amazing Isabel. Then Julie, with her problems—you can't imagine how hard it's been. I don't complain; I never would—but there have been sacrifices. Do we love her any less because she has issues?"

"I know how much you love her."

"*Both* my children. And you'll love both of *yours*," Scotty said.

"I know. Of course," Beth said, slowly eating the rest of the cracker. "I'm just scared, Scotty. I never thought this would be my life."

"None of us ever think our lives would be our lives," Scotty said. She stared hard at Beth and wondered what she was planning. What had she really meant when she'd said she couldn't handle it? Scotty had plenty of problems, and Beth had no idea. Beth had the perfect house, money, a business, a career. It gave Scotty a strange, shameful thrill to know that Beth had screwed up. Everyone idolized her. Scotty felt glad that Beth could turn to her. She was the only one Beth was expressing her doubts to. And it was up to Scotty to support her.

Two clients from the soup kitchen walked out of the building. Rosalie, whose children had been taken from her by DCF, and Martin, one of the most tragic cases of all—a brilliant man who chose the wrong path in life.

"Hi," Beth called to them, waving. "How are you doing?"

"I'm great, Beth," Rosalie said. "I'm going to see my kids on Saturday. Two hours with them. We're going to the aquarium."

"That's fantastic, Rosalie!" Beth said. Scotty watched her. Even in her own despair, Beth was so enthusiastic in supporting other people.

"You've got to take them to the Treworgy Planetarium too," Martin said. "At Mystic Seaport."

"Oh, I love the Seaport," Scotty said, entering into the spirit.

"Have a good day, you guys," Beth said. Rosalie and Martin waved and were on their way. Scotty had the feeling they were heading to the package store. She knew drinkers when she saw them.

"Everything will work out," Scotty said to Beth when they were alone again.

"Are you sure?" Beth asked.

"Honey, you have morning sickness. You can't think straight when you feel like you might throw up at any moment."

"You're right about that."

"Let's take a little walk," Scotty said. "It will clear your head."

"Thanks, Scotty," Beth said, giving her a big hug. "I don't know what I'd do without you. Life is going to get crazy when people find out." She touched her belly.

"Well, I'll be there for you no matter what," Scotty said.

She held out the cellophane pack, and Beth took another cracker.

"Chew it slowly," Scotty had said. "Too fast and you'll get sick. There you go; that's the way."

It had touched her, the way Beth had listened to her. Respected what she had had to say. Complied with Scotty's suggestions, even about eating a saltine.

Sitting on the beach, Scotty reflected on how it had seemed almost as if Beth were a child instead of Scotty's best friend.

PART III

47

November 16

Lulu counted the months without Beth. Summer ended; fall sped along. The holidays, starting with Beth's birthday, would be here soon, and no one wanted to face them. A blast of Arctic air, extreme for November, slashed down from Canada. At dusk, when the light was lavender, Lulu bundled up in her red fleece jacket and drove north, past Mathilda's stone gates, to one of the oldest cemeteries in Connecticut.

She parked on the road, slung a brown leather bag over her shoulder, and climbed to the top of the hill. Heronwood Cemetery was surrounded by a wall built before the Revolutionary War. Colonists were buried here, graves dating back to the seventeenth century. The first time she had visited, on a late May afternoon two decades before, had been with Beth. Although Beth had had her driver's permit, she hadn't had her license yet, and Kate had been on a flying trip with Mathilda, so Lulu had driven her here. Beth had wanted to visit her mother's grave.

They walked past stones and crosses so old, time and the elements had scoured the engravings down to nothing. Other graves still bore ancient etchings of angels, death's heads, sailing ships. Helen Woodward's headstone was at the northeast end of the graveyard beneath a Norway spruce. A great horned owl roosted above, fast asleep in the middle of the day. The ground was covered with pellets of hair and bone. Beth knelt on the grass. Lulu sat beside her.

"It feels so weird to be here," Beth said. "I don't know what to say."

At first, Lulu thought Beth was talking to her, but Beth faced the stone. She traced the engraving of her mother's name and dates with her finger, leaned close, and whispered.

"Well, I do know. What I want to say, anyway," Beth went on. "I miss you. Do you know how much I miss you? Are you really here? Be here, please, Mom."

Lulu looked away, embarrassed. Should she leave? But Beth seemed barely aware of her presence. Lulu looked up into the branches of a nearby white oak, watched a downy woodpecker hop up a groove in the bark as if it were a well-worn trail.

"Dad didn't do it," Beth whispered, touching the stone. "I mean, I know what they say, but I can't believe it. I *don't* believe it, Mom. He wouldn't have; he couldn't have; he loves us. I think it was those people, only those people, the Andersons. Joshua and Sally—they have such normal names. They look like regular people; Kate and I saw them in court. They look normal, but they're evil. Dad's not evil, Mom. He's nothing like them. He wouldn't have done that to you. They did it on their own. It was their idea, not Dad's. You know that, right?"

"Beth," Lulu said softly.

"Kate believes it was Dad, though. She said it was his plan, and that's even worse than what the Andersons did. She's glad he's in prison. But we're his family; he couldn't have told them to tie us up. He would never have let us be hurt. Let you die. Mom, you and I know that, even if Kate doesn't."

Beth was sobbing. She braced herself against the stone, as if it was keeping her from falling over. Still on her knees, she put her arms around it, embraced the gravestone as if it were actually her mother, not just the marker of where she was buried. Lulu had tried to pull her away, but Beth had wrenched her shoulders from Lulu's hands and clung more tightly to her mother's stone.

Lulu walked to the spot now. The massive Norway spruce was gone, probably felled by a storm. Twenty-three years ago, Helen's grave had stood alone here. Now it was one of four— Mathilda's, Ruth's, and Beth's. Lulu stared at the newly engraved name, letters scored deeply into the granite:

Elizabeth Woodward Lathrop, *Beloved by Her Family*

"And friends," Lulu said, kneeling on the ground, just as Beth had done. She stared at the dates. She and Beth had come here one Saturday in late spring; Beth's father's and the Andersons' trials had lasted all through the winter, and by the time Lulu and Beth had visited Helen, the lilacs had already bloomed and leaves were on the trees. It had been a bright, sunny day.

But now, all these years later, Lulu had come to the graveyard alone, and it was evening. The moon closest to the autumn equinox was the harvest moon, and tonight it would be full. Lulu had waited until this moment to visit Beth for the first time since her death; it seemed not only appropriate but necessary.

She sat still. The cold air had silenced the crickets. The night's first owl called from a pine up the hill. She turned her head to look and saw the moon. Just starting to come up, it was large and orange and filled the eastern sky. It seemed to rise fast, nearly clearing the tree line, just like the moon in the painting.

"Beth," she said out loud. "What did we start?" And what would Kate think if she knew? That sliced Lulu's heart more than anything.

Proof of love, Beth had said to explain her reasons. *And proof of the opposite.*

Love had its own internal logic. What made sense at the start could spin out of control, turn into a mystery. An adventure of revenge could become tragedy. Had they thought of their act as vengeance? Beth hadn't called it that. She had wanted to be bold and defiant, to send Pete a message, to take what was hers and, in doing so, reclaim her life.

The moon was a silver disc. Its light dappled through the pine boughs, oak and maple leaves. Lulu stared into the glade beyond the graveyard. She was sure she saw an apparition, a young girl dancing in the moonlight.

She reached into her leather bag and removed a pocketknife, the blade sheathed in bone. She'd had it since she was twelve and taking sailing lessons. The instructor had told the class that all sailors needed to carry a knife at all times, that it could save their lives. The wind had such strong force, filling the sails, driving the boat forward, tightening lines that could trap a person, wrap around a wrist or an ankle, drag a person overboard. With a knife, you could cut yourself free, save your own life.

Lulu held her knife now. So often she had wished Kate had had one with her in the gallery basement. She could have sliced their bonds, rescued herself and Beth and their mother. It had seemed fitting that Lulu had brought this one to Beth's house that hot day this past July, the week before Beth died. They had stood in the bedroom.

"Why do I feel like a pirate?" Beth had asked, holding Lulu's knife.

"You're Grace O'Malley," Lulu had said. "Rebel woman, pirate queen, a quadrant of the Compass Rose, pillager of idiots, leader of your clan."

"My clan," Beth had said, hand on her pregnant belly. Earlier that day, she had let Lulu feel Matthew kick. "And I am about to pillage."

The dancing girl in the painting by Ben Morrison might have been any of them, but it had always reminded Lulu of Kate. The house looked as if it belonged in Black Hall. The moon cast a spell.

Within seven days, Beth was dead. Lulu knew that what they had done that day had been the catalyst for Beth's murder. She opened the pocketknife now and cut her finger. She watched four tiny drops of her blood fall onto Beth's grave. Despite the frost, the earth was still soft, and the blood drained into the dark soil and disappeared, as if it had never been there.

Lulu held the tip of her finger till the bleeding stopped. A few snowflakes began to fall. She stared at Beth's headstone for a few minutes, focused on the date of her birth: November 21, five days away. The stark realization that Beth wouldn't be here for it filled Lulu with more sorrow than she'd ever felt in her life. The owl had fallen silent. Lulu imagined she had flown out for a night's hunting. The only sound was wind in the leaves. She slipped the knife back into her satchel and walked through the graveyard to her car.

48

Tests on the unpainted side of *Moonlight* came back. Reid sat at his desk in his home office, scanning the data. He was partly surprised by it. He had not expected the blood to be Pete's—the romantic gesture of a drawn heart wouldn't be Pete's style, and besides, since meeting with Winnie, he had taken his focus off Pete. It had started to make sense the blood might be Beth's—given the hiding place known mainly to her and Kate—but he hadn't seen the Tallulah Granville component coming. The left side of the heart had been sketched with Beth's blood, the right side with Lulu's.

There was also a tiny smudge—not red at all; it looked like a coffee stain, blood possibly older than the lines in the heart, or perhaps it had been there since the painting had been made. It had been left by a third person. Although the DNA wasn't in the database, the markers indicated it belonged to a female.

Lulu had been fingerprinted for her various airline jobs. Her DNA was on file because she had once been a suspect in an assault. Reid hunched over his desk, reading the report. Five years ago, a woman named Danielle Marvin had accused Lulu of domestic violence. They were both pilots at different airlines, sharing an apartment in Greenwich Village. Danielle claimed Lulu attacked her one night. The file revealed photographs of Danielle with bruises around her neck, a bite mark on her shoulder.

From the start, Lulu denied it. She claimed she had moved out a week before and that Danielle had become obsessed with her. Lulu had, in fact, filed for a restraining order, and it had been granted. Reid read the copy that was in the electronic file. The order of protection was based on an antistalking statute and detailed ways Danielle had installed spyware on Lulu's laptop and a GPS tracker in her luggage. She told friends and coworkers that she and Lulu were lovers, while Lulu maintained they were just roommates. At the time, they each were based at JFK, and Lulu stated that the Village apartment was just a pied-à-terre for layovers in New York.

According to the restraining order, Danielle arranged her schedule around Lulu's, contriving to be in the same cities at the same times. They had some friends in common but separate social lives. Lulu said Danielle would often show up at the same restaurant, pretending it was a coincidence.

The assault on Danielle occurred just after 10:00 p.m. in her apartment on Sullivan Street.

She accused Lulu of attacking her in a jealous rage after a stroll through nearby Washington Square Park because Danielle had told her she wanted to break up with her. Danielle asserted that it was Lulu who had the obsession, who stalked her, not the other way around.

In Lulu's sworn statement, she said that at the time of the assault, she was with Richard Guerin, a curator at the Museum of Fine Arts, Boston. It was their first date, and they were seeing Lucia di Lammermoor at the Metropolitan Opera. Reid was interested to learn that Richard was a longtime client of the Harkness-Woodward Gallery, that he'd been introduced to Lulu by Kate.

Lulu had voluntarily provided DNA and bite impressions. Richard had corroborated her alibi. She'd been cleared of the crime, and no perpetrator had ever been arrested. If she had been involved, her airline job would have been history.

Reid pushed his chair back from his desk, stretched, turned his head from side to side to relieve stress. His gaze fell on the news clippings from his career, including the crime against Kate, Beth, and their mother. He had recently tacked up newspaper and magazine stories about Beth's murder, along with the time line he'd worked out about Pete's movements in the months before Beth had been killed.

He realized, as he often did, that if anyone saw his wall, they'd say he was obsessed. He always told himself that his fixation on the Woodward sisters, particularly Kate, was chivalrous, stemming from a desire to avenge what had been done to them as teenagers. But was that so different from what Lulu said Danielle had done, for which she had obtained a restraining order?

Yes, it was. Night-and-day different. He was positive of that. His confidence was shaken only at night, when he couldn't sleep, an unending tape of details from Beth's murder running through his mind, interrupted only by a what-if scenario—him and Kate at the gallery, the kiss that didn't happen.

That was the part that veered into the realm of obsession. He had never felt passion for any other subject of an investigation before. The other night he'd woken up sweating, dreaming of Kate. In the morning, he'd felt this ridiculous wave of shame—*Why should he? Who could stop a dream?*—but it had made him feel like heading to the Y-Knot on Bank Street and getting drunk. He hadn't sought whiskey or any alcohol as a solution for years, but shame and frustration were powerful motivators.

He stared at the heart and the small spot in the corner.

He looked up the address he had for Lulu Granville and headed over to question her about

486

the bloody heart. Maybe she could tell him who the third woman had been, or perhaps it was historical, left by someone long dead.

And even though Lulu had been cleared of the charge of biting Danielle, Reid couldn't get the image of those scratches and bite marks on Pete's back out of his mind. Early on, Pete had said he'd gotten them during sex. It seemed crazy, but could they have come from Lulu? Pretty much the only thing worse than having your husband cheat on you with an employee would be having him be with one of your best friends.

When he arrived at Lulu's house, Reid found no cars in the driveway, and no one answered the door.

49

It was Beth's birthday, and the sun had not yet risen when the phone rang and woke Kate.

"Hey, old sweetheart," Lulu said. "Let's go flying. What do you say to a hike on the Block?"

Block Island. One of Beth's favorite places in the world, a perfect place to go on her birthday.

"Yes," Kate said, already climbing out of bed. "Let's go."

She had to drop Sam off at Isabel's so she could catch a ride to school. On the way to Black Hall, Sam talked about Beth. She asked Kate to tell her something surprising about Beth, something she'd never heard before.

"She was a champion tree climber," Kate said. "Everyone thought of your mother as being quiet, scholarly, completely wrapped up in art. But one of her favorite things to do was to see how high she could go."

"Where?" Sam asked.

"There was a Norway spruce behind our house—not Mathilda's, but the one where we lived with our parents, in town. It was so tall, Sam, maybe twice or three times as high as our house. The trunk was sturdy and so thick with branches at the bottom, but up toward the top it was scraggly, and the limbs were sparse. Your mom would climb a little higher each time . . ."

"That sounds more like something you would do."

"You'd think so, but I was too scared—I never got more than halfway up. I'd feel the tree swaying, and it would seem like the branches wouldn't hold me."

"What would she do up there?"

"Peek into birds' nests on the way up. And then look out—she said she could see across the Sound, even past Plum Island, all the way into Gardiners Bay. When she came down, she'd be covered with sap—all over her hands and legs— and she'd be beaming. She called it 'visiting the sky.' "

"Why didn't I know this?" Sam asked. "She and I could have done it together."

"Well, she stopped at some point."

"When?"

"Um, when she was a teenager."

"After your mom died?"

"Yes," Kate said.

Sam fell silent, and Kate felt she'd made a mistake by telling that story. It showed how brave and exuberant Beth had been, and how tragedy had killed that part of her. It had taken so much of the fun and the thrill of life out of her.

"Sam," Kate said. "She found her passion.

Maybe she stopped climbing trees, but she . . ."

"I know," Sam said. "Loved art. Loved the gallery."

"No. I was going to say loved you. You were everything to her, Sam. You were her sky."

Sam didn't reply, but when they parked outside the Waterstons' house, she gave Kate a quick and unexpected hug. "Thanks for telling me that about Mom," she said.

"Anytime," Kate said, wanting to hold on to the feeling of closeness with her niece.

She watched Sam walk up the steps. Scotty greeted her at the door, waved to Kate. It was still so early—Sam and Isabel would hang around for a while, then catch the school bus. Kate picked up Lulu, and they headed for the airport. Just knowing she was about to go up into the air made her feel lighter, took weight off her shoulders. She felt Beth with her. They would visit the sky together.

Their Piper Saratoga looked lonely and neglected on the side of the tarmac. Dead leaves had skittered around the wheels, caught beneath the chocks. Rainstorms had stuck them to the wings and windshield like brown paper. Kate and Lulu did their best to brush the debris off, knowing the flight would do the rest.

Lulu was pilot this leg, and Kate would fly home. They took off toward the southwest, Long Island Sound glittering below. One sweeping turn revealed the faded autumn colors of Southeastern Connecticut. The rising sun lit the land, acres of trees dropping their last leaves.

They banked over Napatree Point. A thousand feet below, the long, narrow sandspit curved outward into Block Island Sound, creating Watch Hill's sheltered harbor. Nothing could have protected the point from the hurricane of 1938, when the winds blew ninety-eight miles per hour with a gust of one hundred twenty recorded in New London. A fifty-foot storm surge washed away forty houses from Napatree; one hundred people in Westerly were killed. Kate stared down at the sandy spit; she and Beth had walked there every summer. She closed her eyes—everything seemed so vulnerable.

Tom Francis, a pilot friend, moored his boat in Great Salt Pond during the summer and let his friends borrow the old Jeep he kept at the airport. Kate got the key from Margie at the desk, and they set off for Rodman's Hollow, 230 acres of pristine open space.

Kate and Lulu were at their best when they were on the move. They sometimes tried meeting at cafés or restaurants, but sitting still at a table never felt like enough. It didn't have to be hiking in the Anza-Borrego Desert or kayaking the Colorado River; they loved local expeditions just as much.

They parked in the lot off Cooneymus Road,

grabbed their backpacks, and followed a trail into the glacial hollow. Beyond the tawny fields and coastal scrub, the bright-blue Atlantic glittered. Migratory birds, resting on their journey south from the boreal forest, darted around the thicket. A yellow warbler, perched for ten seconds on the silver-tipped branch of a bayberry bush, looked like pure gold.

"I have to tell you something," Lulu said.

"Do I want to hear it?" Kate asked. "Lately when you say those words to me, we stop speaking."

"Well, when you put it like that, I've changed my mind."

They kept walking. Kate stared at the five massive wind turbines just offshore, tall and white and gawky in the morning light. A red-tailed hawk circled overhead, a black shadow against the blue sky.

"Go ahead," Kate said, stopping dead in the middle of the trail.

"You sure?"

"Just get it over with," Kate said. She felt off balance, scared of what she was about to hear. "Whatever it is, you couldn't have told me before?"

"I didn't want to," Lulu said. "But it's Beth's birthday. It has to be now or never."

She looked pale as she pulled her phone from her back pocket. Head bent, she scrolled through photos.

"Let's see," she said, her voice shaking slightly. "October, September, August, July . . . okay, here we go." She glanced into Kate's eyes. She hesitated, then handed the phone to Kate.

Kate held it and stared at Beth smiling out of the screen. She felt a shiver of normalcy, as if Beth were still alive, could appear at any moment, could be with them enjoying her birthday. Beth had a sly twinkle in her eyes. She stood in her bedroom. She wore an orange sundress, and from the size of her belly, Kate knew the photo couldn't have been taken long before she died.

"Swipe through," Lulu said. "There are eight photos and a video. I took them all the same afternoon."

Next was a shot of a pocketknife in a bone sheath, laid on the bed's summer-weight white comforter; Beth standing in front of *Moonlight* on the wall; *Moonlight* now facedown on the bed, Beth holding the knife like a dagger above it; the painting cut from the frame; the pale-red heart drawn on the back; the canvas yellowed with age, its edges unraveling; a selfie of Beth and Lulu grinning at the camera, each holding up a blood-smeared index finger; then a five-second blurry video.

"Proof of love," Beth said steadily. She reached out to Lulu. The camera shook as Lulu accepted the knife, and the clip stopped.

"What did you do?" Kate asked now, trembling as she looked into Lulu's eyes.

"Isn't it obvious?" Lulu asked.

"No," Kate said.

"She hated him," Lulu said. "Pete. He'd lied to her for so long, took so much of who she was. She had to show him. That painting was hers. The empty frame was a symbol—that's all he was, an empty space, and that was all she was leaving him. She wanted him to know there was someone else. The heart was her proof of love— for herself, for Sam, for the baby, for Jed, for us, her blood sisters."

"Okay," Kate said, her voice breaking. "Then . . . ?"

"I put the knife into my pocket," Lulu said. "Rolled up the painting and hid it in Beth's briefcase. Then Beth took a nap. But God, Kate, I did it to her. I caused her death."

Kate's mind slipped out of gear, a car rolling backward down a hill. She pictured the knife. It couldn't be; she couldn't bear the thoughts and images racing through her mind.

"You're telling me she died that day?" Kate asked, her voice barely a croak. She took a step closer to Lulu.

"No," Lulu said. "Not that day."

"But you were there when she died?" Kate asked.

"What?" Lulu asked. "Are you *kidding?*"

"Whoever took the painting killed her," Kate said.

"She stole it herself!" Lulu said. "I just told you—it was a message to Pete. Jesus, Kate! He killed her the day he left to go sailing."

"How do you know?"

"He had to—it's the only way it fits. You know it too."

"Then what did you mean by what you said—that you *did* it?"

"I meant that I helped her cut the painting from the frame—she asked me to—and seeing the painting gone must have set him off," Lulu said. "He got Beth's message, figured out she was going to leave him. He couldn't have missed it. He'd never be able to stand Beth having the upper hand, making a fool of him. She was laughing when she took it; the idea of it made her feel strong, so happy. If I hadn't supported her, even egged her on, she might not have done it. It was just a symbol. We never imagined the consequences."

"Why didn't she ask me to help her?" Kate asked, feeling so helpless about the distance between them; it seemed that every day she was learning of more and more ways Beth had evaded her.

"You didn't even know about Jed, or that she was leaving," Lulu said quietly, almost as if apologizing for the fact.

That statement smashed into Kate, a baseball in the chest. It came down, again, to the fact Kate didn't understand love, or being in love, could never appreciate a romantic or vengeful gesture, because she'd never had a relationship that would require it. Her sister had known she wouldn't understand. She walked away from Lulu. She began to run toward the ocean, but she heard footsteps crunching fallen leaves behind her, Lulu keeping pace.

Old stone walls marked the end of the trail. A hard left led onto a coast path, hugging the top of the clay bluffs above the Atlantic. The sea was dark blue. The gigantic white windmills turned relentlessly.

The hawk had caught a rabbit in the open field. At Mathilda's when Kate was young, she would hear owls grab them at night, and they would scream as they died, but this rabbit was alive, stock still in fright as the hawk perched on its back, talons dug in. The hawk flapped its wings, lifting the rabbit five feet into the air.

"Stop!" Kate yelled, tearing through the tall grass, waving her arms. The raptor wheeled, lost its grip. The rabbit fell to the ground.

Kate approached slowly. It lay still on its side. Deep red, raw claw marks scored the gray-brown fur along both sides of its spine. At first, she thought it was dead, but there was life in the glossy black eyes, watching her as she leaned over.

"Oh," she said, kneeling beside it. "Oh . . ."

"Poor thing," Lulu said. "Didn't have a chance against a red-tail."

Kate bent her head so she could look directly into the cottontail's eyes. They stared straight at her. Not a whisker twitched, the stillness of shock. Blood oozed from the tracks left by the hawk's talons. She placed her palm on the rabbit's side, felt the light, panicked flutter of its heart. The vulnerability of small creatures, the ones who couldn't be saved. The phrase came to her mind and filled her eyes with tears. In that moment, all she could see was Beth.

She felt Lulu's hand on her shoulder.

"Come on," Lulu said. "Leave her—let nature take its course. You don't want to watch her die."

"She's not going to die," Kate said. She took off her soft fleece jacket and placed it in the grass. She closed her hands around the rabbit. Lifting her, she felt surprised by her weight. Laying the rabbit on her jacket, she wrapped her body tight, the way she'd seen Beth swaddle Sam when she was a baby. Her purpose was to immobilize her and prevent further injury. She expected her to thrash against her touch, but the rabbit seemed to snuggle against her right away.

The rabbit must be so scared, she thought. She had once flown a family and its pet parrot from Westerly to Chicago, and they had kept the cage covered to keep the bird calm. She emptied her backpack, handing Lulu her water bottle, phone, and wallet. Gently, she placed the rabbit inside and closed the zipper.

The whole way back to the Jeep, and then driving quickly to the plane, the rabbit didn't move. Although it was Kate's turn to pilot, and she'd been craving the exhilaration of flying them back to Groton–New London, she took the passenger seat.

"I'm so sorry, Kate," Lulu said. "I know you're really mad. If you want to cancel for later, us all getting together at Mathilda's, I understand."

"We're not canceling," Kate said. "It's Beth's birthday."

Lulu nodded, banking north toward Connecticut. Kate closed her eyes, missing out on the spectacular, endless blue-sea view, and held the backpack against her chest, the warmth radiating through the fabric telling her the rabbit was still alive.

50

Kate dropped Lulu off and headed to the veterinarian. They'd barely spoken the whole way from Block Island to the airport, from the airport to Lulu's cottage, except to agree to meet at Mathilda's after Sam got out of school at 3:30.

Dr. Laurie Banks practiced in a barn on the edge of Mile Creek. Kate had been here before, accompanying Beth to take Popcorn for shots. Dr. Banks took one look at the rabbit and shook her head.

"I'm not licensed to treat wild animals," she said. "You have to take this one to a wildlife rehab." She leaned closer, though, examined the hawk's gouges. "It really doesn't look good, though. The rehabber will probably euthanize it."

Kate stared at the rabbit's wide dark eyes and saw life force and knew she wouldn't let that happen.

"Can you at least tell me if it's male or female?"

Dr. Banks turned the rabbit over carefully and looked beneath the short white tail. "Female," she said.

Kate nodded.

"Here's the name of the closest rehab,"

Dr. Banks said, handing Kate a slip of paper.

"Thanks," Kate said.

"It could be a long shot," Dr. Banks said. "It's unlikely she'll survive. It's probably kinder to put her out of her misery. The wildlife vet will make that decision."

"Okay," Kate said.

The vet brought out a cardboard crate for transport and placed the rabbit inside. Kate carried her to the car, set her on the front seat beside her. She started to drive toward Montville, the address Dr. Banks had given her, but instead she stopped at CVS, bought hydrogen peroxide and bacitracin, and headed for home.

On her couch, she set the cottontail on a towel. The bleeding had stopped. She gently washed the cuts with warm water, then hydrogen peroxide. The gashes were clean. She applied the antibiotic ointment to prevent infection as carefully as she could. The rabbit's fur felt impossibly soft.

Popcorn investigated. Kate didn't want him to scare the rabbit, but Popcorn was so cautious it seemed okay. Kate slung her arm around his neck, burrowed her face in his fur. The dog had been Beth's. Beth had instinctively known how to care for him, and she'd wanted to. Beth had had a husband and a daughter and a lover and all the people she'd helped at the shelter and the soup kitchen. Kate had kept herself as separate as possible from all creatures.

"What should we name her?" Kate asked Popcorn.

He circled, lay at her feet. Kate heard him sigh as he settled. The rabbit was perfectly still, except for her breath. Kate's hand rested on the sofa beside her, and she felt the warmth of each exhalation. On the coffee table was a blue bowl filled with small oranges. The scent filled the room. It smelled like a citrus grove, both sweet and tangy. Beth had loved oranges. They had been her favorite fruit. And she had been wearing the color in those pictures Lulu had taken.

Kate held her hand above the rabbit's head and felt energy passing between them. All her senses were engaged. Beth was still with her. She felt warm breath on the back of her neck and actually turned around to see if her sister was standing there. She had the sudden feeling that she was coming alive in a different way.

Kate's gaze fell upon the bowl of oranges, and the rabbit's name came to her. "You're Clementine," she said. "You're going to get better."

She carried Clementine to the other side of the loft, away from the windows, where it was dark and toasty. She put her back into the crate. It was 2:30, nearly time to leave to meet the others. She'd have to gather tall grass from Mathilda's yard, arrange it in a nest for Clementine. And food—she'd need to learn what wild rabbits liked to eat. She'd seen families of them in the meadow, hopping through clover. She wondered where she could find clover in late November.

"It will be all right," Kate whispered. She thought of Lulu and Beth, the ritual of drawing a heart on the back of the painting. She cringed to think of the secrets they had kept from her.

Since July, her heart had ached more than she thought was safe. She'd thought maybe she would collapse. Her sister was gone, and she'd never see her again. The feelings were similar to what she'd felt when her mother had died, when it had seemed that if someone she loved could be taken so violently, there might be no reason to go on.

Sitting with Clementine, feeling sudden and deep commitment to saving her, she saw clearly what she'd known all along—that she'd already been doing that with Sam. She had decided, without putting it into words, that she would be her niece's person. Less than a mother but more than the somewhat distant aunt she had always been. She might have thought she was shut down, but she had loved as deeply and totally as anyone else all along. She just hadn't let herself feel it.

Sitting cross-legged on the floor, she stared through the crate's open door and watched Clementine watching her. She remembered being eleven, rescuing a feral cat that had lived behind the gallery, the last pet she'd ever had—loving every second with Maggie, feeling her warmth as she snuggled against her side.

After those hours in the basement, Kate couldn't even look at her sister. She had been too numb to grip her hand, to hold her little sister tight, to bond together and try to dispel the horrors of that day and night.

Kate's love of her sister had never left her, but after their mother had died, after the brutality of the ropes, she'd stopped being able to open her heart to physical, hands-on caring for any living being. You never knew when they would be taken from you.

She thought about what Lulu had told her. If not for the photos and video, she would have had a hard time picturing Beth with the knife, cutting *Moonlight* from the frame, and she couldn't help feeling angry at her sister. Beth had staged a fake crime, reminiscent of what their father had done with the same painting.

"Beth," she said out loud. Then she closed her eyes and listened. She ached to hear her sister's voice. After a few minutes, she leaned down to stare into the rabbit's big beautiful eyes.

"You're going to be fine, Clementine. It will all be okay," Kate said, unable to stop herself from reaching into the crate, gently touching the head of her injured cottontail. "I love you more than you could ever know," Kate said, and she wasn't completely sure whether she was talking to Clementine or to Beth. She stood up. It was time to meet the others and celebrate Beth's birthday.

51

Scotty and her family lived in a winterized beach cottage overlooking the boat basin at Hubbard's Point, and at this time of year, she never felt quite warm enough. The November wind whistled through every window. Most boats had been hauled for the season, but gazing out her kitchen window, Scotty saw that there were still two tied up in their slips. Lobster pots were piled on the bulkhead between them. Late fall and winter weren't bad times to be lobster fishermen, if you were hardy enough.

Isabel and Sam had gotten off the bus after school, had a quick snack, and were up in Isabel's room with the door closed. She had no idea what they were talking about. It was time for Scotty and Sam to head to Mathilda's—Isabel would stay here and babysit Julie—but try prying the best friends apart. It had been the same for Scotty and the rest of the Compass Rose when they were that age.

Scotty walked into the pantry and stood looking at the liquor. She wanted a drink badly. Often she let herself have a small one at this time of day. She used to wait till 6:00, the official cocktail hour, but lately she'd begun telling herself an hour or two earlier didn't make a real difference. She didn't drink to get drunk—just to take the edge off.

But other than her two days a week at the food pantry, she didn't usually have to drive anywhere. She actually missed volunteering on the days she wasn't there. She knew it would be frowned upon, but every so often she'd take a walk with one or more of her favorite clients and treat them to a cocktail. Why not? They were all adults, and if it brought a little pleasure into their painful lives, she was happy to provide it.

Beth might not have approved of her sharing alcohol with them—many had substance abuse issues. But Beth had understood almost everything else that mattered to Scotty.

They talked about how it felt to have teenage daughters, how unnecessary they'd started to feel. Both Isabel and Sam had found their independence on what had seemed to Scotty the early side—they'd embraced the belief they didn't need their moms the same way. They had lives of their own, and the last thing they wanted were mothers hovering.

But of course they did need their mothers, more than ever. These were crucial days—that's how Scotty thought of it: mere days, six hundred or so, before they went off to college. The comfort of years stretching ahead—a seemingly endless time for the entire family to nestle together, for Scotty to savor the closeness with her older daughter—was over.

Beth had thought she had that luxury too. Even though life had changed, with Sam growing up, they were still together, and Sam, although perhaps not in the same way as she had in middle school, needed her guidance and love. Beth had loved that girl, and she had been so ready to love Matthew. It was supposed to last forever.

Scotty shivered, thinking of the terrible loss. Beth, gone from their lives. Today, on her birthday, the emptiness was almost unbearable. She stared at the vodka bottle, then abruptly turned her back on it. She had to stay strong. And sober for today.

Kate and Lulu would be expecting her and Sam, but she knew they wouldn't mind if two more joined them. She knew in that moment she couldn't leave Isabel at home on Beth's birthday, and that meant she'd take Julie along too. Her children were everything.

She paused. The last talk with Beth had been so upsetting. Her sweet Beth, so hurt by the men in her life. Was that why Beth had refused to give either one of them, Pete or Jed, the satisfaction of knowing he was the father? Scotty had no use for Pete, and she couldn't see much good in Jed. He was an ex-con, probably drawn to Beth for her money and the connections she could make for him in the art world. He certainly didn't deserve any respect, not after tempting Beth away from her marriage.

Money, clearly. And the prestige of the gallery. Beth must have realized he didn't have good motives. That had to be the reason Beth wouldn't tell him whether he was or was not Matthew's father. Although Jed wasn't honorable, it wasn't fair to keep that fact from him. If he was about to be a parent, he deserved to know, and it was terribly unfair of Beth to not tell him. Everyone had loved Beth, but very few had realized how deeply flawed she had been.

There were certain rules in life that had to be adhered to. You simply couldn't come between a person and his child. That would be selfish and unforgivable. The important thing was to celebrate Beth's life. To be with everyone who had loved her as much as Scotty had.

"Girls!" Scotty called from the bottom of the stairs. "Hurry up; it's time to go! Dress warm— it's cold out!"

52

November 21

It's my birthday.

It's so strange to be here instead of there on this day. On any day.

You're not supposed to ask for gifts; if they are freely given, you are grateful. But you can't expect them.

Am I allowed to wish for one?

The gift I would like is for them to know, to exact payment. They are my beloveds, my sister, daughter, and best friends. In some ways I believe they've known all along, for how could they miss it?

Or maybe my own experience has been colored: of trusting and loving, then turning my back and my skull being smashed—hearing the bones in my head crack. Then feeling hands around my throat, seeing that wild gaze—so charged with fury, but then emotion draining away, staring into my eyes with no emotion as dispassionately as someone trying to loosen a particularly tight lid from a jar. It has colored my judgment, made me believe that there could be no questions—none at all. That is the drawback of knowledge. It gives you a singular point of view that you cannot, in fairness, expect others to share.

I would have liked to have remained blank as I died, to not give the satisfaction of my panic and desperation, but I wasn't that strong, or perhaps a better word would be *disciplined.* I so quickly lost track of what I wanted—to remain calm. My survival instinct made me want to fight with everything I had. But instinct wasn't enough. I started to die the minute that sculpture, the owl I had loved so much, struck my head. I would have withheld my fear if I could. I believe it was accepted as a gift.

Although I couldn't scream—the grip around my neck was too tight—I could hear the terrible choking, gurgling sounds coming from my throat, the fine bones breaking under the pressure of strong thumbs. In that most human of moments, I thought I sounded inhuman.

I reached for those hands, wanting to pull them away, but I couldn't even reach them. My muscles tensed, softened, and my arms fell slack. I imagine the power bestowed by my weakness. Is it odd that I didn't wonder why this was happening to me? Every cell in my body knew, so why bother asking the question? The point is, while being murdered, I was purely there on the bed, physically and therefore mentally present in the moment, experiencing my own death.

And Matthew's death. My son had been moving

and dancing and kicking for weeks. He was even more active in my womb than Sam had been, and that is saying a lot. I was sure she'd come out a champion tennis player. Her prebirth serve-and-volley game was strong.

Matthew was ready to be born. If he could have arrived in July, instead of October when he was expected, I believe he would have. He had such an exuberant life force. I felt I already knew him. When he kept me awake, his feet contentedly tapping, I could picture him learning to walk early, chortling with pleasure as he toddled after Popcorn, a dancer who would grow up singing and laughing.

He had a wonderful personality.

He fought even harder than I did. Even as my own life faded away, I felt Matthew twisting and punching. His little fists balled up, moving in slow motion in the fluid in which he swam. My heart beat oxygen into his. Every breath I took was a breath for Matthew. When I stopped being able to breathe, so would he. That was the only thought that pulled me away from the physical act of dying. The sorrow that my son, already so alive, would lose his life before he had the chance to truly live it. I felt such heartbreak for his father—that his father would never know his beautiful son.

So many misconceptions about the moment of death. They say your entire life flashes before your eyes. You have time to make peace with your regrets, to forgive and let go of resentments, to fill your heart with love. I can see why people want to believe that in the minutes before death, a person can find perfect peace. For me, that did not happen. My entire wonderful life was wiped out, as if it had never been, in violent thrashing, despair, pain beyond belief.

I would have thought it was pure anger that drove my killer—a crazed moment that would surely end as the rage stopped, when realization that this was happening, that I was dying, would have halted the whole thing. But it didn't. That's when I saw that terrible calm enter the eyes staring down at me.

I was so focused on that familiar, once so-loved face, during those long minutes of death. At the very end, when I'd stopped breathing, before the last spark of consciousness left me, I heard the sigh. My vision was gone, but I heard footsteps across the room, the sound of the air-conditioning cranking up, and my sensation was of cold air blowing from the vent, a harbinger of cold beyond human understanding, the ice of death.

Until those final moments in my frigid room, I couldn't spare a thought for my daughter. There was no clinging to the girl that I love, no sense of goodbye. It was all me and Matthew, because we were together, and my death was his death.

But at that last instant, when my life flickered and extinguished, it was Sam I thought of. It was all my daughter. I gave my entire self, my spirit, to Sam. It was all I could do for her, my daughter, my girl. The dead mourn the living, the loss of closeness and the future. I won't be there to teach Sam what I knew about growing up, and I have lost the chance to be guided by her.

When she was little, she would come to the gallery after school and paint and draw. The works that inspired her most were so different from my beloved American Impressionists. After my grandmother and Ruth took a trip to India and Nepal, Mathilda acquired several fifteenth-century Tibetan paintings and a hundred-year-old English translation of *The Tibetan Book of the Dead*. The illustrations were colorful, painted in shades of red and green on parchment, filled with images of protector and wrathful gods, bodhisattvas, and Green Tara, the mother of Buddhism. Sam was fascinated with all the characters, but hungry ghosts moved her most, and she drew an entire book of stories about the desperate souls who died in violence and misery, who haunted the earth without ever finding peace.

What would Sam think, to know that I have become a hungry ghost?

After my mother died, when I was too sad to do anything but dream about heaven, I read the book of the dead and learned that the bardo state lasts for forty-five days after death. The bardo is a ghost world, a period of time before a person is reborn. It gave me comfort to imagine that after a month and a half in the bardo, my mother could find peace in another life. I looked for her everywhere: in feral kittens, a bobcat that stalked the meadow, a new baby at the beach.

Will Sam remember those Tibetan-inspired drawings she did of beings in the bardo? Will they make her think of me?

Many more than forty-five days have passed since my murder. My death was in July, and now it is November, my birthday. A single birth, a death, and there has been no rebirth, no respite from wandering. I'm left to believe that there never will be. My violent end leaves me ravenous for justice, a hunger that hasn't been sated.

Being a mother was the best part of my life. Scotty had nothing on me in that department—I remember how I scared her, upset her, in that moment early in my pregnancy when I wavered, when I thought having Matthew might change everything too much, upset the order of things. It was just a few seconds, but it angered her. I didn't appreciate her feelings enough; I wish I had been more sensitive.

Motherhood. Yes, Scotty understood more than anyone what it meant to me. When I think of Sam now, what she is about to face. How will she manage? I remember how I felt when my mother died. Scholarship and achievement had been my way of healing from what the Andersons had done. But once I conceived Sam, nothing else mattered in the same way. I wanted Kate to have this too—the eternal connection to a child, the transformation from a victim who had suffered at the hands of others to a powerful woman able to give life. Lulu too—our dear and not-so-dear secretive mystery girl Lulu. It sometimes felt so unfair to me that only Scotty and I had experienced motherhood. But frankly, not everyone deserves it—not just the childless, but not even every woman who's become a mother.

I need Kate now. If justice is to come, my sister will deliver it. She is strong and furious, more single minded than anyone I know. It has served her well in the air, in her work. She thinks I look down on her for not having the life I do—family, children, my garden. But I don't—she would never have created the mess I did. I took the painting, one I already owned, to prove to myself I deserved my own life.

The complication of Jed. I tried so hard to keep them both happy: my husband and my lover. Giving Jed the photo of Matthew from the sonogram, encouraging him to think he was my baby's father before I knew for sure. Playing with someone's feelings, when the stakes are so high, is serious business. Leaving Pete with an empty frame on the wall. Lies and manipulations I hadn't known I was capable of. They felt good at the time—vital, even. A good girl all my life, it felt exhilarating to step out of line. But why couldn't I have been content with my children, living surrounded by the art that has sustained me from the beginning?

I lost myself in love. And then I lost my life.

53

On Beth's birthday, Reid drove to New London to meet Tom for lunch. He had plenty to keep him busy at his desk, but the date made him uneasy, and he really needed to get away from the office. He had been sure he would have wrapped up the case by now. He had wanted it for Beth.

He parked in the Saint Ignatius Loyola Church parking lot at the end of Bank Street—just a few blocks from Kate's loft. He walked slowly toward the Black Whale, keeping his eyes open for her. He had told Tom to meet here because Tom was lecturing at the Coast Guard Academy this week, and New London would be convenient for him. But he knew there was another reason. He hadn't spoken to Kate in over two weeks; he felt ashamed of having nothing to report, but he wanted to run into her.

The place was packed with people from the courthouse up the street—lawyers, defendants, jurors, cops. Reid recognized half of them and said hello as he made his way through the restaurant. He spotted his brother in his Coast Guard uniform, sitting in a booth in the back.

"Hey," he said, sliding into his seat.

"Thanks for meeting for lunch," Tom said. "I was surprised to hear from you. You've been so busy."

"I needed a break," Reid said.

The waitress came over, and they both ordered fish and chips. Reid asked for a coffee.

"What's going on?" Tom asked.

"Nothing, and that's the problem," Reid said, drinking the instant the waitress set down the cup, burning his mouth. "Ouch."

Tom watched him, and Reid recognized the expression: half-amused, half-concerned.

"Here," Tom said, reaching into his glass of water, fishing out a handful of ice cubes. "It'll stop the burn. An old Coast Guard trick."

Reid took the cubes, nodded across the table. Tom never stopped being an older brother. He thought about siblings, how strong the bond was. He wondered how Kate was handling the day. It must have shown on his face.

"What's going on?" Tom asked. "You okay?"

"It's Beth's birthday."

"Oh, man," Tom said, leaning forward, watching Reid.

"Probably a really hard day for Kate and Sam," Reid said.

"And you too?" Tom asked.

"A little," Reid said. "But let's talk about something else. How was teaching?"

"I'm done for the day," Tom said. "It's always

good to be at the Academy, see the kids coming along."

"So the Coast Guard will be in good shape with the next generation?" Reid asked. Their platters of fish and chips arrived, and he realized he didn't feel hungry. He sat back, listening to Tom talk about the seamanship class he'd just taught. It made him think of sextants and celestial navigation and the astronomy professor at Osprey House, and when he glanced toward the lunch counter, there he was.

"The astronomer," Reid said.

"Who?" Tom asked, his mouth full.

"Martin Harris," Reid said. "The guy I told you about? Who knew too much about Beth's crime scene?"

"Right—connected to Pete by the stars," Tom said.

"Give me a minute," Reid said. He left his brother sitting there and walked around the counter, right through the swinging door into the kitchen. It was a small space that smelled like fried food, noisy with clattering dishes and the hiss of the griddle.

Martin Harris carried a big rectangular gray plastic bin full of dirty dishes from out front, placed it in a deep stainless-steel sink, and turned on the water. Reid waved at Alma, the cook. They knew each other from his many lunches at the detectives' table over the years. He raised his eyebrows in a question, pointed at Harris, and she nodded her okay. *Thanks,* he mouthed.

"Mr. Harris," Reid said.

Harris glanced over his shoulder, his eyes as bloodshot as ever.

"I'm working," he said.

"I see that," Reid said. "I only want a few minutes of your time. Your boss doesn't mind. Let's step outside."

Harris looked over at Alma, who was busy at the stove. He led Reid out the back door into an alley. It ran the length of the block behind the church. People were milling around outside the parish house, lining up. He realized they were waiting to go into the soup kitchen.

"That's where you eat sometimes, right?" Reid asked.

"Yes, it is," Harris said.

"It's strange to me, Martin, that when I asked you about Beth Lathrop, you didn't mention you ate there. Because she worked there."

"Yeah, she and her friend. Two nice ladies from a fancy town," Harris said. "Serving food to people like us. Who'd a thunk?"

"So you did know Beth."

"Not really," Harris said. "Yes, I'd see her at meals sometimes, and she was really nice. I didn't mention it because I didn't do anything, and I knew you'd think something bad."

Reid didn't say anything, held his emotions

inside. But he thought of Beth feeding Martin Harris, being kind to him, having no idea of the kind of crimes he had committed, making herself vulnerable to what he could do to her.

"We never got together outside here or anything," Harris said, sounding nervous. "I barely even talked to her, just thanked her for the food. I hang out more with her friend."

"Jed Hilliard?" Reid asked.

"Who, that artist guy?" Harris asked. "I know him from here, but we're not friends or anything."

"Then who is it you hang out with?"

"You know, the other lady from Black Hall. She's really nice. She buys us drinks once in a while, and she'll join us." He laughed. "She's a hoot." Then a serious look crossed his face. "But she is really broken up."

"About what?"

"Beth, of course. They were so close. You could tell, just seeing them here. When she talks about what happened . . ." Harris closed his eyes tight, as if it was too awful for him to contemplate.

"What does she talk about?" Reid asked, feeling sweat run down his back.

"The death. What was done to Beth. The bruises. Those bone chips, pearls in the blood. The lace around her neck, the way it dug in . . ."

These were the things Harris had said before that had caused Reid to suspect he had been at the crime scene, or that Pete had told him about it. Harris was practically salivating now, and Reid saw him in the grips of a fantasy, made more thrilling by the fact the ingredients had come from someone so close to Beth.

"Did she tell you how she knew those details?" Reid asked.

"No, and I didn't even ask. She's tight with the family. I figured Beth's sister told her, or you did, or someone involved with the investigation. I was just happy to listen."

I bet you were, Reid thought.

"Thank you for your help, Mr. Harris," Reid said, filled with urgency, knowing what he had to do. He left him standing there in the alley and ran back into the Black Whale to tell his brother he had somewhere to be.

54

These feelings of pure connection were unfamiliar to Kate. When it was time to meet the others, she found herself not wanting to leave the house without Clementine. Online literature regarding the rescue of wild animals encouraged the rescuer to place the animal in a warm, quiet, dark place where it wouldn't be disturbed. Kate had found the perfect corner of her loft and done that. But when she knelt on the floor and saw Clementine lying on her side, watching her with those wide velvet-brown eyes, she fought the urge to take her along.

"You're coming with me," she said after a minute, not even feeling foolish for speaking out loud to a rabbit.

She put Clementine's crate on the car seat beside her and turned up the heat. Popcorn squeezed into the back. She drove straight to Mathilda's. All the leaves were off the trees bordering the private road up toward the house. The bare branches interlocked overhead, forming a dark canopy against a white sky. Snow was forecast. Kate could feel it coming. The air was charged with static electricity.

It was only 3:15, and she was the first to arrive. She stopped at the head of the hillside meadow, got out of the car with the basket she'd brought from home. She left the car running to keep the heat going for Clementine. Popcorn went bounding through the field. The only sound was the November wind blowing through an acre of hay, whispers from the sea. She tugged handfuls of tall grass. When she got home, she would weave them into a bed for Clementine. Crouching down, she ran her hand over a patch of dry clover, picking a bunch for her food.

The first snowflakes fell. She glanced down the hill, pictured how it looked when it was covered with deep snow. She felt a pull back to childhood. She could see children on sleds. Beth in a red snowsuit, Kate in blue. They would tear down the hill, top speed, hitting bumps, steering the best they could and hoping the long glide at the end would stop them short of the lily pond. The pond usually froze solid by mid-December, but Kate still worried about breaking through the ice.

Rescuing Clementine helped her remember how protective she'd felt of her sister, of how it had helped to care at a level deeper than words, to feel it in her skin. They had had so much fun, sledding down and running back up the hill, but Kate's mind would be busy formulating plans for what she'd do if Beth went into the icy pond. Kate weighed whether it would be better to kick off her boots, toss her down jacket aside first—without them she'd be more buoyant—or whether the extra seconds would mean less time to save Beth. It wasn't actual fear, just a measure of how seriously she took her responsibility as a big sister.

"You ready?" she remembered saying to Beth. Kate was nine. She sat behind Beth on the sled—a Flexible Flyer that had been their mother's when she was young—her arms and legs wrapped around her sister, holding her tight.

"Don't go so fast this time," Beth said.

"You don't have to be scared."

"I don't want to fall off," Beth said.

"I've got you."

And they pushed off and flew down the hill again, shrieking with the thrill of it all.

After that, Beth couldn't get enough. The speedier they went, the better. Kate had loved watching Beth find her inner daredevil.

When Kate had filled her basket with enough grass and clover, she checked her watch. The others should be arriving at any time. She continued up the hill on foot, leaving her car parked on the side of the driveway. She opened the door to the garden shed, where the sleds had been stored. They were still there—their red runners rusting, the oak boards weathered and lettering nearly invisible with age. The shed's interior was colder than the outside; she saw her breath.

Ice skates hung from pegs on the wall. Six pairs: Mathilda's and Ruth's, Kate's and Beth's, and Kate's parents'. There was a time when the whole family had been happy together. Kate closed her eyes and saw her father building a bonfire down by the pond. Mathilda had filled thermoses with hot chocolate, and after skating, everyone drank from green pottery mugs, blowing on the steaming chocolate to cool it off while warming their frozen fingers on the hot cups.

Kate and Beth had always squeezed together on the rough wooden bench. They'd shared warmth through their jackets, arms pressing together, listening while the grown-ups talked. Back then, Kate had always been happiest when there was as little room as possible between her and Beth.

When she heard tires crunching on the gravel, she called Popcorn and drove the short distance to the turnaround in front of the house. She saw Pete's car parked there. Her blood boiled. She had told him he couldn't stay, but typical Pete, doing just what he wanted. She didn't want him here ever but especially not on Beth's birthday.

She reached into Clementine's crate, gently touched her soft fur. It reassured Kate to feel her breathing in and out. Lulu pulled up the drive, then Scotty. Kate saw that Scotty's car was full— Isabel in front, Sam and Julie in back. They'd all come to celebrate Beth. Popcorn bounded out of the car.

Everyone piled out, hugged each other. They all wore warm coats, and they squished together in a big circle and didn't want to let go.

"I didn't expect him to be here," Kate said, gesturing at Pete's car when they broke apart. She glanced at Sam, not wanting to hurt her, but unable to hold back her real feelings—especially today.

"Should we go somewhere else?" Lulu asked.

"Well, he is Sam's dad," Scotty said. "Beth's widower."

"He said he didn't want to celebrate," Sam said. "Maybe it's better we leave."

"We're not leaving," Kate said. "He is." She had started toward the house when she heard Julie squeal.

"Bunny, a bunny!" Julie said, her palms pressed to the passenger-side window of Kate's car.

"That's right," Kate said.

"What's wrong with her?" Julie asked. "She sleeping?"

"She got hurt," Lulu said. "Kate rescued her."

"Want to see her; let me get close," Julie said.

"Oh, come on," Isabel said. "It's freezing out here."

Kate agreed, but Julie was so insistent, and she had planned to carry Clementine inside anyway.

"Her name is Clementine," Kate said, crouching beside Julie.

"Little rabbit," Julie said, reaching out one finger but not quite touching Clementine's twitching nose. At the same time, she glanced nervously over her shoulder. "Don't want to go in there."

"In where?" Kate asked.

"Inside the house. Reminds me of Sam's mom."

"It's good to remember people we loved," Kate said.

"It was strange, very," Julie said. "Don't want to go in. I will stay with Clementine."

"God, Julie," Isabel said. "Don't be so annoying! This is about Mrs. Lathrop. We're thinking about her on her birthday."

"I will stay with Clementine," Julie said, scrambling into the car.

"Julie, get out here right now," Scotty said.

Kate leaned past her, face to face with Julie. The girl who never looked her in the eye suddenly did.

"Are you afraid of something?" Kate asked.

"I don't like pretend talk. To Sam's mom." Her eyes darted to Lulu, then to her mother.

"Did something happen?" Kate asked, alarmed by Julie's panic. "That makes you feel this way?"

Julie put her hands over her ears. "Stop it, stop. Mommy, no one listening like before, no one listening. Just talk to air, talk-talk." Again, she looked at Lulu—whether in fear or a sort of pleading for understanding, Kate was unsure.

"Come on, sweetheart," Scotty said, hugging Julie, "everything is fine."

"Hey, where's Sam?" Isabel asked.

Everyone stood still and looked around. Sam wasn't there.

55

Pete wanted to feel amused to call this *home*. It had belonged to the great Mathilda, but he was here now. He sat in the recliner he'd brought from Church Street, making himself at home. He ate a big handful of Georgia peanuts, his favorite kind, from a tin Beth had given him for his last birthday. And today was her birthday. It made him feel terrible. *Melancholy* didn't cover it. He couldn't even enjoy the satisfaction of being in Mathilda's house.

Kate had forbidden him to stay here, and even Nicola wasn't very welcoming. That was their problem. He closed his eyes, going over the details for the many-hundredth time, sure that if he could put the pieces together, he would be able to figure out what had happened. He grieved Beth, and screw anyone who thought otherwise. But the events of the year prior, all the fights with Beth and Nicola, could cause him trouble, make him look bad, if they were brought into the open. And he knew the detective still thought he did it.

His back had healed from the scratches, the bite. He hadn't meant to scare Nicola so badly that day. It had been a week before Beth had died, and Pete had been totally sick of women—of being torn in half. It was a beautiful day in July. Tyler was fussy, didn't want to take a nap, so they loaded him into the car, went for a ride.

They wound up in the state forest near a waterfall. Tyler had finally fallen asleep in his car seat. Pete and Nicola sat in the front, windows open, listening to birds and the sound of rushing water.

She started in—*When are you leaving her? When can we be together?*—and he snapped.

"What the hell do you even want with me?" he asked. "All you ever do is complain about what I'm not giving you."

"Why don't you realize that it's what I want to give you that's killing me?" she said. "Not being able to do everything I want to do for you, for Tyler . . ."

He shook his head. "I can't even remember the last time you kissed me."

She smiled. She leaned across the console and kissed him the way she used to, the way that used to make him go crazy. Then he felt her hand between his legs. Next thing, they were out of the car. He took off his shirt, laid it on the ground for a blanket, and they made love right there in the open, not caring if anyone came along.

"Is that better?" she asked, smiling up at him.

"Yeah," he said, rolling off her and smoothing her hair back from her face. She was so beautiful, young and bright eyed. If only they could go back to the way they'd been when they first started. "Can I ask you to be more patient?"

"I'm trying."

"Doesn't seem it," he said. He hadn't meant it to sound harsh, but she reacted as if he'd slapped her. Her face turned bright red, and her eyes brimmed with tears. "Here they come. Here come the sobs, right on schedule."

She pushed him away, hard, and tried to get up. He grabbed her wrist, yanked her down. Anger boiled inside him. She provoked him every chance she got.

"You know what I'm giving up for you?" he asked. "I have a wife, a daughter. Beth fucking told my mother about us—now I'm going to have to face that. For what? This? Someone who cries every time I open my mouth?"

She was weeping now. Sitting on his shirt, hands over her eyes. He had had enough. She wanted to walk away just now? He'd see how she liked it. He stood up, hurried toward the car. He'd leave her right where she was, let her walk down the road. He'd be waiting there, but just then he wanted to really show her what could happen if she kept this up.

"See you at home," he said over his shoulder.

"Pete!" she cried.

Pete glanced in the back seat. Tyler was still sleeping.

"I'll take good care of him," Pete said, dangling

the car keys. "Just think about the way you act, how you're pushing me away. You're the one destroying us."

"Don't leave," she cried.

He opened the car door fast, wanting to speed away.

"Don't you take my son!" she screamed, and he felt her on his back—clawing, biting him as if she were an animal. He yelled, trying to shake her off, but she held on tighter. It was as if every emotion in the universe filled him, turned her into a monster, tore around them like a tornado.

When she finally stopped, and Pete had wheeled to grab her in a tight hug to keep her arms from flailing, it turned into an embrace, and he was the one sobbing, telling her he didn't know what to do, that he never would have left her alone in the woods. Meanwhile, his back was on fire. It felt as if she had bitten a chunk out of his shoulder.

And Nicola was whispering into his ear, "Forgive me; I'm so sorry—I didn't mean to hurt you." They had driven back to the house, where she had dressed the nasty wounds, dabbing at them with hydrogen peroxide, covering them with gauze.

Reason it out, he told himself now, sitting in Mathilda's house. *If you can give the police more of the truth, you're off the hook. Tell Reid about the fight with Nicola.* But it would make her look terrible. Pete didn't want Reid going

536

after her. What if he thought she was violent? He could become suspicious of Nicola, think that she could have been the one to kill Beth, shift the investigation to her.

As a child, his passion had been chess. He had grown up in the part of Providence you wouldn't want to be seen in, and most Saturdays and Sundays he would take the bus to the East Side, where he would wait for a spot outside the Chess Shop on Thayer Street and with total confidence take on all comers.

He played Brown and RISD students and professors, retired physicists, math prodigies, and a Russian grand master who had coached Boris Spassky, but his greatest teacher was Max Brandt, a homeless man who slept in Prospect Terrace Park and who regularly beat everyone. It just went to show that the educated, the so-called elite, could easily be bested by someone overlooked by society.

Pete had learned that staying one move ahead was pleasant but nowhere close to the rush of letting the opponent think he was winning and blindsiding him with an attack he didn't see coming. Max had shown him that over and over.

Beth's death wasn't a game of chess. It was nothing but sorrow for most of the people in her life—including Pete. But dealing with the police, his friends, her sister, Sam, even Nicola, required careful maneuvering. Pete couldn't expect anyone to understand his point of view. He was alone in this, as he had been in most things.

Throughout his entire life, he had been told by his mother how brilliant he was. His entire extended family had acknowledged that he was the brain of the family, and many had been resentful. He'd gotten into Saint George's, one of the best prep schools in the country. If he had wanted, he could have gone to any Ivy, but he hadn't gone that route.

Pete was modest about his looks, but he couldn't help being aware that women who'd been buttoned up their whole lives enjoyed the attention of a handsome bad boy who happened to be brilliant. He had dated several possibilities before Beth: another heiress, a principal in a private equity firm, a top-earning sales rep for a major pharmaceutical company. Beth had had the most potential. And surprise: he had actually loved her. In the early days of their relationship, what was not to love? She'd believed in him, almost as much as his mother had. She had handed him the keys to the gallery, the art world, and the quiet blue blood society of shoreline Connecticut.

By the time their marriage was in trouble, he'd found Nicola. As a graduate student at Bard, Nicola would be attracted only to the smartest men, and she had chosen Pete.

Beth had stopped appreciating him the way he deserved. She had at the beginning of their relationship, but it had dwindled away. She had demeaned him and had never let him forget that she owned everything.

He thought back to their early days, when he had been so full of hope and dreams. He was working for the insurance agency that had under-written the art stolen from the Lathrop Gallery. Pete researched the case thoroughly. Back then it had been called the Harkness-Woodward Gallery. Once Pete understood the dynamics of how Garth Woodward had hired the Andersons to steal *Moonlight* and tie up the family in the basement, he decided it was time to meet the daughters.

He showed up at the gallery for an opening. They were both there, Kate and Beth, but Kate barely gave him a look. Beth did the opposite—drew him in with her warmth and bubbly personality. When he told her where he worked, no doubt stirring up traumatic memories, she didn't turn away.

He remembered the sensitivity in her eyes.

"Are you in your field because you love art?" she asked.

"It's my passion," he lied.

"Did you know that your company and our gallery have a long-standing connection?"

"Yes," he said. "And I am so sorry for the

reason that you needed us. For what you and your family went through."

"Thank you," she'd said, her eyes welling. He gazed at her with all the comfort in the world; it was as if they had known each other forever—an instant bond. He wanted to give her the feeling that no one could understand what she had endured more than he could. She soaked it up— he knew what she needed, and he gave it to her. His instincts were perfect when it came to what women needed.

Greater things had happened to the gallery since he had married Beth and taken over as president. He had acted as press agent, getting articles in several art magazines and major newspapers. Because of Pete, the Lathrop Gallery had a presence on all the major social media platforms. He tweeted once a day, posted photos on Instagram, and had attracted over five thousand followers on Facebook—an impressive number for a small family-owned gallery. But she had not appreciated him.

She had never let him forget that the money came from her family. What she'd failed to fully realize was that being born rich was nothing more than blind luck. It had nothing to do with IQ. He had once—before Sam was born—tried to get her to take the Mensa test, and she had literally laughed. Not that she would have passed.

Last December, when they were decorating the

gallery for Christmas, Pete had stood at the foot of the ladder while Beth had balanced the star on top of the tree, and he had felt like giving the ladder a good shake. God help him, he thought of it now, and given how she'd died, he felt more ashamed than ever about that single impulse. In that split second, when he had been so angry with her, he would have loved to see her crack her head open on the edge of the desk.

"Fuck," he said out loud to himself, "fucking bastard."

But it wasn't all him—the whole family had put each other through the wringer. The damn painting. *Moonlight*. It had gone missing last year, and now it was again. When he'd seen that empty frame, his heart had literally stopped in his chest. Beth had just stared at him, eyes full of blame, when he'd pointed it out to her. Of course she'd probably think he took it, and he couldn't explain to her—or even, after she died, to Reid. Not without betraying someone he loved more than the world.

"Dad?"

At the sound of Sam's voice, he got out of his chair.

"Sam, what are you doing here?"

"Everyone's outside," she said, gesturing at the front window. "We came to celebrate Mom's birthday."

"Kate's here?"

She nodded. "And Lulu and Scotty. Isabel, Julie, all of us."

"Are you doing okay?" he asked.

"Well, it's her birthday. So . . ."

"Yeah. I know."

She brushed her long hair out of her eyes, and he caught sight of the scars on the inside of her left arm. Were the cuts fresh, or were they scars from months, a year ago, that were healing? *She's cutting because of you,* Beth had said. *Because of you and Nicola and your baby, because she's afraid of losing her father.*

"You still doing that?" he asked. Pointing at first, then walking over to her, gently holding her wrist. "Please tell me you're not."

"Not as much," she said. "Sometimes, though."

He traced the scar she had made last year, just before going to camp. Beth was at the gallery, cataloging new acquisitions. He went to the bank, but instead of returning straight to work, he drove home—he knew Sam had been upset with him, and he wanted a father-daughter moment, to reassure her as she was getting ready for camp that she was his number one, his oldest, his baby, and always would be.

He walked into the house through the front door, heard rummaging in the closet, saw Sam emerge. She jumped as if he'd caught her doing something wrong—the look on her face was pure guilt.

"What are you doing in there?" he asked.

"Nothing, Dad. Just looking for my boots and rain slicker. It gets a little wet up in Maine, ha ha."

"You sure?" he asked. "What happened to your wrist?"

She glanced down at it, saw the smudge of blood. "Huh," she said. "Must have snagged it on a nail or a hook or whatever."

Later Beth would tell him about Sam's cutting, but that day he didn't have a clue.

"Well, did you find your slicker?"

"Yeah," she said. "It's in there. I'll grab it when we drive up. Why are you here, anyway? Why aren't you at work?"

"I came to talk to you," he said.

"Why?"

"Because you're going to camp," he said. "And I want us to be okay." He thought of the day Sam was born, of how thrilled he had been, how he had imagined for her the life he had never had. That July day he felt pressure in his chest, as if his heart were expanding, wanting to burst out of his skin. He stepped forward to hug her, but she pulled back.

"Be okay?" she asked with a guttural laugh.

"Sam."

"Dad," she had said. "Don't. Talking will just make it all worse. I have to go; I told Isabel I'd meet her." And she'd run out the door.

Now, on her mother's birthday, she stood in Mathilda's living room, looking at him with sad eyes.

"That scar," he said, pointing, "looks better."

"I call it *Memory of Moonlight*," she said.

"Maybe it's better you just forget it."

"*Forgotten Moonlight*?" she asked. "Don't you think that's impossible, considering what I did?"

"I suppose it would be."

"Why didn't you ever tell Mom?"

"Because I wanted to protect you."

"She would have been mad."

"You taking the painting off the wall, putting it in the hall closet. Didn't you think you might trigger her? Make her relive that earlier time? Didn't you think it would hurt her?"

Sam stared at the small white scar. "I bled on it too. I didn't mean to do that. I felt horrible. The painting's so valuable."

"It was just a tiny smudge on the back of the canvas," he said. "And the painting's value is nothing compared to you, Sam. You're who we love, who matters, not some piece of art." He swallowed. Had she come in here to confess something else about the painting? He knew the police had found the canvas rolled up in the gallery basement, the back scrawled with a blood heart. "Honey, did you take it this time too?"

"No, I swear," she said, shaking her head hard.

"Okay, I believe you. But why did you do it before?"

"Because everything was falling apart," Sam said in a low voice, not meeting Pete's eyes. "I wanted you to think someone broke into our house, so you'd pay attention. So you'd stay home. We're a family."

She walked toward him then, banged right into his chest and let him hold her while she cried, rock her while she said, "I'm sorry; I'm so sorry I hid the painting. I want her back, Dad. I want you to be together—I want us all to be together."

"I want that too," he whispered. More than he had meant anything in his life, he meant that, which was why when Sam tilted her head back and asked her question, it cut him like a knife.

"Dad, you have to tell me. Promise me you'll tell me the truth. Did you kill her? Did you kill Mom?"

56

The sky was white, and snow was intermittent. Scotty's cheeks stung from the cold, and Kate's were bright red. She watched Lulu stomping her feet to keep them from freezing. Scotty bundled both Isabel and Julie close to her. Everyone faced the house.

"She must have gone inside," Lulu said.

"To talk to her father?" Scotty asked, giving an exaggerated shiver. "Let's get her out of there, away from him, and go warm up somewhere." She hoped it would be someplace with a full bar. Surely drinks all around would be welcome—they could toast Beth for her birthday.

"I'll go get Sam," Isabel said, striding away toward the front door. Julie trailed after her.

"Girls!" Scotty called.

"I'm sure it's fine," Lulu said, grabbing her arm. "Pete's not going to do anything, and Sam will be more likely to come with Isabel than a bunch of ancient aunties."

Scotty instinctively recoiled from Lulu's touch. It was something about the pointed look in Lulu's eyes, as if she were staring into Scotty's soul, trying to put the puzzle pieces together, or possibly wanting to rewrite her own history, wiping out the parts that Scotty knew. She glanced at Kate, who seemed not to notice the interaction.

"What's your problem?" Scotty asked.

"I was going to ask you the same thing," Lulu said.

"You've been acting weird toward me," Scotty said.

"I was just thinking about how close we all were," Lulu said. "And then how many secrets we kept from each other."

"I've gotten over the Jed part of it all," Kate said. "At least I'm trying to. Whether I like it or not, she had her reasons for not telling me. And so did you two."

Scotty watched as Kate reached into the pocket of her jacket, pulled out a folded piece of paper.

"I made a copy of this," Kate said. "I don't know if Beth ever showed you . . . maybe it's the one thing between her and me that you don't know about, haven't seen yet." She smoothed out the black-and-white image. Scotty's knees nearly buckled when she realized what it was.

"A sonogram," Lulu said.

"Matthew," Scotty said, reaching for it.

"Who was his father? Pete or Jed? Will we ever know?" Kate asked.

"At this point, I'm not sure it really makes a difference," Lulu said softly.

"It does," Scotty said, her voice harsher than she intended.

Both friends turned to look at her.

"Only someone who doesn't have kids could say it doesn't," Scotty said. "Believe me."

"The baby's gone," Kate said. "No one needs to raise him. But he still has us to love him."

"Still," Scotty said. "The father deserved to know."

"And she decided not to tell him," Lulu said.

"You were behind her in that," Scotty said. "In that way, you encouraged her worst self."

"Beth didn't have a worst self," Kate said. "Don't say that."

Scotty took a step closer to Lulu. "I tried to help her. I really did. I wanted to support her in all she was going through."

"What are you talking about?" Kate asked.

Scotty stared at the sonogram. It reminded her of the joy she'd felt seeing Isabel's, then Julie's, sharing the moment with Nick. He had been as thrilled as she was. He had always been there throughout her pregnancies.

"Why did he have to start running?" she asked.

"What?" Kate asked.

"Nick. Turning into a running fool. Jogging away from us."

"Come on, Scotty," Lulu said. "He was just training for the race."

Scotty shook the cobwebs from her mind.

"Pregnancy is one of the greatest times of a couple's life. The way Nick used to look at me, hold me. I wanted that for Jed."

"Jed—he's the father?" Kate asked.

"Mm-hmm," Scotty said.

"When did she tell you?" Lulu asked.

"That last day," Scotty said. "I'd gone over to help with her garden—she really wasn't feeling good. It was so hot out, and I didn't like thinking of her digging in the dirt, weeding, getting over-heated."

"Wait," Lulu said. "The last day—of her life? In July?"

Scotty nodded, picturing the perspiration on Beth's face, how Scotty had gently wiped it from her brow.

"You were the last to see her? After Pete left?" Lulu asked.

"Who said it was after Pete left?" Scotty asked, feeling pressured. "Kate knows. It was *before*."

"Yes," Kate said to Lulu. "Scotty was over there early in the morning."

"Beth liked to garden in the shade, before the sun rose over the trees. But even then—it was scorching. Lulu, you keep talking about support. Well, that's one way I helped Beth—planting mint and thyme and petunias and lobelia. And encouraging her to tell Jed the good news—that he was the dad."

"But she didn't want to," Lulu said. A

statement, not a question, with implied criticism.

"No, she didn't want to," Scotty said, narrowing her eyes. "And that was wrong." She felt startled by the vehemence in her own tone.

"Did you see her go into the house? When Pete was still in there, before he left?" Kate asked.

Scotty scrunched up her face, not only trying to recall the exact sequence but calibrating how to tell it to Kate and Lulu. She had been so hung-over; maybe things would have gone differently if she hadn't gotten so drunk the night before. She had still had alcohol in her bloodstream when she'd arrived at Beth's. She really needed to do something about her drinking.

"Yes," she said. "I did. I convinced her to leave the rest of the gardening till sunset—it would be so much cooler then. I told her to go inside and lie down in the air-conditioning." She choked up. This was the part she hated to remember. She wished she could erase it from her mind. "I keep thinking, if I had just stayed. If I hadn't sent her in there, to him. To Pete. I should have just stayed out there, insisting she tell Jed—I could have driven him to her. She could have had the happiness of telling him he was the father, instead of going into that house, and . . ."

"It wasn't your fault," Lulu said. "You couldn't have known."

"When I think of what was done to her," Scotty said. She pictured Beth's fractured skull, blood pouring from the caved-in side of her head, and she felt so sick she had to keep herself from throwing up. "You know, my girls hadn't even had breakfast by the time I got home. I walked in and cut up a pineapple and some ice-cold watermelon, put everything on the table for the girls, for when they woke up. Isabel would stay in bed all day if she could, but that day it was humid; she was up and waiting for me. Julie too."

On other summer days, she might have heard the screen door opening, seen Nick running water at the sink after his jog. She'd watch him taking a long drink, his body glistening with sweat. She could actually smell it now—not dank and awful, but the scent of the man she loved.

She would push from her mind the suspicion that he was having an affair, or wanted to have one, with one of those women he ran with. They used to be happy. They used to have a great marriage. She looked from Kate to Lulu. These two would never understand. But Beth had.

"Cheating," she said to Lulu and Kate now. "I never even thought about it before Pete and Nicola. They opened the door to it, such a terrible door. And Beth walked through it, straight to Jed. I would have expected her to be stronger."

"Scotty!" Lulu said.

"I'm grateful, Scotty," Kate said. "That she saw you that day; she spent some of her last morning with one of her best friends."

Scotty's eyes filled. "She did. I made sure of it. And after Isabel woke up—it was still so early, but God, it was so hot she just couldn't stay in bed—I called Beth. Isabel and Julie were right there at the table, listening to me talk to her on the phone."

"When did you go over and find the UPS note?" Kate asked.

"The what?" Scotty asked, distracted by the sound of a car coming up the driveway. She peered down the hill, but it hadn't rounded the corner yet.

"Never mind. Back to the phone call. What did Beth say when you talked to her?" Kate asked. Scotty understood her friend's thirst for every memory of her sister. She got that, and she would make sure Kate received what she needed.

"Well, Isabel and Julie were right there next to me, eating their breakfast. I was gazing at them, thinking of how lucky Beth and I were to have daughters. So I said, 'Sweetheart, I'm here for you. We might disagree about a few things, but you know I love you. And when Sam gets back from camp, we'll have a mother-daughter day.' "

"And what did Beth say?" Kate asked, thirsty for more.

"That she couldn't wait. That we could go to Watch Hill and have lemonade at the Olympia Tearoom, and watch Julie ride the carousel, and maybe the older girls too . . ."

"No, she didn't," Julie said, crouched by the shed.

"Julie!" Scotty said, shocked to hear her voice. "I thought you were inside with Isabel, getting Sam."

"Air talk, Mommy. You talked to the air, not a person."

Scotty tried to laugh, noticing how Kate looked puzzled and Lulu looked suspicious.

"What is 'air talk,' Julie?" Kate asked.

"When Mommy talked to no one. On the phone, saying words, but no one to listen. The phone line just ringing and ringing."

"What are you talking about, Julie?" Scotty asked, grabbing her arm and giving it a shake. "Don't lie! You know it's wrong."

"Not lying!" Julie cried out.

"Just stop this. Be quiet; go find your sister."

"But, Mommy," Julie said, tugging on Scotty's sleeve. "I picked up the phone in your bedroom, Mommy, and you were talking to no one. Sam's mother not on the phone. No one on the phone. And we weren't eating breakfast, either. It was lunchtime already."

"Julie, the adults are having a conversation," Scotty snapped. "Do you want a time-out?"

"Daddy was gone to the boat. Remember? Mr. Lathrop came to pick up Daddy and they left, and it was after that, lunchtime, you called and talked to the air. Lunchtime, Mommy."

"Beth wasn't talking?" Kate asked. "When your mother called her?"

Julie shook her head.

"For Godssakes," Scotty said. "I came home for breakfast. I called Beth. We had a conversation before the men left, and she was fine."

"Lunch, not breakfast," Julie said. "And talk to air, ringing phone, not Mrs. Lathrop."

"There was no one on the line?" Kate asked, and Scotty felt her gaze burning straight into her.

"Don't listen to her," Scotty said.

"It was lunch, tuna fish, not breakfast. That's when you got back from Mrs. Lathrop. Blood on you here," Julie said, touching the side of her neck and under her chin. "I told you, Mommy, wash it off, wash it off."

Scotty didn't listen to the rest. She saw the way Kate's face crumpled and turned red, how she lurched toward her, and Scotty turned away. She began to walk, then run, toward the house. She was running just like Nick ran, away from what he didn't want—in his case her—and she ran away from what *she* didn't want: the sight of Kate's eyes when she realized the blood Julie had seen had been Beth's, from when Scotty had bashed her head in—when Kate realized what Scotty had done to her sister.

57

Kate was frozen in place, watching Scotty walk into the house. A black car sped up the drive, kicking gravel out behind. Scotty. Beth. White sky. Snow. Beth. Lulu chasing Scotty into the house. Beth. Scotty, no. Scotty. Now this car, this black car, coming fast. Kate couldn't move, couldn't feel. She was a statue. A sculpture in Mathilda's garden. Sculpture. Owl. Beth. Beth.

She stared through the windshield, saw Conor's eyes. Wild eyes. Staring at her. Conor jumping out of the car, door left open. She saw him running to her now, as fast as anyone has ever run, and the ice broke into a million pieces, and Kate stopped being a statue. She flew at Conor, crying now, grabbing him as hard as she could.

"It was Scotty!" she screamed.

"I know," Conor said, holding her. "I know, Kate. Where is she now?"

"In the house," Kate said, sobbing. "And Sam's in there."

58

Reid walked through the front door and found Scotty sitting on the marble stairs. Lulu stood beside her. Isabel and Julie huddled together, leaning against a grandfather clock. Everyone was very quiet. Sam was nowhere in sight. He sensed Kate behind him but didn't turn around. His gaze was on Scotty.

She was wearing a heavy wool coat, and the heat seemed to be getting to her. Beads of sweat appeared on her forehead. She didn't wipe them away. Reid saw her trying to look behind him; he wanted to block her view of Kate.

"Scotty," he said. "Do you know why I'm here?"

"A misunderstanding," she said. "My daughter has a disability. She didn't know what she was saying. I'm sure if I can just explain."

"Mom," Isabel said. "Please just tell them you didn't do anything."

"Well, of course I didn't!" Scotty said.

Reid watched Lulu walk over to Scotty's daughters, bend down, and whisper something. She put her hands on each girl's shoulder. Isabel struggled, as if she didn't want to comply, but within a few seconds, Lulu had led Isabel and Julie into another room of the house.

Now Reid could hear Kate breathing heavily behind him. He didn't want to look away from Scotty, to make sure she wasn't holding a weapon, that she couldn't hurt anyone else, but he threw a quick glance, saw Kate looking pure white, like a ghost with fire in her eyes.

"How could you do it, Scotty?" Kate asked.

"Sweetie, don't even—" Scotty began.

"You can't call me that," Kate said. "Not after what you did."

"Detective Reid, Kate is really upset right now. It makes sense, doesn't it? It's Beth's birthday. We're all very emotional. I think it's best if I take my daughters home . . . ," Scotty said.

"It's better you stay right there," Reid said.

"I actually have to get home to my husband," Scotty said. "He'll be expecting me."

When Reid had run back into the Black Whale and told Tom what Harris had said, and that he was going to drive to Hubbard's Point to arrest Scotty Waterston, it had been Tom's idea to check to see where she would be—because it was Beth's birthday, and it made sense the best friends would be spending it together. So Reid had called Nick, and Nick had told him Scotty and the kids would be joining Kate, Lulu, and Sam at Mathilda's to celebrate Beth's life. He expected they would all be having dinner together.

"I talked to your husband," Reid said. "He's the one who told me you'd be here."

"Well, I've had enough of being here," Scotty said. "This day isn't turning out to be at all what I'd hoped. Not a very good way to honor Beth."

"I also talked to your friend Martin," Reid said.

"He's not really a friend," Scotty said, sounding nervous. "Did he say he was?"

"He said you buy him drinks. And tell him the news."

"I don't tell him anything," Scotty said, her gaze darting to Kate. Reid looked, and Kate seemed spellbound—as pale as before, the fire in her eyes still smoldering.

"You told him about Beth," Reid said.

"Well, he cared," Scotty said. "She was important to everyone at the soup kitchen. They wanted to hear how the case was progressing."

"Scotty, he knew an awful lot about things. And I have to admit—I wonder how you knew them," Reid said.

"Oh, come on," Scotty said, with another glance at Kate. "Word gets around. People talk! We all want this to get solved, put behind us."

Kate cleared her throat. She stepped forward so she was standing next to Reid.

"You know what I want?" Kate asked, staring straight at Scotty. "To know what she said when she saw what you were doing to her."

"Please, Kate . . ."

561

"And I want to know," Kate said, her voice low and calm, "why, after you hit her, after you strangled her, why did you do that with her underwear? Wrap it around her neck?"

Reid needed to know the same thing, and he knew he should stop Kate and take Scotty back to headquarters to question her, but Kate took a step closer to Scotty, stood right beside her.

"Those bruises between her legs," Kate said, her voice rising. "Did you do that to make it look good? To make it seem like a stranger attacked her? Did you do that, Scotty? Was she still alive when you were making it look as if she'd been raped?"

"Kate, no, I swear!" Scotty said. Reid reached behind to grab his handcuffs from his belt.

"You did it," Kate wept, crouching beside Beth's best friend. "You did, Scotty, and she knew it. That's what I hate to think of more than anything. That Beth knew it."

Reid watched as Scotty reached for Kate's hand, and Kate let her hold it for a few seconds before she tore herself away.

59

Kate sat in a chair in the library, *West-Running Brook* and *The Lives of the Artists* on the pile of books where she had left them months ago, the day she had come to look for the blood hearts. She leaned to better see out the window, making sure she could see Sam walking through the field with Popcorn.

Conor had arrested Scotty, put her in handcuffs, and taken her to the state police barracks in Westbrook. Nick had picked up Isabel and Julie. Pete had been somewhere; Kate hadn't cared.

"Why did she do it?" Kate had asked.

"She lost her mind," Lulu said.

"No, there's a reason. A clear reason—there has to be."

"Kate, there's no way this will ever make sense."

And Lulu was right about that.

"Staging it all," Kate said. "With Beth's underwear. Making her look like that . . ."

"To put the blame on someone else?" Lulu asked.

"I don't know what went through her mind," Kate had said. "She went crazy."

"She was drinking more. A lot. And things weren't going so well with Nick. Maybe they were falling apart. But what did Beth do, to make her do it?"

Kate was watching Sam out the window. Sam had found an old tennis ball and threw it for Popcorn to chase. He retrieved it and bounded back to her.

"Nothing," Kate had said after a few moments. "There's nothing she could have done to deserve it."

"I know," Lulu had said. "But in Scotty's mind? What was she thinking?"

Kate didn't take her eyes off Sam. Now she was petting Popcorn's head; now she had her arms around his neck. The way she held him, cheek against his fur, reminded Kate of Beth.

"Beth loved two men," Lulu had said, trying to answer her own question. "Was that it? She cheated on her husband. She refused to tell the men whose baby it was. Everybody but Scotty is a sinner."

"She was . . . our friend," Kate had said, fighting waves of fury and hate. "I don't care why she did it—she killed Beth."

Lulu had given Kate a little shove, making her push over slightly, squeezing onto the chair beside her. Kate had felt the warmth of Lulu's arm around her shoulder.

The front door slammed, and Sam walked into

the room. She was lit from behind, from sunlight pouring through the tall window. She looked like an angel holding a rabbit. She placed Clementine on Kate's lap and sat at her feet.

"It was Mrs. Waterston?" she had asked.

Kate nodded, hardly able to see through her tears. What would it be like for Sam, to know her closest friend's mother had killed Beth?

"It wasn't Dad," Sam said, choking as she said the words, tears pouring down her face. "At least it wasn't him. But oh, Aunt Kate. She was like family to us." She couldn't speak for a few seconds. "I can't stand thinking of Mom knowing it was her. Feeling her best friend kill her."

Kate stood up to hug Sam. Her niece's words flowed through her, and for that instant Kate was Beth, imagining how it felt to have the life crushed out of her by someone she had loved her whole life.

"I saw the detective take her away," Sam said. "She had handcuffs on. Isabel was screaming. Julie was crying."

Kate nodded. She had seen and heard them too.

"Mom had to visit her father in prison, and now Isabel's going to have to go there to visit her mother. Will she and I even stay friends?"

Kate hugged her because she didn't have the answer. She remembered the old phrase: *best friends forever.* It hadn't worked out that way.

Outside, tires crunched on the gravel. Kate heard a car door slam. The sound startled Clementine, and she scampered across the room. Sam went to look out the window.

"Who is it?" Lulu asked.

"Detective Reid's back," Sam said.

Kate watched Clementine hide beneath the desk chair. She walked over to the desk and reached for *The Lives of the Artists*. She opened to the last page, saw the heart and all their initials. *K, L, S,* and *B*.

Footsteps sounded in the hallway. She didn't turn around. She heard Pete's voice greeting Conor. Someday Conor would apologize to him for getting it wrong, or maybe he wouldn't. She heard Lulu saying they should leave, that it was time to go home. She heard Sam trying to coax Clementine out from her hiding place, but still Kate didn't turn around. She couldn't take her eyes off the page where four young girls had once written their initials in blood.

They had been sisters and best friends; they had made promises to each other. There would be no secrets. There would be only love.

"Come on," Lulu said gently. "It's time to go."

Kate stared at the page. She heard low voices behind her.

Leaning down, she kissed *B* for Beth.

"Kate?" Conor said from the doorway.

Kate stood tall and walked toward the detective. He put his arms around her, and they stood together, rocking back and forth.

"You okay?" he asked, leaning back enough so he could look into her eyes.

She shook her head but felt a small smile deep inside.

He gazed at her as if he could see into her soul, as if he knew what she was thinking: that she could never really lose her sister. She crouched to pick up Clementine. She held her gently in her arms, felt her heart lightly beating through her soft fur.

Then together they had all walked out of the room.

60

May 5

Oh, Kate.

We walk through the meadow holding hands. Up the slant of the hill we go, until we near the top, up above our grandmother's house. It is late afternoon, the first Tuesday of May, and golden light washes over the green grass, and the air is warm. Those cold days of November have long passed, and the earth is starting to bloom. My fingers interlock with my sister's. In her other hand, she carries a small carton with handles and holes for air.

Can you feel me with you? I ask her.

Yes, she says out loud.

I believe she can, although it is hard to know. The unshakable certainty I had last summer, when my body died, has given way to a sense that being definite is an illusion. It doesn't actually matter. Nothing is solid; nothing is black and white. Love is fluid, and so is peace, without shape or edges, fresh water flowing from the river's mouth into the sea.

She named her rabbit for my favorite fruit, for the color of the dress I wore the day Lulu and I cut *Moonlight* from the frame. I once despaired over that act, feeling that if I hadn't done it, I might have lived. Telling Scotty that I had done it deliberately to hurt my husband had filled her with poison. How could I not respect my husband when she loved hers so much, when he was turning away from her?

Now Scotty is in prison, just like my father. My father desires retribution; he would like to see her die. What happens to Scotty is not my concern. I left her behind on my last day, when she followed me upstairs from the garden, when I pointed out the blank spot on the wall where *Moonlight* had hung, when she told me she was tired of my life.

Those were her words: "I am sick of your life."

So she took it from me.

Lulu wasn't wrong: everyone but Scotty was a sinner.

I have a journey to take. Scotty will go on trial, and she will tell the truth—that I attacked her, slapped her when she accused me of cheating, of not respecting my husband or myself, of not even respecting my lover enough to tell him he was Matthew's father. Kate and Sam have suffered all along; they were collateral damage of her act, and they will see this through. They will do it for me.

Kate. I say her name. *Kate.*

Her name is contained—it is hard, while my

name is soft. Say it out loud: *Beth.* It sounds like a breeze. Then say *Kate:* it starts with a sharp *K* sound and ends with a hard *T.* I used to think, after our mother died, that her name was perfect for her. She had shut herself off in a castle to protect herself, with rock edges of impenetrable walls. I used to feel her watching me, perplexed, wondering how I could stay open to the world after what had been done to us.

And for so long, she stayed that way.

I don't take credit for what has happened to her in these last months, but I think her love for me, missing me, has let her realize that life is so short, over in the blink of an eye. She rescued Clementine because she couldn't save me. The rabbit with soft fur healed and is alive because of Kate's care.

Kate's love helps me forgive myself for my own death. The choices I made, the people I hurt. But now I know—the best of us waste our time repenting, forgiving everyone but ourselves. And the worst don't even realize there is anything to forgive. Hungry ghosts wander the earth, trapped in the bardo, seeking redemption that had been there all along.

It is time for me to leave. Letting go of my sister's hand will be my last act in this world and may well be the hardest thing I have ever done. We've finally found our way back to each other. I desire peace—I need it; it is the natural order—

yet I yearn to stay. If only I could be reborn; if only this connection could last forever.

Now we have reached the top of the rise. Mathilda's roof glints silver in the dying light. The Connecticut River is painted pure gold, running south to Long Island Sound. In the far distance, the salt water sparkles deep blue, and the two lighthouses at Saybrook Point have blinked on. Kate stops when she sees their beacons.

We stand there together, watching the sun set. In the east, a full moon rises. This night will never be truly dark; moonlight will illuminate this hill, the river, the sea. Kate crouches down and looks into the cardboard crate. Clementine's dark-brown eyes watch her with gentle vigilance.

"It's time," Kate says.

I know, I say.

"I don't want you to go," she says. "Just when I've found you."

I love you, I say.

"Forever," she says.

And ever.

She slips her hand from mine, and I feel myself start to fade, to merge into the moon's pale glow.

Have you ever seen anything so beautiful? I want to ask, but I find I can't. Words lose their meaning; feelings are all that exist. I look down the hill and see the man with dark hair climbing up through the tall grass, coming toward us.

"I will visit you here," my sister says, reaching into the crate to pet Clementine's head, to trace with one finger the scars left by the hawk's talons.

You don't have to visit me anywhere, I say. *I am with you; I am in you; I always will be. Love Sam for me, love Lulu, love each other.*

Kate draws a heart in the grass. There is no blood this time; there is no need for it. The pressure of her finger makes its mark. I kiss the top of my sister's head. She opens the door to the crate, and Clementine inches out. She hops a foot away, seems to look back at Kate, then races through the field and disappears into the hay.

"I love you," my sister says. Her voice is quiet and happy. That is what I take with me—the sound of Kate's happiness.

The moon rises above the tree line, and I lift with it.

Acknowledgments

Thank you to Thomas & Mercer, especially the brilliant Liz Pearsons and my wonderful editor, Charlotte Herscher.

I am forever grateful to my beloved friend and agent, Andrea Cirillo, and everyone at the Jane Rotrosen Agency: Jane Berkey, Meg Ruley, Annelise Robey, Christina Hogrebe, Amy Tannenbaum, Rebecca Scherer, Kathy Schneider, Jessica Errera, Danielle Sickles, Sabrina Prestia, Hannah Rody-Wright, Chris Prestia, Julianne Tinari, Michael Conroy, Donald W. Cleary, Ellen Tischler, Gena Louque, and, forever, Don Cleary.

Many thanks to my dear friend and film agent, Ron Bernstein.

I'm very thankful to Patrick Carson, my extraordinary social media manager.

Epic gratitude, as always, to William Twigg Crawford.

I am grateful to Sergeant Robert Derry of the Connecticut State Police for sharing his insight and expertise.

About the Author

Luanne Rice is the *New York Times* bestselling author of thirty-four novels that have been translated into twenty-four languages. In 2002, Connecticut College awarded Rice an honorary degree, and she also received an honorary doctorate from the University of Saint Joseph. In June 2014, she received the 2014 Connecticut Governor's Arts Award for excellence as a literary artist.

Several of Rice's novels have been adapted for television, including *Crazy in Love*, for TNT; *Blue Moon*, for CBS; *Follow the Stars Home* and *Silver Bells*, for the Hallmark Hall of Fame; and *Beach Girls*, for Lifetime.

Rice is a creative affiliate of the Safina Center, an organization that brings together scientists, artists, and writers to inspire a deeper connection with nature—especially the sea. Rice is an avid environmentalist and advocate for families affected by domestic violence. She lives on the Connecticut Shoreline.

Center Point Large Print
600 Brooks Road / PO Box 1
Thorndike, ME 04986-0001 USA

(207) 568-3717

US & Canada:
1 800 929-9108
www.centerpointlargeprint.com